IN PRAISE OF

THEN CAME FAITH

"…I anticipate every book by Louise Gouge…she never fails to deliver a good story filled with realistic details, leaving me with a sense of having been a part of the story!"

EVA MARIE EVERSON
Author of *The Potluck Club* Series

"Louise Gouge paints a very vivid picture of a life that touches so many aspects of our own lives and presents a story that becomes so much more than a story; it becomes an adventure that leads the reader to stronger faith."

BISHOP LOUIS CAMPESE
Anglican Church in America

"Reading *Then Came Faith* is like stepping back in time. Louise Gouge tells a captivating story set in the reconstruction period when hate and destruction were rampant. Readers will struggle along with the characters as they try to make sense out of a senseless time with no easy answers, wondering if love can truly conquer hate. *Then Came Faith* is a good novel that sweeps you along to the end and is hopefully the first of many."

LAURAINE SNELLING
Author of the *Red River* and *Dakotah Treasures* series,
A Promise for Elli, and *The Brushstroke Legacy*

"Louise Gouge has written another page turner with strong and careful character development whose post-Civil War lives are intertwined in multilayered complexities, budding cross-cultural romances even as the deep Southerners face the consequences of a Union occupational army placed to instill the rule of the re-united States, to protect African Americans freed from slavery, and Northern missionaries and reconstructionists. Conflicts arise between those who hold differing interpretations of Christian ethics. Gouge has skillfully positioned the protagonists in thought-battles, each articulating to themselves different ecclesiastical truths. This strategy gives the reader insights into how individuals struggle to define and act righteously within their faith, and how conflicting religious convictions can be negotiated in the face of national hatred turning into romantic interpersonal love."

SUE-ELLEN JACOBS, PH.D.
Professor Emeritus, University of Washington

THEN CAME FAITH

A NOVEL

LOUISE M. GOUGE

Emerald
Pointe
BOOKS

09 08 07 06   10 9 8 7 6 5 4 3 2 1

Then Came Faith
A Novel
0-97851-372-X
Copyright © 2006 by Louise M. Gouge
Represented by:
Wendy Lawton
Books & Such Literary Agency
Central Valley Office
P.O. Box 1227
Hilmar, CA 95324
209 634-1913
wendy@booksandsuch.biz

Published by Emerald Pointe Books
PO Box 35327
Tulsa, OK 74153-0327

O taste and see that the LORD is good; blessed is the man that trusteth in Him.

Psalm 34:8 KJV

CHAPTER ONE

✳ ✳ ✳ ✳

A burst of raucous male laughter sent a chill down Juliana Harris' spine, but she refused to look toward those responsible. Shielding her face with a white lace parasol, she stood quietly beside her Saratoga trunk on the hot, dirty wharf and wished to be invisible. From time to time, she peeked out from under her parasol toward the distant street, but she dared not leave her baggage to find a carriage. *Where on earth is Miss Randolph?*

The ship on which Juliana had arrived just two hours earlier had brought some sixty passengers, all of whom seemed to find their friends and transportation with no trouble. Soon they had all dispersed, and Juliana searched in vain for the one who had invited her to come to New Orleans. Far down the wharf, several blue-uniformed soldiers appeared to be inspecting cargo, but she could not leave her belongings to ask for their help.

To keep herself calm, she counted her baggage for the third time. One trunk and six boxes of different sizes and shapes. All had arrived, but still she kept checking.

The afternoon sun lit the wharf, and a hot August breeze scattered the acrid smells of dead fish, oily machinery, and perspiration to every corner. Juliana pulled up her fan from where it hung on her wrist and waved it with vigor in front of her face, so as not to appear as frightened as she felt. Where *could* Miss Randolph be?

Around her, men of varied hues carried great bundles of cargo to and from nearby ships. Their vulgar language scorched her ears, and their bold glances brought a burning blush to her cheeks. The only other female on the wharf was a loud, disreputable looking woman in a gaudy, low-cut dress selling some sort of food from a basket. By the swaying of her well-rounded hips, she appeared to be offering more than just food. Juliana felt an urge to deliver a scathing sermon to them all but restrained herself, for she realized her crossness came as much from anxiety as from her sense of moral outrage.

Lord, please deliver me from this place. I know You didn't bring me all this way to forsake me.

"I beg your pardon, miss. May I be of assistance?"

Juliana tilted her parasol back. Before her stood a young gentleman in a well-made but tattered white suit. When he lifted his broad-brimmed straw hat and bowed, his curly blond hair fell into a frame around his boyish face. His soft smile and sky-blue eyes exuded kindness but also revealed weariness beyond his years. He must have suffered horribly during the war. Had he been a soldier?

"I'm sorry, miss, I don't mean to be forward." His words poured out like honey, rich and warm and sweet, in a charming, well-bred southern drawl accented with a whisper of French. "However, this is not a safe place for a young lady traveling alone. May I summon a carriage for you?"

Juliana thought her heart might burst right on the spot. What a perfectly…perfect young man, an answer to her prayer.

"Why, yes. Thank you so much."

For the briefest instant, a frown flickered across his handsome face. "May I inquire as to your destination?"

"Why, yes, of course. I'm going to the Garden District to the home of Miss Amelia Randolph on First Street. Well, actually, it's her father's home. He's—"

The man stiffened. "I know who he is." His tone became sharp and dismissive. He turned to three men lounging nearby, the ones whose boisterous laughter had assaulted Juliana's sensibilities. "Make yourselves useful. Carry these bags out to the street." He spoke as one used to giving orders.

"Yes, boss. Yessuh." The men hurried to obey.

Glancing over his shoulder toward Juliana, the man lifted his chin, all kindness gone from his expression. "Follow me, miss." A slight hiss punctuated that last word, as if he were now reluctant to address her in a proper manner.

"But, wait…" If Juliana had not jumped aside, the burly, dark-skinned men might have knocked her down as they gathered her baggage. On the round top of the Saratoga trunk, they balanced three of the smaller boxes. Two men carried it while the third grasped the other three by their ropes. All three hastened to follow the young man, who strode on a walkway between two long buildings toward a busy thoroughfare.

Lord, help me. Had she made a terrible mistake to trust this temperamental person? Now she had no choice but to lift her hoopskirt and run after them. Arriving breathless at the street, she whispered a prayer of gratitude that the man seemed about to keep his promise.

With an imperious wave of his hand, he summoned a carriage. To Juliana's relief, the driver appeared reputable, if shabby. What would she have done if her now-reluctant knight had palmed her off on some seedy fellow and sent her to who knows where? Her temper rising at his rudeness, she nonetheless feared to ask why he changed his demeanor toward her, lest he abandon her before the task was completed.

He gave orders to the men, who secured her baggage to the carriage's rear platform, and rewarded each with a coin.

"Miss." He thrust out his hand but spoke no further, even when assisting her into the open conveyance. Once she was seated, he handed a coin to the driver. "The Charles Randolph residence." The curl of his well-formed lips shouted his distaste at speaking the name. Then he turned away.

"Wait. Oh, please, sir, wait." Still breathless, Juliana panted out the words.

The man wheeled about, his face still wearing a sneer. "You have nothing to fear. This driver is trustworthy."

"But I must repay your expenditure." She tried to smile, but her temper pulled her lips into a line. "And surely I may know the name of my gallant knight."

He breathed out a mild snort. "There's hardly a need for that." He lifted his hat and gave her an exaggerated bow. "Good day, miss." Again he turned and strode away.

"Gitup." The gray-haired Negro driver slapped the heavy reins against his horse's bony haunches. The animal leaned into the harness, and after a moment the carriage moved forward.

"How incredibly rude," Juliana muttered as she plopped back against the seat. What a disagreeable man. What an unpleasant beginning to her mission. The voyage from Boston had been rough toward the end, for the ship had skirted a hurricane in the Gulf of Mexico. Now that she was on land, would her life be just as rough as the voyage? She pulled out an embroidered handkerchief and dabbed perspiration from her face. It would not do to arrive at the Randolph home all wilted, no matter how weary and cross she felt.

Why was that person so discourteous? She had prayed for help, and the Lord had sent it. The man appeared to be a gentleman, and her own behavior had been proper when she accepted his assistance. If he thought she was not a lady, he never should have spoken to her in the first place. What on earth ailed the man?

With a self-bracing sniff, she tossed her head, tightened her bonnet laces, and looked about at the bustling city. Every imaginable type of person filled the streets. She noticed in particular some men wearing remnants of tattered gray uniforms. Did they have no shame? With the Confederacy outlawed and disbanded, they should find other clothes. Yet the blue-uniformed northern troops patrolling the streets did not pay particular attention to their former enemies.

In general, the busy street reminded her of her home city. Unlike Boston, however, New Orleans needed to recover from the war, and she had come to help. From now on, her life would be useful and satisfying and a grand adventure. Unless, of course, everyone here reacted to her as that reluctant knight had. So much for first appearances. Handsome to the point of perfection, and rude to the point of sin. She would dismiss his memory from her mind.

And yet, stinging disappointment lingered in her heart.

⊷⊶⊷⊶⊷

André strode back toward the wharf, cursing himself for his careless misjudgment. Any fool could see the girl was a Yankee. Why had he permitted himself to be drawn to her pretty face and quality clothing? Why had he let that helpless look in her fine dark eyes generate his sympathy? The instant she spoke, he knew where she had come from. He should have left her to her own devices or those of that murderer, Randolph.

Where was the man, anyway? Didn't Yankees know how to protect their women? Did they have no sense of decorum or even humanity? Without a doubt, they did not. For during their monstrous war of aggression, they had swept through the South, destroyed homes, and left countless decent families destitute. Unutterably cruel and sadistic, they had nearly scorched the life out of the South. With Yankee soldiers still occupying the whole city, why hadn't any of them noticed one of their own ladies in distress?

Randolph. The name stuck in André's craw. One day he would find a way to repay the man. One day, when the scattered pieces of André's life could be salvaged.

"Master André?" Cordell fell into step with him and held out a shipping log. "They're all counted and ready to load. Would you like to sign this, sir?"

André stopped and surveyed the meager cargo of imported coffee. How pitiful compared to the massive shipments of cotton his father's plantation had exported to worldwide markets before the war. Now André was a mere middleman. Still, he felt fortunate to have anything at all to ship upriver.

"Master?" Cordell eyed him with a furrowed brow.

"Cordell, I've told you to stop addressing me that way. You are no longer my…" André could not say the word "slave." Such a vulgar term had never been in his vocabulary, and thanks to that Yankee congress and the late Mr. Lincoln, "chattel" no longer applied. He clapped his companion on the shoulder. "I am your employer, and you are my employee."

Cordell nodded agreeably and gave a little shrug. "Yes, sir." Once again, he held out the shipping log. "Boss man, you be ready to sign this h'yeh paper?" A mischievous grin lit his light-brown face.

Accepting the log and pen, André suppressed a grin and nudged Cordell with his elbow. "That's even worse. Don't you go acting that way around them." He tilted his head in the direction of the men he had hired to carry the young woman's baggage. They now slouched idly on some old crates.

Cordell looked at the group and frowned. "Mr. André, they're not all that bad. They just don't know what to do with themselves."

André studied the three for a moment. Perhaps Cordell was right. If they were the worthless type, they already would have spent their money on liquor. "You have something in mind. What is it?"

"Well, sir, we need more men to tend the house and work in the warehouse."

"I won't be able to pay them until we build things up a bit more. I can't even pay you." And to think he had used almost the last of his change to help a Yankee. What a misplaced act of honor that had been.

"Yes, sir, but we could provide for them. Food, a place to sleep, that's all. The more hands we have, the sooner we'll be back on our feet."

André stared at the trio. Their posture indicated indolence, yet as they talked among themselves, he sensed despondency as well. Fools. Why had they not stayed with their former masters to help rebuild whatever the men had left after the Yankees had done their dirty work? That same lack of loyalty in his own chattels galled André. His father had always treated them as family, yet as soon as Father died, most of them abandoned Mama. Only Cordell, Aunt Sukey, and sweet little Gemma had remained to hold things together until André returned home.

"You'll take charge of them?"

"Yes, sir." Cordell beamed. "Yes, sir, I will. May I bring them out to the house this evening? That is, if they'll come?"

André regarded him for a moment. Something new, something different shone in his pleased expression, but André couldn't put his finger on it. "Yes, you do that." He dipped the pen into the inkwell Cordell held and signed the shipping log. "First, make certain the coffee is loaded on the riverboat. If they're still around, then you can talk to them. I'll go find those groceries Aunt Sukey asked for. I'll see you back at home around seven."

"Yes, sir." Cordell took the log and gave his usual servile bow, but when he turned to follow orders, he squared his shoulders and walked away whistling.

André exhaled a quiet laugh, but not from humor. A whole new order would rule his world from now on, and he would have to adjust. Everyone would. But no one could have told him all those years ago, when he had willfully broken the law and taught Cordell to read and do sums, that his former body servant would prove to be a competent businessman. A worthy right-hand man, in fact, as André struggled to salvage what he could of his former life.

The urge to whistle Cordell's tune brought a pucker to André's lips, but it was stifled by the unexpected memory of a fair-haired, dark-eyed young woman in a yellow summer dress and matching bonnet. The very moment he had observed her courage as she searched for her negligent host, his soul had been deeply stirred.

His soul? Hadn't he lost that forever through four long years of fruitless war, death, and defeat? Yet when he saw the girl, he longed to protect her to his dying breath.

So why on earth did she have to be a Yankee? ✳

✦ ✦ ✦ ✦

"I cannot tell you how sorry I am, Miss Harris." Charles Randolph chomped on his unlit pipe and paced back and forth before the fireplace in his large, bright drawing room. His average height, slender frame, and plain countenance did not match the energy in his brown eyes. "We had no way of knowing exactly what day the *Morgan* would arrive, but I left word that a messenger was to be dispatched as soon as the ship was sighted. It's unforgivable that they did not honor my request."

Juliana took in a breath to respond, but Amelia spoke first.

"My stars, I can't imagine how frightened you must have felt." Seated on the sofa, the dimpled brunette gripped Juliana's hand. "Thank the Lord you found a reputable driver."

"What's the matter with that dock master, or even the ship's captain, that they didn't make sure you were attended to?" Mrs. Randolph sat on Juliana's other side, an arm around her guest's waist. Even thinner than her husband, she appeared fragile, as though she might blow away in a stiff wind.

"Oh, Mother, why do you ask?" Helena Randolph glared first at her mother, then at her father. "They deliberately refused to help Miss Harris simply because she is our guest. Father, isn't there something you can do?"

Mr. Randolph eyed his daughter with a patient expression. "My dear, the war is over. Yes, the North may have prevailed, but we are not conquerors. We are all Americans again, and Louisiana is once again one of the United States of America."

"Tell that to those horrible Southerners who treat us as if it were our fault they rebelled against the Union," said Helena.

Already feeling at home within the circle of the Randolph family, Juliana listened with interest to their lively conversation. Despite the serious subject matter they were discussing, they were just like her own loving family. Now that she was safe with them, the whole affair seemed far less threatening. After all, the Lord had protected her, even if His agent had been a disagreeable, reluctant rescuer.

"I'm sure it was just an oversight." She patted Amelia's hand. "Let us speak no more about it."

Amelia responded by hugging Juliana. "Oh, how good it is to have you here. There is so much to do, and we are sorely lacking in helpers."

"Then let us make our plans. What do you need?"

"My goodness, Miss Harris," Mrs. Randolph also gave Juliana a squeeze, and her blue eyes exuded maternal kindness. "I believe what *you* need is a little nap and a hearty supper. We'll have a relaxing evening. Tomorrow will be soon enough to make your plans."

The others chorused their agreement.

"Miss Harris…"

"Now, Amelia, you must call me Juliana."

Amelia beamed. "Oh, I shall, I shall. You are everything that Mr. Starbuck said, and I shall love you as I love my own sister. I'm so glad he suggested that you come to New Orleans to help me educate the Negroes."

"Do tell us about Isaiah." Helena's widened eyes revealed a strong affection for the person under discussion. "We enjoyed his visits while he was here serving our country. We were terribly sad to see him assigned to the Atlantic coast. What is he doing now?"

Juliana dreaded breaking her heart. Best to get it over with.

"I'm pleased to say that Isaiah and my eldest sister, Lacy, were married the day before I set sail for New Orleans. They are very happy, and we are so grateful that he returned home safely from the war to marry her." Juliana watched Helena form a brave smile and sniff back tears.

"Ah, how grand." If Mr. Randolph knew of his younger daughter's fondness for Isaiah, he covered it well. "We often enjoyed his company during the occupation." He chuckled. "In fact, all the young naval officers visited us frequently, for there were few homes open to them."

"Thank the Lord, the war is over," Mrs. Randolph said. "But how we miss our fine, brave young men. Few people here have anything to do with us these days."

"Surely that will change in time." Juliana glanced about the group. "Surely everyone will have the good sense to reconcile and rebuild the South together."

Mr. Randolph cleared his throat and stared out the window for a moment. "That is our prayer."

"Indeed it is." Mrs. Randolph stood. "Now, Miss Harris—Juliana—let me take you to your room."

"Mother, we can take her." Amelia jumped up from the divan, pulled Juliana to her feet, and beckoned to Helena. "It will be like a party."

Mrs. Randolph slowly stood. Her slight wince indicated some sort of pain in her legs. "Yes, that will be fine. Enjoy yourselves, my dears."

They climbed the elegant, winding front staircase to the second floor, and the sisters led Juliana to a bright, airy front corner room with tall windows. Helena plopped across the four-poster mahogany bed that was centered on an interior wall. She stretched out the bed's gauzy canopy and gave it a little shake.

"We mended these, so they should keep the mosquitoes out at night."

"Helena…" Amelia glared at her sister.

"Oh, don't look so cross," said Helena. "The Southerners weren't the only ones to suffer during the war. We couldn't get material for new draperies or even new clothes." Her lips puckered into a little pout. "I've had to wear Amelia's old dresses and shoes, and those soon became too small." She jumped up from the bed and stood beside her sister. "See, I'm four years younger but just as tall."

The sisters stood just over five feet tall, several inches shorter than Juliana. She gave Helena a sympathetic nod. "I'm the youngest daughter, too, and I've always worn my two older sisters' castoffs." She thought of the bolts of fabric she had brought for her hostesses but decided to keep the gifts a surprise. Etiquette required that she present them to Mrs. Randolph.

"But I thought your family was wealthy."

"Helena!" Amelia shook her sister's arm. "What a rude thing to say. You may be the youngest, but you're sixteen now and far too old to make such an improper remark." She walked to the bed and straightened the white chintz bedspread where Helena had mussed it.

"Oh…" Helena shot Juliana a glance of concern.

Juliana returned a merry smile. "I don't mind. Yes, my father inherited some money. When he became a minister, he used a portion of it to build Grace Seaman's Mission in Boston and invested the rest in enterprises that helped maintain the ministry. We never went hungry, but my mother was a frugal Nantucket girl. She's the sweetest, most unselfish woman you could know, but my sisters, brother, and I always tried to guess what new way she would find to squeeze a penny."

"Hmph." Helena gave Amelia a triumphant smirk. Amelia responded by swatting her with a small pillow from the fainting couch.

Now Juliana laughed out loud. Although it was too early in their friendship for her to join in such high jinks with these two, she already felt right at home.

"I suppose I should unpack." She glanced at her luggage, which was stacked where the servants had placed it, beside a mahogany wardrobe in one corner of the room.

"We can help, can't we, Helena?" Amelia walked across the large room and lifted Juliana's hatbox. "Just tell us where you want everything."

Juliana glanced about. "Oh, thank you. I heartily accept your offer. That smallest box can come over here by the dressing table. Just put the hatbox on top of the wardrobe. My dresses are in the top compartment of the trunk. Would you please help me hang them in the wardrobe?"

Three pairs of busy hands soon had placed Juliana's belongings in their appropriate spots. Weary from her journey, Juliana permitted the sisters to put her to bed for a much-needed rest before supper.

As she slipped into pleasant dreams, the Randolphs' amiable countenances mixed with her own family's faces…and that of a handsome young gentleman with war-weary eyes.

✦⊹⊱✺⊰⊹✦

The late afternoon sun cast a harsh August intensity upon the columned white mansion, magnifying the chipped paint and broken eaves and a hundred other flaws. Three months after his return from the war, André still felt a mixture of warmth and sadness as he approached his childhood home. Even as he mentally listed all the repairs the house needed, he fought back thoughts of what should have been.

Little Jim-Jim should be here to greet him and take his horse, but thanks to the Yankee presence in New Orleans, the boy had run away even before the northern congress had signed away southern rights to their chattels.

The horse André rode should have been his noble mare Salome, not this pathetic animal. Today, poor old Max had made it to town all right, but André hadn't the heart to ride him home with the added burden of fifty pounds of flour on his back. Instead, André led the bony creature through the dusty streets to his quiet neighborhood on Prytania Street. Only in passing did he wonder what had happened to Salome and the rest of Father's fine stable. Stolen? Eaten by the Union troops as they occupied New Orleans? During the war, once-civilized men had forgotten all rules of decency.

André led Max to the stable behind the house and removed the flour sack, other provisions, and saddle. He groomed the horse using a brush with half its bristles gone. Max nudged him. Chuckling at the horse's apparent gratitude, André patted his haunches and then scooped oats from a large bin and into the feed trough.

"Eat heartily, old boy. I don't know where Cordell found these oats, but he's managed to produce more than one miracle to keep this place going while I was gone."

André glanced around the nearly empty stable. Other than Max's well-worn bridle and saddle, no harnesses hung on the walls. No carriages sat polished and proud, ready to carry the Beauchamp family to business or pleasure. Only one small cart stood in the corner, and Max wouldn't be able to draw it out of the yard, much less back from town laden with supplies. Cordell must have been forced to sell whatever the Yankees hadn't stolen.

André's empty stomach growled just as a flash of rage burned through his belly. His head down, he leaned against Max and swallowed hard. *Dear God, how hatred hurts.* But he could not escape the bitter thoughts or the physical pain they generated.

"Massuh André?"

Gemma's soft, sweet voice broke into his anguish. He swallowed again and relaxed his clenched jaw before he turned to respond.

The fair young quadroon stood in the stable doorway like a vision from the past—his sweet first love. Long, soft black curls framed her flawless, almost-white face, with its straight nose and full, pink-tinged lips, a perfect, well-blended combination of her one-quarter Negro, three-quarters white ancestry. Her amber eyes sparkled like polished gold under beckoning black lashes. She had grown taller while he had been away, and her body, even hidden beneath patched clothes, had grown more womanly.

A different kind of heat spread through André's belly. This was what he needed, the warmth of a woman. Not just any woman. Gemma. She had waited for him all these years. She had stayed when all the others left. Her loving embrace would soothe away all his fiery pain.

His pulse quickened, and he took a step toward her. "Yes, Gemma. What is it?"

Without meeting his gaze, she ducked her head and frowned, even took a step backward. "Aunt Sukey told me to tell you to come on in and eat something." She turned away and started back toward the house.

"Gemma…"

She stopped and half turned but still did not look at him. "Yes, Massuh?"

"We haven't talked since I came home. I mean, really talked. Come sit a spell with me here in the stable."

Even in profile, he could see her eyes widen while her back stiffened.

"Miz Beauchamp needs me, sir. Aunt Sukey just sent me out to get you. I gotta get back to your mama." She gulped hard and seemed to tremble.

"What is it, sweet girl? What's the matter?"

She must need comforting, too. André reached out to pull her into his arms, but she stepped away.

"I gotta go, Massuh. Let me go. Please."

He exhaled a silent breath. "Yes, go to Mother. And tell Aunt Sukey I'll be in soon."

He watched her as she walked across the back lawn toward the house. She had been a pretty girl. Now her beauty hit him hard in his gut.

Why had she refused him? Was she tired? Was it an inconvenient time of the month?

Guilt pierced the edges of his conscience. She may have been a chattel all her life, but she was still a woman, and he had been away four years. He must woo her, just as he had when he was sixteen and she was twelve. He would bring back the smiles and laughter. It would be like before.

For a moment, doubt darted across his mind. Did Gemma want him as much as he wanted her? But then he chuckled at his foolish uncertainty. After all, she had stayed to be here for him when he came home. With most chattels deserting their rightful owners and with her fair complexion making it possible for her to pass for white, why else would she have stayed? ✳

CHAPTER THREE

✶ ✶ ✶ ✶

*G*rasping the strong brown hand of the carriage driver, Juliana stepped to the ground. "Thank you, Jim-Jim." She shook her skirt to straighten it. Beneath her cotton gown, petticoats, and hoopskirt, perspiration made her underpinnings stick to her legs in a most unpleasant manner. She should have known New Orleans would be far hotter and more humid than Boston.

"Yes, ma'am." The slender young man smiled amiably and turned to help Amelia down from the four-wheeled, open phaeton.

"Please wait for us, Jim-Jim." Amelia said. "You are free to sit in the phaeton with the top up to stay out of this blazing sunshine. In fact, pull it up there under those trees where you'll be cooler." She glanced around the shopping district on Canal Street. "I'm sure no one will bother you."

Concern darted across his dark brown face, but he nodded. "Yes, ma'am. I won't go no place."

"If anyone accuses you of loitering and you don't want to give my surname, just say..." Amelia's smooth forehead crinkled. "Just say..."

...Tell them you're waiting for Miss Harris, for that is the absolute truth. No one knows me so as to find fault with my name." Juliana took Amelia's elbow and turned her toward the sidewalk. When they had walked several yards from the driver, she leaned close to her friend. "Why would anyone question him? Don't drivers usually wait for their employers?"

Amelia glanced back at Jim-Jim before answering. "Even with Union soldiers keeping order in the city, you can't imagine the trouble the rebels are causing Unionists and former slaves who now work for them. Jim-Jim was a slave, of course, and when our Union soldiers told him Mr. Lincoln signed the Emancipation Proclamation, he left his master, even though slavery was still legal here in Louisiana. He's a good worker and takes so much pride in receiving a salary for his labor."

The women paused outside a millinery shop so Amelia could finish her explanation in a whisper. "Even though the war is over and we won, people around here are finding ways to keep their former slaves in some kind of bondage. They can't go just anyplace, and if a white man stops them, they have to account for what they're doing and anything they might have in their hand. If it's a weapon, they can be put in jail. For my part, I think Jim-Jim should go out west or up north and find a new life. His former owner is sure to raise cain if he finds out for whom he is working. And that man *will* find out."

Juliana peeked back at the young driver, who now lounged in the well-kept phaeton under a shady tree. "What do you think the man will do?"

"Well, he's a Beauchamp and a former naval officer, so he'll do something." Amelia's sweet face was marred with a mixture of disgust and concern.

"I understand why a naval officer might feel some antagonism, especially after the way our navy blockaded nearly all their war efforts. But what's so special about the Beauchamps?"

Amelia glanced both ways, pausing until two men passed by and were out of earshot. "Mr. Beauchamp was accused of plotting to kill our General Butler during the occupation, so the army hanged him. When Captain Beauchamp came home and found out, he was heard to say he planned to find out who betrayed his father and take revenge." She shuddered. "And these people claim to be Christians."

Juliana mirrored her shudder and then blew out a soft breath. "Humph. You'd think losing the war would be just the thing to show these people how wrong they were. God would not have permitted the North to prevail if the South had been in the right."

Again, Amelia glanced around them. "Let's not discuss it any more, at least not until we're safely home. Even in broad daylight, we can't feel completely safe. Let's go in here. The owner is one of us."

The store's glass windows displayed more merchandise than Juliana had expected so soon after the deprivations of the war. Inside, hats and bonnets in all the latest styles sat on head-shaped stands or on white shelves along the walls. The shop was filled with sunlight, and a breeze blew in through a back door.

"Welcome, ladies." A pleasantly plump, brown-haired woman perhaps in her thirties came from behind a curtain and stood behind the oak counter. "Oh, it's you, Miss Randolph. How nice to see you. Is your family well?"

"Yes, thank you, Mrs. Dupris. I'll tell Mother you inquired." Amelia nodded toward Juliana. "This is my friend, Miss Harris from Boston. She brought us some bolts of the most beautiful fabrics I've ever seen—some gingham and cambric, and even a few bolts of gingham and lawn. We're going to make dresses and bring the remnants for you to make our bonnets. We've come to purchase some lace and ribbon. Can you match these samples?" She produced several fabric swatches from her reticule, the small drawstring purse Mother had given her, and laid them on the counter.

Juliana smiled at Amelia's chattiness. Her gifts had brightened the Randolph ladies' lives, just as she had hoped.

"How lovely." Mrs. Dupris examined the material with her eyes and fingertips. "Soft but strong. Very nice. Excellent quality. Yes, I'm certain I can match each one."

She produced a three-by-three-foot board on which were pinned strips of ribbon and lace in a wide variety of colors and patterns. She placed the display on the counter, and the three women leaned over it to discuss the best matches. Once they had decided, Mrs. Dupris pulled the appropriate spool from the shelves behind her. As she measured and cut, she eyed Amelia.

"Is your family all right?" Her intense stare seemed to ask a deeper question.

Juliana wondered about the repeated question, especially because it came from a shopkeeper. But apparently Amelia comprehended the woman's purpose.

"Yes, so far. I think things will settle down soon. We cannot depend solely on the military presence. We must all work to restore some semblance of peace among the people of New Orleans."

Mrs. Dupris emitted a soft, unladylike snort. "Peace? With all the subtle threats we Unionists get? Aren't you just scared spitless to come out without your father's protection?"

Amelia blushed, and Juliana felt her own face grow warm at the woman's forceful speech.

"What's your father planning to do, anyway?" Mrs. Dupris continued to cut their lace, and Juliana watched to be certain her measurements were correct.

"Planning to do?"

"Why, isn't he going to go into politics? To take over. To beat these people at their own game."

"Politics?" Amelia batted her eyes in seeming confusion, and Juliana almost laughed. She had seen her new friend use that ploy just this morning in a dispute with Helena. "Why, I can't imagine…"

"I keep telling my Pierre to jump into it. He and your father should put their heads together. They could run this city and get it straightened out fast. There's enough Unionists here to…"

"Oh, my, look how late it is." Amelia glanced up at the clock on the wall behind the counter. "We'll never be home in time if we don't hurry."

The false innocence in her tone veiled Amelia's distaste for the woman's remarks. Juliana copied her friend's expression and nodded in agreement.

Their purchases made, the two left the shop and ambled down the Canal Street sidewalk, gazing in storefronts and chatting about various goods—the only safe conversation they could have in public.

"Shall we go in here?" Juliana indicated the store where they had stopped. "I believe it's just what I'm looking for. I'd like to open an account so we can purchase our slates and chalk and other school supplies." Not to mention she had a sudden craving for some hore-hound candy.

"Umm, I don't think we should go in there. Mr. Fontaine lost both of his sons at Vicksburg. I'm sure he doesn't want to serve Unionists."

Juliana drew in a soft gasp. "Oh, dear. How tragic." She could not dismiss the man's grief, no matter how much the South was at fault for it. But would he refuse to serve her? Might she be in danger?

She stared through the front window. What possible harm could come to her in a public business? Other customers milled about the large establishment. It would be perfectly safe. "He doesn't know me. Why don't you go back to the carriage, and I'll be along soon."

"Oh, I don't think you should…"

"Nonsense, dear. You go on, and I'll join you soon."

When Amelia did not move, Juliana laughed and gave her a tiny push, as she would her own sisters. Lacy and Molly had learned it was never a good idea to get between Juliana and her candy. "I'll be all right."

With obvious reluctance, Amelia turned back toward the spot where their phaeton waited. Several yards down the sidewalk, she turned, and Juliana gave her a reassuring nod. Then Juliana marched through the front door of the store.

Perhaps ten customers—both men and women—searched the shelves for their own private treasures, while children sat or stood around a large glass case filled with candy jars. They must have been waiting for their parents to approve their choices.

What a grand display of sweets. All sorts of colors and flavors: caramel, peppermint, licorice, and her favorite, golden horehound. Juliana's mouth watered. But rather than join the children and drool over the treats, she forced herself to be responsible. She ambled about the store and located the writing slates and chalk, and then found a tattered copy of Charlotte Brontë's *Jane Eyre* priced at only ten cents. The novel about a determined English orphan would provide inspiration for her students, especially her older girls.

By the time she had found all her purchases, the children and most of the adults had departed. Juliana approached the front counter and placed her own selections on it. The store clerk was arranging merchandise on a side display and seemed not to notice her.

"Good afternoon, sir." Juliana was tempted to mimic a southern accent, but she had never been good at acting.

The balding middle-aged man turned and eyed her up and down but did not move to wait on her.

How rude.

"Yes, miss." The hiss at the end of his second word reminded Juliana of the disagreeable man who had rescued her at the docks.

"May I pay for these purchases, please?" She gave him a sweet smile.

He snorted. "No one can ever say Gérard Fontaine turned down a dollar, even a Yankee dollar."

"Oh, thank you, sir. You're so kind." Maybe she wasn't such a bad actress, after all. "You see, I have just come to New Orleans to establish a school for unfortunate children. I hope to do much business with you, for I shall need slates and chalk and books and all sorts of supplies. I would like to open a credit account, and I have a letter from my bank in Boston to guarantee it." She reached into her reticule and fished for the document.

He moved over behind the counter and glowered at her. "Never you mind that, missy. I'll not be giving credit to a Yankee, no matter who guarantees it. Cash on the counter"—he slammed his hand down—"or it's no sale."

When his palm hit the wood, Juliana jumped back, but anger quickly replaced her fear. How dare he? But she would not respond in kind, for that would achieve nothing.

"Ah. I see. Of course. I understand. Cash only." She gave him a tight smile. "Will you please add up my bill?"

The man snorted unpleasantly. He snatched up a slate and began adding the cost of Juliana's purchases. When he finished, he thrust the slate in front of her.

"Five dollars."

"Five dollars? But you've added incorrectly, Mr. Fontaine. It's only three seventy five. You see, here you carried too much..." She started to point to his error.

He slapped down the slate and once again Juliana jumped.

"Take it or leave it. You Yankees have a lot to pay for, and I don't mean this." He jerked his hand over the pile of merchandise.

What shall I do now, Lord? She stared at him evenly until something in his expression sent a chill through her. She lowered her eyes.

"Five dollars, then." She used a soft, soothing tone, as one would if confronted by an angry dog. Again she reached into her reticule.

"Three seventy-five."

A stern male voice behind Juliana resonated with authority. Before she turned, she knew who had spoken. To her chagrin, tears stung her eyes, and she nearly cried with relief for his help. But when she looked up at his stormy countenance, it was laughter she had to stifle. This handsome rebel had once again been forced to be her reluctant knight.

"Now, Captain..." Mr. Fontaine began.

"I am no longer in the military, Mr. Fontaine. Mister will suffice. Now, accept this customer's three seventy-five so I can make my purchase." He placed a can of tea beside her goods and glanced down his straight nose at her. "Don't just stand there. Pay the man."

Juliana's heart thumped, and her fingers shook as she pulled cash from her reticule and counted out the required amount. "There. Three seventy-five."

Mr. Fontaine's eyes darted back and forth between Juliana and the man he called "Captain." He seemed to do battle with himself over whether or not to accept the payment. But his respect for this former officer must have swayed him, for he scooped up the money and deposited it in a box. Then he lifted the tea tin.

"That'll be ten dollars. Shall I put it on your account, sir?"

"You've forgotten to wrap these purchases." His tone once again stern, the young man nodded toward Juliana's goods.

Mr. Fontaine muttered to himself as he pulled thick brown paper from a roll beneath the counter and cut it with scissors. One glance at the other man seemed to prompt him to take care with the way he wrapped the merchandise, securing it with heavy twine. At last he thrust the bundle at Juliana, and she gasped as she took it. When she had carried all her items to the counter, they had not seemed nearly so heavy.

"Thank you." She spoke to Mr. Fontaine, but he was busy marking the young man's purchase in a book. She looked up at her rescuer and offered a trembling smile. "Thank you."

Did his haughty façade soften for an instant? She must have been mistaken, for his response was a quiet grunt.

She struggled toward the door, all the while praying she would not drop the package and shatter the writing slates. In the corner of her eye, she noticed the forgotten horehound candy, but it was too late to go back. In fact, she would never come back to this store, not for all the candy in the world.

She wondered how she would open the door, but again the young man appeared in time to rescue her. Without a word, he pulled the door open and stood back to let her pass.

"Oh, thank you so much."

As she exited, her hoopskirt first pinched inward to fit through the door and then whooshed back into its dome shape, caught in the breeze, and swung back and forth like a church bell. And she without a free hand to stop it! Oh, how she hated this ridiculous fashion. But if the man noticed her chagrin, he gave no indication.

He also did not move away from her but rather stood and stared down at her, his expression unreadable. For some reason, she found herself trapped in his gaze, unable to move.

"So you've come here to teach 'unfortunate' children." It was a statement.

"Yes."

"And what will you teach them? How the South was wrong to secede from the United States and form the Confederacy? How evil their parents are? How our suffering and our losses are our own fault?" His lower jaw jutted out as he spoke, and his eyes blazed.

Juliana shifted her package, and her reticule's chain strap slipped from her shoulder and dug into her forearm. Her discomfort fueled the anger surging in her chest. "Should you not ask me whom I shall be teaching? Will it offend you to know I plan to teach Negro children and women how to read and do their sums so they can make lives for themselves now that you are no longer taking care of them?" Mother would have chided her for this sarcasm, but Juliana could not stop herself.

Once again, his expression seemed to soften for an instant. The returning frown seemed forced. Almost a pout, in fact.

Juliana breathed out a sigh and turned away. *Lord, please don't let me drop the slates.*

"I will carry your package. Where are you going?"

Was it the heat of the day or the stress of the moment? Juliana nearly lost her balance when she turned back to him. He grasped her elbow and steadied her. She surrendered her burden.

"Thank you, sir. Thank you, indeed." Profound relief swept through her. What had changed his attitude toward her? "My friend's carriage is just up the street."

They walked without speaking. Each time she glanced up at him, he appeared deep in thought. She considered that accepting his help this time might not be entirely proper, but she had prayed not to drop the slates. Once again, God had answered through this man.

Their short journey ended beneath shady oak trees where the phaeton waited. Amelia started toward Juliana but stopped, a look of shock appearing on her face.

"Juliana…Miss Harris, where have you been? I've been beside myself with worry."

Was Amelia actually wringing her hands? Juliana grasped her friend's gloved fingertips. "There were so many choices. It took a while to make up my mind."

Juliana's companion approached Amelia's driver. "Hello, Jim-Jim."

The youth could not meet the man's intense stare. "H'lo, Massuh."

"Tie this package safely to the carriage." He handed over Juliana's purchases.

"Yes, Massuh." Jim-Jim hastened to obey the order.

"Miss Harris. Miss Randolph." The young man swept off his straw hat and bowed low, almost with exaggeration. He straightened, turned, and strode away.

Juliana and Amelia stood unmoving for several moments. Then Amelia grasped Juliana's shoulders and gave her a shake.

"What on earth were you doing with André Beauchamp?" ✳

CHAPTER FOUR

✯ ✯ ✯ ✯

"Here's your tea, Mama." André set the silver tray on the low table beside his mother's blue brocade *chaise lounge*. "Won't you sit up and have a cup?"

With tender care, he drew her up to a sitting position and sat beside her to pour the freshly steeped beverage into a delicate china cup.

"Sugar?"

His question brought a lazy smile to her lips.

"Why, François, how many years have we been married, and you still ask if I want sugar?" Her warm, sweet laugh seemed an effort for her. "How forgetful you are. Two lumps, of course, as always."

"Of course." André's hand trembled as he lifted the silver sugar tongs and placed two lumps in the cup before handing it to her. He must control himself, for she would never comprehend his display of emotion. It might even prevent her recovery.

During four years of war, he had never faltered, no matter how horrendous the losses on his ship, for his men needed to see him stand firm. Why could he not summon that same strength and self-control now?

"My darling, this tea is delicious." Despite the weariness in her tone, Mama's aristocratic English accent infused her comment with authority. "Won't you have some?"

André cleared his throat. "No, thank you, Mama."

"No, of course not. You always prefer your coffee. Won't you have Etty bring you some?" She waved her hand passively toward the door.

He hesitated before answering, but her lazy expectancy demanded a response. Dr. Tanner had urged him to accept her misperceptions, but he could not agree. "Don't you remember? Etty is no longer with us."

Mama gave him a long look. "No longer…?" She turned toward the window, and her eyes lost their focus.

André swallowed hard. When her attention drifted off this way, he could hardly bear it. He gently removed the teacup from her grasp and set it on the tray.

"Mama." He put his arm around her and pressed her head to his shoulder. "Dear, sweet Mama, you must not leave me. You're all I have."

She pulled back and looked at him as if he were a stranger. Then her vision seemed to clear and her expression turned troubled. "Oh, François, where are the boys? I'm so worried about Elgin and André. Where could they have gone?"

André couldn't keep the tremor from his voice. "Mama, I'm here. I'm André. Look at me, Mama. See *me*."

Confusion filled her face, and she expelled a deep, weary sigh. "Oh, dear." She leaned away from him and laid her head against the arm of the *chaise lounge.*

His eyes moistened, so he forced away the tears with a bracing breath. He stood and pulled her legs up on the couch, then laid a thin coverlet over the light dressing gown she wore. Tea service in hand, he paused at the door to be sure she was resting.

Her shiny, thick blond curls had grown dull and sparse over the years. Her cherubic face, always so girlish, now wore deep lines around her eyes. Her plump, pouting lips had thinned, as had her once-round form.

André's heart surged with love and pity—and resolution. Whatever it took, he would restore her life as best he could. Despite Dr. Tanner's warnings, he would bring her out of this phantasmic despair. Together they would grieve over Father's and Elgin's deaths. Then they would go on to build a new life.

With each descending step on the back staircase to the kitchen, André felt his determination grow. With Cordell at his right hand in this new coffee import business, he would earn enough money to rebuild the cotton plantation. They would find more good workers like the men Cordell had hired. Aunt Sukey could stay here at the house in town and keep things running smoothly until Mama was well. The plan was good. He could do it. He would do it.

Aunt Sukey stirred the contents of a pot on the kitchen stove as she had every day since André could remember. Like Mama, she had grown thinner over the years, but she had assured him none of them went hungry during the war. He supposed that was the one good thing about his loved ones being in an occupied city.

Sweat beaded on her light brown forehead and dampened the flowered handkerchief that held back her hair. "Did Miz Felicity like her tea, Mr. André?"

He set the tray on the worktable in the center of the room. "She did indeed, Auntie."

She tapped her spoon on the edge of the cast-iron pot, laid it on the small stand beside the stove, and put a lid on the pot. Wiping her hands on her well-worn white apron, she reached for the tea service and set it next to the dishpan.

"The tea's still hot if you'd like to have some." André poured himself a cup of coffee from the pot at the back of the stove.

"Why, thank you, sir." Aunt Sukey's face beamed.

"Pour yourself a cup and come sit with me." He pulled out a chair and sat at the table.

"Yessuh." Again, happiness shone on her sweet countenance. In her younger days, she had been a beauty, and even now, her smooth brown face evoked admiration. She took an old tin cup from the cupboard for her tea, but she would not take a sip until he drank some coffee.

Something in her demeanor had bothered him since he had returned home. She seemed too servile, too eager to please him. This woman had helped to raise him, had even smacked his hands a few times when he had grabbed forbidden sweets as a child. Before he left for the naval academy at sixteen, she had sat him down for a talk about how to stay out of trouble, echoing his father and discussing subjects his mother never, ever would have mentioned or even seemed to know about. As much as it had pained her, she gave her blessing when her own son was sent along as his body servant. Why would she now act more like a chattel than when she actually had been one?

"Auntie, we haven't had much time to talk since I came home."

"No suh."

She looked in his direction but not into his eyes. Few slaves dared to raise their eyes to their masters'. But this was Aunt Sukey, who had once stared him down until he wept with shame for throwing dirt at the laundry drying on the back line. Fondness—no, love—filled his heart for this good woman.

"You must know how grateful I am for the care you've given Mama."

She looked down at her cup. "Couldn't do nothin' else."

"But you could have." He tilted his head to catch her gaze, but she avoided him. "When Etty and May and Clarence and Jim-Jim and all the rest left, you could have gone, too. Why didn't you?"

Now she looked up. "Why, how could I do that? Before Massuh François died, he made me promise to take care of the missus."

A queasy feeling filled his stomach, as it did every time he thought of his father's death. He studied the coffee grounds at the bottom of his cup. He'd had far too much chicory during the war, but now was not the time to ask her not to mix chicory into his coffee.

"I'm so sorry for bringin' that up, Mr. André."

Now she looked square into his eyes with sorrow written in her own. Or did those faint tears reveal something deeper? True grief? What a devoted servant. What a treasure.

"It's all right, Auntie." *No, it isn't.* "Tell me, was Mama…uh …*well* before Father…um…" André cleared his throat. The warm sympathy in Aunt Sukey's voice and demeanor weakened his control, what little he had today.

"Yessuh, she was. Miz Felicity was fit as can be. Bright and cheerful, full of faith, like always, even after the Yankees came and took Massuh François away. She'd given a party that night, and some of them Creole folks had come down from their high horses to come over for it." She stopped, and a frown creased her smooth forehead. "I'm sorry, sir. Massuh François was Creole, and you're half. I don't mean to…"

He breathed out a mirthless chuckle. "Don't give it another thought. They disowned my father for marrying English and snubbed my mother from the first day she came to New Orleans. Why would I care what they think?"

"Well…" Aunt Sukey gave him a little grin—a real one. "I gotta say this for them, once the war started, they was awful proud of *you*. Lot of their boys went off to the war, and lots didn't make it back. You was an officer. I guess that made you all right in their eyes."

He chuckled again, more at her pleased expression than her words, for it showed her own pride in him. Then he sobered. "When did Mama begin to…to decline?"

She looked down, and her tears returned. "She never believed them Yankees would hang him. Nobody did. Everybody knew Massuh was a kind, peaceable man. He never would have tried to kill that ol' General Butler." Her lips curled as she said the Union officer's name. "No suh." She gave a quick shake of her head. "Never. But somebody said he was in charge of the plans, and they took him away right in the middle of Miz Felicity's party."

His fists clenched, André leaned forward. "Who, Auntie? Who was the liar? Was it Charles Randolph?"

She shook her head. "Some say so, but I couldn't tell you yes or no. We all knew Mr. Randolph's a Unionist, but he's a Christian man, too. He wouldn't lie so somebody'd hang. What good would that do when the Yankees already had New Orleans?"

A subtle change came in her sad expression, a slight furrowing of her forehead. "Mr. André, they's somethin' I ought to tell you—"

Laughter at the back door stopped her. Cordell and Gemma entered, each carrying an armload of vegetables from Aunt Sukey's garden. The moment they saw André, their laughter ceased. He could almost see Cordell's thoughts as the expression on his caramel-colored face changed from surprised to servile to remembering his new station. André might have laughed had it not stung his heart so deeply. They had grown up together, had been bosom friends despite their positions in life. Why couldn't Cordell just relax and accept the new order of things? After all, André's parents had always treated their chattels well.

His relationship with Gemma was proving even harder to amend. His attempts to woo her had fallen flat. If not for the flattering attentions of one or two New Orleans belles when he met them on the street, his ego might have suffered. Even now, Gemma refused to look his way but busied herself cleaning the vegetables in the dry sink.

"Mr. André," Cordell placed his load of carrots with hers. "What can I do for you?"

"Nothing at all." André put his hands behind his head and tilted his chair on its back legs. "I'm just relaxing here with Aunt Sukey." What had she started to tell him?

With a gasp, Aunt Sukey jumped up and hurried to the stove. Grabbing her spoon, she lifted the lid from the pot and stirred the contents. "Ooee! Just about burned these beans. Mr. André, you gonna have to stay outta my kitchen. You distract me when I'm cooking."

Cordell and Gemma stared at her, their mouths agape. But when André laughed heartily, they also surrendered soft, nervous chuckles.

This was the way he wanted it—everyone in his household feeling comfortable and safe. His parents had always treated their chattels like family. By remaining a part of the Beauchamp household when they could have left, these three dear ones had shown they thought of themselves as family, too. And as family, they would make a new life together.

Maybe he should move Gemma out of the room she shared with Aunt Sukey and into her own bedroom upstairs. That might make her feel more amenable to his wooing.

Somehow the thought didn't sit well in his mind. How could he make her his mistress again when he was not in love with her? The thought jolted him. Of course he loved her. Even now, he could imagine kissing that fair, creamy neck as she bent over the dry sink hard at work on supper vegetables.

He set his chair aright and stood, shaking off the feelings his thoughts had provoked. He must be patient with her, with all of them. He must care for them and for Mama. Reluctant but proud, he was the head of this household now. ✳

CHAPTER FIVE

✶ ✶ ✶ ✶

"Five hunnert in advance for the year."

The disagreeable man waved his smelly cigar right under Juliana's nose. His stained, oft-mended suit held the odor of whiskey, and she could only guess how many days it had been since he bathed or shaved. His destitute appearance belied the fact that he owned this small, wood-framed house she wanted to rent.

"Will you have it cleaned before our lease begins?" Amelia stood nearby, a perfumed handkerchief held to her dainty nose, for the cluttered room reeked of all manner of waste.

"Clean it yerselves if you want it." Mr. LaRue stuck his cigar between his stained lips and leered at Amelia. "No matter to me whether you take it or not. I'll find somebody who'll pay five hunnert or even more. Not many places for rent in this neighborhood. It's old, but it's a good address."

"Oh, I'm certain it is." Juliana modulated the sarcasm in her voice as best she could. "We shall rent it, Mr. LaRue." She glanced around once more. The tall, narrow windows brought in light, an important feature if they were to save money on oil for their lamps.

The pleased surprise on his face almost made her laugh. "Five hunnert in advance."

"Yes, so you said. Now, there's only one more matter to attend to." Juliana exchanged a glance with Amelia. "You must know *in advance* that we intend to establish a school for Negro women and children in this house."

He grimaced but didn't respond.

"It must be written in the lease that you know our purpose and have permitted us to rent the house *for that purpose.*"

He turned toward the front window, removed his battered bowler hat, and ran stained fingers through his greasy hair. The struggle in his expression revealed just what she had expected. The man needed the money, and, his bold claims notwithstanding, he had not been able to find a renter. No wonder, considering the disrepair and filth in the two-room house.

"I don't want no trouble." Indecision still clouded his face. "But they's mostly coloreds in this neighborhood now. It's the school part I don't know about. Used ta be before the war it was against the law to teach coloreds to read. Can't see why things'd have to be any different now."

"Everyone needs an education, Mr. LaRue." Juliana sensed he was weakening. She straightened to her full height and spoke with an air of authority. "I can have my banker wire five hundred dollars in United States funds to your bank as soon as we sign a lease with provisions we both agree on."

Greed glistened in his dark eyes. He clapped his hat back on and grinned as if he had won a prize. "That's fine by me. I'll write something up."

"You mustn't trouble yourself." Juliana offered a pleasant smile. "Our lawyer will take care of it."

"Lawyer? Now, see here, missy…"

"Why, Mr. LaRue, there's no cause for alarm. Lawyers simply translate the law for those who cannot comprehend it. A lease prepared for us by a lawyer will protect us both. And of course, if you object to any of the provisions, you can refuse to sign, and we will move on to find another house for our school."

Confusion deepened the age lines around his eyes, as though he wondered how Juliana had gained the upper hand. She retained her pleasant smile and reached out a gloved hand.

"Do we have a bargain, sir?"

He scowled but thrust his cigar in his mouth and shook her hand. "Awright, then, we have a bargain. You know where to find me when you get that paper from the lawyer."

Juliana and Amelia restrained their delight until Jim-Jim had driven them away from the house. Both young ladies were eager to discuss their plans.

"We should send out the word about the school right away." Amelia still held her white linen handkerchief and used it to dab perspiration from her upper lip. "No doubt many of our potential students will want to help clean the house."

"And paint it." Juliana wondered if any local stores had paint or if she would have to send to Boston for it.

"And repair the furniture."

"Will former slaves know how to repair furniture?"

Amelia cocked her head and stared at Juliana. "Of course. They didn't just pick cotton. They did all the work on the plantations. You'll be amazed at their varied abilities."

Juliana's face grew even warmer than the hot day warranted. "Oh, how silly of me. I should have realized that." She drew out her fan to cool herself. "And so, we will need the furniture repaired and will have to purchase desks and chairs and books and…"

"Did you notice the built-in bookshelves in the east room?"

Juliana nodded. "We'll start our library there."

"Oh, my." Amelia bent forward and stared up the street in the direction they traveled. "That looks like…it *is*…your friend, Mr. Beauchamp."

Juliana located the oncoming rider and drew in a sharp breath. Indeed, Mr. Beauchamp leaned forward astride an old horse and slapped it with his straw hat to force the poor animal to a hard gallop. Man and beast threw off sweat and foam as they swept past the carriage, swirling up clouds of dust from the dry street. In spite of their speed, Juliana could see the expression on his face.

"Why, he looks terrified." She twisted in her seat to watch him turn at the corner and disappear beyond some houses. Flouncing back to face the front, she tried to contain her alarm. "Poor man. Whatever could have him in such a state?"

"And in his shirtsleeves, too. Strange for a man who always dresses so properly." Amelia reached for Juliana's hand. "I'm sorry for calling him your friend."

"Never mind, dear. I would gladly be his friend if it would lead to his salvation. From the look of things, perhaps even now the Lord is bringing him to his knees through some calamity."

Juliana thought her heart would burst. How she longed to follow her golden-haired knight as he faced whatever caused his terror. *Lord, please help him through this trial, and please help me to quit dreaming about him unless You're going to save him.*

They resumed their chatter about the school until they reached the house, where the Randolphs' elderly Negro butler met them at the gate.

"Oh, Miss Amelia, Miss Juliana, come in quick." Gray-haired Jerome helped them from the phaeton before Jim-Jim had a chance to jump down from his seat. Always a picture of reserve and control, the old man hurried back toward the front door.

"Jerome, what is it?" Amelia caught his anxiety as they rushed into the house.

He turned to her with a worried expression. "Oh, Lawdy, miss, it's Mr. Charles."

"Father? What happened? Tell me…"

"Oh, Miss Amelia, he been shot. He been shot. Hurry on up the stairs. We sent for the doctor, and Miz Rachel and Miss Helena is with him now."

While the other two hastened up the stairway, Juliana stopped at its foot, and her legs threatened to buckle. A vision of terror-stricken André Beauchamp astride a galloping horse flashed through her mind.

"No…no." She gripped the banister and bowed her head against it. "Lord, please, *no.*"

Had her gallant knight become an avenging murderer?

Jumping from Max before the horse could fully stop, André dashed up the back steps and into the kitchen.

"Aunt Sukey!" He raced through the hallway and up the staircase. "Aunt Sukey!"

Aunt Sukey emerged from his mother's bedroom and closed the door. "Hush, Mr. André, hush now." She waved him away. "Now go on downstairs. Everythin's awright. Miz Felicity's gon' be awright."

André slumped against the wall. "Then why did you send that boy to tell me she fell?" He straightened and started toward the bedroom.

Her eyes were filled with worry, but she touched his arm. "Now, chile, don't go disturbin' her. Yes, she had a fall down the front stairs, and I was scared she was hurt. That's why I sent the boy to git you. But she musta just fell down the last few steps, 'cause when she come to, she walked back up the steps herself, jest leaning on me a bit."

"Did she say anything? Did she say why she came downstairs?"

"Well, um, I don't rightly know." Aunt Sukey wiped her eyes and shook her head. "She musta had one of her wanderin' spells. I sure do hope she don't start to feel pain later on. By the time I put her to bed, she didn't even recall she'd fell." She gave him a sidelong look, as if uncertain he would believe her.

André exhaled a fierce blast of air from his still-heaving lungs. "Thank God."

"Yessuh, that's right. Thank the Lord." She now gave him a large grin.

He heaved a few more breaths to clear his lungs after his frantic ride. Poor old Max. He would have to tend to him soon.

"Where's Gemma?" An unpleasant thought swept through him, and his tone grew sharp. "Where was she when Mama fell?"

Aunt Sukey frowned. "Now, son, she's with your mama, but she ain't at fault. She just stepped out to the backhouse for a minute. She's with Miz Felicity all day every day. The girl's got to breathe sometime."

André gave her a short nod. "I suppose. Yes, of course she does."

"Now, your mama do have a little bump on her temple, but Gemma's put some cool cloths on it." Aunt Sukey lifted her hand in appeal. "Honey, the girl feel so bad about it. Please don't fault her. Please don't make her feel worse."

André paced the hall, still trying to calm himself. He suddenly felt drained. All his dread—terror, actually—had been for naught.

"I'm going to look in. I can't go back to work until I see for myself she's all right."

Aunt Sukey nodded. "Yessuh, I understand."

He carefully opened the door, wincing at the noisy creak of the hinges. When was the last time they had been oiled? Another neglected task to add to his growing list.

Gemma sat on a chair beside the bed in the shadowy room. Her expression revealed her anguish over the mishap. She hurried over to him.

"Oh, Massuh André, I'm so sorry."

"Shh. Never mind, sweet girl." He patted her shoulder, resting his hand briefly on its soft roundness. "You go on downstairs and see what Aunt Sukey needs you to do. I'll stay with Mama."

"Yessuh." She edged around him and left the room.

In the dim light that found its way through the shuttered and draped windows, André studied the small lump on Mama's temple. The tiniest bit of blood oozed through the broken skin. He sat beside the bed and applied a cool, damp cloth to the wound. Tender grief surged through his breast and welled up into his throat. Her injury was small, but she was so delicate these days—not at all like her former, hearty self—that he could not bear to see her suffer in any way.

"Mama," he whispered. "Sweet Mama, I'm here to watch over you."

She did not stir.

The memory of the Yankee girl he had passed on the way home flitted across his mind. She had looked so startled. She must think him a madman. He emitted a silent, ironic laugh. Why should he care what she thought? But their two encounters haunted him. She had come here to help people, to start a school, to teach those who were less fortunate. Despite his attempts to dismiss all thoughts of her, he could not deny his admiration.

Mama rolled over and blinked in the darkness. "François?"

"It's me, Mama. André. Are you all right?"

"Why yes, my dear. Of course I'm all right."

Several minutes passed in silence.

"François?"

André groaned. The battle to make her recognize him weighed too heavily right now.

"Yes, Mama."

"Why did Cordell want to take me downstairs? I was too tired to go, but he insisted."

André shook his head. More delusions. "Mama, Cordell has been at the warehouse with me all morning."

"Oh. Oh, my." She looked at him with troubled eyes. After a moment, she said, "My dear, it's been so long since you've read to me. Would you read to me now?"

The thought pleased him. She had asked for nothing before this. It was a good sign.

"What shall I read, dear one?"

"Why, the Psalms, of course. You know they're my favorite."

Something twisted hard inside André's gut. The Psalms. The Bible. The book of the One who had betrayed his godly father. It wasn't enough that God had abandoned the Confederacy; He had also permitted an evil man to lie and murder the finest Christian André had ever known.

Mama watched him expectantly, a half-smile on her lips. He walked to her elegant mahogany desk and retrieved the book. Was it his imagination or the heat of the day? The book nearly burned his hands.

He opened to the Psalms and held the book up to catch the dim light from the window.

"Blessed is the man that walketh not in the counsel of the ungodly…" ✳

CHAPTER SIX

✷ ✷ ✷ ✷

Juliana shook off her anguish and hastened upstairs to the master bedroom, where Amelia and Helena stood at the foot of the bed, comforting each other. Mrs. Randolph held a handkerchief to the bleeding wound on her husband's chest. Another injury on the side of his head had already clotted into a grotesque red and black mass. The unconscious patient lay shirtless and still.

"Mrs. Randolph, you must permit me to do that." Juliana moved to the trembling woman's side. "Amelia, help your mother to sit down. Has anyone sent for a doctor?"

"Yes. Oh, I do hope he arrives soon." Mrs. Randolph fussed with her husband's jacket, clearly not knowing what to do. "I must stop the bleeding."

"Please let me help. I tended many injured soldiers at our mission in Boston."

"You did?" Mrs. Randolph surrendered her place. "Yes, yes, of course. Please do what you can." She accepted her daughters' assistance to a nearby chair.

Above his heart, the wound in his chest oozed a slow, steady stream of dark red liquid, giving Juliana hope. Bright spurts would mean his heart was pumping out his life's blood. If the bullet had been visible, she would have demanded a knife to remove it before infection could set in. If the doctor did not arrive soon, she would dig for it anyway. For now, she ripped a sleeve from Mr. Randolph's shirt, balled it up, and pressed it to the wound. With her free hand, she carefully examined the mass on his head but couldn't tell if a bullet had entered.

"Amelia, please bring a pan of warm water. I want to clean this."

"Right away." Amelia ran from the room.

Juliana studied Mr. Randolph's gray complexion. Other than the flow of blood, only a slight pulsing in his neck indicated that he still lived. She stared hard at Helena, who trembled and wrung her hand-kerchief as if on the verge of hysteria.

"Helena," Juliana used a stern but gentle tone. "Go fetch old linen sheets and rip them into strips about six inches wide. We'll need plenty of bandages."

Helena gulped back her tears and ran to obey.

"We made it all through the war without their doing anything more violent than throwing rotting animal carcasses on our front porch." Mrs. Randolph looked almost as pale as her husband. "Why did they do this now? Why do they blame us?"

"There's no sense to it, is there?" Juliana glanced over her shoulder. "Ah, Jerome, you're still here. Please bring Mrs. Randolph some tea."

"Yes, Miz Juliana." The elderly man had regained his composure but still wore a distressed expression as he hurried out.

Lord, please put Your healing hand upon this good man. Juliana released her pressure from the wound to inspect it. The blood came more slowly now—a good sign.

In the presence of the frightened Randolph women, she had affected an air of calm experience. Inside she was a quivering mass of uncertainty. A memory flitted across her mind—her own family kneeling around the bed of her younger brother during one of his many illnesses. God had always healed Samuel, and He could help the Randolphs now. In addition, prayer would comfort the Randolph ladies.

"Mrs. Randolph, gather the household. We shall kneel here and pray."

Mrs. Randolph's eyes brightened. "I've prayed from the moment the servants brought Charles inside. But you're right. We should all seek the Lord's comfort together."

In a short time, the mother, two sisters, and four servants knelt about the room while Juliana tended the patient. In the activity of gathering them, Mrs. Randolph had regained some strength. Once again she was mistress of her house.

As they prayed, Juliana brushed away her tears with the back of her hand. She needed to see in order to clean the matted blood from Mr. Randolph's head wound. Gently dabbing warm water into the thick hair around the bloody lump, she reached its core and bit her lips to stifle a gasp. No bullet lodged there, but a shallow gash cut into the skull four inches above his left ear. A shudder swept through her. What if she had caused more injury by cleaning around it?

Dr. Mayfield, a uniformed Union physician, arrived within an hour. With gentle diplomacy, the sober young man sent the prayer meeting to another room but kept Juliana at his side.

"Miss Harris, I can see you are an excellent nurse," he whispered while examining Mr. Randolph. "If you were not a lady, I would offer you employment in my infirmary."

His bold pronouncement did not offend Juliana, for doctors in Boston had told her much the same thing. Assured that she had done no harm, she gulped back tears of relief.

"Thank you, sir." She peered over his shoulder. "How is he?"

"Gravely wounded, I'm afraid. But you knew that." He glanced at her before turning back to his work of removing the bullet from Mr. Randolph's chest. "You were asking me if he is going to live. I wish I could say yes, but I cannot. Once I remove this slug and patch up the wounds, only God can mend him."

His words echoed her own faith but brought both relief and despair. How often as she nursed dying soldiers had they begged her to promise them that they would live? She could never make such a guarantee but rather pointed them to Christ to assure them that whatever happened to their bodies, their souls would live on with Him. Yet, while Mr. Randolph was ready to meet his Maker, his family desperately needed him.

"Mercy."

The word slipped out in a whisper. Dr. Mayfield glanced at her again and smiled. His kind, pleasant face had the worn look of a man who had been a wartime surgeon.

"Yes, mercy. It *is* all we can hope for now, is it not?"

After he had used large tweezers to remove the bullet and the particles of fabric it had forced into Mr. Randolph's chest, Dr. Mayfield applied antiseptic and stitched the wound closed. With Juliana's assistance, he wrapped Helena's bandages around the patient's slender chest. Then he straightened up and rolled his shoulder and neck. Sweat poured from his face.

"Would you mind if I took off my outer coat?"

"Not at all, doctor."

Juliana helped him remove his blue woolen coat and laid it on a chair. She offered him a linen rag to wipe his face.

He smiled his gratitude.

"Now for this one." His expression once again sober, he bent to examine the head wound and exhaled. "Mmmm."

"Is it…?"

"Not deep, but still serious."

For the first time, Juliana noticed how gently his long, slender fingers touched the wound. She could imagine the hand of Christ touching her injured friend in this manner. Would that the kind doctor's hands held the same healing power.

＊❖＊

André awoke slowly, his mind clouded from the lack of air in the room. He lifted his head from the edge of Mama's bed and watched her. She wore a serene expression, as she had from the moment he began to read the Psalms.

He struggled to shake away his mental fog. He should get back to the warehouse. Cordell would need his signature for the coffee shipment. And André needed to bring home some supplies for Aunt Sukey. He would have to take Max with him…

Max!

Fear slammed into André's stomach. As quietly as he could, he left the room and dashed down the back stairway. Aunt Sukey wasn't in the kitchen, and neither was Gemma. He ran out the back door to the stable.

Both women knelt beside Max, who lay on the hard dirt floor. His legs jerked with irregular spasms, and he groaned out a pitiful whinny.

Gemma looked up with sadness filling her eyes. "Mr. André, he fell down." She caressed Max's head and brushed away her tears. "He jus' dropped down to the ground."

Aunt Sukey slowly shook her head. "He won't live, a sick old horse like this. You gonna have to..." Her expression finished her sentence.

Burning pain gripped André's stomach, and he swallowed hard to keep from heaving. What madness had taken over his life? Not once in his twenty-four years had he ever mistreated or neglected a horse. He had spent many boyhood hours in these stables learning from the family's groom how to care for the animals. Yet now, because of him, here lay a once-fine horse suffering because he had ridden him to exhaustion.

André longed to kneel down and burrow his face into Max's mane, but that would have to wait. He turned and strode back to the house. Twenty-five yards had never seemed so far to walk.

In the study, he pulled a key from his pocket and unlocked the tall wooden gun cabinet. Setting his hand briefly on several different weapons, he chose the old Jennings rifle his father had preferred for hunting. But then he realized that if the gun's one shot didn't kill Max, André would have to reload, and Max would suffer even longer. André searched for his father's pearl-handled, six-shot Colt revolver. It was not in the cabinet. With a muttered curse, he grabbed the rifle, powder, and shot, loaded the weapon, and returned to the stable.

"Goodbye, ol' Max. Goodbye. You been a good ol' horse." Gemma petted his head one last time and then stood with Aunt Sukey.

"Don't you want to go to the house?" André said.

The two women shook their heads and clung to each other.

André knelt and patted the horse. "Goodbye, old boy." With a shudder, he stood and, with careful aim, ended the beast's suffering.

Aunt Sukey gasped, and Gemma yelped.

"Find someone to haul him away," André said to Aunt Sukey.

He strode back to the house, returned the rifle to its place, and secured the gun cabinet. Refusing to acknowledge the pain in his stomach, he marched from the house out into the street and down toward the docks.

He would not think about Max. He would not think about Mama's fall. He would go to the dock and sign the shipping log and write more letters to coffee suppliers.

A hot breeze blew through his sweat-soaked shirt, and he hesitated for a moment. He had left his tan frock coat at the warehouse. Should he return home and get another? André snorted. Let all the fine young ladies see him walking the streets in his shirtsleeves. What did he care for society's conventions? Without a shred of decency or mercy, he had just ridden a faithful family servant to death. He was nothing less than a murderer. But where was the sorrow? Where was the shame? All he felt was ice in his heart and a raging fire in his belly. ✳

✦ ✦ ✦

"It is my sincere hope that you will never encounter another tragedy like this." Dr. Mayfield leaned forward in the gold wingback chair and spoke to Juliana in a whisper. "But again I must commend your nursing skill. Because of your experience, you were able to take charge of the situation and provide much-needed help for this good family."

Heat rose to Juliana's cheeks at the intensity of the doctor's gaze. "Thank you, sir." Helping him to tend Mr. Randolph had exhausted her, but the effort also had given her great satisfaction. In the fading daylight that shadowed the bedroom, she studied the patient and felt gratified to see his breathing had deepened.

Dr. Mayfield cleared his throat. "One thing I must mention."

"Yes?"

The doctor's demeanor grew stern, but his voice remained soft. "You must never wash a clotted wound. By breaking the scab, you can cause further loss of blood and possibly irreparable damage. Always wait for a doctor."

Juliana gasped. "Did I…?"

He shook his head. "No. The bullet grazed his head but not deeply. When I washed the rest of the scab away to check the wound, I was prepared to staunch the blood flow." He gave her an encouraging smile. "Please do not reproach yourself, dear lady. You were very brave."

The admiration in his eyes brought another rush of heat to her cheeks. "Doctor, your skillful hands saved Mr. Randolph's life…yours and the hand of the Lord."

"We are only His instruments, are we not?" He stood to check Mr. Randolph's breathing, then sat back down, released a weary sigh, and rested his head against the back of his chair.

Juliana's heart warmed. Tired as he was, Dr. Mayfield would not leave until his patient was out of danger. What a gentle man. Even his words of reproof had been softened with kindness, which hadn't often been the case with the doctors in Boston during the war.

In a short time, Dr. Mayfield's soft snore brought a smile to her lips. She could like this man very much. He was a Christian who truly depended on the Lord. Of medium height, he had a slightly stocky, muscular frame. His pleasant face, while not handsome, exuded peace and inner strength.

How sad that André Beauchamp did not possess those same graces. She considered the look on his face as he had ridden past the carriage. Did he shoot Mr. Randolph? Or had Juliana made a hasty judgment simply because he had ridden in haste? Whatever anguish she had observed in those brief seconds, she had not noticed guilt. Or had she only seen what she wanted to see? Even now his tall, well-formed body and handsome face danced into her thoughts. Without doubt, she felt more attracted to him than any man she had ever met.

Juliana, Juliana, what are you thinking? Here before me is a Christian gentleman whose every waking moment is spent saving lives. And yet my heart reaches out to one who may be a murderer. Dear Lord, let me not be led into temptation.

She thought for a moment. *And please don't let it be Mr. Beauchamp who shot Mr. Randolph.*

✦✦✧❋✧✦✦

By the time André reached the docks, the late afternoon sun bore down with its final blast of heat for the day. Reeking sweat drenched his body, and he burned inside with a bellyache and ill humor. At his warehouse, he found Cordell hard at work with their three employees loading a shipment of coffee and other merchandise onto a cart.

"Mr. Beauchamp"—Cordell insisted on formality in front of the other men—"Mr. Dupris is in your office. He's been waiting for over an hour for your appointment. I told him you had an emergency. Is Miss Felicity all right?" His eyes clouded with concern.

André gave him a curt nod, and Cordell responded with an understanding look. They had been together since infancy and knew every nuance of each other's personality. Later André would explain about Mama—and Max.

As André strode through the warehouse to his office, a strange mixture of disgust and hope replaced his former misery. Although Dupris boasted an Old New Orleans Creole heritage, he had fraternized with the Yankees after they took the city in 1863. After the war had ended the previous April, he said he had been spying in hopes of finding some way to help the Confederate cause. André hadn't had time to check out his claims, nor had any of his acquaintances. Right now every man spent his days piecing together the last remnants of his former life. For André, that might mean doing business with a man like Dupris.

"André!"

Dupris stood and advanced with a pudgy, outstretched hand. André shook it with reluctance. But Dupris grasped his hand firmly and pulled him into a fraternal embrace, a clumsy feat for the shorter man whose protruding belly suggested he had not gone hungry during the war. Dupris stepped back and studied André up and down.

"Look at you, the war hero—Captain André Beauchamp." Dupris smiled, revealing a gold upper tooth.

"The war's over, Dupris." André tried to ignore his revulsion at the man's touch.

"How are you? How's your family?" Dupris grimaced. "Forgive me, my friend. It was a thoughtless question. Your poor father..."

With a light shrug, André moved to his cluttered desk. "What do you want, Dupris? Why this appointment?" He searched for his frock coat without success. Hadn't he left it on the back of his chair? Father never would have done business in his shirtsleeves. André peered under the desk. No coat.

"Ah, that's the question these days, isn't it? Why are former acquaintances becoming fast friends? Why are former enemies now our very lifeline?" The dark-haired little man rocked on his heels, glancing at the extra chair in front of André's desk where he had been sitting.

André gave an indifferent wave of his hand to invite Dupris to sit down. If the man found his host's bad manners objectionable, he didn't show it. André dropped into his own chair and glared across the desk at Dupris's fawning smile.

"Talk." André wondered if his rudeness would send Dupris to some other hapless soul, but after today's tragedies, he didn't care one way or the other.

Dupris leaned forward. His eyes sparked with enthusiasm. "You have your coffee imports and other goods for sale. I have market contacts all over the northeast. We'll make a fortune."

André snorted. "Contacts so soon after the war? How does that happen? Besides, you're a pure-blooded Creole. Why would you step out of your little enclave for a partnership?"

Dupris's smile took on a bit of strain. "I thought you knew. My wife is from Pennsylvania. Like your dear departed father, I married outside the *enclave,* and you know what that means." A slight sneer darted across his mustachioed lips. "Let them keep on inbreeding." With a twitch of his shoulders, he resumed his irritating smile. "The contacts are through my wife's people all the way up the Ohio River. That's a lot of customers for your coffee."

André settled an even look on Dupris. The man was probably close to forty. He had hustled countless deals for many years before the war. During the war, there's no telling what he had done in complicity with the Yankees. André, at twenty-four, with only his naval training and service behind him, felt acutely aware of his own lack of business experience. Father or Elgin would have known whether or not to trust the man. Still, André's being the middleman who transferred goods from foreign markets to a local distributor seemed simple enough. But to deal with this man? Even now, Dupris's toadying smile turned his stomach.

"Why don't you import your own goods?"

Dupris gave a self-deprecating shrug. "Contacts, my friend. I've lost all my local contacts and never had any abroad. But up north…"

"So you said." André expelled a long breath. "Do you have any capital?"

"Some." The look in Dupris's eyes did nothing to encourage André's trust.

"Well, until I receive payment for my last shipment to Indiana, I don't have any. The banks my father did business with collapsed over a year ago."

"Aha, problem solved. A fella named James Robb is opening a new bank with the backing of some New York capitalists. He's eager to get the cotton trade going again, but with your family's good name, you could get cash to increase your coffee trade."

Yankee money! But it might be just what he needed. André did his best not to appear eager. Maybe this was the answer to everything. He would talk with Cordell on the way home and see what he thought of Pierre Dupris and his ideas. André might even decide to go directly to this Robb fellow without this former turncoat.

"Come back tomorrow. I'll think about it and let you know."

Dupris bounced out of his chair and snatched up his black stovepipe hat. He thrust his hand across the desk toward André, a conspiratorial grin on his face. "Partner."

André shook his hand and gave him a slow, reserved smile. "Maybe."

Once Dupris had gone, André stared at the pile of papers on his desk and scratched his head. Some day he would have to get it all organized and filed. Right now, he would just like to find that frock coat. Old and worn, it was still the best he had for business until that shipment sold upriver—if indeed it sold. Competition was growing rapidly.

Earlier that morning he had inspected the now-darkened warehouse, so he retraced his steps but found nothing. Adding to his annoyance, he remembered that his father's favorite pipe and leather pouch of fragrant cherry tobacco were in the coat pocket. He had been trying to learn how to smoke it. Father always said his pipe settled him down in the evening. André needed something to soothe away the burning inside. This evening, he would have to try the other pipes in the study to see if any suited him.

"Mr. André, there you are." Cordell peered around a stack of wooden crates and grinned. "What are you doing back here?"

"Have you seen my tan frock coat?"

"No, sir. But I do have this log for you to sign."

André suddenly realized his neglect of duty. "Ah, yes." He took the offered pen, dipped it in the inkwell, and signed. He would not ask if the shipment was in order. Cordell was proving to be meticulous in business matters, just as he had been as André's body servant. And Cordell had never lost a single article of André's clothing.

"André."

Only in their most serious moments did Cordell address him that way. André frowned, bracing for more bad news.

"That Charles Randolph…"

André's stomach turned at the name. "Go on."

"He got shot this morning."

"What?" André felt a strange chill sweep through him.

"Yes sir. Somebody shot him. They sent for that Yankee Dr. Mayfield, so I don't think Mr. Randolph died, at least not right away. Nobody knows how he's doing now."

André swallowed hard. *Never rejoice over iniquity,* his father always said. But he had difficulty not rejoicing over this man paying for his evil lies.

"Imagine, shot right in front of his own house, right there in that quiet, decent part of town not five blocks from our house. Thank the Lord none of the Randolph ladies were hurt." Cordell clasped the shipping log. "I'll take this to the captain and send that coffee on its way."

André stepped back with a gasp, as if he had been slapped. Randolph had been shot in front of his own home. And where was Miss Harris when it happened? The pretty schoolteacher had been in harm's way because of her association with the man. He must go there and be certain she was all right.

Wait. Cordell had said Randolph was shot this morning. André had ridden past the ladies some time after noon. He breathed out his relief. She hadn't been there to see the shooting, which undoubtedly would have sent her into a swoon or a fit of terror.

For a frantic moment, he searched his memory to think of a friend who could host Miss Harris. His father's cousin? His ancient grandfather, who had never once spoken to André although they lived in the same city? Some boyhood friend whose family should have offered help to his mother after Father died? No. Not one relative or friend came to mind who would open their doors to this good-hearted lady and keep her safe from harm now that her patron was incapacitated. Propriety forbad André himself from ensuring her safety.

Or did it? ✳

★ ★ ★ ★

"Do you like the opera, Miss Harris?" Dr. Mayfield sliced into the chicken breast on his plate and ate with flawless manners. Seated in the Randolphs' formal dining room, they had left their patient resting in Amelia's care so they could eat a midnight supper.

"Yes, very much so." Juliana tasted the collard greens on her plate and wondered how she could politely leave them where they were.

"Perhaps you've heard that there is an exceptional opera house here in New Orleans. Next week, an Italian tenor will arrive for an extended engagement." The doctor's forehead furrowed. "I hope you won't think me callous for mentioning it. We doctors often take our minds off of the seriousness of our work by speaking of lighter matters."

"I understand."

He drank some coffee and returned to his chicken. Juliana felt a twinge of disappointment—and then guilt. Even though she admired the doctor and would gladly accompany him to the opera, she should not desire such an excursion at a time like this. But perhaps he was merely making conversation and hadn't planned to invite her at all.

"Would you—?"

"I think—"

They both spoke at the same time, and both laughed.

"Please go ahead." His eyes sparkled, and the lines around them deepened. In spite of his weariness, his plain face was almost handsome.

"I think it's grand that New Orleans is resuming its cultural events. This should bring people together and help them forget their differences."

He stared at her for a moment. "Ah, Miss Harris, what a pure and uncomplicated view you have of things. Would that our nation could be reunited without difficulty. But I fear President Johnson's Reconstruction plans will not sit well with everyone."

Juliana set down her cutlery and sipped her coffee. "But they have no choice. The war is over. The Confederacy is no more. The only sensible path is to work together to rebuild the South with an entirely new social order and economy. Surely southern leaders will realize this. Former slaves must be educated. They must have land and jobs. And of course they must have the right to vote. Isn't that what we fought for?"

"Yes, but I fear…"

Helena rushed into the dining room, anxiety etched across her face. "Dr. Mayfield, Amelia sends for you. Please hurry."

Juliana and the doctor hastened to follow Helena to the second-floor bedroom where Mr. Randolph tossed and turned in a feverish delirium.

"Use the sheets to keep him from thrashing about." Dr. Mayfield pressed down on the patient's shoulders while the sisters struggled to secure him with the bedding. *"Lord, don't let him tear the stitches.*" "Miss Harris, please bathe his brow with cool water. Miss Randolph, do you have any ice?"

"I'll send for some." Amelia hastened from the room.

Juliana wrung out a cloth and wiped Mr. Randolph's face. The raging heat of his skin felt as if it would scorch her hands. Into the early morning hours, she and Dr. Mayfield worked to bring down the fever. The doctor administered a second dose of morphine, and the ice further helped to quiet him.

Mrs. Randolph had not been awakened with news of her husband's condition; Dr. Mayfield had prescribed rest in another room for the fragile woman. When exhaustion claimed each of them, the sisters, Juliana, and the doctor took turns sleeping in the soft wing-back bedroom chairs or on the bedroom fainting couch. During Juliana's watch, she pondered the propriety of this arrangement, which would be shocking under any other circumstances. Yet what could be done? They all needed to stay near Mr. Randolph.

Then, unbidden, her thoughts drifted to her earlier suspicions about Mr. Beauchamp. While everyone in this family had heard about his threats against Mr. Randolph, they hadn't heard the threats themselves. Juliana simply could not believe that the young gentleman who had come to her rescue two times would shoot down his neighbor outside his own home, no matter what his supposed crime might be.

Amelia had told her that Mr. Beauchamp thought Mr. Randolph had conspired against and lied about the elder Mr. Beauchamp, his one-time close friend. And of course that was not true. How sad that the younger Mr. Beauchamp had been misinformed.

In the morning, Juliana would send a wire to her parents asking them to pray for Mr. Randolph's recovery. If Juliana's father were here, he would use his considerable powers of Christ-like love and persuasion to convince the young man to forgive his enemy without qualification. Then he would bring the two men together for reconciliation, whereupon it would be revealed that Mr. Randolph had no part in the tragic wartime hanging.

With her elbow on the chair arm, Juliana rested her chin on her hand and contemplated the situation. *That's it!* Of the four Harris children, she considered herself the least like her saintly father. But she did feel the same burning desire to see every soul come to Christ. Why couldn't she persuade Mr. Beauchamp first to turn his heart to God and then to reconcile with Mr. Randolph? If Father could do it, so could she.

Yet, unlike Father, she could not simply go to Mr. Beauchamp's house for a pastoral call. What plan could she devise to speak to him and yet remain within the bounds of propriety?

※

"Every man needs a chance to redeem himself." Cordell walked alongside André on their way to the warehouse. "Mr. Dupris had a hard time during the war, like everybody else. More than that, folks turned their backs on him and his missus for colluding with the Yankees. But he's a good businessman."

A clattering wagon passed them on the street, giving André time to consider Cordell's words. Dupris wasn't the only one to have dealings with the Yankees. As distasteful as that was, André might have to overlook such things to make business deals. "Can you think of any rumors or information that might suggest he would engage in dishonest practices or cheat a partner?"

As they neared the warehouse, Cordell shrugged his shoulders. "I never heard of him cheating anybody. Of course, there's..." He paused, frowning. "But that might just be rumor."

"What are you talking about?" André felt a slight burn in his stomach.

Cordell's frown deepened, and he gave a wincing shrug. "I don't like to speak ill of a man when I don't know the truth of it. But if you're thinking about doin' business with him...well, more than one fella has said Mr. Dupris has a business interest in Althea Dawson's place."

André chuckled, and the heat in his stomach cooled. "Is that all? What's the harm in a gambling establishment? My father sometimes gambled, and I've been known to lose a little gold at the tables myself."

Cordell shook his head and glanced at the busy crowds milling around the docks. He leaned near André and spoke softly. "Now you know more goes on at Miss Althea's place than gambling. The upstairs stuff. The girls she keeps up there." A blush crept up his neck and reddened his light brown cheeks.

This time, André laughed out loud, and then sobered. Poor Cordell. He might be a good businessman, but he was as simple as a child when it came to what went on between men and women. André clapped Cordell on the shoulder. "Not a man in this town would fault him for that, or Miss Althea either, except maybe the priests and preachers. And I'm not too sure about some of them."

Cordell gave him a weak smile and lifted his hands in resignation. "Well, then, I suppose you could go ahead and see what you and Mr. Dupris can work out."

"Good. I'll do that."

They entered the warehouse, an old building much in need of repair. André studied the rotting beams above yesterday's shipment of coffee from Brazil. If they didn't get them fixed soon, boards might break away and fall on a stack of crates or barrels, destroying his goods. Then where would he be?

In the heat of the morning, the smell of decay seemed stronger than usual, stirring André's agitation. He needed to find a steamship captain who would take this cargo upriver right away and on credit. That is, unless Dupris's Yankee banker would give them a loan to pay for the shipment.

Cordell went off in search of the three men he had dispatched to the warehouse just after dawn. They now slept above the Beauchamp stable in the groom's old lodgings, and they had proven to be dependable, hard workers. André just needed to find out which one was the smartest in the bunch. He would send that man over to the Randolph house with one of Aunt Sukey's desserts and vague words of condolence. The youngest of the three might appeal to the Randolphs' servant girl, and he could ask some pertinent questions about Miss Harris, making sure she was unharmed.

André reached his office, removed his black frock coat, and hung it on the coat rack. This one had been Father's, and clever little Gemma had taken it in to fit André, even restyling it a little bit, just as she had done with all his clothes. He could not imagine what happened to the other coat. When he suggested to Cordell that one of their "boys" had taken it, Cordell firmly vouched for each one.

Now he had to deal with this messy desk. What *were* all these papers?

He had not been one for organization until he attended the naval academy, where the skill had been seriously "encouraged." Even there Cordell stayed near and took care of his clothes and other personal belongings. But with all he had to do these days, André didn't have the heart to add body-servant duties to his responsibilities. And of course there was no money to hire anyone else to do the job.

"Mr. André?" Cordell stood in the doorway, his crooked grin brightening his light-brown face. His gaze swept over the mess on the desk, and he bit away a laugh and stared down.

Releasing an exaggerated groan, André ran his hands up his face and through his hair. Then he laughed, too. Something about Cordell's attitude toward life had always made André feel certain that everything would be all right. But this time, a strange uneasiness quickly robbed him of that assurance. ✷

✫ ✫ ✫ ✫

"Etty, are you certain this lovely creation came from Mrs. Sutter?" Mrs. Randolph studied the beautifully decorated, four-tiered lemon cake on the kitchen table, her blue eyes glistening.

Juliana's mouth watered as she looked at the pretty confection. Would they have to wait until after dinner to have a piece? *Silly girl, remember you're a guest.* With difficulty, she kept her feet from dancing about in anticipation.

"Yessum, Miz Randolph." Etty nodded. "Jus' a half hour ago or so, Miz Sutter's new houseboy, Kester, brung it to the back door sayin' as how Miz Sutter hopes Mr. Randolph gits well soon. He says she wants to know how everybody's doin' over here, including you, Miss Juliana." The short, slender girl gave them an artless smile.

Juliana wondered if thoughts of Mrs. Sutter's houseboy was responsible for the vibrancy of Etty's expression.

Mrs. Randolph dabbed her eyes with a handkerchief. "What kindness! I had thought all of our southern friends hated us, for we've not had one social call from them since Fort Sumter. Mrs. Sutter is even showing you notice, Juliana. Truly, it is remarkable for a woman of her importance to reach out to Northerners so soon after the war." Her breath hitched slightly, and she placed her hand on her bosom as if to still her heart. "Why, this is not a cake. It is nothing less than an olive branch…a peace offering."

"Mother, may we have some now?" Helena leaned over the cake and inhaled its fresh aroma. "I think it must have been baked just this morning. See how the frosting glistens?" She waved a finger above the dessert and seemed to have difficulty not dipping into the creamy icing.

Her hopes rising, Juliana eyed Mrs. Randolph, but the woman's unfocused gaze in the direction of the kitchen window made it clear she was not thinking about the same thing as her daughters and houseguest.

"Just imagine," she said, "this could be the beginning of reconciliation. With this sort of kindness, we women could do so much to help bring people together again."

"Mother, that's just grand. Now, about the cake…" Amelia sounded mildly annoyed, but Juliana noticed something else in her expression. What was Amelia thinking?

"I must go right over there this afternoon and thank her," Mrs. Randolph said.

Amelia and Helena traded a look that bespoke conspiracy.

"But we should taste it first so you can tell her how good it is." Amelia turned to Etty. "Please get us some plates and forks."

Mrs. Randolph's attention returned. "No, no, not so close to dinner. Haven't I taught you girls anything? Why, look at Juliana. She's not behaving like a child over this."

Juliana gave them a bright smile that felt more than a little tight. "Your mother knows best. Don't you agree?" She lowered her chin and swallowed hard so they couldn't see she was feeling very childish indeed for drooling over the cake.

"I truly must go thank her." Mrs. Randolph glanced about the kitchen. "What shall I take in return? Flora, do we have anything prepared?"

The Randolphs' German cook shook her head, loosening some red curls from their precarious pinnings. "No, ma'am, but I could have something prepared by one o'clock. Vould sugar cookies be acceptable?"

"Yes, your cookies are delightful. Now, Etty, would you go see if my blue walking dress is fresh? Helena, would you like to go with me? We must not delay in acknowledging Mrs. Sutter's gift." Mrs. Randolph's face flushed with excitement. "Oh, this is wonderful."

She swayed toward the table, and all the women in the room reached out to steady her. Amelia reached her first.

"Mother! You must sit down. Etty, a chair, please. Helena, help me."

The sisters lowered Mrs. Randolph into the seat while Flora fanned her with her apron. Her heart racing, Juliana leaned close. This family did not need more grief.

"Let me see if you have a fever." She touched Mrs. Randolph's now pale face and neck. "No, I don't think so. Do you have these spells often?"

Mrs. Randolph's forehead crinkled. "Oh, my head." Hand to her temple, she inhaled with effort and winced. "They only began after Mr. Randolph was…was…"

"Shh, never mind." Juliana patted Mrs. Randolph's free hand. In the four days since her husband's wounding, Mrs. Randolph had not once been able to say her husband had been shot. He still hadn't regained consciousness, but his breathing and pulse were even, and his wounds showed no infection.

"I simply must go see Mrs. Sutter." Mrs. Randolph tried to get up but sat back down with a wince.

"No, Mother," Amelia said. "You're in no condition to be out in this heat. You can wait a day."

"Or I can go," Helena said.

"Um, well…" Amelia gave her sister a doubtful look.

"Sweet Helena." Mrs. Randolph took her younger daughter's hand. "You're so bright and mature. But your inexperience in southern society…"

Helena bit her lip and nodded. "I think I would be frightened to death." She turned to Juliana. "Mrs. Sutter is quite…formidable."

Juliana glanced about the group. "Amelia, you and I could go."

Amelia looked from her mother to her sister to Juliana. "I can't. Mrs. Sutter's son, Blake, is home recovering from his war wounds. He courted me before the war, and I…I did not wish to accept him because of his views on certain issues. He expressed great bitterness when I *did* accept…" She broke off with a half-sob.

Juliana put an arm around Amelia, whose fiancé had been missing since late in 1864. His commanding officer had written to the family about his concerns that Captain Billings had been imprisoned at the infamous Andersonville Prison in Georgia. With the prison closed since the previous May and still no word from Amelia's fiancé, the family feared he was one of the hundreds of unknowns who lay dead and buried in unmarked graves.

"Then that leaves me. I think my mother would say it's perfectly proper, especially since Mrs. Sutter inquired about me by name." Juliana took Mrs. Randolph's hand. "May I go for you?"

Mrs. Randolph gave her a wincing smile. "Yes, please do," she whispered. "Tell her I will call on her soon."

Juliana tried to subdue her own rising concerns over the forthcoming visit. Back home, she often had accompanied her mother on social calls, some of them to "formidable" Boston society matrons, who always turned out to be much kinder than their reputations. Yet this time she might seem like a foreigner to the woman she was visiting.

Mrs. Randolph took to her bed, and the younger women ate their dinner and the long-awaited cake.

"I have never comprehended southern ways, Juliana." Amelia pushed her sweet potatoes around her plate. "So I have no insights to offer as to how you should behave with Mrs. Sutter. However, your lovely manners would be pleasing to anyone in their right mind." Her tone caused Juliana to wonder if Amelia held some bitterness toward the South or even toward Mrs. Sutter. No wonder, considering Captain Billings's absence. Juliana would be certain to pray about it. She doubted there was any family in the entire nation that had avoided sorrow and loss during the war.

Arranged prettily on Mrs. Sutter's cake plate, the cookies were still warm when Flora placed them in a basket and carried them out to Juliana, who waited in the phaeton.

"Ve'll see who's the better cook, ja? Mrs. Sutter's Irish Amy or me."

Flora shook with laughter, and Juliana laughed, too. Did any two cooks ever agree on whose cooking was the best?

"Oh, I'm sure it's you, Flora." *But that cake was nothing short of divine.*

Jim-Jim clucked the bay mare into a brisk walk through the dry, dusty streets. Traveling three blocks one way and two blocks another, they arrived at the elegant Sutter mansion on Prytania Street. Juliana noticed that her driver shot several nervous glances at the house next door as they pulled up to the wrought-iron fence surrounding the white-columned house. But her own nerves were too much on edge to inquire why.

Lord, calm my nerves. Please help me to be a true diplomat and help restore this friendship.

She took as deep a breath as permitted by her corset—and the two slices of cake she had eaten—exhaled, and squared her shoulders. Jim-Jim escorted her to the door and banged the brass knocker before handing her the basket of cookies.

A black butler perhaps forty years old, wearing a shabby but clean black suit, opened the door. "Yes, Miss?" He scowled for a brief moment at Jim-Jim, then turned back to Juliana.

"Miss Harris to see Mrs. Sutter on behalf of Mrs. Randolph."

The man's dark eyebrows arched and his chin lifted, but his expression was now kind. "Yes, Miss Harris. Please come in."

"Please wait in the carriage," Juliana whispered to Jim-Jim.

"Yes, Miz Juliana." He seemed reluctant to leave her.

The butler escorted Juliana to a large, bright drawing room. The Louis XIV furniture needed new upholstery; its formerly brilliant red and blue brocades had faded to pinks and grays in many spots. But the fine mahogany wood gleamed from regular polishing. The butler invited Juliana to be seated in a chair near the white marble hearth. Then he gave her a slight bow and left the room.

This was only the second southern home she had ever entered. How different the architecture and furnishings were from those in Boston, but they were just as pretty. She loved the tall French windows that let in a profusion of light and fresh air. With shorter, milder winters than Boston, New Orleans had found the styles that provided comfortable living for its citizens. The owner of this house must have traveled to France and brought back the delicate Limoges lamps and figurines now gracing the mantelpiece and end tables.

"What do you want?"

A stern female voice broke into Juliana's musings. She stood and faced the middle-aged woman, who, despite her medium height, did indeed appear formidable. Her fair skin was marred by a sneer, and she glared at Juliana without a hint of kindness. This couldn't be right. Perhaps the butler had misunderstood her.

"Mrs. Sutter, how do you do? I'm Juliana Harris. Mrs. Randolph sends her regrets, but she is ill and could not come herself. However, she did send over some cookies to express her gratitude for the lovely lemon cake you sent to her this morning." Juliana spoke in a breathless rush as she took the plate containing the cookies from the basket.

"I did no such thing. Why would I send a cake to a Yankee?" The woman's expression remained unchanged. "And why would I want Yankee cookies?"

Juliana stared at her for a moment, feeling the blood drain from her face. "But this is your cake plate…" *Oh, what a foolish thing to say!*

"That most certainly is *not* my plate."

"But your young man, your servant, brought the cake…"

"I have no *young* male servant, thanks to you Yankees." Her venom-filled voice shattered Juliana's struggle for composure. "Now, if you'll excuse me, I have more important things to do than talk with the likes of you." The woman turned and strode from the room, her elegant but faded yellow gown rustling as she went.

Juliana's face felt as if it were on fire. The butler waited by the doorway to see her out. She blew out a breath of frustration.

"Would you like a cookie?"

She held out the plate toward him. His dark eyes widened, and he glanced over his shoulder to where his mistress had exited.

"Go ahead. She'll never know."

"Oh, no, miss, I couldn't. But I do believe I recognize this here plate from the folks next door." He nodded to the left.

Juliana stared at him for another moment. What on earth was going on? Anger shot through her. Had someone played a prank? Had they deliberately misled Etty this morning? Or told an outright lie?

"Thank you." Putting the plate back into the basket, she followed the butler to the front door and went out to the phaeton.

"Jim-Jim, I'm going next door."

The young man hung his head. "Yes, Miz Juliana."

"What's the matter?"

"Nothin', Miz Juliana." He helped her into the carriage and took his place.

At the similar white-columned mansion next door, Jim-Jim drove through the open gate into the courtyard and pulled up short of the *porte-cochere*. Juliana again went through the troublesome routine of climbing down from the carriage in her hoopskirt without losing her dignity. She huffed out a breath, straightened her bonnet, and marched to the front door, basket in hand. Jim-Jim hung back, but she didn't care. Lifting the brass knocker, she banged it loudly against the green door; like the rest of the house, much of its paint was peeling. *Serves them right.* She ignored the guilty twinge she felt over entertaining such an unkind thought.

After some moments, the door opened.

Mr. Beauchamp stared at her, his mouth slightly open as if he were at a loss for words.

Juliana stared up at Mr. Beauchamp for longer than propriety permitted, unable to think of one coherent thing to say to him.

"Miss Harris."

"Yes. And you are Mr. Beauchamp. My mother would be scandalized, but I suppose we may now consider ourselves to be introduced, whether properly or not." Juliana's temper rose as she spoke.

He began to chuckle, which fueled her anger further. "Why, yes, Miss Harris, I suppose we might do that—with all our unexpected encounters."

She longed to turn and leave and knew that she surely must. But his sky-blue eyes, so merry with laughter, still held her captive. In their previous meetings, he had not seemed so light-hearted…or handsome. Juliana pulled in a shallow breath. It was all she could manage. Her anger subsided to a strange, warm feeling deep in her chest.

He cleared his throat as if to sober himself, but his countenance continued to beam good will in her direction. "Won't you come in?" He stood aside and waved a welcoming hand toward the entrance hall.

Endless thoughts warred in her mind until one took preeminence. "No. No thank you. That most assuredly would *not* be proper."

"Ah, yes. Of course." He nodded. "When my mother is well, perhaps…"

"Oh, yes. Of course…perhaps. I hope she recovers soon." *What's wrong with his mother?* But she dared not ask.

"Thank you." He leaned against the doorjamb and glanced at the basket. "To what do I owe the honor of your call?"

Juliana stared down at the object in her hands. "Oh. This? I'm returning something of yours." She opened the basket and pulled out the plate of cookies. "I believe we—by that I mean you and the Randolphs—may consider yourselves, um, ourselves, even."

He straightened and took the plate, a frown forming on his brow. "What…"

Anger shot through her again. "The very idea of your sending a cake to Mrs. Randolph in the midst of their family tragedy and using Mrs. Sutter's name, when you surely must know that Mrs. Sutter will have nothing to do with dear Mrs. Randolph, the kindest lady I've ever met. I am so glad I came in her place, for it would have broken her heart to be thrown out of that awful woman's house—her former friend, for heaven's sake—as I was just now."

"In Mrs. Sutter's name…?"

"Oh, don't act so innocent. I have a brother and two sisters. I know a mean trick when I see one. Your young man brought over a lovely cake, which was quite delicious, I'm forced to say, and told the Randolphs' maid that it was from Mrs. Sutter."

Mr. Beauchamp groaned and slumped back against the door-jamb. "I will strangle that boy with my own two hands."

He straightened up again, reminding Juliana of how pleasing his height was, six feet tall to her five foot four. *Oh, why on earth am I thinking such a foolish thought at a time like this?*

"Do you mean to tell me you don't know about this? And who is 'he' whom you plan to strangle?"

"Miss Harris, please accept my apology and convey my further apology to Mrs. Randolph. My new servant gets confused sometimes. And just in case you're wondering, I did say 'servant.'" He gave her a meaningful stare and then looked down at the plate in his hands.

"Sugar cookies. My favorite. I'll wager Flora baked them. I'm sure they'll be just grand."

How easy for him to blame it on a servant. But Juliana's anger had faded at his sincere apology. At least it seemed sincere.

"I'm appalled at your treatment at the hands of Mrs. Sutter." His eyes exuded even more sincerity. "Please understand she spends all her days nursing her son, who was so badly wounded in the war."

"Yes, I know what it is like to nurse a wounded loved one." She stared hard into his eyes and was rewarded with a painful flicker. Guilt? But then why would he have sent the cake?

He looked beyond her and raised one hand toward the carriage. "Hello, Jim-Jim."

Jim-Jim sent back a weak, "'Lo, Massuh."

"You don't need to torment him that way. He's obviously afraid of you. Did you hold him in slavery?" Juliana tried not to spit out the words, but once again her sarcasm got the better of her.

The pleasantness left Mr. Beauchamp's handsome face and was replaced by a paternal sneer. "I would not expect you to understand how we lived before the war of northern aggression, Miss Harris."

"Wh—"

"Don't." He lifted his chin and stared down his nose at her. "Don't preach at me. After all, you did win the war. Isn't that enough?"

Once again they seemed trapped in each other's stares, as though to garner some insight, some bit of wisdom that would explain it all.

"No, Mr. Beauchamp," Juliana said at last. "It is not enough. Now we must bind up the wounds…on both sides." Her voice broke, and so she turned and fled to the carriage before he could see her tears.

He did not call out or follow. Juliana felt a hint of disappointment.

✯ ✯ ✯ ✯

CHAPTER TEN

*I*n an instant, Miss Harris's parting words cooled André's anger. He started to call out to her, but what would he say? She would never understand his world…his old world. Still, her innocent, childlike belief that the wounds of the war could be healed brought a bittersweet ache to his chest. She just didn't understand the way things were. As she walked toward the carriage, she held her head high with seeming resolution; another lady might have displayed arrogance under these circumstances. But Miss Harris had come to New Orleans for an unselfish purpose, not for frivolity or personal gain. He had read that in her lovely brown eyes.

She climbed into the carriage with a gracefulness rivaling that of any southern belle. Jim-Jim clucked to the well-fed horse, and they pulled away.

Why was André standing there like a fool? Did he hope Miss Harris would turn back to wave at him? To acknowledge him, even with a scornful frown? But she did not. André felt his heart pulled to follow, to try to explain what she would always find incomprehensible.

He stared down at the plate. Cookies. They could turn a sensible man back into a boy. Where had Flora found fresh orange peel at this time of year? Perhaps in the same market where Aunt Sukey had found the lemons for the cake. As tempting as they were, he would wait and share them with Mama when she awoke from her nap.

He looked up just in time to see the carriage disappear around the corner. Shaking off his disappointment, he turned and entered the house. The whoosh of the closing front door sent the aroma of the cookies up to his nostrils. All of this anguish over a cake and some cookies—which reminded him…

"Cordell!" His bellow reverberated throughout the entire house.

Within seconds, Cordell came from the study. "Yessir, Mr. André."

"What in the world?" Aunt Sukey rushed in with flour on her hands.

Gemma scurried down the stairs without a word, which cautioned André that he might have awakened Mama.

He waved the women away. "I just need Cordell. Wait, Aunt Sukey. Take these to the kitchen." He placed the plate in her hands.

"Why, Mr. André, I sent that cake over just this morning." Aunt Sukey chuckled. "They must have thought it was pretty good." Her arched eyebrows and hopeful expression required a response.

"Why, most certainly. Miss Harris—and the Randolphs, of course—send their highest compliments."

Aunt Sukey beamed. "Good, good. Now I'll just put these in the kitchen to serve Miz Felicity with her tea." She walked out humming, and Gemma followed.

Cordell regarded André with a worried frown. "Sir, you seemed…upset when you called me. Is there something wrong?"

"Where is Kester?"

"I told him to clean out the stable in case you decide to buy that horse from Mr. Collins."

André strode through the house's center hallway to the back door with Cordell hurrying to keep up.

"Is there a problem, sir? He delivered that cake all right, didn't he?"

Rubbing his stomach to stop the fire within, André felt his anger growing as they walked out the door and across the yard toward the stable. "Yes, he delivered it." André stopped and faced Cordell. "I thought you said Kester was reliable."

"Yessir, he is. I'd stake my reputation on it." Cordell's lip formed a determined line.

André resumed his pace. "Don't sell your own honor for someone like him."

"Sir?"

André blinked to adjust to the dimness of the stable. Kester was sweeping out a back stall, and dust clouds floated on shafts of light all around him. The smell of leather and horses lingered, an ever-present reminder of days past.

"Kester." André tried to keep from bellowing this time.

The boy poked his head above the side of the stall. "Yessuh?" He propped the broom against the wall and hurried over to André, brushing dust from his face and clothing as he came.

André suddenly felt ashamed at the sight of Kester's tattered pants and shirt, which barely fit his adult frame. His parents would never have let their town chattels be dressed like field hands. He wondered if Aunt Sukey had some of the old house servants' clothes that this boy could wear.

"Kester, you took the cake over to the Randolph house."

Kester's eyes widened, and he nodded. "Yessuh, but I was cleaner then."

André waved his hand with impatience. "Of course you were. But why did you tell Mrs. Randolph's maid that the cake was from Mrs. Sutter?"

Kester cast a glance at Cordell. "Well, suh, I-I…well, Mr. Cordell said not to make too much of it bein' from you. The important thing was to find out about Miss Harris. When I comes back to the house, you was at the dock, and I been cleaning the stable since then."

"That doesn't explain why you used Mrs. Sutter's name."

Again, Kester shot a fearful look toward Cordell, who still wore his worried frown.

"I thought if the important thing was to find out about Miss Harris, it didn't matter who sent the cake. I only jus' mentioned Mrs. Sutter and how ever'body over here in this neighborhood was concerned 'bout Mr. Randolph and how was Miss Harris. I feel awful bad if it made you a problem. I thought—"

"You *thought?*" André shouted. "You were told to do something very simple. Who gave you the right to think for yourself?"

Kester stared at André for a moment, his mouth opened as if he was trying to answer. He swallowed with a noisy gulp. Then the fear left his eyes, and he straightened to his full five feet seven inches. "As I recollect, Mr. André, it was Mr. Abraham Lincoln who give me the right."

A physical blow to the chest could not have stunned André more. No man in his ship's crew had ever dared such insolence, such insubordination. No Negro had ever spoken such defiance to him, whether chattel or free person of color. André turned to Cordell and read shock in his eyes—along with silent approval of the boy's words.

"Then you can go to blazes and work for Mr. Lincoln." André spun around and strode out of the stable into the fiery heat of the late afternoon. In seconds, Cordell caught up with him.

"Mr. André, he's just a boy. He doesn't have good sense about these things."

André stopped, his fury burning a hole in his chest that rivaled the sun's blistering rays on his head. "I won't tolerate that kind of attitude from anyone, whether sailor under my command or colored boy working for me for wages."

Cordell winced and glanced toward the stable. Kester stood watching. "Only trouble is, if he goes, we lose our other two men. They're family, and they promised to stay together."

André muttered a curse. These men worked hard for him, trusting he would pay them when his goods sold upriver. During the war, he had learned to keep dependable men close and to reward a job well done. He stared hard at Kester, who calmly looked back at him, no longer defiant.

"Tell him to watch his attitude."

Cordell grinned. "Yessir." He turned toward the stable, but André gripped his arm.

"And about what he said to the Randolphs' maid…tell him that misleading someone is just the same as an outright lie."

"Yessir." Cordell started away again, but André still held his arm.

"And tell him to finish cleaning out that stable."

"Yessir." Cordell sprinted off to obey.

Returning to the house, André wiped his sweaty brow on his shirt sleeve, leaving several gray streaks on the dull white fabric. Hot day, hot belly, insolent servants, and dismay over his conversation with Miss Harris. What could happen to make things worse?

But seated at his desk in the study, perusing the news in the *Daily Crescent* and sipping Aunt Sukey's fresh lemonade, his mood grew mellow. After all, despite everything that had happened, the cake had accomplished its mission. André knew Miss Harris was safe.

✦┄▷◉◁┄✦

Juliana tried not to look at Mr. Beauchamp, but as the carriage neared the corner, she could not resist turning back to catch one more glimpse of his house. There he stood staring at the plate of cookies. She once again faced the front. Why had she expected him to be looking her way? She had angered him, and after today's two encounters, she knew these Southerners would never change their ideas. And now Juliana faced the task of shattering Mrs. Randolph's hopes of reconciliation with Mrs. Sutter. What a cruel blow after almost losing her husband, who still was not out of danger. Was she foolish to think she could do any good here?

Jerome met her at the front door, and for a moment she feared more bad news. But he wore a huge smile.

"Miz Juliana, Mr. Randolph woke up. Glory be, he woke up. Dr. Mayfield is with him and the ladies now."

"Oh, how wonderful. Thank you." Juliana handed him the basket and hurried up the stairs. In her room, she discarded her reticule, bonnet, and gloves, and hastened down the hallway to the master suite.

Amelia opened the door to Juliana's soft tapping and pulled her into an embrace. "It's a miracle," she whispered. "That's what Dr. Mayfield says."

Juliana tiptoed across the darkened room. Bending over Mr. Randolph, Dr. Mayfield checked the stitches on the patient's head. The doctor glanced across the bed and smiled, which as usual made his plain face handsome.

"Mr. Randolph, here is our heroine. If not for Miss Harris, I cannot assume that you would have fared so well."

Juliana felt her cheeks grow warm at the compliment.

Mr. Randolph winced as he turned his head toward her. His thin face now wore deeper age lines than before his injuries. But his weak smile soothed some of the afternoon's pain from Juliana's heart.

"You have my gratitude, child." Mr. Randolph's soft voice crackled from disuse.

"Shh, don't speak of it. The doctor saved your life, not I." Tears stung Juliana's eyes. She reached across the bed and gently squeezed his hand, then looked at Mrs. Randolph, whose face glowed.

"How I wish this could have happened before you went to see Mrs. Sutter," Mrs. Randolph said. "She will be so pleased with our good news, don't you think?"

Juliana walked around the bed and embraced her. "Everyone who has a good heart will rejoice with us."

"Tell us about your visit," Amelia said. Her tone was pleasant, but she wore a guarded expression.

She must have seen through Juliana's deflection of her mother's question.

"Oh, my, not now." Juliana sat in one of the wingback chairs and fanned herself with her hand. "Goodness, this heat…"

Not until dinner did she permit the Randolph women and Dr. Mayfield to pry from her the details of her brief interview with Mrs. Sutter. Mrs. Randolph took it better than her daughters did.

"It was too much to hope for, wasn't it?" She appeared sad but not broken. "Now that Charles has awakened, we'll have to decide whether or not to stay here in New Orleans. If everyone hates us so much that one of them tried to kill him outside our own home, who's to say they won't try again and succeed the next time?"

Helena murmured her agreement, but Amelia shook her head. "I will not leave. God has given me a purpose with our school." She glanced at Juliana. "I will not be forced to abandon it through fear."

"That is an admirable sentiment, Miss Randolph," Dr. Mayfield said. "That is also my reason for staying here after the war ended. As to these Southerners, I believe cooler heads will prevail as they try to put their lives back together." He turned to Juliana. "Will you stay as well?"

Juliana could not ignore the eagerness in his eyes, and again she blushed at his attention. Both he and Amelia had voiced such courage. How could she do any less?

"I will stay until the Lord guides me elsewhere," she said.

After supper, Dr. Mayfield once again checked Mr. Randolph's condition and then bade the family good night. He asked Juliana to accompany him to the front door.

"We spoke the other evening of the opera. May I be so bold as to ask if you would accompany me tomorrow evening to hear that Italian tenor? I feel certain there is no danger. And of course, Miss Randolph and Miss Helena are welcome to come, too. After the sorrows this family has faced and your own unfortunate experience this afternoon, I believe a diversion is in order for all of you."

Juliana controlled her smile so it wouldn't appear too broad or too eager. "Doctor's orders?"

He chuckled—a deep, warm baritone laugh that pleased her. "Doctor's orders."

"Then I suppose we must accept."

After seeing him out the door, Juliana found Amelia and Helena sewing in the drawing room. She picked up a length of lace and a collar and set to work. When she reported his invitation, they accepted with delight. Helena's eyes glowed with particular fervor.

"If that rude old Mrs. Sutter doesn't want Flora's cookies, I'll take them." Helena set aside her sewing and rose. "May I bring some for you two?"

"Um, well, you see"—Juliana looked from one sister to the other—"as it turns out, her butler recognized the cake plate and sent me next door to…to Mr. Beauchamp's house. Mr. Beauchamp was, um, pleased that we liked the cake."

"I knew it!" Amelia cried. "I could see your reserve the moment you entered Father's room." She eyed Juliana with suspicion. "Why do you suppose you keep meeting André Beauchamp by accident this way?"

"I'm sure I have no idea. And I'm sure this will be the last time."

"Well, I certainly hope so," Helena said.

Amelia put in her agreement. "Never mind that he sent the cake. I don't trust him. You should avoid him at all cost."

Juliana gave them a vague nod. Yet deep in her heart—Dr. Mayfield's attentions notwithstanding—she did indeed wish to meet Mr. Beauchamp again…by accident, of course. ✻

CHAPTER ELEVEN

★ ★ ★ ★

André leaned back in the faded velvet chair and stared across the opera house. In a cloistered box high above the auditorium's main level sat Augustus Beauchamp accompanied by an elegant quadroon. André hid a sardonic smile. His grandfather had good taste, but where did he get the money to maintain the young woman now that southern cotton fortunes had been shattered? Had the wily old devil stashed his gold in some French bank? Had he held back his wealth from the Confederacy while others went bankrupt to support the cause?

The old fellow himself seemed frozen in time, the very image of the man André had last spied in this same room just over four years ago, right after the war began. His posture was straight as a pine tree; a great shock of white hair rose up and back from his high patrician forehead, emphasizing the height that André had inherited. His large, startling blue eyes stared toward the stage's closed curtain rather than searching out friends and acquaintances in the noisy, packed room. Augustus Beauchamp had always held himself to be above the crowd,

A deep longing wormed its way into André's heart, a longing he had first felt as a five-year-old. That was when he saw a man who looked so much like his father that he had tried to approach him. He was at the races, where Father was running one of his champions. Father had left André with Elgin while he went to make a bet. In the excitement, André had glanced at the man and dashed toward him. Elgin, who was six years older, had tackled him to the ground and pulled him back to their spot beside the racetrack rails with André squirming and yelling out his rage all the way.

That night, through his tears, François Beauchamp had told his sons that Augustus, his own father, had disowned him for marrying an Englishwoman rather than someone from his own Creole community. Then Father had promised that he would never disown them or stop loving them, no matter what they did.

In time, André came to understand. Augustus never did anything overt to harm François. How could he? To his way of thinking, his son had ceased to exist. To his way of thinking, he had no grandsons. The pain of Augustus's rejection had remained with Father all his life.

And now, André could not comprehend his own feelings for the old man. Why should he waste his time and emotions caring for someone who refused to acknowledge his existence?

"There he is." Pierre Dupris nudged André's arm and jolted him from his reverie. Dupris nodded his head toward the second box. "James Robb, the banker who's going to make us rich." He grinned broadly and waved in Robb's direction. "We'll catch him at intermission."

André held a shudder in check but wondered why he bothered. Dupris was completely unaware of his own boorishness. André glanced beyond his companion.

"Tell me, Mrs. Dupris, do you like the opera?"

"I think I can learn to like it." The unfortunate woman's complexion grew red clear to the roots of her brown hair each time André addressed her. "I come from farm people, and we never got to see this sort of thing." Nature had graced her with one pretty attribute—a friendly, honest smile that almost made up for her husband's sleazy grin. Almost. How had nature put these two together?

"Johnson," Dupris called out. He jumped up from his seat and scooted past his wife to ensnare some other unlucky victim.

Poor Mrs. Dupris. André tried to think of some pleasantry to say to her. But she had busied herself with reading her program and fanning herself, which sent waves of her strong, homemade perfume André's way, threatening to incite a headache.

Maybe coming to the opera with the Duprises had been a mistake, but André had more than one purpose in being here. After the incident yesterday with Kester, he had felt his alarm growing. If the boy's attitude persisted or grew worse, André would fire all three men and find some workers who had more respect for their betters. Let those brash Negroes join with other former slaves who roamed the streets without purpose. Yet that created another problem that was already of concern to decent citizens. What would these useless men do when they grew hungry and desperate? Form mobs and attack the defenseless?

André had been trained to lead, and his achievements as a naval officer had proven his skill. He would gather men who had given their all to defend the Confederacy and now must be prepared to give all again to defend their loved ones and their very lives. Many had come back home from the war to find their property destroyed and their way of life shattered. They must band together to restore order to the South.

But with the Freedmen's Bureau and Johnson's Reconstruction plans now being implemented, André realized he must test the waters in social settings like this or find himself on the wrong side of the law; he should have paid attention to the situation sooner. The time had come for him to shake off his lethargy and reestablish boyhood friendships, for these men would be the leaders of tomorrow.

He looked around to survey the audience, searching for those likely to join him. They shouldn't be too hard to find.

Miss Harris.

André thought his heart had stopped.

She stood at the top of the aisle, graceful, beautiful, almost ethereal in her pink gown, with her honey-blond hair swept up in the back and ringlets framing her flawless face. Her beatific smile was aimed at the Randolph sisters and—was that the Yankee doctor? Mayfield, wasn't it? From his posture and gestures, the good doctor clearly preferred Miss Harris over her companions. A burning knife of jealousy cut into André's heart and started it beating again. Without conscious thought, he rose from his seat.

"Forgive me, Mrs. Dupris." He was being a cad to leave her alone. Where had her husband gone? "May I?" He started to cross in front of her.

"Of course." Although Mrs. Dupris granted him permission and even pulled in her full lavender skirt so he could pass, her eyes betrayed her dismay.

André could not continue. His parents would have been mortified, and he would have disciplined any of his men who deserted a lady in this manner. With a slight shrug, he did not pass but stood by her chair.

"On reconsideration, I believe my business can wait. I must ask you to forgive me for not remarking earlier on your lovely gown, Mrs. Dupris. Lavender becomes you."

A blush once again spread over her face, and she fanned it with fury. "Why, thank you, Mr. Beauchamp."

As if some heavenly force were rewarding him for his gallantry, Miss Harris and her party moved down the aisle toward him. She looked his way, and his breath caught. He smiled and gave her a slight bow. She spoke to her companions. A moment later, the four reached André's row and focused their attention on Mrs. Dupris, who looked up with surprise and then rose from her chair.

"Why, Miss Randolph, Miss Harris, Miss Helena." She stood between André and the newcomers, obstructing his view of Miss Harris. "How nice of you to stop."

"Good evening, Mrs. Dupris," the young ladies chorused.

André noticed frowns in the glances sent his way by the Randolph ladies. Was his cravat crooked or his evening coat too worn? Silly girls. They didn't even know him.

"Mrs. Dupris, have you met Dr. Mayfield?" Miss Randolph asked.

While the others expressed pleasure at seeing each other in this setting, André peered around his companion at Miss Harris. She seemed to be leaning to the side so she could see him, too. Before he could speak, Mrs. Dupris appeared to comprehend her position as the matron of this little gathering. She eyed each person, resting her gaze at last on André. Her blush seemed particularly profuse.

"Mr. Beauchamp, have you met these folks?"

"I've had the honor of meeting Miss Harris." André would have bowed, but Mrs. Dupris still stood in his way. "However, I've not been introduced to these other lovely young ladies or this gentleman." André injected an affable tone to his words as he studied the doctor. A sturdy fellow, to be sure.

Mrs. Dupris presented André to the Randolph sisters, who curtsied and murmured polite comments in return for André's compliments. Then Mrs. Dupris introduced the doctor, and the two men shook hands. Dr. Mayfield's firm grip both impressed and annoyed André. The Yankee seemed to be decent enough, but André could not discern how Miss Harris regarded him.

The opera house's gaslights dimmed. Miss Harris and her party bade André and Mrs. Dupris farewell and hurried to find their seats. Pierre Dupris returned to his chair with a pleased expression on his face. An uneasy feeling crept through André's chest. Who else was his "partner" doing business with?

✦·⊹·▨◈▨·⊹·✦

Seated four rows down from Mr. Beauchamp and on the opposite side of the aisle, Juliana wondered how she could peek back at him without being rude. How odd that he accompanied Mrs. Dupris, for she had said such hateful things about Southerners that day in her store. They certainly made a strange pair—he a society gentleman, and she a shopkeeper.

Dr. Mayfield leaned toward Juliana. "Is that Mozart?" he whispered.

She nodded. "The accompanist is excellent, isn't he?"

Her eyes seemed to move of their own accord to look back over the doctor's shoulder. A man now sat between Mr. Beauchamp and Mrs. Dupris, probably Mr. Dupris. Juliana forced herself to look back to the stage as relief mingled with guilt. The object of her reluctant interest had not improperly escorted a married woman to the theater after all. Yet, by looking at another man, she herself was not giving her own escort proper respect.

Still, she could not help but hope that during the intermission she might have another, more successful opportunity to speak with Mr. Beauchamp. His charm and courtesy to her party just now showed he held no ill feelings toward her despite their disagreement yesterday. Oh, why on earth did she feel this longing to be in his company when it would surely lead to more unpleasantness?

Intermission proved to be a disappointment. By the time Juliana could stand and turn around, Mr. Beauchamp and his friends had left their chairs and disappeared. She could not be so rude as to search for them. Instead, she focused on her own party.

"Amelia," Juliana said, "how is it that you didn't know Mr. Beauchamp? Didn't you say your parents and his were friends before the war?"

"We moved to New Orleans shortly after he left for the naval academy late in 1857. My father found a good friend in the late Mr. Beauchamp, whom he regarded as a dedicated Christian." Amelia glanced around and lowered her voice. "Even though the war damaged their friendship, you can imagine our shock when Mr. Beauchamp was charged with conspiracy to assassinate General Butler. My father still cannot speak of his death without deepest sorrow, even tears. That makes it all the more insane that someone would accuse him of betraying Mr. Beauchamp."

"Goodness, may we talk about something else other than that arrogant rebel?" Helena touched Dr. Mayfield's arm and batted her eyes. "Doctor, what do you think of Señor Blanco? Have you ever heard a man sing such high notes?"

Juliana hid a smile. Helena's brown eyes sparkled with unbridled admiration. The dear girl had not yet learned how to hide her feelings. While the doctor and the sisters discussed the singing talents of the tenor, Juliana surreptitiously glanced across the auditorium. She was rewarded with a view of Mr. Beauchamp looking in her direction. If anyone should notice, the blush in her cheeks would divulge her heart's longing just as surely as Helena's wide-eyed gazes betrayed their owner.

She forced her attention back to Dr. Mayfield's humorous story of a singer he had heard in New York who should have abandoned the stage for hog calling. The ladies laughed, and the doctor chuckled. Juliana could see the tensions of his profession disappear from his countenance in this pleasant company. She felt no alarm over her friend's interest in Dr. Mayfield. Once Helena matured a bit more, they might make a charming couple.

With that thought, something settled deep in Juliana's heart, but she could not guess whether it would lead to her happiness or to unimaginable pain.

She turned and boldly stared at Mr. Beauchamp, who had returned to his seat with the Duprises. As if compelled by her silent will, he turned her way.

And so Juliana smiled at him. ✳

Chapter Twelve

✶ ✶ ✶ ✶

Seated at his father's desk in the study, André relived the moment over and over. When Juliana had turned and smiled at him at the opera, he thought his heart would burst with happiness. Later, throughout his meeting with several other men concerning the ex-slave problem, he continued to think of the invitation that smile implied. In spite of all their differences, she wanted to see him as much as he wanted to see her.

But he would never be able to stomach going to the Randolph house. He had nothing against the Randolph sisters or their mother. Charles Randolph, wounded though he was, was another matter. Just to think of entering the man's house ignited a fire in André's belly. So how could he court Miss Harris without impropriety? The quandary brought forth many foolish imaginings.

The only way he managed to gain some sense of perspective was to concentrate instead on Miss Harris's apparent ignorance of how dangerous her charitable work could turn out to be. With her sweet innocence and lack of worldly experience, she did not understand that some people might threaten her life for teaching coloreds to read. He had heard plenty of anger over that very issue last night.

He said little in the meeting but had observed who was there and noticed their level of commitment to restoring a semblance of the pre-war social order. Unlike most of the men, he had no objections to educating Negroes. Where would he be right now if he hadn't taught Cordell to read when they were boys?

The problem as he saw it was curbing the activities of the uneducated former field hands. Someone mentioned reenacting Black Codes, which would confine the blacks to certain areas of the city and prevent them from owning weapons. André found that to be a reasonable proposition, with the caveat that dependable men like Cordell could carry papers attesting to their character, as certain slaves had done in the past.

Until these things could be established, André feared many of the men would resort to violence, perhaps taking aim at a Yankee woman for starting a school. Whoever had shot Randolph might also regard her as an enemy. The thought brought more than a little concern to André.

He turned to his father's portrait on the wall beside him. "How can I protect her? What would you do?"

Immediately, André knew the answer. François Beauchamp would have prayed, a practice he himself had given up about the time General Lee surrendered and President Davis tried to flee the country to avoid prosecution for treason.

"Very well, Father, have it your way." André looked up at the ceiling and lifted his hands in mock supplication. *"Almighty God..."* Something within him cringed at his irreverent attitude, as if his father's portrait had come alive and rebuked him for blasphemy. Without contrition, but at least with a tone of respect, he whispered, *"Show me how to protect Miss Harris from those who would harm her for her good works and from her own naïveté about human nature."* André turned again to the portrait, sensing approval from the good man pictured there.

He shook off his foolishness and began to rummage through the papers before him on the desk. Coffee and citrus shipments from South America, silk from China—so many possibilities for products to import and distribute upriver. One advantage to the war's end was the full reopening of the Mississippi River, not to mention the flood of pioneers bound for the western frontier. But if he couldn't get funding, all of Dupris's contacts up north wouldn't make any difference. Their appointment with James Robb tomorrow would be the deciding factor in whether André had a future in commerce.

Until then, why not find out where Miss Harris planned to establish her school? He could help her find the right section of town where no one would know or care what she did. And then, with a word in the ears of the right men, André might be able to make sure the school was off-limits to the more militant men. A perfect idea.

"Cordell!"

Rapid footfalls sounded on the staircase, and Cordell soon appeared in the study doorway dressed for business in one of André's old suits. "Yes sir? You ready to go down to the warehouse?"

André eyed him with fraternal affection. What would he do without Cordell? "Not today. I have something else for you to do. Sit down."

Wearing an expectant expression, Cordell took a chair on the opposite side of the desk.

"You know Miss Harris and Miss Randolph plan to open a school to educate former chattels," André said. "What I need for you to do is find a good, safe location in one of the colored sections of the city that I can recommend to her...to them. What?"

Cordell had that look on his face that sometimes pleased and sometimes annoyed André, depending on the situation.

"Sir, the ladies already rented a place from Mr. LaRue over in Faubourg Tremé. It's a two-room frame cottage in the middle of some shotgun shacks. They'll have plenty of willing students nearby and probably some who won't mind walking a long way to get there. The word is out, and folks are eager to get started."

Momentary disappointment shot through André until he realized the practicality of the situation. With the location problem solved, he would find other ways to help.

"Only problem is," Cordell continued, "the house is pretty beat up. Needs cleaning, painting, a few new floorboards and some roof work, maybe a Ben Franklin for the winter."

"Good." André leaned forward, his head filled with plans. "I want you to see that everything she—they—need is taken care of. You and I will go over to the lumberyard and get some paint for both the inside and outside. Let's find out who has roofing supplies. I'll trade some coffee for some shingles, if need be. And I want you to send Kester, Eddie, and George over to start cleaning it up."

"I'll see if they want to do that, sir." Cordell busied himself making a list of André's instructions.

"Want? What do you mean 'want'?" André snorted. "They're lucky to have what they have, a roof over their heads and food to eat. They'd better *want* to do what I say."

Cordell paused in his writing. His even, frowning stare bored into André. "André, don't think for a minute those boys don't know they have it good. They're working hard for you, and they're grateful for what you've done. But just like you don't march over to Mr. Randolph's house, there's places they might not want to go either. Now that nobody owns them, they don't have to go where they don't want to go. And that's a fact, sir." Cordell glanced down at his list and chewed his lip. Then he looked up again. "You know I don't mean any disrespect."

André stifled a bitter retort and leaned back in his chair with a sigh. "So, what about you, Cordell? Are you doing what you want to do? Why do you stay? Why don't you take Aunt Sukey and go north where your talents will be better appreciated?"

Cordell shook his head. "Now don't start in on that kind of foolishness, André."

"No, I mean it. Why?"

Again, Cordell stared evenly at André. "Because we're family." He stood and held up his list. "Now I'll get right on these things. And I'll make sure the boys help out one way or the other." Without waiting to be dismissed, he left the room.

A strange mixture of respect and reassurance filled André's breast, although he couldn't say exactly why.

As Juliana and Amelia's carriage drew near to their schoolhouse, they exchanged glances of concern.

"Who are all those people?" Amelia craned her neck to study the busy crowd. "Jim-Jim, can you see what they're doing?"

"Not too well, Miz Amelia." He rose up from the driver's seat of the carriage for a better view. "Why, land sakes, Miz Amelia, they's carrying everything out of there."

Alarm filled Juliana. "You mean they're stealing things?" Not that there was much of value to steal.

"No, Miz Juliana," Jim-Jim said. "They's cleaning out the mess." He chuckled. "My, my, look at that. Working in the yard, too."

The ladies turned to discover Negroes of all ages had formed a chain to carry junk from the house. Others raked the dirt yard with brooms made of sticks and branches. One man stood by the door and studied each item as it was carried from the house. Then he decided whether to send it to a cart to be carried away for disposal or set aside to be repaired for use. The busy workers were laughing and talking, as if at a garden party. Juliana and Amelia laughed, too.

"Before we call, God will answer," Juliana said. "Let's get busy."

She and Amelia accepted Jim-Jim's assistance as they climbed from the carriage. They donned the aprons they had brought and approached the house. Juliana waited for Amelia to speak first.

"How wonderful for you to clean out the house." Amelia addressed the man at the door. "Thank you. My goodness, you've accomplished so much. May I ask your name?"

"Percy, ma'am." The dark-skinned man had short, curly white hair and a kindly twinkle in his black eyes. His posture seemed bent in a permanent bow, but he bobbed even lower to show his respect.

The other workers stopped their tasks and gathered around the ladies.

"Tell me what you've done so far." Amelia peeked inside the door.

"We just about got the place cleaned out. They's not much useful but one old bed and some chairs that need fixin'." Percy scratched his head. "Don't know how you gonna git everybody in those two rooms." He waved his arm to take in the thirty or so people surrounding them.

Juliana's heart lilted with excitement. How little faith she'd had, fearing they would have to search for helpers and students.

"We can teach you in shifts," she said.

"Ma'am?" Percy asked.

"We can teach the women and children in the morning and the men in the afternoon." To Juliana, it seemed the logical solution.

"Yes, ma'am." Percy did not appear convinced, despite his affirmative answer.

"What would you suggest?" Amelia asked.

Percy's face lit up, and he straightened a little. "Well, ma'am, since you asked and since I been thinking on it, a lot of us—men and women, too—have paying jobs." The pride in his voice brought a tender ache to Juliana's spirit.

"We got to go to work all day, so we want you to teach the chi'drun. Then they can teach us in the evening—that is, if you think that's all right." Percy wore a hopeful expression, as did others in the group.

"Why, that sounds just perfect," Amelia said. "And if any of the adults need extra help, we'll find a way to meet with you, perhaps on Sunday afternoons."

The plan agreed upon, Juliana and Amelia entered the house. One room had been emptied, and three women were on their knees scrubbing the floor. Once again the two friends exchanged glances, this time with smiles.

Throughout the morning, the work continued, and soon the remaining needs became apparent. Percy explained that he had been a carpenter on a plantation, so they appreciated his recommendations. Paint, boards to restore weakened areas of the floor, a few replacement windowpanes—all before desks or benches could be brought in. Finding some of the needed resources might prove to be the biggest problem. But having a carpenter who also possessed leadership skills delighted Juliana and Amelia. At each step of the way, they could see that God was blessing their enterprise.

Just before midday, Juliana stepped out into the sunshine for some fresh air. She couldn't help but notice that the Negro women did not wear such cumbersome clothing as society dictated for her and Amelia. Most of them wore simple, modest dresses that long ago should have been consigned to the ragbag. Wearing a corset, hoop, and petticoat, she felt a bit useless for some of the tasks at hand—not to mention very hot on this late August day.

A wagon drawn by two mules came clattering up the road. Juliana shielded her eyes from the sun to view the newcomers. Had the Lord brought more pleasant surprises? Indeed, He had. In the driver's seat of the wagon sat Mr. Beauchamp, and in the rear sat four Negro men. When they drew up to the house, Juliana wondered why Mr. Beauchamp wore a frown.

"Good morning." She went to greet them.

Mr. Beauchamp wrapped the reins around the brake and jumped down from the wagon. "Good morning, Miss Harris." He removed his straw hat and bowed. "You are a vision of loveliness, if I may say so." His gracious words did not match his frown.

"Th-thank you." Those clear blue eyes always unnerved her. "How nice to see you. Did you enjoy the opera last night?" Remembering the bold way she had smiled at him brought warmth to Juliana's face.

He shrugged, but a hint of a smile came to his lips, his very nice lips, which were a bit full for a man, especially the lower one. "It was tolerable, but not outstanding." He looked beyond her, surveyed the house, and then stared down at her again. "I see you have many helpers. And here I had hoped to come to your rescue and help you clean up this place. Now I see my paltry offerings are not needed." He gestured toward the wagon containing not only the four men but also some boards and other building supplies she could not quite identify.

Juliana wished for a fan to cool away the heat flooding her face, but she hadn't brought one. "Oh, no, not paltry at all. We were just discussing, Miss Randolph and I, where to find boards and paint and nails and—" She was babbling, and from the grin he was trying to pucker away, she knew he noticed. "And so, Mr. Beauchamp, I think you have indeed rescued me *again,* and I'm grateful. Won't you come inside and see what we've accomplished? We will welcome your recommendations for further improvement."

"I would be delighted, Miss Harris. Permit me." He held out an arm for her.

She set her hand on it, feeling the strength of his forearm even through his coat sleeve. *My goodness, this day grows hotter by the minute.*

Once they stepped inside, Mr. Beauchamp changed from solicitous escort to critical inspector. He walked from one room to the other and back again, thumped the walls, tested floorboards with a booted foot, and emitted an occasional "hmm," as if trying to decide what course of action was needed for each problem. At last he stood, hands on hips, and stared up at the ceiling.

"Before we repair and paint that, we need to check for rotten rafters and joists. Then the roof needs to be sealed and new shingles will have to be laid down." He stood on tiptoes and reached up to press a drooping bit of ceiling. "Hmm. Maybe we should just tear this out right now and rebuild it before anything else."

A soft groan came from Percy, who had been watching Mr. Beauchamp.

"What is it, old man?" Mr. Beauchamp asked.

Percy wilted a little at his gruff tone, and Juliana quickly stepped between the two.

"This is Percy," she said. "He's a carpenter. Percy, didn't you climb up into the rafters a while ago and inspect them?"

Percy stepped forward, and Juliana could see that his hands shook. "It's all right, Percy," she said. "Mr. Beauchamp is here to help. We're all here to help."

Mr. Beauchamp dropped his hands to his sides and relaxed his posture. "Ah, an expert. Tell me, Percy, what was your assessment?"

"Sir?"

"Are the rafters and joists in good condition, or should we replace them?"

Again Mr. Beauchamp said "we"—not as if he was taking ownership of the building but as if he was joining them in their endeavors. Juliana's heart filled with warmth that had nothing to do with the heat of the day, and she sent up a silent prayer of thanks.

Percy straightened a little bit. "Well, suh, they's a few bad timbers up there, but I think we can save the ceiling."

"Hmm." Mr. Beauchamp considered Percy's words and nodded. "I'm all in favor of saving what we can. Come with me, Percy. I have some boards in my wagon. Let's see what we can do with them." He nodded toward the door, and the old man followed him out.

With some difficulty, Juliana resisted the urge to follow as well. What a wonder she had just observed. After thinking the worst of Mr. Beauchamp with regard to his treatment of former slaves, she had seen his true character. He was a good man. He *could* change his old views.

"Don't you *dare*." Amelia crossed the room and gave Juliana's shoulders a gentle shake.

"What? What are you talking about?" Juliana hadn't noticed that Amelia was in the room.

"You and Mr. Beauchamp."

"I and—"

"I'm not blind, Juliana. You look at Mr. Beauchamp just like Helena looks at Dr. Mayfield." Amelia's eyes exuded sadness. "And just like poor Dr. Mayfield looks at you."

"Oh, dear." Juliana's face flamed, but she wasn't certain whether it was from embarrassment or annoyance. All too often, her two older sisters had chided her for her romanticism and mothered her in other ways. Although she dearly loved them, she had been relieved when they married and moved away from home. She did not need Amelia to take their place. Yet, like them, Amelia apparently had seen Juliana's heart in her eyes.

"'Oh, dear' is right." Amelia sniffed. "That *man*." Her tone resounded with disapproval.

Unable to bear her censure, Juliana hurried out the front door. Mr. Beauchamp and his workers had begun to stack the contents of the wagon beside the house. At the sight of him carrying several boards over one shoulder, her heart leapt to her throat. What a very fine figure of a man. What a fine man in every way. Why shouldn't she be friends with him?

"Miz Juliana!" A bright little girl, dark as midnight except for her sparkling brown eyes, ran to Juliana and held forth a wilted dandelion. "This is for you."

Relieved to have this delightful distraction, Juliana laughed. She knelt down and drew the child into her arms, choosing to ignore the dirt from the ground or the dust from her precious young friend, which now clung to Juliana's face and clothes.

She glanced over little Pearl's shoulder at the cause of her disagreement with Amelia. Yet, try as she might, she could not think of a single reason she should not be friends with Mr. Beauchamp. ✺

✶ ✶ ✶ ✶

*I*f André had been uncertain of the depth of his feelings for Miss Harris before, he now knew that he loved her completely. He had loved her since the moment he had seen her that day on the wharf, alone, frightened, and very, very brave. Now, with her arms around a pretty little black child, she appeared nothing less than the embodiment of angelic goodness. Her laughter rang out like exquisite music, and her light-blue hoopskirt billowed out like a cloud around her to complete the picture, one that seemed to confirm that she was not of this earth.

His eyes still on her, André tripped on a rock and dropped his load of lumber. One board bounced back, striking his shin, and pain shot up his leg. He bit back a curse. "Ah!"

Miss Harris appeared beside him in an instant. "Goodness gracious, are you all right?"

André's face blazed with embarrassment over his clumsiness. But one quick glance at her sympathetic expression proved too tempting. He set his hand on her dainty shoulder and pretended to steady himself.

"Why, ma'am, I do believe I'll need to sit down."

"Oh, my!" she cried. "Percy, please bring over those chairs." She pointed toward the salvaged items from the house.

Percy hurried to help, followed by two other men who carried the wooden chairs into the shade at the side of the house and then assisted André as he sat down.

"You all right, suh?" Percy's honest concern showed André that he had won over the old man.

Some of the women and children gathered around. André touched his shin and winced more than the injury warranted. He had suffered far worse bumps in his life without any such attention. Still, with Miss Harris seated beside him, so ready to shower him with sympathy, he must not disappoint her.

"Mmm," he moaned softly.

"Shall I look at it?" Miss Harris started to reach down.

He stayed her hand. "Why, no, ma'am. I'm sure that wouldn't be proper." She didn't need to see how slight the wound was.

"I've been a nurse at my father's mission for years, Mr. Beauchamp." Her tone sounded rich with understanding.

At the thought of her gentle touch on truly sick individuals, André felt his heart surge with warmth…and a bit of shame. "No, no, it's nothing." Did his voice sound a little strained?

She wrinkled her pretty forehead, as if she didn't believe him. "Very well, then."

"Miz Juliana," Percy said, "some of the womenfolk have brought over dinner. Can we offer you somethin' to eat?"

"How lovely. Thank you." Miss Harris started to get up.

"Now, miss, you sit still," Percy said. "We'll bring it over."

"Do you know where Miss Randolph is?" Juliana asked the group of onlookers.

"She's inside with the children," one of the women said. "They spread out a blanket on the floor for a picnic."

André stifled a sigh of relief, and Miss Harris seemed satisfied with the arrangement. The workers dispersed, and André had Miss Harris all to himself as they dined on hot cornbread, dandelion greens, and chicory coffee. André wondered at their ingenuity, for this neighborhood appeared to have so few resources for survival. Miss Harris was grace personified in accepting this lowly fare. Only by watching closely could he tell that she did not care for greens, for she took very small bites and chewed with determination before gulping them down. At one point, she stopped chewing and winced, as if she had bitten down on a pebble. But then she gamely resumed her meal.

"I must commend you for your service to the sick." André took a sip of coffee and withheld a grimace. He hated chicory.

Miss Harris grew pensive. "My sisters and I could do nothing less, considering the terrible things done to our brave fighting men… oh!" She blushed scarlet and looked away. "Oh, dear."

André felt a bit of warmth creep into his face, too, but he could not bear another argument with her. "Dear Miss Harris, the war… happened. If we are to be friends—and I hope you wish for that as much as I—then we must face it honestly." He stared away for a moment, struggling to find something conciliatory to say. "Uncommon courage was displayed on both sides."

She nodded and busied herself with her small dinner.

"You have sisters?" He must close this chasm before it widened.

"Yes." Her expression lightened. "Two bossy older sisters and one younger brother who's a pest. My sisters are married and now have husbands to order around. My poor brother must be bored with no one at home to tease." Her laughter tickled his heart. "I miss them all dreadfully. And you?"

Why had he brought up this subject? Of course she would respond in kind. He took a gulp of coffee. "No sisters. My only brother died of yellow fever."

She touched his arm with such gentleness that he wished he could pull her into his arms for comfort. "I'm so sorry, Mr. Beauchamp."

He willed away his mood and stared down at her. "Please call me André."

Understanding flitted across her eyes. "I suppose that would be acceptable, but only if you will call me Juliana."

He chuckled. "Why, I would be honored, Juliana." He liked the way it felt to speak her name.

"That's actually my middle name." She wrinkled her pretty little upturned nose. "My first name is Dorcas, but I've never cared for it."

"Ah, named for the biblical woman who did such good works. Prophetic, I think."

Juliana laughed. "I'm sure there were times when my parents wondered over their choice. They always—"

"Miss Harris." Miss Randolph rounded the corner of the house as if on a rampage. "There you are."

"And here you are, Amelia." Juliana glanced at André. "We should get back to work. How's your injury?"

"Completely healed, I'm sure, by the pleasure of your company." André stood, forbidding himself to wince, for his shin did ache now. "If you ladies will excuse me, I'll go to the lumberyard for another load of supplies."

André took Cordell and Kester, leaving Eddie and George to continue helping with the work. Seated beside André in the driver's seat, Cordell hummed a nondescript tune, an annoying habit he had developed of late. Usually it meant he wanted to say something and didn't know how to begin.

"Well?" André nudged him with his elbow.

"That Miss Harris…" Cordell grinned and stared off in the distance.

André glanced toward the back of the wagon where Kester dozed on an old blanket.

"Yes. That Miss Harris." André's heart swelled. No matter that renting this wagon had put him further in debt to Fontaine. No matter that the cost of the building materials had been charged at an exorbitant rate of interest, and André had no idea how he would pay for any of it.

Oh, yes. That Miss Harris…his Juliana.

✦❘❘❘✦❘❘❘✦

Juliana ignored Amelia's scowls. She refused to feel guilty for having dinner with Mr. Beauchamp…André. Everything he had said and done pleased her. How could Amelia continue to dislike him when he was donating supplies to their school?

Instead of seeking Amelia, Juliana joined some women who were sorting through a pile of clutter brought outside from the second room. They welcomed her with smiles and friendly comments. When she and Amelia had first arrived, these same women had been shy and silent. Now they spoke as if she was a part of their community.

"Don' know where I'll git clothes for my boys," one woman said as she shook the dust from a piece of ragged cloth before inspecting it. "They's growin' so fast."

Others spoke of similar problems.

"My girl's thirteen, and she's bustin' outta her clothes, too. Gonna be a woman soon." Claudeen, another mother, laughed softly, but Juliana sensed a note of worry in her voice.

Maybe the time had come to send another telegram to Papa and Mother. They could have a clothes drive and ship their collection to Juliana. These dear people had so many needs that the task of helping them seemed daunting, but Papa's church back home had promised support.

"Mm-mmm!" Winnie, one of the younger women, stared beyond the group. "Now there comes one of God's finest creations."

"Oh, mercy, you know it," Claudeen said.

"Hush up, you hussies." A gray-haired old woman clucked her tongue. Her snapping midnight eyes swiftly silenced her younger companions. "Show some respect."

Juliana followed the women's gazes. A tall, well-formed Negro man strode up the street toward them. His dark brown skin glistened with perspiration. Yet his black suit, tall hat, and dignified bearing immediately evoked esteem, for he walked with a confidence unmarred by arrogance. This must be what Frederick Douglass had looked like when he was younger.

"Do you know him?" Juliana asked.

"He's the reverend," the old woman said in a hushed tone.

"Ladies." The man lifted his hat and nodded to the group, but he seemed on a mission. He walked past them toward the men, who were sorting wood.

The younger women sighed, and Juliana wanted to giggle. When a handsome man appeared, reverend or not, all women were alike. She guessed the single women wouldn't have admired him so openly if he had been married.

Soon the man returned, accompanied by Percy.

"Miz Juliana," the old man said, "this here is Rev'rend Curtis Adams. He's the leader of our community." His eyes shone with pride. "Rev'rend, this here is Miz Juliana Harris of Boston."

"Ma'am." Reverend Adams removed his hat and bowed, but when he straightened, Juliana saw caution in his eyes.

"Reverend Adams." She dipped a curtsy. "I'm so pleased to meet you."

As his eyebrows rose and his face rounded in a broad smile, Juliana noticed that the symmetry of his handsome face was broken by a savage gray scar slashed across his right cheek. She gulped back a gasp. Some cruel slave master had no doubt done that to him.

"Miss Harris, I am honored." He nodded to her again. "Your generosity to my community is much appreciated."

He spoke in deep, rich tones and pronounced his words carefully. Juliana could imagine him delivering a powerful sermon.

"We're so happy to be here doing the Lord's work," she said. "You must meet my fellow teacher, Miss Randolph. I believe she's inside working with some of the children."

"I've already had the honor of meeting Miss Randolph and her family. Mr. Randolph is a good friend. Our church has been praying that the Lord will fully heal him."

"Thank you, sir," Juliana said. "His color was good this morning. Dr. Mayfield predicts a complete recovery."

"Praise the Lord," Reverend Adams boomed out in his melodious voice.

"Praise the good Lawd is right," Percy echoed with equal enthusiasm.

Reverend Adams glanced at the group of women, who stood watching with interest. "Miss Harris, may we speak to you and Miss Randolph in private?"

"Certainly." Juliana led the two men to the house and found Amelia reading to a group of nine or ten children seated on the floor around her.

Amelia looked up, first frowning at Juliana and then brightening at the sight of Reverend Adams. She rose and greeted him, responding with gratitude to his well-wishes for her father's health.

"Children," Reverend Adams said, "I want you to go find your mamas."

Without a word and with obvious admiration for the reverend, the children quickly obeyed and scampered from the room, each receiving a pat on the head or back from him as they went. He even sparred for a moment with one of the older boys.

Once they were out of the room, Reverend Adams grew serious.

"Miss Randolph, Miss Harris, I will come right to the point. I need two things, and I believe you are the ones God has chosen to provide them."

Juliana looked to Amelia to respond.

"We'll do what we can," Amelia said. "What do you need?"

"First, I need a church building where my people can gather. The two rooms of this house would be just the right size if this middle wall were removed." He knocked on the wall. "I don't believe this is a bearing wall, do you, Percy?"

"No, suh." Percy shook his head. "It's not. But…"

"What a grand idea," Juliana said. "Oh, Amelia, wasn't it clever of Mr. Smith to write that clause into our lease with Mr. LaRue?" She turned to Reverend Adams. "We can make improvements to the house as we see fit as long as it doesn't cost Mr. LaRue anything."

Percy joined in as both ladies laughed.

Delight sparkled in Percy's eyes. "Lawd, Miz Juliana, Miz Amelia, you sure are a godsend."

"What was the other thing you need, Reverend Adams?" Juliana asked.

His jaw tightened, and to Juliana it seemed as if a hint of wounded pride marked his expression.

He pulled from his pocket a battered old Bible and held it up.

"I need for you to teach me how to read this." ✶

✳ ✳ ✳

"But I've heard you preach." Confusion filled Amelia's expression. "You hold up your Bible and quote scriptures flawlessly. How can it be that you cannot read?"

Reverend Adams's shoulders slumped a little, but then he straightened, and his eyes snapped with intensity. "I listen with great care to other ministers when they read the Bible. I ask questions so I will not sin by misspeaking the Word of God. My mind captures those holy words, and the Lord Himself writes them into my spirit and seals them into my memory. I repeat them day and night to myself and to anyone who will listen."

He set his hand on Percy's shoulder, and the expression in his black eyes softened. "Percy has been a spiritual father to me. Not only did he save my life, but he listens to my recitations when he should be getting some sleep."

Percy chuckled. "Never could read myself, so hearin' the Word of God is rest unto my soul. The Lawd takes care of the body."

Juliana's heart surged with wonder and joy. These revelations confirmed as nothing before that her coming to New Orleans *had* been God's will. "Reverend Adams, you will be welcomed in our class."

She tried for a moment to envision this community leader seated as a pupil among the children. He hadn't wanted anyone to hear him ask for reading instruction, so Percy might be the only one who knew he couldn't read. But it would not be proper for either her or Amelia to give him private lessons. Only one solution presented itself.

"After all," she said, "we need a school superintendent. With you in attendance, we can be certain the children behave."

Amelia must have comprehended her thoughts. "What a good idea. I've had a few concerns about the older boys, but if you're here, Reverend Adams, they won't misbehave."

As if he too grasped the situation, Reverend Adams laughed with relief. "Oh, yes, ma'am, that is a real concern. Even the best-behaved boy will kick against the traces from time to time, as well I know." In what appeared to be an unconscious gesture, Reverend Adams passed his hand over the scar on his face and down his neck.

Juliana burned to ask what had happened to him, but that might offend him. As their group walked out the front door into the cloudy afternoon, she decided to ask in a roundabout way.

"Percy, how did you save Reverend Adams' life?"

Percy shook his head. "Nothin' nobody else wouldn't do."

Reverend Adams put his hat back on and wagged a finger at the older man. "Now, don't you go actin' like it was nothin'." His pronunciation relaxed for a moment before he turned back to the ladies. "On the plantation where I was born a slave, I was at odds with certain practices and suffered for it."

"They jes' about beat the boy to death." Percy's eyes filled with tears.

Reverend Adams looked away, as if the memory haunted him anew. "Then they sold me over to Pinewood Plantation to take me away from my mother and sisters." He swallowed and shook his head. "But God had a plan for me in all that mischief, just like He did for Joseph in the Bible."

He nudged Percy's shoulder. "Percy nursed me for many a night, talking all that time about the Lord. I had no choice but to listen." He emitted a self-deprecating laugh. "Pretty soon his words began to reach into my mind and heart. I had always found it easy to condemn the evil that others did to my loved ones and to me. Now I saw my own evil. Not my rebellion against a cruel master, but the hatred I clutched like gold in my heart and the murder I knew I was capable of…and wanted to commit. I saw that my own efforts had brought forth nothing but more misery for me and those I love, for the wrath of man worketh not the righteousness of God.

"I came to see that the only hope to be found in my miserable existence was in the Lord Jesus Christ. I surrendered my anger, my hatred, my very will to Him. He saved my soul and restored my health. Then and there, I promised the Lord I wouldn't just take His salvation for comfort when things got bad. I knew I had to go about the work of serving Him with every bit of strength in my soul and body."

Juliana pulled a handkerchief from her sleeve and wiped away tears. Amelia did the same.

"How remarkable." Juliana sniffed into her handkerchief. "How truly wonderful. God has certainly given you the gifts to serve Him and His children. And listen to you talk. The scriptures aren't the only words you've memorized. Your diction and enunciation are excellent."

Reverend Adams bent forward with a little bow. "Thank you, ma'am. I try, I try, and I know under your tutelage, I can only improve."

Once again amazed by his choice of words, Juliana looked for traces of pride in his eyes but saw only humility, much like the godly meekness always reflected in her father's face.

Reverend Adams stared beyond the others, and his countenance clouded.

Percy turned that direction. "Now, Curtis…"

"It's all right, Percy." Reverend Adams wet his lips. "The Lord's just testing me to see if I meant what I just said."

Juliana turned to see what had drawn their attention. André Beauchamp once again drove near with a wagonload of supplies. He jumped down and gave orders to his men and then strode toward Juliana and her companions. The smile on André's face faded as he drew closer.

"Ladies." He tipped his hat and bowed. Then he straightened and lifted his chin. An arrogant sneer marred his handsome face. "Hello, Curtis. I see you've recovered from our last encounter and grown right tall over these past four years." He scanned Reverend Adams up and down. "Mighty fine clothes you're sporting there. Coming up in the world, are you?"

Reverend Adams clenched his fists and pulled in a deep breath, returning a strained smile for André's rudeness. "Good afternoon, Mr. Beauchamp."

The eyes of the two men locked in silent warfare. The air between them crackled like an electrical storm. Waves of stinging heat washed over Juliana. She must diffuse this situation. "Reverend Adams has just been saying—"

"Reverend?" André emitted an explosive laugh and continued to glare at the minister. "Do tell."

Now Juliana understood. It was André who had beaten Reverend Adams. His own words condemned him. Unable to take a breath, she swayed, feeling as if Satan himself had appeared and slapped her down. Amelia reached out to steady her.

André whipped his attention to Juliana. Every nuance of his posture and expression accused her. "May I speak with you privately?" He bent his head toward the wagon, where his men and others unloaded supplies. He turned and strode away.

"No." Amelia held her. "Don't go."

Juliana glanced at Reverend Adams and Percy. They regarded her with tranquil understanding.

"I must." Juliana pulled away from Amelia and followed André.

At the wagon, he stopped and spun about. "What are you doing with that Negro?"

"He…He's the leader of this community. He's…"

"Do you mean to tell me you're coming under the influence of that n—"

"Don't!" Juliana cut in. "Don't you ever use that word in my presence, especially about someone *you,* Mr. Beauchamp, almost murdered."

He stared down at her. Time seemed to halt as she looked up into the dreadful, endless abyss of his soul. At last he expelled a dismissive snort. "If you intend to instruct me in things you know absolutely nothing about, then I will gladly remove myself from your presence for good, *Miss* Harris."

He turned and looked at the last item in the wagon, a bucket of nails. He yanked it out and dumped it upside down on the ground.

"Cordell!" He gave a curt wave of his hand, and his four men came running. Once they were in the wagon, he snatched up a whip and drove the mules away in a fury.

Juliana stared after him. The flash of anger she had felt only moments before dissolved into deep sadness. Not for the awful truth she now understood about André Beauchamp or for her own bruised heart, but for all of the South. She believed with all her heart that God had made His will clear in the defeat of the Confederacy. Had He not given them a chance to repent of their evil practices and become new men—a whole new society?

Amelia gathered Juliana into her arms. "You see?"

Juliana leaned her head against her friend's. "Yes." Then she pulled back to look at her. "But if he—they—won't learn, we know who will." She scanned the property, where her new friends and pupils worked to build their schoolhouse and church. "Let's get busy."

⟡

"André, slow down." Cordell grasped André's forearm to stop the whip. "These aren't your mules."

André pulled back hard on the reins, and the mules almost stumbled to a stop, snorting hot breaths all the way.

"You want to drive?" he spat out.

Disappointment clouded Cordell's eyes. Feeling as if a hot iron had scorched his soul, André flushed with shame. A memory shot through him—old Max heaving in his death throes because André had ridden him so hard.

"Here. You drive." Softening his tone, André thrust the reins at Cordell, returned the whip to its stand, and then wiped sweat from his face with both hands.

"Yes, sir." Cordell slapped the reins and clucked to the animals until they moved forward. "What happened back there?"

André glanced back at the other men, each of whom held on to the side of the wagon as if fearing for his life. "I'll tell you later."

No, he wouldn't. Cordell had never approved of the discipline administered to chattels who lacked his own easygoing manner. And André never wanted to revisit that horrific day when he and Elgin...

He closed his eyes and saw Juliana's sweet face turned up to his, her eyes blazing with accusations he could never answer. She would never understand.

What had Curtis told her about that day on the plantation? André felt no surprise that such a violent, disobedient, lying slave could fool other Negroes into believing he was an upright person. But why did Juliana...Miss Harris have to believe him? Because she was entirely too innocent and, yes, *ignorant* of the truth about these people she was so eager to help, that's why.

Wasn't their inherent inferiority obvious to her, this race of people unfit and unable to take care of themselves? Why was she trying to lift them up when they did not deserve it and would never be grateful for her sacrifices?

So how had he responded to her accusation? By whipping these poor mules in her presence, which only proved to her that he was capable of the cruelest deeds. How would he ever redeem himself in her sight? With Curtis an influential part of her school project, André would never go back.

After taking the mules and wagon back to Fontaine's store, André and his men walked home. As if the events of the day were not enough, during their nearly two-mile walk from downtown to the Garden District, a late afternoon rain poured down on them, drenching them to the skin and splashing mud on their shoes and clothes. Aunt Sukey would have a fit over all the extra laundry she would have to do. But André slogged on through the torrent, determined to let it wash away the last of his anger. After all, tomorrow he would meet with James Robb and get his loan. Then the future would be his.

Once he had cleaned up and had supper, André's nightly visit with Mama revived some of his anxiety. She insisted that she had seen Cordell that afternoon, but Cordell had been at work with him all day. When André tried to dissuade her, she grew despondent.

"I've been trying to remember something." Her voice slurred as she lay in her bed ready for sleep. "Oh, what is it? It's something you should know, André."

André bent down and kissed her. "You'll think of it in the morning, Mama. Rest now." At least she had stopped mistaking him for Father.

According to his new custom, André went to his study for the evening to check over his paperwork for the next day. Cordell had organized everything for his meeting with the banker. Since Dupris insisted they leave Cordell out of the affair, André needed to be familiar with the details for himself. Yet every time he tried to make sense of the figures, Juliana's fair form seemed to glide across the pages of his ledger like shadows from the nearby flickering candles.

"Miss Harris," he reminded himself, as though by speaking her surname aloud, he could put some distance between his mind and his heart.

"Mr. André?" Gemma said from the doorway.

André glanced up and inhaled a quick breath. How beautiful she looked this evening. "Come in, sweet girl. What can I do for you?" He waved her over and pointed to a chair in front of the desk. "Sit down."

She glanced at the chair but remained standing in front of his desk, her eyes not meeting his.

"Sit down," he said again with as much gentleness as he could. He would not have another female thinking he was a brute.

Gemma shook her head and gave him a shy smile. "That's all right. I jus' come in to ask you somethin'."

André leaned back in his chair and enjoyed the pleasant feeling her presence ignited. This was what he needed, the comfort of someone whose affection he could count on. He stood and walked around the desk, coming just short of touching her. She stepped back and bit her lip. What a shy, sweet creature.

André reached out and pulled a lock of her long, soft black hair over her left shoulder. Then he repeated the action on her right side.

"I like seeing your hair down."

Her eyes widened, and she swallowed. "Maybe I can ask you another time."

She started to leave, but he tugged her into his arms and bent his head toward her.

"Mr. André. Please…"

The pathos in her tone hit him in his gut. He released her and stepped back.

"What are you afraid of, sweet Gemma? Don't you want to be close to me like we were before?"

She stared at the floor, shaking her head. "No, sir. I mean, I'm grateful to be working here taking care of Miz Felicity, but…"

They stood in silence for a moment. For the second time this day, shame surged through André. Why was he playing this stupid game? Not only did Gemma not want him, but he didn't really want her, except to use for his own selfish purposes. He almost reached out to pat her arm but changed his mind, lest he frighten her further.

She shot a nervous glance his way and then started from the room.

"Gemma, wait." He stepped toward her. At her wince, his insides twisted sharply. "I'm not going to touch you again." He kept his tone light, soft. "Tell me why you came in here. What do you want?"

Her expression lightened a little, and she gave him an innocent half-smile, which made her look much younger than her nineteen years.

"Cordell tells me there's this school where I could learn to read. He taught me my letters, but I'd like to read some more, maybe even learn how to write my name."

In the flickering candlelight, hope danced in her beautiful amber eyes…hope and something else. He wondered what dreams resided in that lovely head.

After all the frustrations of the day, *this* he could accomplish— doing something for no other reason than to reward a faithful servant who had never asked for anything.

"Why, of course you can go to school, Gemma. I think we can find an old slate for you to use and maybe some chalk. If we have to get someone in to help watch Mama, then we will."

Tears brightened her eyes. "Thank you, Mr. André. I promise to work extra hard at night to make up for it."

He smiled and nodded his head. "I know you will. Don't be concerned about it." He longed to give her a friendly pat on the shoulder, as he would Cordell, but he feared she would misunderstand. Only by keeping his distance would she see that no price tag came with his generosity.

Not until after she had left the room and he had returned to his desk did the full import of her going to school strike him. What a perfect solution to his dilemma. His little Gemma was just the person to keep an eye on Juliana. ✳

CHAPTER FIFTEEN

* * * *

Augustus Marchet Beauchamp will receive you.
Thursday, September 1, 1865, 11 A.M.
1415 Charter Street
AMB

André read the handwritten missive repeatedly as he sat at breakfast in the kitchen. Aunt Sukey's delicious ham, eggs, and grits lay untouched on his plate. When the letter had arrived earlier that morning, he had been stunned. An invitation, no, an *order* from his grandfather. André had always assumed the old man was unaware of his existence or at least did not care whether he lived or died.

"What do you think?" He handed the invitation to Cordell, who was busy eating his eggs across the table from André. "Why should he summon me in this arrogant manner, as if he were some grand potentate calling for a slave? And why now? Why today?"

Cordell's eyes flickered for a moment before he read the letter again. "He might just be used to giving orders and not intending to be rude at all. And look here"—he held it up and pointed—*"will receive you.'* Maybe he's just saying if you go over to his house, he'll receive you." He raised his eyebrows and gave André a knowing look. "Now that's a change after all these years, 'cause you know if you'd gone over there before the war, his people would never have let you past the front gate. This here almost sounds like he's giving you a choice. He's inviting, and you can accept if you want to."

André snorted. "Some choice. Come *now,* this morning, or never have another chance to meet him. But I can't afford to miss that meeting with Robb at one o'clock."

Cordell nodded, but then he chuckled. "That might not be a problem. Those Creoles still like to take their long lunches, especially the older ones. He'll probably want you out of his house by noon."

André laughed. "Good point."

The laughter felt so good that it lifted his spirits. The old man wanted to see him. He wanted to get to know his only living grandson. What would André say to him? And what should he wear? The suit that was acceptable for his appointment with Robb now appeared too threadbare for meeting the family patriarch.

Family? Did Augustus regard André as family? Of course he did. Why else would he have summoned him? André could hardly wait to go.

After breakfast, Cordell once again went over the shipping figures with André until he felt confident in what he would say to Robb. Then Cordell reverted to his old job, polishing André's worn half-boots and helping him find the right clothes. Cordell dug out a well-made brown morning suit from before the war that still fit through the shoulders, although Gemma had to hurry and let out the trouser legs. After Aunt Sukey ironed the trousers and his white shirt and helped him tie his cravat, they all proclaimed André's appearance fit for presentation to the august Augustus.

With his papers for the later meeting tucked in his inside coat pocket, André set out. Yesterday's rain had washed clean the Garden District yards and perked up lawns and flowers, infusing the neighborhood with fresh scents. Morning sun had hardened the ruts in the roads, causing passing carriage wheels to wiggle and wobble all over the streets. People with their varied activities filled the sidewalks and yards.

As André strode across town toward the French Quarter, he felt like a boy on an outing. The closer he came to Charter Street, however, the more he harkened back to his days as a young midshipman at the naval academy when he had been called before the superintendent for getting into mischief.

He knew nothing about his grandfather. Despite Augustus's austere public appearance, was he jovial in private? Did he smoke a pipe, as André's father had? Or did he prefer cigars? André had neither time nor money to bring a gift. Maybe he should have dug out one of his father's gold stick pins or other jewelry.

This was foolishness. On an already hot day, he was working himself into a sweat over a situation he had not chosen for himself. In all his life, he had done nothing to offend Augustus other than be born of the woman the old man hated simply because she was from England rather than France or his own Creole community. Cordell's parting words came to mind.

"You never can tell what good might come of this. We'll be praying for you."

André could always count on Cordell to say the right thing.

With ten minutes to spare, he arrived at the address, a gated, tree-lined property with a two-story house set back several yards from the narrow road. A young colored boy unlocked the gate and pointed him toward the oak front door, where a butler granted him admittance.

"This way, Massuh André." The middle-aged Negro took his straw hat and led him upstairs to the drawing room, an elegant chamber with well-maintained French provincial furniture and large vases filled with fragrant, multicolored bouquets. "Please wait here."

André did wait. Shortly after he arrived, the clock on the mantel-piece chimed eleven o'clock and, after what seemed like hours, eleven-thirty. Then, at eleven thirty-five, fighting to gain control of his temper as one would an angry dog on a leash, he walked toward the drawing room door, wondering what the butler had done with his hat. Behind him, he heard a door slam shut. He swung back around, a rebuke ready on his lips. But then he stopped, unable to move or speak.

Augustus Beauchamp looked as if he had stepped from a larger-than-life painting of some European nobleman or king. His height—more than six feet and unbowed by his seventy-six years—was greater than André's by at least two inches. His straight white hair rose above his high forehead like a crown and swept down to his shoulders like a cape. Few wrinkles lined his handsome face, and those that did only added to his dignified appearance. But his large, icy blue eyes cut into André's heart, freezing out the last bit of warmth he had felt in antic-ipation of this interview.

André lifted his chin and smirked. Who did this man think he was?

Augustus emitted a caustic laugh. *"Quelle surprise! Le garçon est ni un pleurnichar ou une chiffe molle."*

André stiffened. So the old buzzard would insult him in French. Had he really expected him to be a spineless fool or a whining puppy? What arrogance! What bad manners! He would rebuke the old man in kind.

"Bonjour, Grandpère. Quant a vous, votre arrogance n'est surpassée que par vos mauvaises manieres."

Augustus grunted out a cutting *"Touché.* Now come back in here and sit down." He whipped his hand around in a commanding gesture and then thrust a finger toward a decidedly feminine chair.

André ambled over to the room's dominant chair, an almost throne-like piece of furniture in front of the fireplace. Made of heavy mahogany with a red leather seat, it boasted an ornately carved back of two rearing horses, with one horse's front hoof protruding in the center. A man of Augustus's height would be forced to sit erect in this chair. Anyone else would find his neck against the hoof—or under Augustus's heel. André eyed the old man, whose expression dared him to sit there. He shrugged and moved to a sturdy divan where he sat back and stretched out his legs as if he had visited this room all his life.

"Nice house."

"Ha!" Augustus nudged past the footstool in front of his chair and lowered himself slowly. His movement suggested he might be in pain, but his face remained immobile.

For a moment, the two men studied each other, their faces hard. André felt like a prized horse up for sale. He wanted to ask if his grandfather would like to inspect his teeth. His assessment of the man was no less unforgiving. How could André's warm, loving father have been the spawn of this cold mannequin? With great difficulty, André refused to ask why he had been summoned. Let the old man lead in this ridiculous interview.

"Don't bother with that Yankee's money." Augustus spoke firmly but not as one would give an order.

A chill swept down André's neck, but he did his best to hide it. How did Augustus know about his plans to borrow money from James Robb?

"I don't much care for Pierre Dupris," Augustus continued, "but if we keep an eye on him, he won't rob you blind. He might even prove to be a useful partner."

We? André shifted in his seat and ground his teeth. A nervous flutter erupted in his belly and grew hot. He had every reason to get up right now and leave, but he could not.

Augustus lifted a bell from the table beside him and rang it. A door opened behind André.

"Bring coffee." Augustus set the bell down, and the door closed again. He once again studied André.

"*I* will lend you the money for your import business. I know of a worthy steamship we'll purchase to take the cargo upriver. You can command it yourself. No need to hole up here in New Orleans like a whipped puppy just because the North won the war. You're a young man. You should see more of this country, have a little more experience in life."

André's insides roiled with conflicting emotions, but self-respect won over pragmatism. "You don't think commanding my own ship during the war was experience enough?"

For the briefest moment, he thought he detected paternal pride on the old man's face. But it was quickly covered with an indifferent shrug. "You had some successful runs, but the Union blockade worked against your earning any real glory. Now, about my proposition."

Proposition? Not orders?

"Go on." André tried to sound nonchalant. Could Augustus see his trembling?

The door behind him opened again. A beautiful quadroon, the one he had seen at the opera, carried a tray to the table in front of André. She gave him a serene smile as she sat down.

"*Monsieur,* may I pour you some coffee?" She was darker than Gemma but still had features more white than black. Her black hair was parted in the middle and pulled into thick buns that covered her ears. Seeing her up close, André noticed the beginnings of age lines around her eyes and mouth, but they added character rather than diminishing her beauty. A delicate scent of jasmine emanated from her and wafted throughout the room.

"Yes, *merci.*" André's belly burned hotter now, but he would not refuse the drink.

"This is Jacinta." Augustus gazed at the woman with obvious fondness. André could see she was far more than a servant. A possible chink in his armor?

He stood and took her hand to kiss it. "Jacinta. Spanish for purple hyacinth. You are well-named, *mademoiselle,* for you are indeed a beautiful flower."

"*Merci, monsieur.*" A tinge of pink touched her cheeks. She withdrew her hand to give him a steaming cup of coffee.

Even Augustus seemed pleased by his comment. Could it be these two led a lonely life shut away in this quiet house on a quiet street?

Augustus cleared his throat. "My proposition."

André felt a shift in the room. Was it Jacinta's presence that modified his grandfather's behavior, or was the old man actually vulnerable to André's opinions? André took his time sipping his coffee.

"Delicious." He smiled at Jacinta, a friendly smile without flirtation. The coffee scalded his stomach.

One glance at Augustus revealed to André that he must not delay his answer for long. How he wished Cordell were here to advise him. They had agreed applying for a loan from James Robb was a good idea. He might be a Yankee, but most Southerners agreed he was honest, as attested to by the cotton farmers who had borrowed from his bank. André didn't doubt his grandfather's honesty, but what strings would be attached to this offer?

"Let me think about it."

Augustus shook his head. "You don't need to keep that appointment. I'll send a boy to cancel it."

André felt as if he had a vise closing around his chest. Did his grandfather know everything about him?

"*Monsieur,* will you stay for dinner?"

Jacinta spoke in a rich, warm, almost maternal voice. So soothing was the sound of it that André suddenly craved what he had missed for so long—family.

"Your decision first." Augustus leaned toward André only to be scolded by Jacinta's look and "tsk." The old man actually looked somewhat abashed. Had Jacinta influenced him to send for André? Had all of this been her idea?

André expelled a long breath. Too many uncertainties accosted him. If he still knew how to pray, he would do it. *God* was all he could think, and he did not mean it in vain.

"Yes." The word slipped out before the thought settled in his mind. A sense of peace—even joy—swept down his body. His belly cooled. This was the right thing to do.

"Humph!" Augustus grunted out his pleasure. He rose from his chair and turned to Jacinta. "Dinner." He gave André that imperious gesture again. "This way."

André stood and clenched his teeth. If only in this could he assert some of his own will, so be it.

"Thank you, but I must go home. Aunt Sukey is preparing my favorite meal."

"Another time, then." Jacinta gave him a gracious nod.

"Ah, yes," Augustus said, an odd gleam in his eyes. "Susette. She was…a fine cook."

"You will excuse me?" André bowed and walked to the door.

"André."

André's heart leapt. His grandfather had never before spoken his name. He turned back; he did not know what to expect.

"The Yankee woman," Augustus stood tall, and without a doubt, this time his words were an order. "She is not for you."

André stared at him for a moment and then marched out the door. ❁

✫ ✫ ✫ ✫

The instant Juliana bit down on the strawberry preserve-covered biscuit, pain shot from her bad tooth clear down into her neck as if she had been stabbed by an ice pick. She grabbed her jaw. "Ah!" Her whimpering cry immediately drew the attention of everyone around the breakfast table.

"Is it your tooth again?" Amelia's eyes exuded sympathy. "You must go to the dentist. There's no other way to be rid of that pain."

"Yes, Juliana, you must go," Mrs. Randolph said. "I was told by one of our young soldiers that southern dentists have a remarkable record for dealing with bad teeth. If you can secure the services of one of these men, by all means, go see him."

Dr. Mayfield eyed Juliana with a frown of concern. "Dear lady, if only I had known you suffered from a toothache. I've been training with Dr. Saunders, who served as a dental surgeon in the Confederate army. He has taught me how to evaluate whether a diseased tooth requires extraction or filling and to see to the proper treatment. May I be of service to you?"

Still holding her aching jaw, Juliana shook her head and blinked away tears brought on by the pain. "No...ouch...thank you." The doctor seemed eager to help her. Perhaps too eager.

Helena giggled. "Juliana, your eyes are as round as saucers. You should let Dr. Mayfield help you. After all he's done for Father, surely you can trust him to fix a little tooth. I would trust him completely." Helena's eyes were quite round, too, as she stared at the doctor.

Dr. Mayfield leaned toward Juliana and spoke in his most soothing tone. "I cannot promise it won't hurt, but you'll feel much better afterward."

Juliana sniffed back her tears. "But I don't want to lose a tooth. My mother lost several, and she..." She stopped, feeling disloyal. Her mother's pretty face had been marred when her left cheek had sunk inward with no teeth to support it.

"I understand," Dr. Mayfield said. "But perhaps I can save the tooth. If I don't treat it, it will only get worse."

Juliana glanced around the table to see encouragement on every face. She exhaled a painful sigh. "Very well, then. Perhaps some day next week?"

"Juliana, we begin our classes on Monday." Amelia wore a scolding frown. "You must not delay this."

"Why not this afternoon?" the doctor said.

At the coaxing of her friends, Juliana at last and reluctantly nodded her agreement.

After checking Mr. Randolph's progress, Dr. Mayfield pronounced him ready to sit up for an hour in the morning sunshine. The whole household participated in the arrangements. While Jerome and Mrs. Randolph dressed the patient in light clothing, the young ladies took pillows out to a lawn chair in the back yard. Flora brought out a tray loaded with a coffee service. Dr. Mayfield and Jerome carried Mr. Randolph out into the sunlight. And Helena crowned the affair by placing a broad-brimmed straw hat on her father's head and a kiss on his cheek.

Although pale and drawn, Mr. Randolph still managed to tease his ladies about this and that. Since her arrival almost a month earlier, Juliana had admired the Randolphs' devotion to one another, for it reminded her of her own family. Now her heart warmed to see their playful side re-emerge.

Unspoken in the activity, yet clearly understood by all, was that danger still might threaten Mr. Randolph. Although he had been shot down in front of the house, who was to say he was any safer in the fenced back yard? Mrs. Randolph donned her bonnet and sat near her husband. Without being asked, Jerome stood nearby and surveyed their surroundings.

Dr. Mayfield made certain Mr. Randolph was comfortable and then announced that he had other patients to see. Juliana accompanied him to the front door.

"I'll bring my dental tools when I return." He stood at the door as if reluctant to leave.

"Oh, all right." Juliana touched her cheek. "But, really, I think it's better."

Dr. Mayfield challenged her with a teasing grin. "Teeth don't get better, Miss Harris."

Juliana looked up at him. If her entire left jaw didn't hurt so badly, she might have enjoyed this moment of mild flirtation. The doctor, whom she had first thought plain, possessed a decidedly pleasant face, especially when he smiled. His hazel eyes, which tended to be more blue than green when he wore his dark blue uniform, never failed to twinkle when he looked at her, thus proving Amelia had been right. The good doctor cared more than a little for Juliana. Despite her previous resolve to leave him to Helena, she knew that without too much effort she could persuade her own heart to return that affection. Except that her heart stubbornly insisted on grieving for a different prospect, now lost to her forever.

Juliana lowered her eyes. "I promise to be a good patient, Dr. Mayfield."

"Miss Harris, forgive me if I am being too bold, but would you please call me Robert?"

Juliana sighed softly and looked back at him. She simply could not do this. But his expression revealed raw vulnerability and a tenderness she had not seen when she had last stared into another, bluer pair of eyes. So she playfully pulled away and gave him a coy, sidelong look.

"Why, Dr. Mayfield, such a notion. I hardly know you. Perhaps in the future…" Indeed, she could see this man winning her heart under different circumstances.

He chuckled and nodded. "Yes, perhaps. Good morning, Miss Harris. I shall return this afternoon. Now don't run away."

"Hmm. What a good idea." She laughed, too. "Perhaps I shall."

As she closed the door, Juliana turned to see Helena watching from the staircase opposite the entrance. A pout—no, *distress*—filled her sweet face. She sniffed softly and then fled up the stairs. Juliana chewed her lip for a moment until the jaw movement made her tooth hurt again.

How could she consider surrendering her heart to Dr. Mayfield, whom she did not love, when someone who was as dear to her as a sister clearly loved the man already? She must find a way to divert his affection. Only one plan came to mind.

This afternoon, she would be a very bad patient.

"Do you have any idea what you've cost me? Cost *us*?" Standing in the foyer of the Beauchamp house, Pierre Dupris shouted at André and waved his fat hands about like a windmill. The cigar in one hand threw off ashes onto the carpet and hardwood floor. "Robb said he didn't have time or money to do business with a man who can't even keep an appointment. Now what am I going to do?"

André tried to remain calm. So his grandfather had failed to send a message to Robb canceling the appointment. Would he be as untrustworthy in other things? Now André must try to salvage this situation.

"I sent a boy to say I couldn't come. Didn't he arrive?"

"Well, of course he arrived. But do you think a man like Robb will lightly forget an appointment broken at the last minute?"

Shrugging, André hid his relief. Augustus had kept his word after all. "Never mind that. Come into my study and let me tell you about a meeting I had this morning."

Grumbling all the way, Dupris followed André and plopped into a chair on the opposite side of the large oak desk. Before telling Dupris about his meeting with Augustus, André decided to put certain matters on the table, as Cordell had advised after they discussed the old man's offer. While he considered his words, a feeling of satisfaction filled him. For the first time since he had commanded his ship during the war, he was in charge of a situation. He opened the desk's center drawer as if to appear distracted. Had he really left these papers in such a mess? At Cordell's urging, he had tried to improve his organizational skills. Never mind. He must stick to the business at hand.

"First of all, Dupris, before we shake hands on any deal or sign partnership papers, I want to know just how many pies you have your fingers in."

"What? What are you talking about?" Dupris shifted in his char.

André leaned back in his. He liked playing this cat-and-mouse game, especially when he was the cat.

"I know you had a partnership with Althea Dawson before and during the war. I want that to end. I don't want any part of her little operation." This was a concession to Cordell's sensibilities, but André had promised to require it.

Dupris leaned forward and pounded the desk. "That has nothing to do with our partnership. Do you want to do business with me or not?" He sat back and shoved his cigar into his mouth.

André shrugged again. "I'll find someone else to work with. You're not the only one with northern contacts." A vague thought crept up from the back of his mind. Maybe he could restore his shattered friendship with Miss Harris by asking if her father could advise him on where to ship his goods. Even if not...

Dupris shot him a worried scowl. "Now don't go jumpin' the gun, boy. We can talk this out. For one thing, I recently dissolved my partnership with Althea over some...shall we say, *issues* I'd rather not discuss. What else are you concerned about?"

The man had clearly been disarmed. André put on his captain face, the one that made sailors tremble. Narrowed eyes, firm jaw slightly jutted forward, lifted chin. Problem was, he didn't have any further demands. Ah, yes. One thing.

"You will recognize my man Cordell as my emissary and take his word as though I were speaking."

Now Dupris narrowed his eyes. "You mean I have to kowtow to that n—?"

"Don't." André took a turn at pounding his fist on the desk. He would not have that demeaning term used for Cordell. "You either respect him as you would me, or no deal." Even as he said it, his thoughts shot to Miss Harris's similar defense of Curtis. Her choice of people to respect might be flawed, but she had stood up for what she believed. *Admirable.*

"Bah." Dupris snorted out his disgust and gave a dismissive wave of his hand. "Have it your way. What else?"

André resumed his enigmatic expression and wished Cordell were there to suggest something else to keep Dupris off guard.

"That's it for now."

"All right, then, let's do business. What about that meeting you had this morning?"

André could hardly keep the glee from his voice. If he hadn't blown off some of his exuberance to Cordell earlier, he might just make a fool of himself right now. He cleared his throat and gave a little shrug.

"Augustus Beauchamp has offered to back us. He's planning to purchase a ship…"

"Augustus…Beauchamp?" Dupris shouted, and then nearly swallowed the stub of his cigar. He fell into a fit of coughing and bent over, beet red from neck to bald pate.

André hurried around the desk and pounded him on the back with the hope the man would not die right on the spot. Dupris flung himself back in his chair, gasping, and waved a handkerchief to indicate he would recover. André went to the side table where several decanters sat filled with a variety of golden liqueurs. He poured a small glass of his best port and set it before Dupris. The man drank it in two gulps and thrust out the glass. André poured a second glass and capped the decanter with a decisive "clink." He watched Dupris complete his recovery.

"Augustus Beauchamp. Who'd have ever thought?" Dupris wiped his eyes with his handkerchief and stared at André. "Did you ever think?"

The entire Creole community knew that Augustus had disowned his only son and never acknowledged his grandsons. But André would not give Dupris any satisfaction in this. He simply shrugged. "It never occurred to me, but it does make perfect sense." He sniffed casually, as though discussing the weather. "What do you say?"

"I'd say the man who turned down an offer from Augustus Beauchamp is a fool."

André at last gave himself permission to smile. "Dupris, I think we've found something we can agree on." ✳

CHAPTER SEVENTEEN

✯ ✯ ✯ ✯

"I still think Dr. Mayfield enjoyed himself entirely too much." Juliana sniffed with pretended indignation as she and Amelia traveled in their carriage across the city. The air smelled fresh and clean after last evening's rain, and sunshine lit the city. "And that instrument of torture he used on my tooth looked like the tool my Uncle Jonathan uses to drill holes when he makes furniture."

"You were very brave." Amelia's eyes twinkled. "And you bit him only once." Now she laughed. "When I think of the expression on his face, I don't know who was in worse pain, you or he."

Juliana touched her still-tender jaw. "I couldn't help myself, but I wasn't in pain. The morphine powder numbed my whole jaw, and I had no control over what I was doing."

"Ah, well, now your tooth is filled—with gold, no less, and Dr. Mayfield still thinks you're a very fine young lady." Amelia grew pensive. "Poor man."

"And poor Helena."

Juliana had tried to be a bad patient, but once she had seen the doctor's frightening dental equipment, she had forgotten all her resolve to attempt to deflect his affections. Immobile with fear, she had not moved during the entire procedure—except when she bit him. She swallowed a giggle at the memory of the shock on his face and his "Miss Harris, if you please!" But his tender expression quickly returned, and the touch of his gentle hands was soothing. After he completed the procedure, his devotion seemed undiminished. Helena had fled from the room, surely because not once had Dr. Mayfield looked in her direction.

What a relief that Juliana would no longer need to redirect his interest. With Mr. Randolph improving, the doctor would not have to visit so often. And Juliana's time would now be consumed with teaching and ministering in other ways to her new friends.

As Jim-Jim drove the phaeton through the rutted, hard-packed streets toward the school, Juliana mentally listed their preparations for this new adventure. With all the volunteers who had come to help, Reverend Adams and Percy had assured the young ladies that they would have the house ready for classes. The slate blackboard Juliana had ordered before leaving Boston had arrived early the previous week and had been sent to the school. Her box of primers sat in the back of the carriage. She had planned her lessons for writing, reading, and simple arithmetic. If the students did well, Amelia could teach them more advanced mathematical concepts in addition to history lessons. New benches would be built from the lumber André...Mr. Beauchamp had donated.

Juliana slumped a little in her seat. Why did she have to think of him just now? Although she had tried for five days, she still couldn't forget those three happy hours when he had been André to her, before she had learned how cruelly he had treated those unfortunate people his family had enslaved. Long after he had driven off in his wagon, she had felt physical pain in her chest. Now, morning and evening, she prayed for him to see how wrong he was about Reverend Adams and how evil his former life had been, but no faith supported her words. His anger, no, *rage* at her had been complete. She had done nothing to forgive, yet he would never forgive her. Trying to figure it out gave her a headache. Her toothache had almost been a welcomed diversion.

One tiny spark of hope kept trying to ignite. Mr. Beauchamp could have packed up all his building supplies and returned them to the lumberyard, but he had not. As childish as his dumping the nails into the dirt had been, he had left everything for their use. Perhaps it was an issue of southern honor not to take back a gift. More likely, he simply wanted to get away from her. She must not surrender to any kind of optimism in his regard, for it would only cause more pain. André Beauchamp was a cruel and violent man, and she must have nothing more to do with him.

Optimism about the school was another thing entirely. As Jim-Jim reined the bay mare into the schoolyard, Juliana's heart lifted. There in front of the house stood Reverend Adams, Winnie, another young woman who appeared white, and at least twenty-five children of different ages, from tall, gangly boys clear down to several little girls who couldn't be more than five years old.

Juliana and Amelia exchanged gleeful glances, then put on their teacher faces and stepped down from the carriage.

After pleasant greetings, Reverend Adams herded the students into the building. While he arranged them in order of age, with the youngest seated in the front row, Juliana and Amelia stared about in wonder at the changes to the house.

The middle wall had been removed so completely that no trace of it remained. The ceiling and walls were smoothed over with plaster and painted white. Broken windowpanes had been replaced by new ones. The slate blackboard hung at the front of the room. And eight rows of ten-foot-long benches occupied the center of the room.

"Oh, my, what a wonderful job you've done." Amelia's eyes sparkled.

"You must have worked late every night to finish in time for this morning's classes—and clean everything up, too." Juliana ran a gloved hand over the blackboard. It was spotless.

"Yes, ma'am." Reverend Adams's face shone with enthusiasm. "But we finished it Saturday night so we could have services yesterday. This room was mighty crowded, but we had church."

"Amen." Winnie sat next to the minister on the back row.

"That's just grand." Juliana surveyed her class. "Now, let's begin with prayer. Reverend Adams, will you please?"

Just as she had imagined, the minister prayed beautifully. But unlike the confident black ministers she had heard at the African Meeting House in Boston, Reverend Adams's voice was filled with wonderment and an almost childlike tone. He thanked God for the school, the teachers, and the brave parents who trusted their precious children to his care while they went to work. His voice trembled with such emotion that Juliana knew this man would willingly sacrifice his life for any one of them. At his "Amen," a respectful silence filled the room for several moments.

Amelia made a list of each student's name and the names of their parents. Most of the children could only offer their mothers' names. Just the day before, Amelia had reminded Juliana that slave children had been kept with their mothers unless their masters sold the children to someone else. Often they never saw their fathers or never even knew for sure who they were. The idea appalled Juliana, but she had heard the same story from escaping slaves long before their emancipation. Such awful conditions prompted her to join the abolition movement as nothing else had.

With twenty-six students now enrolled, Juliana began the assessment process. Who knew their alphabet? Who could read a little bit? Who knew their numbers and addition and subtraction? At first the children seemed too shy to respond, but soon they learned it was all right to raise their hands to answer her questions.

The lovely young woman named Gemma sat by herself on the second row from the back. Seated with Negroes of varying brown shades, she appeared to be as white as Amelia. Her narrow, straight nose, high cheekbones, and slender jawline certainly gave no hint of her ancestry. Her clothing appeared in better condition than most of the others, too. Only when Gemma spoke did a hint of her race show through. From the way the others welcomed her, she clearly was among her own people. Yet Juliana was intrigued. Had this woman been a slave, too?

The morning proceeded with no difficulties. Amelia and Juliana arranged their eager pupils into groups according to their ability and began lessons at each level. The two women distributed slates and chalk with the charge that the children must take great care not to break either as they practiced their letters and numbers.

At noon, the children carried their lunches outside. Most had brought cornbread wrapped in cloth and small jars of water. They shared with those who had none. After the adults finished their dinner, Winnie volunteered to play a few games with the younger pupils. She invited Gemma to help her, and Gemma seemed especially pleased to oblige.

Reverend Adams remained indoors with Amelia and Juliana. Seated on the classroom benches, they chatted about the morning's success. But soon it became clear that he had arranged the playtime so he could talk with the ladies.

"Miss Harris, Miss Randolph, last week you were witness to my unhappy reunion with Mr. Beauchamp. I would like to clarify some things about the history of our enmity so that neither of you will misunderstand. May I tell you?"

Juliana's heart seemed to skip a beat. "Oh, yes, please do."

"Must we hear it?" Amelia crossed her arms and frowned. "We know enough about that man."

"With respect, Miss Amelia, I believe I can give you some more information."

She shrugged. "Very well."

Reverend Adams cleared his throat and ran his hand over his scarred cheek. Juliana felt certain the gesture was an unconscious one, for she had seen him do it several times before when he seemed to be considering what to say.

"I must begin with my own story. As I told you the other day, Miss Harris, I was born on the Beauchamps' cotton plantation. I was the eldest child of my mother and had two sisters. We all were field hands working hard to pick our quota of cotton each day; we would be punished if we did not. Sometimes my mother faltered, but my sisters and I worked hard to fill her bag before our own. Late at night, exhausted from our labors, all we wanted was a simple meal and a night of sleep.

"Now there was a man of our race who had sold himself to the devil, for he was the overseer who had to make sure we brought in enough cotton. He gained favor with our master and got better provisions for himself by treating his own people with great cruelty. As if that was not enough, he took a liking to my younger sister."

Reverend Adams's eyes shone with unshed tears, and he swallowed hard. "I will not be so unseemly as to tell you how miserable he made her. I will only say that I could bear her cries no longer. I jumped the man and tried to kill him."

Amelia gasped. "Why, Reverend Adams, you are such a gentle man. How—"

He ducked his head in a humble gesture. "Thank you, ma'am. Maybe I am now, maybe not, but I most surely was not back then. If several of my fellow slaves had not pulled my hands from the neck of that beast, I would have murdered him."

Juliana shivered but tried to keep back her tears. If someone had hurt her sisters or brother, Lord help her, she might find herself willing to defend them at any cost. "Please go on, Reverend."

"My punishment the next day was the beating Percy spoke of."

"Yes," Amelia spat out. "Mr. Beauchamp must have been very proud of himself for doing that."

Reverend Adams shook his head. "No, ma'am. He didn't do it. Not that Mr. Beauchamp. It was his brother, Mr. Elgin Beauchamp. Mr. André was the one who strung me up and held me."

Both ladies gasped.

"No," Juliana whispered. All through the weekend, she had prayed that he'd had no part in such an action. Yet, even if he had not wielded the whip, he had participated in the dreadful deed.

"But you must understand the whole story." Reverend Adams's voice grew softer but more intense. "It was their father who forced them to do it. He said that if they were to learn how to manage the plantation, they must show me and all the others who was boss. Now, you have to understand, slaves had been hanged for less than what I did, so there was even a measure of mercy in the sentence. Have you ever heard of Nat Turner's so-called rebellion?"

Amelia turned to Juliana. "In 1831, Nat Turner gathered other slaves and rebelled against their owners. They killed sixty white people before they were captured and hung."

"Ah, yes. I read Mr. Turner's pamphlet." Juliana managed to keep a pleasant expression on her face. Did Amelia really think she did not know this historical event?

Reverend Adams nodded to Amelia. "I heard they let him tell his story before they hung him. I suppose slave owners were still scared by that. Maybe Mr. Beauchamp thought I was another Nat Turner, and I guess I could have been, 'cause I sure did want to kill some-body…maybe a lot of somebodies."

Amelia put her hand up to stop him. "Do *not* tell me they were justified in beating you." She trembled with anger.

Reverend Adams shrugged. "No, ma'am, I won't. But I will tell you that both of those young men hated what they were doing. Looking back, I believe even old Mr. Beauchamp hated it."

"But the other day, the way you and André, young Mr. Beauchamp, glared at each other…" Juliana began.

"Miss Harris, I begged him to let me go. I begged him to under-stand about my sister. He looked at me, and he looked at his pappy, and there was a war goin' on in his soul. I lost that war. He strung me up and held me, and his brother did the rest. I guess they figured that day they became men. I think that day they became a lot less than men."

All three of them now struggled with tears.

Juliana dabbed her face with her handkerchief. "Reverend Adams, it still seems as if you would excuse what was done to you."

Again, he shook his head. "No, ma'am. Not excused, but forgave."

"But how can you—?" Amelia's tears stopped her words.

"My Lord Jesus was without sin." His voice became filled with passion. "But they beat Him, and they killed Him in the cruelest way they could think of. Yet He forgave them all.

"I was a sinner. I deserved to be punished for trying to kill that overseer—not punished by Mr. Beauchamp, but by the Lord Himself. I deserved to be sent to perdition for all my other sins, too. But He forgave me, just like He forgave those Roman soldiers who put the nails through His hands and feet and that sharp spear into His side, crying out 'Forgive them, Father, for they know not what they do.'

"We *all* have sinned and come short of the glory of God. We *all* need to be forgiven. And"—he looked at each lady in turn—"we *all* need to forgive.

"When I was a lost sinner, I asked the Lord to save me, and my soul was set free. When I was enslaved to man, Mr. Lincoln signed the Emancipation Proclamation, and my body was set free. When the old devil whispered to me that I had every right to hate the Beauchamps for what they did to me and that vile overseer for what he did to my good mother and sweet sisters, I said 'No, suh!' I will not be enslaved again to bitterness. I set myself free by forgiving them."

The sonorous cadence of his voice made Juliana want to shout "amen" like the worshippers back home at the African Meeting House. With difficulty, she held her tongue, for she did not wish to interrupt him.

Now Reverend Adams's face shone with joy instead of tears. "My prayer is that André Beauchamp will understand that he's a sinner, that he'll understand the forgiveness and grace of our Lord Jesus Christ, that he'll understand the peace that passeth understanding. As for me, the moment I saw André Beauchamp last week, I feared the old bitterness would return. But by the grace of the Lord Jesus, I forgave again, and I will keep on forgiving as long as Jesus grants me that same grace to do so."

He looked at Juliana with pastoral kindness. "For your sake, Miz Harris, as the disciple Stephen prayed, 'Lay not this sin to his charge.' André Beauchamp may yet be redeemed."

His words, spoken with such soft intensity, echoed off of the walls like a thundering sermon. And then all grew quiet.

The children burst into the room full of energy but were quickly hushed by Winnie and Gemma. They filed into their rows and sat with expectant expressions on their shining, sweat-dampened faces.

Juliana marveled that they were ready to return to their school work when it seemed most children would prefer to play. More than that, she wondered how she could stand before them and make any sense of her lessons. After all that Reverend Adams had revealed about André Beauchamp, the very thought of him plagued her soul.

Lay not this sin to his charge.

Clearly, the minister had discerned the depth of her feeling for André. Was he telling her to give him another chance? How could she, knowing this horrible truth?

But if God forgives, who am I to hold him accountable?

A quietness settled over her heart. She must see to her responsibility. This was what she had been called to do, and God would give her the grace to do it.

"All right, class, now I have a surprise for you. Jack," She beckoned to one of the older boys. "Please help me to pass out these primers. We're going to read." ✳

CHAPTER EIGHTEEN

✯ ✯ ✯ ✯

"Mrs. Sutter, how kind of you to call. Please come in."

André stood at his front door and reached out to his next-door neighbor. When she placed her hand in his, he bowed and kissed her fingertips. "To what do I owe the honor of this visit, ma'am?"

Mrs. Sutter, once an acclaimed beauty, had not fared well in recent years. Her face now bore deep age lines, and sorrow emanated from her dark blue eyes. Her frail frame and slight tremor gave her an appearance so fragile that he almost pulled her into a protective embrace, as he would his own mother.

"André, how good to see you. You're looking very well." She glanced toward the drawing room. "May we sit down?"

"Of course." He escorted her through the arched doorway and seated her on a gray brocade chair, then sat nearby and gave her his full attention.

Her eyes filled with tears, and she studied her hands in her lap. "Next to burying my beloved husband, this is the most difficult thing

I've ever had to do in my entire life." She inhaled deeply and exhaled an ironic laugh. "Who would have thought things should come to this? We possessed the best of everything the world had to offer right here in New Orleans—the richest city in the country."

André forced himself not to squirm. Had she come to ask him for a loan?

"Now so many of our young men lie dead or broken by that horrible war." She stared toward the fireplace as if lost in thought. Then she shook herself, and her eyes took on a hard glint. "Blake is dying."

"Ah, dear lady, I am so sorry." André's heart ached with guilt. He had only visited his childhood friend twice since they returned from the war. Blake had served in the army and saw far more direct combat than André had in the navy. He reached out and took her hand. "What can I do to be of service to you? Name any task, and I shall execute it."

She emitted another hard laugh. "Will you? No matter how difficult?"

André frowned. "Why, yes, ma'am." Surely she would not ask him to end Blake's suffering. *That* he would not do.

"Very well, then. I want you to go to the Charles Randolph home." She spat out the name. "Tell Amelia Randolph that my son is asking for her."

Despite the warm evening, the hairs on André's arms stood on end. How could she ask this of him? He sat back, unable to speak.

As if sensing the depth of his horror, his struggle, she leaned forward. "You promised."

"Y-yes, ma'am, but…"

"Blake served with honor and courage for our Confederacy." Her voice grew shrill with passion. "He fought heroically, just as you did. His youth, his life were stolen from him by those…"

She seemed about to curse. André felt relieved when she stopped to regain her self-control. "…those *Yankees*." The word itself seemed enough of a curse.

"Yes, ma'am. I know he did, but…"

Mrs. Sutter moved forward in her chair and glared at him. "But *what?*"

André's belly flamed. He could not do this. Yet he must. "Nothing, Mrs. Sutter. I will do as you ask. I cannot promise you that Miss Randolph will come, but I will make a strong case for it."

She sat back and seemed to shrivel up in her chair. "Thank you," she whispered. "Thank you for understanding that I cannot do it myself."

"Yes, ma'am, I do understand." Did she think it would somehow be easier for him? "I'll go right away."

Mrs. Sutter's face relaxed, and some of the years imprinted there seemed to slip away. "I shall be eternally grateful to you." Her brow wrinkled. "You realize, of course, that I cannot bear to be in the same room with her. Tell her my servant will accompany her into Blake's room."

An audacious thought crossed André's mind and swept into his heart. What if Miss Harris came with Miss Randolph? Then she might comprehend that southern soldiers suffered as much as those she had nursed in Boston.

"Yes, ma'am, that seems proper. Perhaps, if Miss Randolph agrees to come, she will want to bring her sister…or her houseguest. Would that be acceptable to you?"

Mrs. Sutter shrugged. "If that will make it more likely that she'll come, then by all means, do what you must."

The moment she left the house, André's heart filled with excitement as if he were a schoolboy, even as a hint of nausea edged into his belly. Now he must go to the Randolph house, the den of that viper who had conspired against his father. How could he do it? Only at the prospect of seeing Miss Harris again.

André ran up the front staircase two steps at a time. In his bedroom, he changed into a fresh white shirt and a blue silk tie. Throwing on his best frock coat, the one he had worn to visit his grandfather, he dashed back down the stairs, almost bumping into Cordell.

"André, where are you going all dressed up? Did Mrs. Sutter need something?"

André grabbed him by the shoulders, hardly containing his glee. "She asked me to go fetch Miss Randolph. Blake is calling for her."

Cordell's eyes filled with sympathy. He nodded. "That sure would be good for Mr. Blake. I'll be praying she'll come."

André stopped cold, slammed by shame. He had only thought of his own desires, not the needs of the dying man. "Yes, you do that. And pray I'll have the right words to say to the young lady." To both *young ladies.* He strode to the front door, wishing he had bought that horse he had been considering, for it would get him to his destination faster.

"You could do that, too." Cordell's words followed him out the door.

Several moments passed before André realized that Cordell had just urged him to pray. He recalled his half-thought prayer at Augustus Beauchamp's house and the good results. Funny how the habit of a lifetime had been so quickly discarded at the end of the war. Maybe it was time to reclaim it.

With each step he took on his five-block walk through the Garden District, André chanted to himself, "Make her come. Make her come." But no matter how hard he tried to think of "her" as Miss Randolph, it was the fair Miss Harris's face that danced in his mind.

◆━▷◈◁━◆

"And so, Miss Harris, if you would like to have one of those imported toothbrushes, I shall be happy to supply it." Dr. Mayfield sat across from Juliana in the Randolph drawing room. While his expression glowed with affection, his tone bore a hint of paternalism. "It may be a difficult habit to acquire, but I think you will appreciate the good that it does for your teeth. If you'd prefer not, then please consider what I said. Rinse your mouth well with water after you eat sweets, and you'll avoid developing another painful cavity."

Juliana could feel the strain in her smile. "I can't imagine putting a brush made of bone and boar bristles in my mouth and scrubbing my teeth, but I do thank you for the advice." If he said one more word about that English invention, she would run from the room shrieking.

"Another method of cleaning teeth was suggested by the late Dr. Levi Parmly right here in New Orleans." Enthusiasm lit his eyes. "As far back is 1815, he suggested using silk thread to remove food particles from between the teeth. He called it flossing."

"Indeed?" Like embroidery floss? How strange. Yet Juliana did sometimes use thread to remove food particles.

"Why, yes," Dr. Mayfield said. "Furthermore, Dr. Saunders observed fewer cavities in those Confederate soldiers who did not care for sweets. Perhaps you might consider modifying your eating habits that way."

Oh, bother! "How fascinating." Much more fascinating was the thought that anyone could *not* like sweets or could possibly give them up. Somehow she must turn this conversation around. "Unfortunately, if there is a sweet to be had, I will race Helena for it. And I can assure you, I will win out over Helena every time."

Dr. Mayfield laughed, and she joined him. Behind her, the side door to the drawing room slammed shut, yet no one entered. Perhaps the pleasant evening breeze from the open window had closed it.

"Ah, Miss Harris, I fear I've been boring you with my medical prattle." Although Dr. Mayfield smiled, he looked somewhat abashed. "There are so many things I long to know about human physiology. It will be a lifelong study."

"How truly admirable. Then you will be interested to know that just yesterday, or was it this morning, Helena was saying her father's injury and convalescence have turned her thoughts toward nursing." In truth, Helena had said she would like to help others in whatever way she could as long as it was not teaching. "Perhaps you could make some suggestions to her."

A sharp rap on the front door echoed throughout the entry. Jerome passed by the open double doors of the drawing room. In a moment, he walked in the opposite direction, and his footsteps sounded on the staircase.

"I wonder who that could be." Juliana traded a look of curiosity with Dr. Mayfield. "Perhaps I should go greet them." A perfect ploy to end their conversation. She rose and crossed the room, with Dr. Mayfield close behind.

The moment Juliana entered the front hallway, she drew back and bumped into the doctor. He gripped her elbow to steady her but then did not release it.

"Mr. Beauchamp!" *André*...

"Miss Harris." Hat in hand, Mr. Beauchamp bowed to her. When he straightened, his eyes went from her face to her arm, which the doctor still held. Juliana thought she saw a subtle sneer cross his lips. "Dr. Mayfield."

"Mr. Beauchamp, good evening." Dr. Mayfield moved even closer to Juliana.

She barely resisted shaking off his too-familiar gesture. Without doubt his intentions were honorable, if not his way of expressing them.

"What brings you here, sir?" Juliana's words came out in a breathless rush.

Mr. Beauchamp's eyes seemed to snap with...with what? In the dim light of the hallway, she could not discern his mood.

"Why have you come here? What do you want?" Amelia ran down the staircase into the entry hall. From the fire in her eyes, Juliana had no trouble sensing her mood.

After a short bow, Mr. Beauchamp stood tall and stared at her. "I would not disturb you, Miss Randolph, without urgent cause." He glanced at Juliana and the doctor, then continued. "In spite of the enmities of the recent war, perhaps you can find it in your heart to speak a few words of kindness to a dying man."

Amelia gasped. "Blake..."

Mr. Beauchamp nodded. "He is asking for you, ma'am. Will you come?" From the movement of his facial muscles, Juliana could see he was struggling for control, but whether of anger or grief, she could not tell.

Amelia sniffed back a sob. "Yes, of course." She gripped Juliana's hand, pulling her away from Dr. Mayfield. "You must come with me."

"Yes." Juliana set her emotions in check, as she often had done at the mission in Boston.

"Miss Randolph," Dr. Mayfield said, "may I be of assistance? May I escort you, since the hour grows late?"

"Oh, yes, that would be so good of you." Amelia turned back toward the staircase, calling over her shoulder, "Juliana, I'll fetch our bonnets and wraps and tell Helena where we're going. Please have Jim-Jim prepare the phaeton." She disappeared around the landing.

Juliana started down the hallway to the back of the house, but Mr. Beauchamp called to her. "Miss Harris, I took the liberty of asking Jim-Jim to prepare the carriage."

She whipped around and stared at him. "Asking…?"

He stiffened. "Yes, 'asking.' I did not order him."

"No, no, that's not what I meant." How could she explain? "You knew Amelia would come, didn't you?"

His expression softened. "Yes, ma'am. I knew my friend could not have fallen in love with a heartless woman."

Tears scalded her eyes. *And you, André, are not heartless either.*

Dr. Mayfield stepped forward. "You have done your duty admirably, sir. Perhaps now you would like to retire and permit us to execute this endeavor."

Mr. Beauchamp stared down his nose at the shorter man, and again his blue eyes snapped. Unlike the visual warfare between

Reverend Adams and Mr. Beauchamp, this battle had a territorial element to it, and Juliana felt as if she herself were the territory. She would have laughed had the situation not been so tragic.

"Oh, no, Dr. Mayfield, Mr. Beauchamp must go with us. Mrs. Sutter will want her son's friend nearby."

The two men continued to glare at each other for a moment until Amelia dashed down the stairs, bonnets and shawls in hand.

"The phaeton?"

"All ready to go." Mr. Beauchamp waved his hand toward the door. "Shall we go?"

Dr. Mayfield grabbed his black physician's bag.

Outside another tragicomedy threatened. The small carriage was intended for two adult passengers, three at most. Once again, the doctor and Mr. Beauchamp seemed to vie for a place. Jim-Jim sat in the driver's seat scratching his head. "I don' know how y'all's gonna fit."

"We don't have time for this." Mr. Beauchamp motioned to Jim-Jim. "Step down. I'll drive."

No one objected to the arrangement, and soon the carriage sped along the street toward the Sutter residence. Juliana took heart as she noticed Mr. Beauchamp's gentle treatment of the bay mare, even as he hurried her along.

The carriage rattled loudly along the quiet, rutted streets, stirring up dust in its wake. Dr. Mayfield's bag added to the snug fit in the small seat. Yet Juliana could not be concerned with matters of comfort. During the entire journey, she prayed that young Mr. Sutter would not die without understanding and accepting the mercy and forgiveness of God. And she prayed that Mr. Beauchamp also would grasp God's loving nature, perhaps this very night. ✼

CHAPTER NINETEEN

✯ ✯ ✯ ✯

*T*he moment they entered Blake Sutter's bedchamber, Juliana noticed that it did not smell like a sick room. A large bouquet of fragrant flowers sat on a table by the door and another on the bedside table. A faint smell of vinegar suggested someone had scrubbed the room clean, probably the solicitous Negro woman who stood on the opposite side of Mr. Sutter's bed. The patient had been washed and shaved, and he sat up against several pillows with his eyes closed as if he were sleeping. Although he appeared gaunt and gray and his breathing sounded labored, Juliana could hear no death-rattle. To her surprise, she saw his hand resting on a Bible.

Amelia approached the bedside, and Juliana stood at its end. If Mr. Sutter should require medical assistance, she would fetch Dr. Mayfield, who awaited downstairs with Mr. Beauchamp. Once they entered the house, all hostilities had ceased—to the credit of both men.

In the dancing light of several candles, Juliana could see the struggle in Amelia's face. Her eyes glistened, and she drew in her lips, as she always did when trying to control her emotions. So then, just as Juliana had suspected, Amelia once had loved this man. Had the cavernous differences between their beliefs driven them apart—she a Unionist from the North, and he a secessionist from the South?

"Blake." Amelia's whisper seemed little more than a sigh.

He opened his eyes and turned toward her. A faint smile—no, a glow lit his face.

"Mammy, I see an angel."

The old woman reached out to pat his hand. "Yessuh, Master Blake, you sure do." She laughed softly, a deep, warm, and throaty hum that softly resounded throughout the room and wrapped them all in maternal love. Juliana almost lost herself in the emotion of the moment, for this woman reminded her of a childhood friend who had nursed her family through many an illness in Boston. Once again, Juliana set aside her own feelings so she might be strong through this difficult moment. She traded a look and a nod with the Negro woman that bonded them without a word.

"Blake." This time Amelia's voice broke. She fell to her knees beside the bed and buried her face in the covers.

Blake set a bony hand on her bonnet brim and tried to shove it back but could not manage the task. Amelia quickly untied the ribbons and thrust the bonnet away. She gripped his hand and pulled it to her lips, bathing it with tears.

"Shhh. Shush now, brave girl. Will you spend our last few moments together weeping?" Mr. Sutter's voice sounded weak and gravelly, yet Juliana detected a thread of strength in it. Was love empowering him now?

"I have never forgotten you," Amelia said. "I prayed for you every day, as I promised I would."

He emitted a wry laugh. "As often as for your fiancé?"

She nodded, sniffing. "Oh, yes. Oh, yes…"

"How did he fare? Home safely, I hope." The honest concern in his eyes revealed the truth of his words.

Amelia shook her head. "Presumed dead…at Andersonville."

He winced as if struck and then gazed upward. *"Ah, Lord, such cruel things we have inflicted upon our brothers, both North and South. How can You forgive us, Your wayward children?"*

Amelia hesitated before murmuring "amen" to his prayer.

They began to whisper together about former times before the war divided the nation—and the two of them. As they talked, Juliana studied Mr. Sutter's eyes as best she could from her position. Something about their coloring and his overall complexion stirred a memory. With a subtle gesture, she beckoned Mammy to follow her from the room into the hallway.

"If you please, I do not wish to interfere, but I believe that if Mr. Sutter were to take in some third-boil molasses, it would improve his condition. Has your doctor suggested that remedy?"

"No, ma'am. His wounds were so bad when he come back that they pretty much give him up for dead." Mammy shook her head. "I fix him chicken and dumplings when I can git a chicken. They's his favorites. 'Lasses is hard to come by 'cause the sugar plantations are mostly deserted now."

"How about calf's liver?"

"No, ma'am. Beef's been in short supply for Southerners here in New Orleans, though the Yankees had it plenty during the war." Her cross tone revealed her distaste for the Northern troops that still occupied the city.

Juliana frowned. Somehow she must persuade these people to try her remedies. "Please wait inside as their chaperone. I'm going downstairs for just a moment."

"Yes, ma'am."

Juliana hurried downstairs and stopped short at the drawing room door. Inside, Mr. Beauchamp and Dr. Mayfield sat facing each other over a chessboard. Both were chuckling.

"Good move." Dr. Mayfield stroked his narrow beard and studied the board. "But I think you'll see"—he moved his bishop—"that should stop your bid for my queen."

Mr. Beauchamp leaned back in his chair and groaned as if in defeat. "Ah, clever move, my friend." He sat up again. "But you are remiss if you think I'll give up in my quest for your queen. She's already mine." He moved a knight and snatched up the white queen. "Furthermore, your king is in check and, land sakes, I do believe"— he moved his castle—"I have checkmate, too."

Dr. Mayfield's eyes narrowed. "Well played, my good man, well played." Though his posture remained somewhat stiff, his tone was amiable. "Shall we have another go at it?"

Juliana wanted to laugh. They were being civil with each other, even having a good time. Perhaps their pleasantry would continue if she joined in the humor of the moment. Remembering family times at home, she decided to tease. She put on her teacher face and cleared her throat to draw their attention. They jumped to their feet and seemed about to knock each other over in their haste to approach her.

"If you please, gentlemen, might your time not have been more usefully spent in prayer for the patient upstairs?" She struggled to maintain her pose, for a smile threatened to break through. "I assumed you would be doing that."

"Miss Harris," Dr. Mayfield said, "I hasten to assure you that is exactly what we did." His dark eyebrows dipped into a frown.

"Yes, ma'am, we did." Mr. Beauchamp nodded his agreement, but an impish gleam lit his eyes. He had caught on to her game. But then he grew serious. "How is Blake?"

Dr. Mayfield continued to look abashed. "Shall I go up? Do you think he will accept my treatment?"

Juliana ceased her levity. "I don't know, but I shall certainly ask. For now, I have advised a treatment of third-boil molasses. At our mission hospital, it brought about improvement in men whose appearance resembled Mr. Sutter's. But Mammy says there is none in the house."

"Miss Harris, should you not leave to me the diagnosing of illness and recommending of treatment?"

Dr. Mayfield wore his paternal look, the one that made her feel as if she were an unschooled child. She bit back a sharp retort, for this was not the time to surrender to her temper.

"I'm certain my Aunt Sukey has some molasses." Mr. Beauchamp strode past her toward the front door. "I'll see what kind it is and be right back."

"Thank you, Mr. Beauchamp." Juliana turned to the staircase and began her ascent.

"Dear Miss Harris." Dr. Mayfield's voice was filled with dismay.

She stopped and looked at him over the banister. The sincerity in his expression subdued her annoyance.

"I am sure the molasses will do no harm," he said. "But do not set your heart on it improving Mr. Sutter's health."

She gave him a placid smile. "*Dear* Dr. Mayfield, if you would count me a friend, then please continue your prayers for him."

———⊕———

Third-boil molasses? Restoring Blake's health couldn't be that simple. Nonetheless, André dashed across the yard to the secret passage in the hedge he and Blake had used as children. Forcing his way through the overgrown path, he crossed his own side yard and bounded up the outside steps leading to the formal dining room. Inside, as he rounded the mahogany table, he heard voices in the kitchen. He hurried through the short hallway between the two rooms just as the back door slammed.

Aunt Sukey stood by the dry sink, her hand over her heart and her eyes wide. "Master André..." She only addressed him that way when she was startled.

"Do we have any third-boil molasses?" André glanced about the kitchen.

"Y-yessuh, right here." She reached into a storage bin and pulled out a quart jar half-filled with a thick, dark brown substance. "Here it is. It's a few years old, but molasses don't spoil."

André seized the prize. "Good." He turned to go then looked back with a grin. "Am I to assume you had a gentleman caller?"

In the light of the kerosene lantern on the table, he could see her light brown complexion take on a deep pink shade.

She didn't look at him. "Oh, Lawd, Mister André, how you do go on."

Something in her expression puzzled him, as did many of her actions of late. But he would have to question her another time.

Retracing his steps, he hastened back to the Sutter home and passed the drawing room door on his way to the staircase.

Dr. Mayfield apprehended him at the bottom step. "Mr. Beauchamp, don't you think…?"

"Yes sir, I do think. I think that if Miss Harris wants third-boil molasses, she shall have it."

The doctor shook his head. "Please let me finish. That's not what I mean. I want you to stop confusing her with your southern charm. That"—he pointed to the jar in André's hand—"is not a remedy for anything other than a sweet tooth, which Miss Harris happens to possess to her own detriment."

"You have brought up two points of contention, sir, neither of which I have time to discuss with you at the moment." André continued up the stairs, ignoring whatever the doctor continued to say. At least the man had the good sense not to follow.

André knew the way through the Sutter upstairs as well as his own. Blake's room lay down the main hallway at the back corner of the house. André opened the door slowly.

On a small chair beside the bed, Miss Randolph sat reading a Bible. Although Blake's gaunt face looked ghostly in the candlelight, his obvious devotion for the lady emanated from his jaundiced eyes. Her presence seemed to have improved the sick man's health. André wondered if Mrs. Sutter had mistaken how ill Blake was.

Miss Harris glided across the room and reached out for the jar. "Thank you, Mr. Beauchamp." She gazed up at him and smiled. "I'll send Mammy for a spoon."

"Please allow me to fetch it for you."

Her smile widened. "Thank you. That would be very kind." She appeared to stifle a laugh.

Self-conscious and a little annoyed, André frowned. "Is something wrong?"

Puckering her lips, she shook her head. "Not at all. You look particularly gallant with leaves adorning your hair like Caesar's laurel wreath."

André reached up and pulled a small leafy twig from his hair just above his ear. If he hadn't been in a sickroom, he would have laughed aloud. He handed the leaves to her. "For you, fair lady. I'll return with that spoon in a moment."

To avoid another encounter with the doctor, he took the back stairs and quickly found a spoon in the kitchen, plucking shrubbery from his clothes as he went. All the way down and up again, his heart surged with happiness. Against all odds, just as in the chess game, he would win his enemy's queen. ❈

Chapter Twenty

☆☆☆☆

In the shade of a live-oak tree, Winnie knelt beside five-year-old Pearl, who covered her eyes and counted. "One, two, *free,* four…"

The other students scattered in twenty-five different directions, hiding behind bushes, trees, the outhouse, the side fences, and any other place out of sight. From the back door of the school, Juliana and Amelia watched and laughed at their pupils' creativity as they devised ways to disappear.

Pearl stopped after "ten," so Winnie prompted "eleven." Soon the child had counted to twenty.

Winnie turned Pearl out to face the yard. "Now say 'ready or not, here I come.'"

"Ready or not, here I come!" the child called out. With a giggle, she began running around the yard with her arms extended. Children appeared from every corner and raced to the safety of the oak tree, easily missing Pearl's hands.

"Here comes some more," Winnie cried. "Tag somebody. Tag somebody."

Gemma ran into the yard holding another small child by the hand. They ran to the tree. "Home free. All safe." She pulled the little boy into her arms and gave him a hug.

Pearl continued to giggle and wave her arms around, clearly not understanding the game. She ran to the tree and smacked it, then ran back out into the yard. Her brother, twelve-year-old Jack, dashed from behind the fence, the last one to run for safety. He saw Pearl's happy confusion and ran close to her.

"Tag me, Pearl."

The child patted his arm, and said, "Tag me, Jack."

Everyone laughed.

"I'm 'it.'" Jack surveyed the group. "Now we'll see who gets home free." He leaned against the tree and covered his eyes. "One, two, three…"

Off the children dashed again.

"Whew!" Amelia stepped back inside the schoolhouse. "Where do they get their energy?"

"I wonder." Juliana joined her, sitting on one of the benches inside. These midday respites from teaching always helped her get through the rest of the day.

Reverend Adams sat in the back of the room staring at the pages of his Bible. A frown creased his dark face.

"Reverend Adams," Juliana said, "is there something we can help you with?"

He looked up and gave them a sad smile. "I just wonder if I'll ever be able to read God's Word. Many of the children are already reading their primers, but I can't seem to remember all the letters in the alphabet."

"Don't despair," Amelia said. "Children always learn more quickly than adults."

"That's so?" His expression filled with hope.

"Yes, that's so." Amelia smiled.

"We've only been here for five days," Juliana said. "Give yourself some time."

He emitted a deep, throaty chuckle. "I suppose I do need some patience." He stood and walked to the front of the classroom, taking a seat near them. "I'm anxious for the day when I can read every word for myself. There's so much of the Bible I've never heard, so much more I want to learn by rote."

"I just can't stand to think that you were not allowed to read." Amelia shook her head. "That was nothing short of evil, just like everything else pertaining to slavery."

"I can't bear to think of these little children being forced to pick cotton all day." Juliana glanced through the open doorway and felt a surge of joy seeing them at play.

"Those were hard times for them." Reverend Adams nodded. "A child would be out picking with the rest of us as soon as he could learn how to do it."

"Good gracious," Juliana said. "Surely some measure of kindness was extended to the elderly." She pictured her frail grandmother, who had recently died, and could not imagine her being forced to work under a hot sun.

"Only the old men and grannies too old for field work stayed in the quarters during the day. The grannies raised the little ones and nursed them if they took sick. Sometimes the lady of the plantation—if she was kind—might send down some medicine. But mostly the plantation owners cared more about their hunting dogs than they did our children."

"But this is a new day," Amelia said. "This school is the beginning of many good things for the people of your community."

"Amen." The pastor's enthusiasm shone in his eyes. "We hear that all over the place, all over the South, colored folks are forming communities like this one where we all can help each other out. We'll be voting soon, owning businesses, going where we want to go."

His tone grew hushed with intensity. "We're *citizens* of the United States of America. Most important of all, we can gather our families back together—husbands, wives, children, those who wanted to marry but weren't allowed. We can get a doctor when our children are sick and pay him from our own hard-earned money. We can work to buy the right food to make our little ones grow strong and healthy.

"Yes, indeed, this is a new day, a time to move on to a happy future." Reverend Adams's voice rang with pride. He held up his Bible. "And I *will* learn to read."

As always, Juliana's heart was stirred by his passionate optimism. Surely God's grace was upon this man. With his wise leadership, his people would build a strong and prosperous community.

On Friday afternoon, the two teachers bade the children goodbye, straightened and locked the schoolroom, and waited for Jim-Jim to convey them home. Reverend Adams and Winnie waited with them, and Gemma lingered too, as she did most days.

"Miz Harris, thank you for lettin' me come to your school." Gemma tried to tuck a loose lock of hair into her upswept coiffure. After the first day of class, she had begun to copy Juliana and Amelia with her mannerisms and speech, and especially her new hairdo. "Can I help you some way to pay back your kindness?"

"Gemma, you already help us by taking care of the children during play time." Amelia took a hairpin from under her bonnet and captured Gemma's unruly strand. She stood back and surveyed her work. "There, that should hold it."

Gemma's eyes moistened, and she reached up to the spot where Amelia had made the repair. "Thank you, Miz Amelia. Ain't no white lady ever touched me so kindly like that."

Juliana started to correct her speech, but the depth of feeling in Gemma's tone and expression stopped her. "Gemma, were you a house slave?"

Gemma nodded. "Yessum. Yes, ma'am."

"Do you still work for the people who held you in bondage?" Juliana asked.

Again Gemma nodded. "Yes, ma'am. It's safer there, and the work ain't...isn't hard. Not like the fields."

She glanced over at Reverend Adams and Winnie, who seemed engrossed in their own conversation. Juliana sensed a romance in the air, but kept her thoughts to herself.

"Safer? What do you mean?" Amelia asked.

Gemma shook her head and stared down, kicking a pebble with her bare toe. "Oh, nothin'...I mean..." A frown creased her forehead, as if something worried or frightened her.

"What are you afraid of?" Juliana reached out to touch her shoulder.

Gemma shrugged. "Oh, nothin' much." She gave Juliana a side-long glance. "Well, I *am* scared my aunt's gonna make me come over to the French Quarter and work for her. She's got a house over there."

"But wouldn't it be better to work for a relative?" Amelia asked. "Someone who cares for you and loves you?"

Gemma's pretty face crinkled with confusion. "You think I ought to work there, ma'am? I mean, you bein' a Christian?"

Juliana gasped. "Oh, Amelia, I think I know what kind of 'house' that is."

Amelia's cheeks grew pink. "Oh, my. Oh, dear. Goodness gracious, no, Gemma, I don't think you should work there."

"She can't make you do it." Another kind of heat warmed Juliana's cheeks. "We won't let her. You're a free woman now, and you can do what you want. What's your aunt's name? We should know in case she comes asking for you."

Gemma glanced again at the reverend and Winnie. "Althea Dawson." She whispered the name as if it were a rude word. "She's always been a free woman of color like her people, goin' way back to the French days. Her brother took up with my mama. She was a slave over at Magnolia Plantation, but they wouldn't sell Mama to him. When I was twelve, they sold me over to..." She stopped for a moment. "Over to this man for his son's birthday present when he turn sixteen. That's the family I still work for."

Juliana gasped. "Oh, Gemma, how awful for you." What unfeeling monsters these southern men had been to their slave women. To give a young man a girl slave could only mean one thing. She shuddered to think of such cruel immorality.

"No, ma'am, not so bad. House slaves have...*had* an easier time than field hands. O' course there's always..." Gemma stopped herself again and looked off in the distance.

"You're still afraid of someone in that family, aren't you?" Amelia asked.

"Oh, not much." Gemma frowned and again nudged the pebble with her toe.

Juliana looked at Gemma's dusty, callused feet. Except for Reverend Adams, none of their students wore shoes, but they all lived within a few blocks of the school. This woman walked barefoot for some distance in order to get her education. Then she had to walk back home to earn her living. Did her former owners force her to work all night to compensate for her time spent at school? Maybe Juliana and Amelia could make it a little easier on her. "Why don't you let us take you home? Where do you live?"

Gemma bit her lip. She appeared to be deciding how to answer. "Over in the Garden District."

"Then you must ride with us." Juliana turned at the sound of clopping hooves. "Here's Jim-Jim."

The young driver secured the reins and jumped down from the phaeton. "Miz Amelia, I ain't late, am I?" His dark brown face wore a worried frown.

"No, Jim-Jim. You're right on time. We let class out early today."

Jim-Jim looked beyond her. "How do, Miz Gemma?"

Gemma gave him a stern look that Juliana could not discern. "How do, Jim-Jim?"

"I'm fine, ma'am." His nod to Gemma held more meaning than a simple pleasantry. Juliana guessed they knew each other fairly well. She also could see that the young man admired Gemma but without the affection of a suitor.

They bade Reverend Adams and Winnie farewell and climbed into the carriage.

Clouds gathered in the afternoon sky, and the air smelled of rain. As the carriage traveled through the streets, Juliana did not have to coax Gemma to talk.

"Miz Harris, is Boston a big city like New Orleans?"

"Yes, Gemma. In fact, it may be even bigger. Before the war, Boston and New Orleans were rival ports."

"Did you always live there?" Gemma's amber eyes exuded curiosity.

"Yes, I was born there."

"Do you have any brothers and sisters?"

Her questions continued, and Juliana answered patiently about her family and her home.

Gemma shyly fingered the smooth cotton of Juliana's blue gingham day dress. "This is pretty. Who does your sewin'?"

"I have a dressmaker back home. She was very busy getting my wardrobe ready before I came to New Orleans." Juliana glanced at Amelia, whose pleasant smile indicated she did not mind being left out of Gemma's questioning. The girl probably had not been schooled in how to engage in polite conversation.

Gemma studied the cloak sleeves and ruched bodice of Juliana's dress. "I can make these. If you need someone to mend and sew for you, I can do it."

"Indeed?" Juliana raised her eyebrows. Gemma's long, slender fingers did appear fit for sewing. "I shall certainly remember that when I'm ready for new clothes."

"Gemma," Amelia said, "would you like to be a seamstress?"

Gemma nodded with enthusiasm. "Yes, ma'am."

"Why, you could have your own business." Juliana said.

"I could?"

"Certainly," Amelia said. "You know, of course, that even before the war, many free blacks owned land and had businesses here in New Orleans. Now that you're no longer in bondage, you can, too."

Gemma grinned and stared off in the distance. "Picture that." She turned back to Juliana. "Do a lot of colored folks have businesses up North?"

"Yes, they do." Juliana said.

"Oh, look. We're home." Amelia set her hand on Gemma's. "We could take you all the way home."

Gemma shook her head. "No, ma'am. I'll walk." Without waiting for help, she jumped down from the phaeton. "Thank you," she called over her shoulder as she ran up the street.

"Hmm," Amelia said. "We'll have to add some lessons in etiquette and decorum to our curriculum, won't we?"

Taking Jim-Jim's offered hand to climb down, Juliana laughed. "Yes, I suppose so. But aren't her enthusiasm and curiosity inspiring?"

"Indeed they are." Amelia took her turn stepping out of the carriage. "Thank you, Jim-Jim." She linked her arm in Juliana's as they walked toward the front door. "What a rewarding week, but I must admit I'm worn out."

"Now we can enjoy two days of rest and some time to ourselves."

"I wonder if Mrs. Sutter sent a response to the note I sent her this morning." Amelia paused at the door.

"I prayed she would permit you to visit Blake."

"Thank you. If she wrote back with an invitation, will you go with me?"

"I would be delighted." Juliana's heart skipped a beat. Maybe she would see Mr. Beauchamp again. Last Monday seemed a lifetime ago.

As if reading her mind, Amelia said, "Now, don't you go getting any ideas about seeing that André Beauchamp again." Her pretty forehead wrinkled into a frown.

"Amelia Randolph, mind your own business." Juliana laughed as she said it, but she had to force down her temper.

"You simply must not accept that man's attentions."

"Why not? You're receiving Blake's attentions. In spite of his illness, you cannot regard his request to see you as anything else."

As they reached the front door, Amelia jerked away from Juliana. "It's not the same. Those two men are not the same."

Juliana forced a smile. "Let's don't quarrel, Amelia."

Amelia blew out a sigh. "No, let's not." Her smile was genuine. "I still want you to go with me. I know you're eager to see if your remedy has improved Blake's health."

"Yes, I am. As I said, I'll be delighted to go."

Their quarrel had ended for the moment, but Juliana did not feel at peace about their discussion. Like Juliana's sisters, Amelia thought she knew what was best for everyone else—an endearing quality except in regard to affairs of the heart. This situation would require much prayer and much patience, the former of which Juliana found easy to do, the latter of which she found more than a little difficult to possess. ❋

CHAPTER TWENTY-ONE

★ ★ ★ ★

André knew this had been a landmark week in his post-war life, but by Friday he began to feel like a marionette. Many times he had to subdue his temper, for Augustus Beauchamp seemed to be pulling string after string to control him. André obeyed only because this seemed the most expedient route to success.

Throughout the week, the old puppet master had sent him three terse messages. First, he had deposited a large sum of money into André's bank account, and André received orders to purchase new clothes befitting a prosperous businessman. Second, he must outfit his stable with proper horseflesh. Last, negotiations were almost complete for the steamship, so André was to go down to the docks and inspect the vessel.

André made an appointment with his grandfather's tailor, who fitted him with several new suits. After the tailor recommended other skilled tradesmen, André's wardrobe soon included boots, hats, and other accessories.

On Wednesday, André bought the sorrel gelding he had already been considering and also a dappled pair for a carriage, which Cordell would select.

On Thursday, André went to the shipyard. On his way to inspect his ship, he saw an old three-masted sloop that reminded him of the *Preble,* the ship on which he had received his first hands-on naval officer training. The sight of the old relic, *Antares,* sent a great wave of aching nostalgia through him. How he wished he could go back to those academy days when innocence and adventure had ruled his life—a distant time long before war turned seafaring into a grave and fearsome responsibility. In those days, he and his bosom friends learned all the skills that made them worthy opponents when they later became bitter enemies, each trying to obliterate the other. How had his former comrades fared throughout the war? Did André even want to know?

Shaking off these useless thoughts, André stepped onto the deck of the *Bonnie June* to perform a thorough inspection. The English-built Clyde steamer resembled his wartime blockade-runner and undoubtedly had been used for that very purpose. In addition to speed, maneuverability, and great cargo capacity on a light draft, the vessel sported a side paddlewheel, an iron hull, and two smokestacks. Had Augustus chosen this ship because he knew André would know it well and quickly adapt to sailing it? Whether or not the old man had such generous thoughts, André found the ship sound in all respects. He sent word back to Augustus to that effect and waited for his next order.

Augustus had not invited him to his home since that first visit. André tried not to let that affect him. After all, if he grieved too much that the old man regarded him as a mere business partner, maybe even a pawn, might that not seem disloyal to his own father and to his gentle, suffering mother? André only knew one thing for certain about the arrangement: he had this one opportunity to succeed in business and to make a new life for himself and, if all went well, the woman he loved.

Augustus seemed to know everything André did, and so André was surprised that the old man did not repeat his order that "the Yankee woman is not for you." Perhaps he had been testing André. Perhaps his agents had not informed him about the supplies André had taken to the school or about last Monday evening's events at the Sutter home.

Whatever the circumstances, whatever the consequences, André had already made his decision. Concerning Miss Harris, he would not be ordered about. In this one matter, Augustus would *not* pull the puppet strings.

Early on Saturday, according to his daily custom, André helped Mama eat her breakfast. Then he decided to take her out on the upstairs gallery for some fresh air. He arranged pillows on a wicker lounge chair and then carried Mama out to enjoy the cool autumn morning. At first she seemed a little confused about her surroundings, but soon the magnolia trees and gardenia bushes in the side and back yards caught her attention.

"Will they be in bloom soon, André? I do love my gardenias so much."

"In the spring, Mama." André bent over and kissed her forehead.

She seemed satisfied with his answer and laid her head back against the pillows, soon drifting off to sleep. André left her there to walk the gallery, which surrounded the second floor of the house.

Everywhere he looked, the house needed repairs. Would Augustus approve his spending money on paint and carpentry? He could accept to a degree that the old man might want to control him in their business ventures, where he had a monetary stake. But how much would he try to control André at home?

In the navy, the rules had been clear: follow the orders of superior officers. As André rose in rank, he had given orders to the men under him. He himself had obeyed his superior officers, who in turn obeyed the admiralty, knowing they had a broader plan that subordinate officers were not always privy to.

Should he regard this as a similar situation? Should he view Augustus as a sort of "high command" so his coldness didn't cut so deeply? He would of course expect André to make decisions on his trips up the Mississippi River. Perhaps decisions about this house could be viewed in the same way. If André was wrong, he felt certain the old man would let him know.

"Of course." André laughed quietly to himself. Augustus seemed concerned about appearances in the business world. The house fell under the same category as his clothing and transportation. Augustus would want him to repair it.

Now whom should he hire? Father had taught Elgin to take care of these matters. Where could André find a reputable carpenter? One name cut into his thoughts: Percy, the old Negro who had helped refurbish the schoolhouse. According to Gemma's report, the man had done a good job. André would need to contact Miss Harris to find Percy. Perhaps she would be impressed by his generosity in hiring the man. Yet despite last Monday's forced trip to the Randolph house, André could not stomach going there again. He would send Cordell this afternoon.

Juliana watched with Mrs. Sutter as Jim-Jim and the Sutters' butler, Eben, carried Blake down the stairs and out the back door. The servants had already brought a *chaise lounge* and several chairs for the ladies onto the broad green lawn right behind the two-story mansion. The two men carefully laid Blake on the cushions Amelia and Mammy had arranged. Amelia sat in the chair nearest the invalid.

"Please sit down, Miss Harris." Mrs. Sutter pointed to a chair near Amelia's. "I'm going to leave you young people to yourselves."

Juliana touched Mrs. Sutter's hand. "I don't think they'll mind if you stay."

Mrs. Sutter's eyes misted. "There's no need. Blake and I have had a good week of talking. I trust him to your care." She put a lace handkerchief to her nose and sniffed. "How can I ever repay you? You've given me back my son."

Juliana subdued her own tears. "God has something special for Blake to do in this world. Don't you agree?"

Mrs. Sutter seemed unable to speak through her emotions. At last she whispered, "Yes, He surely must." She gave Juliana a sad smile. "Will you ever forgive me for being so rude the day you came calling?"

"Shh, please don't think of it." Juliana squeezed the woman's hand. "We'll just go on from today. Agreed?"

Brushing away more tears, Mrs. Sutter nodded. "Agreed. Now you go sit nearby and be their chaperone." She nodded toward the young couple. Then she reached up and kissed Juliana's cheek. "Go, child." She turned and hurried into the house.

Juliana secured her emotions and took a seat several yards from Amelia and Blake. She took out her embroidery and began concentrating on the daisy patterns on her cotton tea towel. In spite of her strongest efforts not to eavesdrop, she could not help but listen to the young couple and glance their way every few moments.

"You look mighty fine in that silver satin gown, Miss Randolph." Blake's face glowed with ardor. "It puts the color of the sky in your pretty blue eyes."

Amelia reached out to touch his face. "And you, my fine young man, look so much better than last Monday night. You must have been a good boy and taken your medicine."

"I must admit there were times I thought it better to eat manna in heaven than swallow that cane syrup." He peered beyond Amelia and grinned at Juliana. "But by the end of the week, I was looking forward to every dose."

Amelia sniffed. "Don't tease about such things."

"Oh, my darlin'," Blake took Amelia's hand and brought it to his lips. "Don't you worry. I'm here as long as the good Lord wants me here."

Grinning to herself, Juliana studied her stitches. She would place this tea towel with the others in her hope chest. But if there was to be a wedding, she doubted hers would be first.

"My Amelia," Blake's voice sounded weak and raspy, but it also had a happy tone to it. "You know why I sent for you the other night."

"Blake, please…"

"*You* please, darlin'. Please listen to me. I'm asking you to marry me. Now, I understand why you couldn't say yes before the war, but that's all over now. God's made His will clear for the country, and I believe He's made it clear for us. Don't pretend you don't love me. I see it in those sky-blue eyes."

Amelia hung her head. "Oh, gracious. What shall I do?"

"What is it, my sweet lady?" He tried to reach out to touch her cheek, but his arm seemed too weak, for his hand fell to his side.

"How can I marry you when I'm engaged to someone else?"

Blake's brow furrowed. "But you said the other night your fiancé died in the war."

"I said he was presumed dead at Andersonville prison. Until I know whether or not he's alive, I cannot marry you."

Blake slumped back in the *chaise*. "Ah, yes. I see." He cast a long look out over the back lawn. "Honor above all. It applies not only to soldiers and gentlemen."

"Yes." Amelia's words were barely a whisper.

He gazed off into the distance, and the expression in his eyes grew wistful. Then he gave a brief, decisive nod and, bracing one arm with the other, was able at last to touch her face. "Then let us pray for his safe return, my beloved. No, I must not call you that. But may I address you as *dear* Miss Amelia until that day?"

She captured his hand against her cheek. "Oh, yes, *dear* Mr. Sutter."

They began to speak of other interests, the joys that had brought them together in those pre-war days of 1858, when no sensible person could imagine the horrors about to overcome the nation.

Juliana looked away to survey the various bushes and trees. She ventured a look toward the house on the right and quickly ducked her head. Mr. Beauchamp stood on the second-floor gallery staring in her direction. How dashing and distinguished he looked in his fine black suit.

Her heart lilted, and her cheeks grew warm. Did she dare to look again? A quick glance toward Amelia and Blake revealed them still deep in conversation. Juliana lifted her eyes to see the man next door. She also lifted her hand and gave him a friendly but surreptitious wave. When he returned the gesture, she could barely contain a giggle. She could just hear her elder sisters' voices—or Amelia's: "Ah, Juliana, in your heart, you're more childish schoolgirl than grown-up teacher!"

⁕⧢⊛⧣⁕

André could not believe his good fortune. He could speak to Miss Harris in person about Percy. He glanced over at Mama, who still lay sleeping on the *chaise.* She always slept for several hours in the mornings. He could make a quick trip next door and be back before she awoke.

Trying to appear nonchalant, he wandered to the back gallery and down the steps. This time he would not dash through the hedge and arrive in her presence covered with leaves and twigs, especially not in these fine new clothes. He walked out the back gate and over to the Sutters' gate. As he swung it open, the rusted hinges screeched out a protest. His home was not the only one in need of repairs.

As he strode across the lawn, he saw that all three were watching his arrival, yet how different were their receptions. Blake wore a weary but pleased smile and even lifted his hand in a weak wave. Miss Randolph's hatred blazed from her narrowed eyes and stiff posture. Why did this young lady despise him so much when it was he who bore the rightful grudge against her father? But he had come to see Miss Harris, and her lovely smile and shining eyes were all the welcome he needed.

"Miss Harris, Miss Randolph." He bowed to each in turn as they returned their greetings, one pleasant, one forced.

"Blake, my good man." He stepped over and sat on the edge of the *chaise,* gently grasping Blake's offered hand.

"André, how good to see you." Blake's grip felt weak, but his steady gaze revealed the firm soul within. "I thank God for you, old friend, and for your safe return from the war."

André refused to give place to the emotions those words stirred. "But look at you, old man, claiming all this attention from the ladies." He glanced at them with an impish smile and raised one eyebrow. "Makes a man want to take to his sickbed."

Miss Randolph gasped, but Blake and Miss Harris laughed.

"I'll trade places with you, if you like," Blake said.

This time André could not respond with levity. "Ah, my friend, if only we could do that." He stared into Blake's eyes, awestruck by the deep peace he saw there.

"Mister Beauchamp, you really mustn't tire him." Miss Randolph leaned forward with a scolding frown. "Mr. Sutter, it's probably time for you to go inside." She looked at Miss Harris as if seeking confirmation.

"Perhaps in another half hour." Miss Harris set aside her embroidery and came to study the patient's face. "I think the sunshine is doing wonders for him. Mr. Sutter, try to take deep breaths as much as you can to draw in fresh air. Sometimes when we've been in our sickroom for a long time, the stale air prolongs the illness."

"Thank you, ma'am. I'll do that." Blake inhaled, coughed, inhaled again, and laughed. "Feels good. I'm ready to go to the races."

Miss Harris's face glowed with satisfaction. "Now you mustn't overdo it or you'll become dizzy. But you have the right idea." She wandered back toward her chair.

André gently clapped Blake on the shoulder. "I won't add to your weariness. I just came over to wish you well." He stood and apprehended Miss Harris before she sat down. "May I speak with you privately?"

She turned and looked up at him with a sweet smile. "Of course you may."

For a moment André could not breathe. He quickly pulled in some air. "Shall we walk out into the yard?" He offered his arm, and she set her dainty hand on it. As they strolled away from the house, André heard Miss Randolph's "tsk!"

"How lovely you look today, Miss Harris, as always." André leaned toward her as they walked toward the back gate, forcing away a needling anxiety. He must return to Mama soon.

"Thank you, Mr. Beauchamp." She turned to face him. "How may I assist you?"

Come for a carriage ride with me. Let us forget our enmity and take a picnic out to the country. For a moment, with her dark eyes gazing into his, André forgot what he had wanted to say. Hardly the behavior of a former naval officer. He cleared his throat.

"I wonder if you were satisfied with the carpentry work on the schoolhouse."

She stiffened, and her smile disappeared. "Yes, it was very well done. Your generous donation of supplies was greatly appreciated, even the nails."

André drew back. "Ah, I had forgotten. Forgive me. That was childish." How could he rescue this moment?

"You wished to ask me something."

"Yes. I am in need of a carpenter, a good one. Would you recommend the old Negro, Percy? Was he the primary planner of the repairs?"

A look of pleased confusion swept across her face. "Why, yes, I would recommend him. He planned and directed all the work. The walls are seamless." She laughed, and her eyes sparkled. "You surprise me, sir. I never know what to expect from you."

The memory of Blake's gray pallor—so like the dying men on Confederate ships during the war—contrasted starkly with the living man just a few yards away. André was filled with awe, for this lady was nothing short of a miracle-worker. "I might say the same for you, Miss Harris."

"Well, then," She glanced back toward the Sutter house. "If that is all…"

"No, ma'am, it's not." Reckless hope shot through him. "I would like to spend time with you." *A schoolboy's words!* "I would like for our meetings no longer to be by accident."

A pretty pink blush filled her smooth cheeks. "I would welcome your calls."

He laughed, and she did, too. They stood in comfortable silence for a moment, yet André longed to tell her many things.

"When I looked over here a while ago and saw you…" He glanced back at his own house and thought his heart would stop. "Forgive me…" Without another word, he swung open the gate and dashed up the alley.

The *chaise lounge* on the second-floor gallery was empty. ✴

✫ ✫ ✫

With a sinking heart, Juliana watched Mr. Beauchamp's frantic dash back toward his house. Should she follow and try to help with whatever caused his alarm? She glanced toward the Sutter house just as Amelia stood and beckoned to her.

"Juliana, come quickly."

Another look toward the Beauchamp house brought Amelia's anxious "Juliana!"

She lifted her skirts and hurried across the lawn. "What is it?" She knelt beside Mr. Sutter. "Are you all right?"

"I'm fine, Miss Harris. The sun's gettin' a little warm, but this lemonade helps cool me off." Mr. Sutter held up a crystal goblet of pale yellow liquid. "Won't you have some?"

Juliana gave him her sweetest smile. "Why, yes, that would be lovely." She then stood and shot a glaring look at Amelia. "Did you need something, dear?"

"Isn't it time to move Mr. Sutter into the house?" Amelia returned a similar glare. "He admits he's too hot."

"I didn't say *too* hot…" Mr. Sutter began.

"Well, by all means, let us move him inside." Juliana started away.

Several yards from Mr. Sutter's chaise, Amelia caught her arm and whispered, "Why are you receiving that man's attentions?"

Without replying, Juliana pulled away and strode toward the house, tossing over her shoulder, "I'll call for the servants."

Anger propelled each step. Why must Amelia be this way? Why did she hate Mr. Beauchamp so much? Juliana looked toward the house next door. Just above the hedge top, she could see the gentleman in question disappear inside an upstairs door. *Lord, please help him, whatever his difficulty.*

Her prayer cooled her temper. "We are here to serve the Lord," her father had always said. A sudden longing for him filled her breast.

"Oh, Father, what would you do?" she whispered. "How did you face those disagreeable Nantucketers who wanted to stop your marriage to Mother?"

Marriage? For the second time this day, she had thought of marriage and André Beauchamp in the same moment. Yet wasn't that what they both were thinking? If each wanted to spend more time with the other, wasn't it so that they could discover if they were compatible? For her part, she longed to know so many things about him.

She entered the drawing room through the French doors. "Hello? Is anyone here?"

Mrs. Sutter and Eben soon appeared from the hallway.

"Is everything all right?" Mrs. Sutter's pale forehead wrinkled with concern.

"Yes, ma'am, everything is fine." Juliana gave her a reassuring smile. "We just think Mr. Sutter has had enough sun for this morning."

Mrs. Sutter laughed softly, and her rigid posture slumped with relief. "I've feared bad news for so long that I hardly know how to deal with the good." She turned to Eben. "Please call Jim-Jim and help us bring Blake indoors."

After returning the invalid to the house and finishing their own lemonade, Juliana and Amelia departed with a promise to return the next week. Mrs. Sutter stood in her front doorway waving goodbye. The young ladies waved back until the phaeton swept them around the corner and they no longer could see her.

Amelia hummed to herself and seemed absorbed in the scenery, but Juliana sensed a sermon was imminent. Would she be reasonable and discuss the matter, or would she simply scold? Or perhaps she simply felt pleased about the visit with Mr. Sutter. Juliana also rejoiced over his progress and her part in it. If not for a family friend, a Gay Head Indian woman who had nursed Juliana's family through many illnesses, she might never have known about the curative effects of dark molasses.

Concern swept through Juliana. *Lord, please help Mr. Beauchamp,* she prayed again. How she longed to discover the cause of his alarm.

⋇⊹⊱❈⊰⊹⋇

Fire ripped through André's belly as he ran up the back steps two at a time and hastened around the corner of the house to the empty *chaise lounge.* He never should have left Mama alone. He should have called Gemma to sit with her. What could have happened to her? He quickly scanned the front of the upstairs gallery and the yard below, but she had not wandered to either place, nor had she fallen.

He darted in the side door and down the hallway. Jerking her bedroom door open, he almost fell into the darkened room. There she sat, serene as a queen on her indoor *chaise*.

Perhaps not so serene. Her pretty face was puckered in a full-blown pout. In spite of his fear, he laughed with relief, then ambled over, sat beside her, and drew her into his arms. How good it felt to hold her and know she was safe.

"Mama, why on earth did you come back in here? Weren't you enjoying the fresh air?"

She pulled away and scowled at him. Her eyes seemed clearer than they had since he came home. "I didn't want to come in, but Cordell said I must. He said the fresh air was bad for me. Isn't that ridiculous? While I was outside, I felt better than I have for ages, but in here..." Her voice trailed off, and her cross frown changed to one of confusion.

André shook his head. "Cordell is working down at the docks, Mama. He's not even in the house."

"But he insisted that I take my medicine." She shuddered. "Dreadful stuff."

André drew her close again. "It's all right, Mama." The pain in his stomach softened but did not disappear. Her delusions cut into him more than her physical infirmities did. All his life he had been proud of her forthright English ways, which set her apart from many other women of his acquaintance. Perhaps this very quality attracted him to Miss Harris, for she too spoke her mind without dissembling.

"Stay here while I fetch Gemma. She'll sit with you."

Mama answered with a renewed pout. "As you wish." Resignation filled her voice, but her eyes flickered with displeasure.

He kissed her forehead and stood to leave. Should he lock the door to keep her from wandering? No, he could not bear to imprison her in her own home. But he would lock all the upstairs gallery doors.

On the way down to the kitchen, he considered her remarks. Despite her strange visions, he felt certain the fresh air had done her some good, for her long-dormant, feisty spirit had begun to emerge with that pout. Ignoring Dr. Tanner's insistence that she should stay in her room until she improved, André would take her outside again in the morning. But he would not leave her there, no matter who visited next door—not even Miss Harris.

How had the young lady responded to his sudden and unforgivable departure? Surely she must think *him* delusional. As he entered the kitchen, he exhaled a sigh of frustration. Just when they seemed about to have a friendly, reasonable discussion, poor Mama had to cause a stir.

"Gemma, please go sit with Mama."

"Yessuh." Gemma gathered her mending, sidled past him, and left the room.

"Everything all right, Mr. André?" Aunt Sukey was kneading biscuit dough on the kitchen table. Her smooth forehead crinkled with concern.

André slumped down in a chair. "Mama thought she saw Cordell again."

Aunt Sukey's eyes widened, and she glanced toward the back door. "He's still down at the docks, but he'll be home for dinner in another hour."

Were her hands shaking?

André eyed her with a frown. "Is everything all right with you?"

She gave him a shaky shrug. "Yessuh, just fine and dandy."

André stared at her. If one of his naval subordinates had acted this way, he would have suspected a lie and would not have rested until he dragged out the truth. But this was his Aunt Sukey. She had never lied to him, never had a reason to.

This was ridiculous. Like Mama, he was imagining things. He should just go to his study and read until dinner time. He stood abruptly, scraping the chair across the wooden floor.

Aunt Sukey jumped back. "Lawdy, Mr. André, don' scare me that way."

André sighed his exasperation. "What are you so skittish about, Auntie?"

"Nothin', nothin' at all." She chewed her lower lip for a moment. "I been thinkin' real serious that I should say somethin' 'bout…" She shook her head, as if she had changed her mind. "I jus' gotta get dinner on the table by noon, that's all."

Tilting his head, he placed his fists on his hips in an artificially cross pose. "Now, Aunt Sukey, have I ever once scolded you for being late putting a meal on the table?"

"No suh, 'cause I never do." Her smile revealed a bit of her old, teasing self.

He wagged a finger at her and chuckled. "Well, you just make sure you keep it that way." He walked toward the door, rewarded by her hearty laughter.

<hr/>

"Please do not mention it again." Juliana spoke as sweetly as she could but without a smile. The afternoon sun poured through the drawing room window with heat that rivaled this unpleasant discussion.

Amelia crossed her arms and tapped her foot, just as she did with unruly students. "Very well. But surely you must know that this threatens to damage our friendship."

Tears now burned Juliana's eyes. "How can you say that? Think of our pupils, our school. They are so much more important than this silly little difference of opinion."

"*Silly* difference of opinion? That man—"

"*Mr.* Beauchamp is"—what was he?—"a friend of mine." Could she really call him that?

"You barely know him. He's not even a true acquaintance." Now Amelia's balled-up hands went to her hips, and she bent forward in a scolding posture. "You were never properly introduced."

"I believe that was remedied at the opera just the other week… *and* last Monday evening when he fetched the molasses for your Mr. Sutter."

"Oh! Will you listen to yourself?" Amelia flung her hands up in a gesture of disgust. "Why do you insist on befriending our enemy?"

Juliana trembled with rage. "Your so-called enemy has shown himself to be very much a friend to the man who owns your affections." With great effort, she did not spit out her anger. "I am going for a walk." She marched from the drawing room to the front entry, there to don her bonnet and gloves and retrieve her parasol from the hall tree.

"Don't you dare go to his house." Amelia's command reached her.

Juliana spun around, barely able to see for her fury. "What a splendid idea. I might just do that."

Outside in the blazing afternoon sun, she marched in the opposite direction of the Beauchamp and Sutter homes. Despite her angry words, she would never do anything so improper as to visit a gentleman without a chaperone.

But *oh,* how she wished she could. ✳

CHAPTER TWENTY-THREE

✦ ✦ ✦ ✦

*J*ust a half block away from the Randolph house, Juliana realized her mistake. Her day slippers were not meant for street shoes. Every pebble on the sidewalk bruised her feet, which slowed her pace considerably. She would not be able to walk off this fit of temper—her worst since leaving home.

From beneath her parasol, she glanced across the street and saw a small park up the block. A wrought-iron bench under a spreading magnolia tree invited her to sit and reflect on her wretched situation with Amelia. If their conflict continued, what would it mean for their school?

After a wagon passed, she consigned the slippers to ruin and stepped into the street, avoiding several deep puddles that had not yet dried from last night's rain. Riders on horseback clopped past, splashing mud that barely missed her skirt. Did they somehow recognize she was from the North and resent her for it?

Safely seated in the cool shade of the tree, she lowered her parasol. The pleasant fragrances of autumn flowers and freshly mown grass seemed to welcome her. She glanced around. Was this private property? No fence surrounded it or separated it from the large Federal-style house that sat some twenty yards away. Juliana sighed. If the owners wanted to chase her away, well, they would just have to come all the way out here to do it.

The street had few inhabitants at this time of day. Most people were probably at home with families enjoying their weekend. Thoughts of her own home filled Juliana's mind. How good it would be to endure her younger brother's teasing once again or to tell her older sisters to mind their own business. At least in her arguments with Lacy and Molly, she felt secure in their love and friendship, no matter what quarrel was involved. And neither sister would be so cruel as to interfere in affairs of the heart, for they wished Juliana to be as happy as they were in love and marriage.

Why did Amelia despise Mr. Beauchamp so much? Surely she no longer suspected him of shooting Mr. Randolph. The authorities would have arrested him if he had committed such a heinous act. For her own part, Juliana discerned deep character in the gentleman's clear, blue eyes. A man who could humbly admit his own childish-ness and a strong measure of shame in dumping the nails into the dirt was someone she could reason with—unlike the intractable Miss Amelia Randolph.

Juliana cut off the direction of her thoughts. She must seek a solution rather than condemn her good friend. She stared out into the street to watch the passersby, and her heart leapt into her throat. Mr. Beauchamp was coming her way on a fine sorrel horse. Should she call out? No, of course not. But then, there was no need, for he saw her and lifted his hand in greeting.

Lord, surely You planned this. Surely our unexpected meetings are Your design.

Juliana tried to school her broad smile into something more guarded, more ladylike, but she could not. He would just have to see how happy she was to meet him "by accident" once again.

⟡

Miss Harris.

André could not believe his good fortune. His business with Dupris would have to wait, for he would not pass her by without stopping to talk, if only for a few moments. He reined Renárd to the curb and dismounted. No fence or post stood nearby, so he led the gelding up onto the sidewalk. Until André had time to train him to ground tying, he would have to keep him close. Hoping that the spirited beast would mind his manners, André approached Miss Harris.

She wore the same yellow dress and matching bonnet as the first time he had seen her…and treated her so rudely. This time, however, her lovely face was not clouded with anxiety but rather was lit with recognition and open pleasure at the sight of him.

"Miss Harris." He doffed his straw hat and bowed deeply. "What a pleasure to see you for the second time today. I hardly know how to comprehend my good fortune."

"Mr. Beauchamp, how nice to see you." She moved aside to make room for him on the bench. "Please sit down."

Risking disaster with Renárd, André complied. The horse nickered, bobbed his head, and then settled down to nibble the short grass on the lawn.

"What a handsome creature." Miss Harris did not seem frightened of Renárd's large size.

"Yes, I was fortunate to obtain him."

"Sir, you must tell me straight away that all is well at your house. When you left so abruptly this morning, I prayed for God's mercy on whatever extremity caused your alarm." Her earnest expression required his candor.

"Thank you. How thoughtful of you to be so concerned. I had left my mother on the upstairs gallery, and when I looked up, I saw that she was not there."

"Oh, dear, no wonder you were distressed. Is everything all right?"

He shrugged. "As well as can be expected."

"I see. Your mother is not well, then?" Miss Harris's eyes shone with the utmost kindness and sympathy.

André felt himself sinking into those dark pools, and so he looked away to gather his thoughts. Would she think less of him if she knew too much about Mama's illness?

"I did not mean to intrude." Her cheeks wore a pretty blush.

He reached out to touch her gloved hand. "Your compassionate interest is no intrusion at all. Mama has not been well since my father was…since he died."

Miss Harris emitted a soft sigh. "I am so sorry, sir. How tragic for her…and for you."

André looked away again and inhaled a deep breath. This subject was not what he wished to discuss with her. This ache in his heart was not the feeling he wished to have in her presence.

"When we spoke of the war before," she said, "we both felt uncomfortable. If we try again, will we argue this time, too?"

He tilted his head and gave her a little smile. "Undoubtedly."

She laughed. "Oh, then let us speak of frivolity—balls and fashion and the weather—and learn absolutely nothing about each other."

He chuckled. "Perhaps you're right. Perhaps until we get beyond our differences, we won't be able to discover our mutual interests."

"Precisely my thoughts, sir." The brightness in her face lifted his heart.

The gravity of this venture seemed to strike them both at the same moment, for they both grew sober.

"May we agree," she said, "that the war was a horrible tragedy? Something no sane person would willingly engage in?"

"Yes, most assuredly. Furthermore, I am horrified to think that your innocent eyes saw the kinds of wounds men sustain in battle. To think that these delicate hands"—he drew her gloved hands into his own, and she did not resist—"ministered to those wounds. What a brave young lady you are."

She shook her head. "Should we ladies be any less brave than our men?" Her eyebrows lowered into a frown. "Even that comment hints of our former enmity, for it pains me to think of 'our' men and 'yours.'" She pulled back her hands and looked away. "You must know…you must understand…" She turned back to him and stared into his eyes, her lips drawn in with a determined expression. "I was a dedicated abolitionist, and I shall never regret it. Nor shall I ever regret that slavery has indeed been abolished."

He took a turn at looking off into the distance. This was the hardest part. If they could not get beyond it, he might as well get on Renárd and ride away for good. With a sigh that came out as a shudder, he felt a pain akin to the agony that filled his breast when he had surrendered his ship to that Yankee captain. Must he now surrender again in order to win her affection? No, he could not, for he had fought that evil war to defend his homeland and his most deeply held beliefs. But…

"We cannot alter what the war did to us," he said. "We can only hope to go forward and find a way to manage our lives with the changes it has wrought."

For a moment, she did not answer. "Yes, that is the only sensible course."

"Your school is an admirable endeavor to that end."

A radiant smile lit her face. "Thank you. Without your generous contribution, we could not have finished the remodeling and begun our classes so soon."

"Are your pupils doing well?"

"Prodigiously well. We have several very bright ones. The children, of course, must learn their alphabet and numbers, but some are very quick. We also have two clever young women and one…" Her expression changed to one of chagrin.

"Curtis."

"Reverend Adams."

André stifled a groan. Would that sly deceiver destroy this budding friendship? How could André diminish the man's influence over her?

"Does he learn quickly, too?" He forced a tone of polite curiosity.

She smoothed her skirt and tugged at her gloves before answering. "Not as quickly as he would like. He is eager to learn how to read the Bible for himself instead of memorizing it when others read to him."

She eyed André, as if to check the sincerity of his interest. "Reverend Adams is a natural leader in his community. He has organized his people to accomplish many things, including settling into homes, planting gardens, and starting businesses." Her eyebrows lifted prettily into a teasing inquiry. "When I speak to Percy about your carpentry needs, shall I tell him to bring along Reverend Adams for the heavier work?"

André chuckled in spite of himself. "No, thank you. I believe that would be too much of a challenge for both of us."

She grew serious again. "Not at all. Reverend Adams would welcome the chance to…"

"Yes? To what?"

She bit her lip and glanced away, then stared back at him with a look of renewed determination. "To express to you his sincere forgiveness for his…his b-beating at your hands."

Her gaze wavered but held. The words had been difficult for her to say, yet no more difficult than for him to hear them.

"Hmm." What else could he say? Never once in his life had it occurred to him that he owed Curtis—or any of his other former slaves—an apology. Was this to be part of the new order of things? If so, it was intolerable. Those chattels who had done their work had been rewarded. Those who had not done well received punishment. Curtis had tried to kill a man and should have died for it. Father had spared his life. Why would he deserve an apology? With great difficulty, André did not stand up and ride away, nor did he answer the implied challenge of her words. But his belly warmed with a familiar discomfort. How mad he was to think he could share a friendship—and more—with this Yankee woman. Why could he not simply leave her now?

"Where did you serve during the war?" Her question sounded as friendly as an everyday "How do you do?"

André drew himself up into his proudest military posture and stared down at her. "In the Confederate navy. I was a blockade runner." He permitted a mischievous smirk to play across his lips.

"Indeed?"

Her eyebrows arched, but André felt certain he saw admiration in her eyes.

"You were an officer, were you not?"

He bent forward with a little bow. "Yes, ma'am."

"Did you receive your training at sea, or did you attend the naval academy at Annapolis?" Now her expression grew serious, and her voice softened.

Something in her tone unnerved him. Would they discover one more reason not to be friends?

"Yes. I would have graduated in June of '61, but my father called me home right after South Carolina seceded, for he anticipated Louisiana's imminent secession. Why do you ask?"

She released a soft breath. "My goodness. Will wonders never cease?"

"What is it, dear lady?"

"My sister Lacy's husband was in your class. Isaiah Starbuck."

André burst out with a loud laugh that surprised them both.

"Forgive me, Miss Harris, but if your sister is as bright and intelligent as you, how could she ever marry such a dullard as Starbuck? Why, the man was a—" André stopped, for her pretty lips drew in and her dark eyes glowered. He affected a polite expression. He could not bring himself to tell her that Isaiah Starbuck had been the worst snitch in their class and frequently had been shunned for it. "He was a brilliant student, flawless in fact. You must be very proud." What more could go wrong for them?

They sat quietly for several moments. Again André wondered if he should leave, yet some force seemed to hold him here beside her.

"Mr. Beauchamp?"

"Yes, Miss Harris?"

"If we have so many differences, should we not simply part company now and never see one another again?" Her face was now hidden by her bonnet brim. "Why do you not simply leave me here where you found me?" Was that a tiny sob in her voice?

He cleared his throat. "Because I cannot." How long had he been here? He should go to the docks. Dupris was waiting for him. "Why don't you go?"

For several moments Miss Harris did not answer. At last, she echoed his words.

"Because I cannot."

In the silence that followed, the burning in his belly cooled. This was the soothing effect her presence had on him. This was why he could not leave her.

She turned back to him and set her hand on his arm. Despite the heat, a pleasant shiver raced up his arm to tease the hairs on his neck.

"I believe God has brought us together, André. We must find His will in this. Are you willing to search with me, to *pray* with me for ways to compromise, to the end that we might indeed be friends?"

Again the dark pools of her eyes threatened to drown him. He could not bear to let one more problem divide them. He could not tell her that his faith in God had died with the Confederacy, for surely that would be the one thing to destroy all his hopes. Rejecting every sane objection in his mind, surrendering instead to the longing of his heart, he drew her hand up to his lips.

"Yes, my Juliana, I am willing."

Her beatific expression almost undid him. "Then will you lead us in prayer now?"

Surely she heard his dry swallow. Now she would comprehend that he was a fraud. He bowed his head and closed his eyes. Without conscious thought, words came forth.

"Our Father, which art in Heaven, hallowed be Thy name."

A gentle peace settled within his chest where once a dull ache had resided. He pressed Juliana's hand to his heart as more words rolled out.

"Guide us. Give us wisdom." André's voice deepened with sudden feeling. *"Father, show us Your will,"* he breathed out.

So profound and sincere were his sentiments, so complete his relief, that he almost stood up and shouted "Hurrah," as when his ship had slipped through the Union blockade. Instead, he leaned over and kissed Juliana, gently, but directly on her lovely lips. Then he stood and bowed low.

"Until we meet again, fair lady."

"May it be soon."

He led Renárd to the street, mounted, blew her another kiss, and rode away. ✳

CHAPTER TWENTY-FOUR

★ ★ ★ ★

*J*uliana touched her lips where André had kissed her. He really should not have done that. She really should have scolded him. But the honesty of his prayer cast a whole new light on their friendship, and so the kiss seemed almost appropriate. The gentle touch of his lips on hers seemed like the touch of a feather, yet it imparted a world of feeling and understanding and possibility.

She had no motive in asking him to pray except to seek God's will, as she always did for everything. She could see that her request had unnerved him, which only made him all the more appealing to her. Once he began, however, she heard the depth of his feeling, his faith. To think that she had assumed he was not a Christian just because he had been a slave owner. He and Blake Sutter had certainly changed her opinion about that. One day she would ask him how he could reconcile such a contradiction. But since the war had solved the dilemma, she would defer the question until a more convenient occasion.

His prayer also achieved another effect. The moment he spoke, peace flooded her soul, and the last bits of her anger dissolved. Now she could go back to the Randolph residence and face whatever Amelia might say to her. She stood, raised her parasol, and began her short trek.

Amelia met her at the front door and embraced her, knocking her bonnet askew. "Oh, Juliana, I was so worried. Where have you been?" She stood back and dabbed her wet cheeks with a handkerchief.

Juliana removed her bonnet, hung it on the hall tree, and placed her parasol in the stand. "Just down the street. I found a nice little park and sat on a bench in the shade."

"Yes, I know the place. Then you had a chance to think about what I said." Amelia still appeared anxious and even a little cross.

Juliana gave her a reassuring smile. "Oh, I had plenty to think and pray about." Her heart lilting, she gave Amelia a quick hug and then hurried toward the stairway.

"Wait," Amelia called. "I have news."

Juliana turned back, her heart catching. "Yes?"

"It's all right, nothing bad. Father just wants us all to attend services tomorrow. Of course, he won't be able to go, but he can see Mother needs an outing. Will you go with us?"

"Why, that would be lovely. I've never attended an Episcopal service, and I'm sure to enjoy it." Juliana had missed attending church since coming to New Orleans. After Mr. Randolph was shot, everyone wanted to stay near home unless necessity demanded their presence elsewhere.

She once again turned toward the stairway.

"Wait," Amelia repeated.

Juliana turned again. Her friend still wore an anxious expression and was twisting her lace handkerchief to complete the picture of distress. Juliana hurried back to her.

"Is something wrong?"

"Oh, Juliana, are we still friends?" Amelia caught her hands and held tight.

"Of course we are."

"You understand my concerns, don't you?"

Juliana looked down. She could not bear to renew their argument. "Yes."

"Then you'll not seek Mr. Beauchamp's company again?"

Juliana laughed, but without mirth. "I have never sought his company." She struggled to keep her voice even. "I simply go about my life, and there he is."

Amelia stiffened. "Then you must ignore him."

"But what if God is placing him in my path?" *I will not get angry. I will not get angry.* A deep breath braced her resolve. Exhaling helped her relax.

With a sniff, Amelia flipped a curly lock of hair over her shoulder. "If anyone is *placing* Mr. Beauchamp in your path, it is the man himself."

Juliana pulled in another deep breath. She could not let this continue. How could today's meeting with André have been anything but God's plan? Even she herself had not planned to storm out of the house in a huff.

"Promise me you will ignore him." Amelia held Juliana's hands tighter.

With great restraint, Juliana did not pull free. "No, I cannot promise that. However, I can promise not to seek him out unless forced to do so by dire circumstances. On the other hand, if I continue to meet him by accident, then I shall know it is God's will for me to accept…to continue this friendship."

Amelia's shoulders slumped, and she released Juliana's hands. "I cannot agree that this is a sensible way to determine God's will. I would despair to think that you might have to learn a painful lesson because of that horrible—"

"Please. Not another word or we shall quarrel again." Juliana once again made her way toward the stairs.

"I say these things because I love you as my own sister." Amelia's voice took on a slightly shrill tone.

As Juliana ran up the steps, she sent back a quick glance. "I know. I feel the same way about you."

Once in her room, she flung herself onto the fainting couch and clutched a pillow to her chest. Amelia had just explained more than she intended in her declaration of affection. Once an older sister, always an older sister. And always, *always* bossy.

Guilt at her uncharitable thoughts swept through Juliana, with doubt not far behind. Was it truly God's will that she and André should form an attachment? She could think of only one sure way to know for certain. Slipping down beside the low couch, she bowed in prayer.

"Father, if I see Mr. Beauchamp in an unexpected place in the next two days, then I shall know it is Your will for us to be friends. If not, then I shall…I shall…"

Juliana released a heavy sigh. She had no idea what she would do, unless it would be to cry.

"Lord, please let it be Your will."

Like a flash-flame in a fireplace, an idea blazed into her mind. Amelia's opinions notwithstanding, this would settle it once and for all.

"Father, if You want me to continue my friendship with André, please have him come to Christ Church Cathedral for the service tomorrow morning."

❖

Nearing the docks, André stopped to chat with several acquaintances as he rode Renárd toward the warehouse. After his pleasant conversation with Juliana, he felt in no hurry to see Dupris and would be glad when their meeting ended. Their business dealings had begun with his partner holding all the advantages. Now André felt a shift in the balance of powers. Whereas Dupris once seemed to act as if André were nothing more than a pawn, now he displayed almost a sycophant's demeanor. Augustus's money had won for André the superior position even though Dupris knew more about the business world.

He left Renárd tied to a post and entered the darkened warehouse. As he expected, Dupris was pacing outside the office, hat in hand.

"Late again," Dupris snapped. "Didn't they teach you anything in the navy?"

André shrugged. "I'm here now. Are you ready to inspect the ship?"

"I had a pretty good look at her outside." Dupris's eyes narrowed, and he gave André an accusing glare. "Your crew wouldn't let me board."

André stepped into his office and retrieved an ebony and silver cane from the closet. "Hmm. I guess I did learn something in the navy," he muttered just loud enough for Dupris to hear.

The other man snorted out his annoyance and muttered a few words of his own.

"We don't have to do this today." André twirled his cane casually. He was feeling mellow; was he just being mischievous to bait Dupris this way? As a boy, he had enjoyed bedeviling his older brother.

Dupris's widened eyes revealed his panic. "No, no, let's get on with it." His tone lightened, and he put his hat back on. "Never put off until tomorrow what you can do today,"

André had him right where he wanted him.

They spoke little during their two-block walk to the Dumaine Street wharf where the *Bonnie June* was docked. André set a brisk pace, and Dupris hurried to keep up. André's thoughts kept straying to a shaded park bench, a lovely young lady in a yellow dress, and the peace that filled him as they prayed. This evening he would ponder it further. Now he must concentrate on business.

The *Bonnie June* sat berthed at the end of the wharf as if eager to be on her way. The gray and black vessel bore a slender red line around her hull halfway to the gunwale and had the rakish appearance of the blockade-runner she once had been. With his heart light from his talk with Juliana, André's spirits lifted higher. His own ship. Once he took the helm of this fine vessel, it would be like shutting a door on the past and opening another one to a bright new future.

As they boarded, Dupris stuck to the center of the gangplank and shot nervous glances at the water below them. André followed him and clapped him on the shoulder. Dupris jumped.

"Nothing to be nervous about," André said. "She's solid."

"Fine, fine, whatever you say." Dupris's voice shook.

André introduced him to Mason Caldwell, the first mate. As former shipmates during the war, they knew each other's habits and could communicate wordlessly with a raised eyebrow or a scratched chin. Caldwell's placid expression belied the clever, gallant fighter within. André had forewarned him not to leave Dupris unattended on the ship until they tested his honesty and found him worthy.

"Pleased to make your acquaintance," Caldwell drawled, sticking out his hand to Dupris.

Dupris' upper lip started up in a sneer until André cleared his throat. He quickly grasped the first mate's hand. "Mr. Caldwell."

The tour took little time. Dupris showed no interest in the inner workings of the vessel but visually measured the largest cargo hold and made notes in a small leather book. When the three men inspected the upper decks, Dupris studied one cabin after another with searching eyes and enthusiastic commentary.

"Why, we could carry passengers, set up gambling, have entertainment. This ship has far greater potential than to be just a cargo carrier."

André and Caldwell traded a look. They had anticipated Dupris's ambitions. With a few noncommittal remarks, André closed the subject. Surely his grandfather hadn't chosen this ship so it could be a river casino.

That evening, as André coaxed his mother to eat her supper, he considered his varied quandaries. He had fallen into the habit of telling her about his day, but she offered few responses.

"Her name is Juliana, and she's from Boston." André lifted a spoonful of black-eyed peas to her mouth.

Mama opened her lips and took the bite but chewed slowly, reluctantly.

"I think I'm in love with her, Mama."

Did her eyes brighten just now? He hurried on.

"Yes, I know. She's a Yankee," he said. "But the war's over, and we have to reconcile ourselves to the outcome."

Mama nodded and opened her mouth to receive another bite.

"You and Father had a lot of differences, too, but you worked them out."

"Yes, we did." Mama gave him a lazy smile. "You just ask him about that. Oh, he has many amusing stories to tell."

André's heart wrenched. She comprehended what he was saying but still had no sense of time or reality.

"I'd rather hear them from you, Mama." André wiped her chin with a napkin and fed her another bite.

"Yes, I will." Her strange response seemed to confuse her. Her eyes lost their focus, and she did not accept the spoon.

André set it down, along with the bowl. She had eaten more than she had the previous night. He would be grateful for this small progress.

"Pray." She blinked, as if struggling to refocus.

"Ma'am?"

"Pray. Now."

This was new. What should he say?

"All right, Mama. What shall I pray about?"

Her smile was slight but sweet. "About your young lady, silly boy."

André breathed out a laugh. She *did* understand.

"All right, I will." He took her hand, just as he had taken Juliana's this afternoon, and held it to his chest. *"Heavenly Father…"*

"Heavenly Father." Her echoing words infused his heart with happiness.

"If it's Your will for me to…to have a deeper friendship and even more than a friendship with Juliana, please guide both of us."

"Guide both of us." Mama's eyelids drooped, and she lay back against her pillow wearing a sweet, peaceful smile.

For the second time that day, André wanted to stand up and shout "hurrah!" And for the second time, the very act of praying had begun to restore his shattered faith. In spite of what happened to the Confederacy, God did listen to His children. He did care about them. Perhaps in time he and all his fellow Southerners would come to understand why He allowed them to be crushed.

André felt a sudden, overwhelming urge to return to church the next morning. How good it would be to worship once again in the house of the Lord. ✳

CHAPTER TWENTY-FIVE

✯ ✯ ✯ ✯

*E*arly Sunday morning, Jim-Jim drove the landau through the streets of the Garden District to deliver Juliana and the Randolph ladies to church. Since coming to the city, Juliana had little time for sightseeing, so her first view of the Gothic-style Christ Church Cathedral lifted her heart with joy. While this church's services were more formal than those at her father's chapel in Boston, she could hardly wait to sit with others and worship the Lord.

"Ah, what a lovely day." Mrs. Randolph looked refreshed and well in her purple satin dress. "How good it is to be out and about. Juliana, I do hope you're enjoying yourself." She had resumed her duties as hostess and manager of her home, and the younger ladies happily deferred to her once more.

"Yes, ma'am." Juliana gave a little wave of her hand. "New Orleans is a pretty city. I hope to see more of it, especially the French Quarter. I understand the varied architecture there is quite interesting."

"Oh, indeed," Mrs. Randolph said. "The Spanish and French influences are everywhere. You'll appreciate that." She turned toward her eldest daughter. "Amelia, you must take Juliana there next Saturday after your visit with Mr. Sutter."

"Yes, of course, Mother." Amelia's voice had a shrill edge to it.

A frown passed over Mrs. Randolph's face, and she glanced at Juliana.

"But then," Amelia continued, "I thought you should be the one to go with me to visit Blake the next time. I think Mrs. Sutter is ready to resume her friendship with you." She patted her mother's hand. "Now that the war is over, you need to restore these old friendships."

Mrs. Randolph's eyebrows arched slightly, but she nodded. "Yes, that's true. Let us see what the week brings about." Again she glanced at Juliana. "Good friendships are important. One must do whatever is necessary to maintain them, despite disagreements."

Juliana almost laughed at her remark. She and Amelia had reached a silent agreement not to let their quarrel spill over to the others in the household, but Mrs. Randolph was a wise woman who knew her daughters well.

"Ah, here we are." Mrs. Randolph's face brightened.

Jim-Jim drove the carriage up to the sidewalk in front of the church. Another young Negro groom took hold of the horses' bridle so he could hand the ladies down.

"Now, Jim-Jim, once you secure the carriage, you must come back in for the services. Remember, you may sit wherever you like now that you are free."

"Yes, Mrs. Randolph." Jim-Jim grinned. "I like to sit up in the colored section with my friends."

"Very well. Just be certain you behave yourself." She gave him a merry smile.

He chuckled. "Yes, ma'am."

Juliana's heart warmed at the exchange. Jim-Jim was always well-behaved. But Mrs. Randolph's teasing showed how far she had recovered from her recent sorrow.

As the ladies neared the tall wooden church doors, Juliana stared upward in appreciation at the cross-topped spire that pointed toward God. A large foyer stood just inside, and through inner doors a sanctuary beckoned. Organ music filled the building with worship-inspiring hymns. Along the sides of the sanctuary, tall stained-glass windows let in sunlight, adding to the warmth Juliana already felt.

Hundreds of people filled the vast chamber. Some searched for a place to sit, and others visited quietly with friends. A spirit of reverence pervaded the room.

Following an usher, Mrs. Randolph led her party halfway down the center aisle where an empty pew awaited them. Juliana was the last to file in.

Once seated, her gaze fell on the man sitting across from her. She gasped and then smiled, barely able to contain a laugh of delight.

"Good morning, Mr. Beauchamp."

André stood and bowed. "Miss Harris, how nice to see you." His blue eyes sparkled in the bright room. In his well-cut black suit, he cut a dashing figure, and his height made her pulse beat faster. What a splendid-looking man. He stepped across the aisle, took her hand, and raised it to his lips. "You are a vision of loveliness. I thought nothing could surpass you in your yellow dress, but you are exquisite in this pink gown."

Juliana's face heated with a happy blush. "Thank you, sir. Might I return the compliment? Most men look somber in black, but you are elegance personified."

"Tst!" Amelia leaned around Juliana. "We are here to worship the Lord, not each other," she hissed. "Mr. Beauchamp, I believe you have lost your place. Should you not go and find another?" She waved her hand toward the back of the sanctuary with a dismissive gesture.

Indeed, someone now sat where André had been. Juliana gave him a rueful smile. "Shall I see you after the service?"

"No." Amelia again interjected herself into the conversation. "We have an obligation, and Mother will not excuse you."

André bowed to Amelia, and his face betrayed no animosity. "Of course." He turned back to Juliana. "Another time?"

"Soon, I hope." Juliana had no doubt that Amelia would chide her for this boldness.

"Oh, yes, dear lady, very soon." He kissed her hand again. Only then did Juliana realize he had been holding it the whole time.

He bowed away from them and turned up the aisle but not before giving her a little wink.

Amelia gasped. She clutched Juliana's elbow and pulled her down into the pew.

"Has he no shame?" she whispered. "Winking in church—why, winking at a lady at all."

The organ music grew louder, preventing the flippant response Juliana longed to return to Amelia. But how could she mind anything her friend might say to keep her from André? Had not God Himself made clear His will? She was completely free to receive André's attentions. More than that, she was free to love him with all her heart.

"Thank You," she whispered.

Amelia leaned against her. "You're welcome."

Again, Juliana almost laughed. Poor, dear Amelia. She meant well, but she was so wrong.

✦❈✦

André ambled up the aisle, not minding where or by whom he sat. His every thought and feeling was lifted up in a prayer of thanks. After a long absence, he had come back to church to reconfirm his faith. Now that he had seen Juliana, it would take some serious concentration to keep his mind on this morning's sermon. Yet her words, gestures, and smile affirmed her continued interest in him. He could think of how to pursue her at a later time. For now, he had several matters to take up with the Lord, and he hoped Bishop Larson's homily might address at least one of them.

He glanced down a row near the back and spied Cordell staring toward the altar. Just as he started to move into the pew to join him, the man turned, and André could see it was not Cordell after all. Their builds, their light-brown coloring, even their profiles were the same, almost like twins. But this man had to be ten years older, and his thick, black eyebrows were a straight line whereas Cordell's were thinner and arched.

The man stared directly at André for a brief moment, and his upper lip curled in a slight sneer. Anger—the old familiar anger at a Negro who didn't know his place—shot through André. Just as quickly, he recalled that his purpose of coming here today was to restore himself to God. Anger at some insignificant stranger would only hinder his communication with the Almighty.

He found a space in the back row just as the opening procession entered the sanctuary. Acolytes and deacons preceded the bishop, all dressed in holy vestments. Peace flooded André's soul as he looked forward to the comfort and reassurance of the familiar liturgy and sacraments, kneeling with other Christians to lift up petitions and standing to offer praise.

The bishop spoke of reconciliation and peace, using Scripture to support his thesis. Sensing in the old man a hint of resignation, even surrender over the Confederacy's losing the war, André felt his military training and experience surging up to resist. Within him the battle raged, and the familiar cry rose up in him. How could a good God desert His children in their righteous cause of protecting their homes and way of life? He had returned to church for spiritual restoration, not to have defeat pounded into him.

"When the children of Israel disobeyed God, they were chastened. When they sought after other gods, He set their enemies upon them. But never, never did He desert them. And He has not deserted us today."

How did the South disobey? Why were we chastened?

A dark face came to André's mind. Curtis—terrified, trembling, pleading for mercy before Father forced Elgin to beat him. André shifted in the pew as the memory of that day pierced his conscience. How could he justify his unwilling participation? Curtis had tried to kill a man. The mercy was in the beating rather than a hanging. When it was finished, Curtis had glared at him with great hatred, as if André had somehow betrayed him. Why did his hate-filled face haunt him now? Was it because the light-skinned Negro who resembled Cordell continued to shoot angry looks his way?

André answered the challenge of his expression with a bland stare. Who was this man? What grudge did he bear toward André? What could André possibly owe him or any other Negro?

What about Reverend *Curtis Adams? What do I owe him? Nothing! We don't owe any of them anything.*

André leaned against the back of the pew. Father had been a kind, benevolent master. He had taken seriously his responsibility to care for an inferior race, to give them meaningful work and to provide for their bodily needs. André had learned to take care of them the same way. Now most of those poor souls wandered aimlessly with no direction or structure to their lives. As for him, if the order of his life had been wrong, why did he still feel such an obligation to care for Cordell, Aunt Sukey, and Gemma, to keep them close and see to their needs?

"Be reconciled with your enemies. Do good to those who have done evil to you. For only in this can we fulfill the law of Christ."

These were the words of a weak man. André's belly burned for the first time since he had sat in the park with Juliana.

Several men stood and left the service, their anger obvious through their hunched shoulders, muttered curses, and stormy faces. Distressed wives and children nervously hurried after them. Fred Stevens caught André's eye and beckoned him with a lift of his eyebrows as he passed by. André felt no urgency to follow. He knew where and when these men congregated.

"Hear the words of our Savior: Love your enemies, bless them that curse you, do good to them that hate you, and pray for them which despitefully use you and persecute you."

Love my enemies? Love the Yankees? Well, there was one Yankee he could love with no difficulty. But the North as a whole? Never.

André sighed. Evil nations had destroyed innocents through-out history. The Confederacy had fallen to such a power. Bishop Larson was simply saying that the only sensible path was to work within the new social order and go on with life. After seeing the horrors of war, André wondered if that might be the only way for any of them to survive.

Did he still believe the Constitution was the greatest document of government ever devised by man? Yes, despite the way the Union had misused it. Could he support the United States again, "my country, right or wrong," as he had at the naval academy? That question was not so easy to answer. The only way to ensure that his country was in the right would be to go into politics, which did not appeal to him at all.

His thoughts had wandered. This was not the reason he had come to church.

Or maybe it was. As he took his turn kneeling at the rail to receive the Eucharist, he lifted his eyes up to the image of the crucified Christ above the altar. In spite of all the losses in his life, he still believed in the goodness and wisdom of God, just as his father had always taught him.

Lord, show me Thy will, and I will obey. ✳

CHAPTER TWENTY-SIX

✶ ✶ ✶

André tipped his chair back against the wall of the Café du Monde and took another swallow of aromatic coffee. Dupris had insisted they meet some other businessmen in this informal setting rather than at the cotton exchange where most men conducted business.

"Never hurts to have too many friends," he had said.

But if these were his friends, André wanted no part of them. Fred Stevens and his cohort, Baxter, had a scheme, probably a sordid and illegal one, and they were searching for partners and a ship. They made it clear they didn't mind dealing with any scum and river rat on the Mississippi, and more than once, they mentioned the *Bonnie June.* Halfway into this so-called meeting, André decided he wanted no part of them, and he was growing suspicious of Dupris. Still, it wouldn't do to alienate any of them. At least not yet.

He leveled his chair with a thunk and set down his cup. The only good thing about this meeting was the fine taste of the coffee. "Well, gentlemen, I don't plan to add anything else to this first trip upriver. When I get back, I might reconsider adding entertainment for passengers. In the meantime, I bid you good day." He rose and retrieved his hat from the peg above the table.

"Say, son, don't be so quick to turn down a good plan you haven't even heard yet." Stevens stood and placed his hand on André's shoulder. "By the way, I was real sorry you didn't come with us yesterday when we left church. We needed to make more of a show to those people. Bishop Larson is a tired old dog with no fight left in him. Somebody just needs to take him out and shoot him. Figuratively speakin', o' course."

Bristling inside, André resisted shrugging off Stevens's hand, but he did duck away with a casual gesture. "I thought his message was very helpful, considering."

"I do declare, boy," Baxter said, "you don't sound much like a naval hero to me. You sure you weren't fightin' on the wrong side in the war? You need to be sure you're friends with the right people these days. Don't go makin' enemies with folks you might need later on down the road. You don't want folks thinkin' you're some sort of Yankee-lover, do you?"

André laughed. "If that's a threat, I'd be pleased to show you how much fight *I* have left in me. As for being a Yankee-lover"—he plopped his hat on his head—"you just never know, do you?" He edged around the table and strode toward the café entrance.

As far as he was concerned, Dupris had just shown his true colors through his choice of associates. Why had Augustus encouraged him to maintain their partnership? Was he a part of all this? Was it some kind of continuing reprisal for Father's marriage to an Englishwoman? If so, André had no idea what he would do next.

One thing he was sure of. God would show him the way.

Was it the hard edge to Amelia's voice? Or her own excessive cheerfulness? No matter how hard they tried to hide it, Juliana could see that their quarrel was evident even to the children. Round white eyes in solemn brown faces drove conviction into Juliana's heart. But how could she stop a quarrel not of her own making? Obviously, yesterday's sermon on reconciliation had not touched Amelia in the least.

"And so you can see from the map"—Amelia tapped a pointer against the map of the United States that hung over the blackboard—"that the country is once again united into one nation. Here are the territories still to be settled…" She circled the western part of the North American continent. "California has been a state since 1850, but soon many of these…"

Seated at the back of the room, Juliana looked back down to grade the older students' arithmetic papers. Amelia really should not tap the map so hard.

Reverend Adams cleared his throat softly. Juliana glanced over to where he sat with perfect posture on the backless bench. His questioning stare bored into her, and she blinked and shrugged. She must find an opportunity to ask for his prayers that Amelia would quit interfering in her life.

The moment the thought left her, conviction returned. What if he asked what the quarrel was about? Would he also condemn her growing friendship with André? No, of course not. He himself had forgiven the worst a slave owner could do.

Juliana sighed and shrugged again, turning away from the minister. How she longed to talk with her father about all of this. But in his absence, perhaps it would be helpful to seek Reverend Adams' counsel. He certainly knew more about how to forgive an adversary than anyone she had ever known.

At the end of the school day, the minister asked to speak with Juliana and Amelia. While Gemma helped the teachers gather and straighten papers, Winnie swept the room, and young Jack took the erasers out back to beat the chalk out of them. After Reverend Adams set the benches in order, he called everyone to the front of the room.

"Miss Gemma, would you please go on over to Miss Winnie's house and see if you can help her work on that quilt for just a short while? She wants to finish it before we get married. When we're done talkin' over here, I'll send Jack over to say the ladies are ready to go home."

"Yes sir, I'd love to help," Gemma said. She and Winnie bade the others goodbye and left, chattering happily as they went.

"Jack, you go on out and ask Mr. Jim-Jim about that fine horse and buggy he has out there. Tell him the ladies will be along directly."

"Yes sir, Reverend." Jack brushed chalk from his brown trousers and dashed out the door.

Juliana glanced at Amelia, who did not return the look but crossed her arms and stared out the window. For her own part, she felt much the way she had as a child waiting for Father to sort out an argument she'd had with her little brother. A little fear, a little anger, and a whole lot of stubbornness; she was *not* in the wrong.

Lord, please help me to be sweet to my adversary, as Papa always taught.

"Now, ladies, what seems to be the problem?" Reverend Adams's voice was filled with humility and sorrow, as though uncertain he had the right to interfere. "How has the old devil stirred up trouble between you two?"

"I'm glad you asked," Amelia said. "You know from your own experience what an evil man André Beauchamp is. Please join me in advising Miss Harris that she must not receive his attentions."

He nodded thoughtfully. "Ah, yes. I saw the direction of his interest the day I met you and he so kindly brought supplies for the school."

If ever Juliana had thought Reverend Adams's lack of education prevented him from being a competent minister of the Lord, this proved otherwise. With insight only a servant of God possessed, he saw right through this silly argument. Why else would he counter Amelia's accusation against André with a compliment for him?

Amelia snorted in an unladylike manner. "He simply wanted to influence her in his favor."

Juliana quietly inhaled to keep from speaking in anger. As sweetly as she could, she said, "Mr. Beauchamp already had my favor, Amelia. And now more than then, I am certain God wishes me to continue my friendship with him."

"Friendship?" Reverend Adams had a twinkle in his eye.

Juliana felt her face warming pleasantly. "Why, yes, friendship …so far."

He laughed heartily now. "Well, Miss Harris, I cannot promise you what the destination of your friendship journey will be, but I do give you my blessing. André Beauchamp was a man of his time, just as we all were. What matters now is what we become in the future. If we, the wounded parties, do not forgive and move forward…if we do not reconcile with our enemies, then how shall our country endure? I have great hope that Reconstruction will bring about peace between Negroes and whites. Sensible men will prevail."

Juliana's heart lilted with happiness. She struggled to keep from turning to Amelia to say, "See, I told you that you were wrong."

"But you don't understand, Reverend Adams." Amelia's eyes brightened with tears. "He shot my father." She turned to Juliana. "There. I said it. Do not deny that you have thought the same thing."

Reverend Adams's eyes widened. "Have the police found this out for sure?"

"No," Juliana said. "And furthermore, they won't, because he didn't."

"Oh," Amelia cried, "how can you be so blind? He rode right past us coming from the direction of my house. He looked terror-stricken. We both noticed it."

"But he had no gun and…"

"If you tried to murder someone, would you keep your gun as you ran away?" Amelia's voice rose in pitch and volume. "He must have thrown it in the bushes or somewhere else."

Juliana felt as if she had been struck in the chest. Yes, she once had feared André was guilty, but now that she knew him better, she could not believe it. She had no idea Amelia felt this way.

Reverend Adams sighed. "Well, I expect the police will find out soon enough who's guilty. We'll pray that they will." He gave Amelia a kindly smile. "If indeed Mr. Beauchamp is the one who did the shooting, you know Miss Harris will break off her"—he smiled ruefully at Juliana—"her *friendship* with him. Till that day, please be reconciled as sisters in the Lord. Seems to me I recall a passage in Philippians about two ladies who argued in the church. St. Paul asked them to get along for the sake of Christ and His church." He stared at each of them for an instant and then waved his hands toward the row of empty benches. "Will you do that for my little lambs?"

Juliana cast a tear-filled glance toward Amelia, who also struggled not to weep. Before Juliana could embrace her, however, Amelia shook her head.

"I cannot countenance your friendship with Mr. Beauchamp."

Reverend Adams sighed again. "Then maybe you can just pray and let God do His work in Miss Harris. You believe God led her here to New Orleans. Now just believe He'll lead her about this."

Amelia's shoulders slumped. "For your little lambs, Reverend, I will try to do this."

Juliana released her own sigh of relief. "Thank you." She watched to see if Amelia would embrace her.

Instead, Amelia took her bonnet from the hat stand and put it on. "We'd better be going. Mother will be concerned if we're late."

They left the schoolhouse, and Reverend Adams sent Jack to fetch Gemma. They stood in silence until Jack came running back.

"She ain't there," he said. "She done gone on home."

"Jack," Juliana said, "would you please say that again? This time say it correctly."

Jack grinned. "Yessum. She *isn't* there. She gone on home."

Juliana and Amelia traded a look and laughed. The laughter flowed through Juliana's heart like a healing balm. Boys like Jack were their whole reason to be here. In that, if in nothing else, Amelia agreed with her.

"Thank you, Jack," Amelia said. "We will see you tomorrow."

Reverend Adams sent them home with a promise to pray about all the things they had talked about.

On the way home, Juliana decided to test their truce.

"Wasn't it lovely of Mrs. Dupris to collect so many remnants of wrapping paper for the children to write their computations on? Our funds can now go to other needs for the school."

Amelia nodded, perhaps a bit too eagerly. "Oh, yes. And I'm so pleased to see how quickly some of the boys grasp mathematical concepts."

"And I'm delighted to see the girls excel in language."

Juliana felt encouraged. Perhaps these were mundane matters they had already discussed, but Amelia's tone was no longer shrill, and her posture had relaxed. She could only hope that their former intimacy would return soon. ✻

CHAPTER TWENTY-SEVEN

✧ ✧ ✧ ✧

André dismounted in front of his home and turned Rénard over to Kester.

"Make sure you rub him down and give him a half quart of oats."

"Yessuh, Mr. Beauchamp." Kester patted Rénard's shoulder and led him away.

André watched him for a moment. Since their confrontation several weeks earlier, Kester had been respectful and hard-working. Just as Cordell had said, he was turning out to be a good worker worthy of André's trust.

In the kitchen, he found Cordell pacing and Aunt Sukey wringing her hands.

"Oh, Master André," Aunt Sukey said, "Gemma ain't come home from school yet. She's over an hour late."

"That's right, sir." Cordell's brown eyes were filled with concern. "Would you mind if I took one of the carriage horses and rode over to the Randolph house to look for her? She might have stayed to visit with the ladies."

Alarm assaulted André. Gemma always hurried home to give him a report on Juliana. Had all of them been delayed? "Yes, of course. I'll go with you."

"Oh, Master André, do find her," Aunt Sukey called as they went out the back door.

Within minutes, Rénard wore his saddle again, and one of the dappled grays was ready to ride. André and Cordell urged their horses to a trot and quickly covered the five blocks to the Randolph house.

As they rode, André's mind reached out in many directions trying to guess where Gemma might be. If she had stayed with the ladies and he went to the door, undoubtedly Amelia Randolph would turn him away. Moreover, he was not yet ready to confess to Juliana that his servant had been spying on her, no matter how honorable his intentions. Only one solution came to mind. When they neared their destination, he pulled up short.

"You go on, Cordell. Miss Randolph won't want to see my face here again."

Cordell blanched. "Yes sir, but will they care about...I mean ...me being colored and all, will they want to help?"

Certainty surged through André, and with it came a realization. "Cordell, these people believe in colored rights. They're the best kind of folks to help us out at a time like this."

"Yes sir. All right then." Cordell kicked his horse forward.

"Cordell?"

He turned back.

"Go to the front door."

Cordell smiled, and André thought he saw tears in his eyes. "Yes, sir." He reined his horse forward and disappeared around a hedge.

Within ten minutes, he returned. The terror on his face revealed more than André had expected. Truth slammed him hard even as Cordell cried out the words.

"She's not there. She left the school before they did. What are we gonna do, André?"

The anguish in his voice betrayed his love for Gemma. How could André have been so blind? So selfish? He urged Rénard close and grasped Cordell's shoulder. "We're going to find her. Let's go over to Faubourg Tremé and ask around. We'll start near the schoolhouse. Someone over there will know something."

He turned Rénard and started to dig his heels into his flanks. Then another thought struck him.

"Wait a minute. Let's pray."

Cordell stared for a moment as if in shock, and he grinned through his tears. "*Yes,* sir."

Each of them sent up a quick petition for Gemma's safety. Then they kicked their horses to a gallop across the city to the colored district.

Even as André rode, shame and regret edged around his mind. Why had he ignored the hints—the tender glances, the subtle gestures, Gemma's refusal of his own advances—that should have told him Cordell and Gemma were in love? Yet he had refused to see what he did not want to accept. How could he have misused these loyal servants that way?

Use the right words, fool. They were your slaves. *By some miracle, they cared enough about you to stay on when they could have left. Cordell is smart enough to go north and make something of himself. Why didn't they go?*

"Because we're family," Cordell had said.

A wave of familial affection swept through André. He lifted another prayer heavenward.

Lord, help us find Gemma, and I promise I'll take better care of all my household, my loved ones, from now on.

"Amelia, we must not quarrel about this, too." Juliana paced the drawing room, endeavoring to control her temper. "That poor young man obviously loves Gemma. We must go to Winnie and ask if she said anything about calling on anyone else."

Amelia sat beside the marble fireplace nibbling her thumbnail. "Do you think I don't care about her? I love Gemma just as much as you do. But we will do no good by rushing out willy-nilly. Why, it will be dark in another hour and a half. Who would see to your safety? That young man said he had help for his search. Those men will find her. *Our* duty is to pray for her safety."

Frustrated, Juliana turned to Mrs. Randolph. "Please let me go. I can take Jim-Jim. We'll go directly over to Winnie's and ask if Gemma mentioned going anyplace else. We'll be back in no time."

Mrs. Randolph nodded her understanding in Amelia's direction, but she turned back to Juliana with a sad smile.

"I will permit you to go only if you promise to come back before dark."

Juliana bobbed her head eagerly. "Oh, yes. Thank you." She hurried from the room and found Etty, whom she sent out to the male servants' quarters with instructions for Jim-Jim. Then she dashed upstairs and donned her riding habit. A carriage would be entirely too slow for this enterprise.

Once mounted, with Jim-Jim following on another horse, Juliana whipped her mount into a gallop. The wind flung her riding tam off her head to flap on its strings against her back, and her hair blew into wild, loose tangles. If not for the urgency of her mission, she would have relished this frantic ride. She hadn't ridden since coming to New Orleans, and it felt good to be on horseback again.

The light-skinned young Negro who came searching for Gemma looked familiar, but Juliana could not place him. Visions of the young woman's evil employer, whoever he might be, danced through Juliana's head, driving her onward. Maybe poor Gemma had fled for fear of his cruel attentions. Did these southern men not realize slavery had been abolished?

Lord, protect Gemma, Lord, protect Gemma. The prayer beat through her in rhythm with the pounding of her horse's hooves.

✦✦✧✦✧✦✦

"Yessuh, I knows Miss Gemma." The Negro youth eyed André and Cordell. "Ya'll come over that day to help with the schoolhouse, didn't you?"

"Yes, and now we're in a hurry." André glanced down the narrow street at the row of shotgun houses. A door-to-door search would take too long. "Is there anyone around here who might know where she is?

"Yessuh," the boy drawled. "Over yonder is Miss Winnie's place. I see'd Miss Gemma there this afternoon."

"Good man." André tossed the boy a coin.

Cordell had already ridden down the street. By the time André caught up, he was knocking on the door. Both of them recoiled when Curtis answered.

"Yessuh, what can I do for you gentlemen?" Curtis wore a black suit and a starched white shirt.

Against his will, André had to admit the man had a certain air about him. Dignified and humble, as a man of the cloth should be. No, that thought was madness.

"Curtis." Cordell reached out his hand.

Curtis clasped it and pulled Cordell into an embrace. "Hello, my friend." He stood back to look over Cordell's shoulder. "Mr. Beauchamp, it's good to see you. What can I do for you gentlemen? If you'll forgive my saying so, you both look like you've been chased by a hungry gator."

Cordell struggled to speak. "It's Gemma. She never came home."

"Gemma? Miss Gemma lives with you?" He stared again at André. "I never knew she was yours." He winced at his own words. "Used to be yours."

André braced himself against the guilt his words produced. "She works for me, caring for my mother. We need to find her before dark. Have you seen her?"

"Just at school today." Curtis glanced over his shoulder. "Miss Winnie, Miss Mabel, could you please come here for a moment?" When he raised his voice, it had a deep and musical timbre.

Two dark Negro women came from the back room, one a younger version of the other.

"Did Miss Gemma say anything to either of you about going someplace else when she left here?"

Winnie and Mabel shook their heads.

"No suh, not that I recollect." Winnie stepped forward, a frown of worry on her brow. "Is everything all right?"

"Gemma didn't come home."

Winnie's eyes widened. "Then you're…" She traded a startled look with her mother, then bit her lip and stared down.

"I'm what?" André tilted his head downward to read her expression but without success.

Winnie lifted her head to look around at everyone but him.

"She, uh, she say she was scared of…of…"

Curtis put his arm around her shoulders. "What's Miss Gemma scared of, honey? It's okay. You can tell Mr. Beauchamp and Cordell. They care about her."

Winnie gulped and wet her lips. "She say she's scared about two things. Her aunt, Miss Althea Dawson, keep pesterin' her about workin' down at her place. Gemma say she scared Miss Althea gonna make her do it. That's why she don't go no place but school and back home."

"What's the other thing she's scared of?" Cordell wore an anguished expression.

Again Winnie hesitated. Again she avoided looking at André. "They's some white men who come ridin' down here from time to time lookin' for quadroons and mulatto women." Now her eyes narrowed, and she stared at André. "They say they want to give 'em work at their rest'rants, but we ain't that ignernt. We know all about that. We know why white men want light girls."

André bristled at the implied accusation of her words and stared, even as he privately admitted it was true, even as he admitted his own guilt. Where once he might have denied it, he could no long say before God that he was innocent.

"What's the name of that place?"

Winnie put her hand on her forehead. "Lawd, I can't think of it. Mama, do you know that place?"

"No, honey, I don't," Mabel said.

"Well, send somebody down to the French Quarter if you remember it. Come on, Cordell." André gripped his arm and pulled him back toward the horses. "We'll try Althea's place."

"Mr. Beauchamp?" Curtis said.

André stopped and turned.

"I will go with you." Curtis stood tall and held his chin high. His eyes bored into André with determination.

"No," André said.

"Yes," Cordell said.

André glared at his friend. "He rides with you."

Cordell smiled for the first time since their ordeal began. "Yes, sir."

The joy in his face cooled André's anger. Maybe it was better to have another man with them after all.

But André would keep an eye on the so-called *Reverend*.

Juliana reined her horse toward Winnie's house, just a half block from the schoolhouse. She waited for Jim-Jim to help her down, and then they hurried to knock on the front door.

"Oh, Miss Harris," Winnie cried as she came to answer, "have you heard about Gemma? She never made it home today." She waved her hands nervously and chewed her lip. "A colored man named Cordell come by with a white man. They lookin' for her. Reverend Adams went with them."

"Yes, Winnie, that's why we're here. A white man, did you say? That must be the one…why, her former owner." This was even worse than Juliana thought. If that kind of man was worried too, no telling what could have happened to her. "Do you know where they're searching?"

"They goin' over to Miss Althea Dawson's place in the French Quarter. She's Gemma's aunt."

"Oh, dear, I hope that's not where she is. Do you have any other ideas?"

"Yes, ma'am. They's two white men who come around looking for light-skinned girls to work in their rest'rant. I don' mean to be ugly, Miss Harris, but it ain't just a rest'rant. It's like Miss Althea's place." Winnie wrinkled her brow. "Oh, I jes' recall it's the Shady Moon."

Juliana gasped. "Oh, my, is there no end to this? Winnie, do you know where that place is?"

"Yes, ma'am, but you ain't goin' there, is you? It's not fittin' for a fine white lady like you to go down there."

"No, ma'am, Miss Juliana," Jim-Jim said. "Mr. Randolph would have my head if I let you go there."

"Jim-Jim, I promised *Mrs.* Randolph I would be home before dark. I have at least another hour to find Gemma. Winnie, will you show me where the Shady Moon is?"

Winnie and Jim-Jim stared at each other for a moment, their eyes communicating both fear and excitement.

"Yes, ma'am, I will."

"Can you ride behind me on my horse?"

Winnie's mouth dropped open and then clamped shut. She gave a quick nod and said, "I reckon I's about to learn."

"Jim-Jim, you go to Althea Dawson's and find Reverend Adams, Cordell, and whoever the white man is. Tell them where we are."

"Yes, ma'am."

Jim-Jim helped the women onto their horse and then mounted his own. They galloped toward the French Quarter, parting ways at Bourbon Street. The ride had invigorated Juliana, and she knew for certain that she could face any challenge.

That is, until she set eyes on the Shady Moon Restaurant. ✳

CHAPTER TWENTY-EIGHT

✶ ✶ ✶

André and Cordell slowed their horses as they neared Althea Dawson's establishment. Magnolias and Lace was an elegant, two-storied Spanish-style mansion on St. Louis Street, a discreet and homey setting that disguised its seamier activities. Several well-dressed white men entered the front door as if attending a dinner party.

André and the others dismounted and assessed the situation for a moment. "Curtis, you know they won't let you in. Stay here and watch our horses. And keep an eye out for anything that might help us find her."

"Yessuh, I will." He took the reins of both horses. "And I'll be prayin', too. You can be sure of that."

André eyed him briefly. The man was useful for something, after all.

Inside the front door, André and Cordell were greeted by an exquisite quadroon of about thirty years, just past her prime for the work upstairs. She stood in front of a long, red velvet curtain that served as a barrier between the entrance hall and the rest of the house,

From her level stare and air of assurance, she appeared to have been promoted to a management position.

"Hello, pretty boy," she said to André. "Come on in. I'm Elena. My, my, you sure are a fine lookin' gentleman. Makes a girl want to go back to work." Glancing behind him, she appraised Cordell up and down. "Honey, you're lookin' awful good, too, but you need to go 'round the corner to Black Lizzy's place."

"He stays with me," André said. "And we're not here as patrons. We're looking for a girl."

The woman threw back her head and laughed. "Now, that's jes' all kinds of contradiction, pretty boy. But I think we can find jes' the right girl for you."

Pulling out a gold dollar, André affected a casual pose and rolled the coin between his fingers. "That's right kindly of you, Elena, but this girl is here by mistake."

Elena followed the movement of the coin with narrowed, greedy eyes. "Honey, ain't no girl here 'cept by mistake."

"She's new. Just came today."

Elena looked directly into André's eyes. "Ain't no new girl here today, sugar." Her stare returned to the coin, and she licked her lips. "I swear it."

André leaned close to her. "Mind if I look around a little bit?"

Elena shot a look at the closed curtain behind her. "I can't do that," she whispered. "Miz Althea will kill me."

André caressed her cheek and spoke in a teasing tone. "I'll make sure she doesn't." His insides roiled with disgust over having to play this game.

The woman moved back and laughed uneasily. "Well..."

André lifted her hand and kissed it, then tucked her fingers around the coin. "Elena. A beautiful name for a beautiful woman."

She coughed out another nervous laugh. "Awright, pretty boy. Don' you git me in trouble, now." She drew aside the curtain and pointed to a large door on the right. "The gamblin's in there." She nodded to a narrow, winding staircase on the left. "You go on up those stairs."

Only when he walked past her, followed closely by Cordell, did André see the derringer hanging from her belt. He felt certain that armed men sat in some dark corner ready to come if trouble erupted. Once the curtain fell behind them, André sent Cordell a silent message of relief with a quick glance and a slight lift of one eyebrow. Cordell let out a quiet breath. They were in!

A long, dark corridor ran in both directions from the staircase landing. André pointed to the one on the right. They would search it first. Revulsion filled him as he quietly opened several doors to check the identity of the busy denizens in the dimly lit chambers. Few of them even bothered to look up to see who had peered in. Fearing how all of this might be corrupting Cordell, he tried to shield him from the sights.

They had almost reached the end of the corridor when a tall, striking mulatto woman came from the farthest room.

"May I help you gentlemen?" Her gracious words did not match her blazing eyes and cold tone.

André drew up to his full height, returned an icy glare, and spoke in his sternest military voice. "Althea Dawson?"

She flinched but stood firm. "I've already paid the judge. What does he want now?"

André hesitated. What judge? Should he find out who was protecting her from prosecution for her illegal business? He felt Cordell's shoulder against his own, reminding him they had come on a more important mission.

"I'm looking for Gemma Dawson. She doesn't belong in a place like this, and you know it."

"Gemma?" Althea's softened voice revealed her confusion. "She isn't here."

"Don't lie to me." André spoke in a clipped tone. "She told her friends you were looking for her, and she was afraid you would force her to work here. Now where is she?"

Althea reached out and gripped his arm. "She's not here, I tell you. I never would have put her to work. She's my only blood family. I wanted to send her to school and find her a decent husband." She released his arm and stood back, glaring at him again. "Who are you? Why are *you* looking for her?"

André peered down his nose at her. "She works for me tending my ailing mother, and I'm putting her through school." He cringed inside at his own lie. He had done nothing more than use Gemma since she was twelve years old. Quickly he pushed aside the sickening guilt. The Lord would have to chastise him later.

Althea continued to eye him suspiciously.

"Ma'am," Cordell said, "you won't be needin' to find her a husband. Miss Gemma and I are plannin' to get married real soon."

She turned her glare on Cordell, assessing him up and down as Elena had done, but with considerably less favor. "I might have something to say about that."

Cordell snorted. "Where you been all these years that lets you think you have a say?"

"We don't have time to argue," André said. "If Gemma isn't here, where do you think she is?"

Althea pulled a handkerchief from her bodice and dabbed her eyes. "I don't know. What happened? When did she disappear?"

Cordell quickly related the afternoon's activities. Althea's tears increased.

"Who would care about a pretty little colored girl like her getting stolen off the streets?" Althea wrung her hands. "We can't even call the police."

André snickered. "How about that judge you paid? Was it Judge Henry?"

Althea's eyes rounded with fear, confirming his suspicions. "You won't tell anyone I said that, will you?"

"Not if you help us find Gemma," Cordell said.

Althea snorted tearfully. "You think I need to be blackmailed to help my niece?"

"Let's go, Cordell." André touched him on the shoulder and started back down the hallway. "This isn't solving anything."

Cordell fell in beside him.

"What can I do?" Althea cried.

"Tell your *people* to watch for her," André tossed over his shoulder.

"I'll do that. You can count on it."

Twilight was approaching when they came back out on the street and told Curtis their news.

"You all right?" Cordell asked Curtis.

Curtis gave them a sheepish grin and held up a couple of silver coins. "A man can make a little money takin' care of horses out here."

Despite their fruitless search, André could not stop his own explosive laugh. "Curtis, you are quite the opportunist. You're going to do all right."

The others chuckled. This brief, light moment seemed to help them all.

"What should we do now?" Cordell's eyes shone with anxiety once more.

Before André could form an answer, Jim-Jim rode up and jumped off his horse. "Mr. André, Mr. André, you gots ta come quick. Miss Harris done gone over to the Shady Moon to git Miss Gemma."

"Miss Harris?" André felt the blood drain from his face. "Are you sure?"

"Yessuh, Mr. Beauchamp. She think she can march right over there and save the world. You gots ta git over there. No telling what they might do to her."

André seized Rénard's reins, leaped into the saddle, and dug his heels into his flanks. As they galloped through the streets, fear gripped him. Juliana had no idea what kind of evil men she would be dealing with. With twilight imminent, why would she risk her life this way? Gemma might not even be there. If something happened to her, it was his fault and no one else's.

And then the worst of realizations struck him.

The Shady Moon belonged to Pierre Dupris.

Juliana helped Winnie slide to the ground, and Winnie in turn helped her dismount the little mare. They lashed the reins to a hitching post across the street from the Shady Moon and looked up at the building's moss-covered balcony. Several young women in flimsy, low-cut dresses stared down and searched the streets, beckoning to passing men and inviting them to come "have a good time."

All her life, Juliana had averted her eyes from the seedy businesses near her father's mission in Boston. Not once had she spoken to the wicked women who worked in such places unless they found their way into the chapel at Grace Seaman's Mission and repented of their evil ways. Now, however, her mother's example of Christian charity welled up inside of her along with a surge of her father's courage. These women needed to be told how to live a better life. But she and Winnie shouldn't go there alone.

"I hope Jim-Jim found Reverend Adams and those other men." Juliana paced back and forth.

"Miss Harris, lookee there. They's some Union officers." Winnie pointed to three men in blue uniforms walking up Bourbon Street.

"Oh, how wonderful. Maybe they'll help us find Gemma."

A carriage clattered past, and when it was gone, Juliana drew back in shock. One of the officers waved to a young woman on the balcony, and then all three men entered the Shady Moon.

Juliana stamped her foot. "Can you beat that? And here I thought our Union men had better sense." *And better morals!*

Winnie shook her head. "A man's gonna do that sort of thing unless he's right with the Lord." She snickered. "O' course, they might just be goin' in for the food. Maybe the gumbo's 'specially good over there."

Juliana sent her a rueful look. "If only that were true."

"Miss Harris!" A young woman emerged from the second floor of the Shady Moon and started to climb over the wrought-iron balcony railing. "Miss Harris, help me!"

"Gemma!" Juliana cried. "Oh, Winnie, she *is* there!"

A burly man dragged Gemma back inside, and the other girls laughed.

"Come on up, honey," shouted a red-haired girl in a blue dress. "We make good money up here and have lots of fun doin' it."

Rage seized Juliana. "I'll be right up, you hussy, but not for that reason."

She marched into the narrow street, but Winnie grabbed her arm.

"Oh, Miss Harris, you can't go in there. You jes' don' know what kind of people they is."

Juliana pulled loose. "They wouldn't dare harm me. I will go in the strength of the Lord." She had no time to pray, but surely God would have her rescue Gemma.

"I's goin' with you then."

Juliana squeezed her hand. "Thank you."

With Winnie on her heels, she marched across the street and barged through the front door into the large entry hall. In the room on the left, men sat around linen-covered dining tables eating and chatting with their pretty female companions. On the right, the darkened saloon was filled with other patrons and women.

"Pardon me, young lady." The maitre d', a middle-aged white man in a black evening suit, came from behind a desk and approached her. "I do believe you've come to the wrong place."

"No, I have not. Now where is your staircase?" Juliana peered around but found no passage to the upper floor.

"Miss." The man's tone and expression hardened. "Please leave before I have you escorted out." He reached for her arm.

Hoping her guess was accurate, Juliana yanked away her arm and dashed into the dining room. Just as she had thought, a narrow staircase stood at the back of the room. The patrons at the tables appeared too stunned to stop her as she raced between tables, eluding the maitre d'. Winnie took another path and reached the stairs at the same time. Juliana had taken only two steps upward when the man caught up and grasped her arm.

"I said get out," he growled.

"Let me go, you heathen." Juliana noticed that several patrons were laughing at the disturbance.

"Ma'am, may I be of service?" One of the Union officers stepped over to the staircase, and his two companions flanked him.

"Oh, yes, thank you." Juliana heaved out a sigh of relief. "My good friend is upstairs by mistake and—"

"What seems to be the problem, folks?" A portly, balding man approached. "Why, Miss Harris, is that you?"

"Who…?"

"We've not been introduced, for I've only seen you from a distance at the opera house. My name is Pierre Dupris, and I'm a business associate of Mr. Beauchamp." He reached for her hand and bowed over it to kiss her fingertips.

"You know André Beauchamp?" Juliana asked. "How wonderful." Questions about the man nagged at the back of her mind, but she must get to Gemma. "Then you will help me?"

"Why, little lady, I'd be pleased and proud." Mr. Dupris turned to the officers. "Gentlemen, we have this under control. Thank you for your interest."

"Are you certain you're all right, ma'am?" The lieutenant who had first spoken eyed her with concern.

"Yes, thank you. This gentleman can help us." She turned back to Mr. Dupris. "You see, my dear friend is—"

"Please permit me to escort you into my office where we can discuss this privately. Is this your maid?" He nodded toward Winnie.

Juliana shook her head. "No, sir, she is my friend."

His eyebrows shot up. "Ah, I see. Well, if you'll just follow me, we can take care of all your concerns."

"Miss Harris." Winnie cast a worried glance around the room. "I don't think…"

"It's all right, Winnie." Juliana took her elbow and guided her after Mr. Dupris. "He's a friend of a friend."

They followed Mr. Dupris far down a darkened hallway to the back of the building. He opened a door and waved them inside. Instead of an office, it seemed to be some kind of storeroom, for it was piled high with boxes and crates. A low cot with rumpled, dingy bedding sat in one corner.

Winnie moaned softly. "Oh, Miss Harris…"

Juliana turned to Mr. Dupris, whose kind expression had turned into a sneer. He reached out and caressed her cheek.

"Do you have any idea," he said in a sinister, suggestive tone, "how much money a pretty blond white woman can fetch?"

As reality blasted into her, Juliana almost gave in to a swoon. Instead, she balled up her fist and smashed it into his jaw with all her strength. A jolt of pain shot up her arm, but in her rage she ignored it.

"You beast! How dare you?"

Recovering quickly, he answered by slapping her in equal measure with the palm of his hand. She slammed into Winnie, and both women fell to the floor with gasping sobs.

"You an evil man fo' shor'." Winnie shook her fist at him.

"Shut up, you—"

Juliana shut her ears to the wicked epithets he hurled at Winnie. What a fool she had been not to realize the depths of depravity that pervaded this neighborhood, these businesses. She sat on the floor staring up at evil incarnate in the person of Pierre Dupris.

Lord, help. It was the only prayer she could think of. Worst of all, she knew she did not deserve help. Why had she let her temper drive her to such foolishness?

"You." He sneered at her. "Get up."

Winnie helped her to her feet.

"Now sit down and don't make any noise." He pointed to the dirty cot.

Someone rapped on the door, and hope sprang to Juliana's heart. When Dupris opened it, she screamed, "Help!"

Dupris grabbed the back of her neck with one hand and her open mouth with the other. "Shut up before I quiet you for good." His hand was jammed into her mouth too far for her to bite him, but still she struggled to free herself.

"Whattayou want?" He asked the large man at the door.

"That new quadroon's kickin' up a ruckus upstairs. Some of the guests are complainin'."

"Bring her down here."

When he said that, Juliana stopped struggling. They were bringing Gemma to her. *Thank You, Lord.*

"You gonna cooperate now?" Dupris bent over her and stared hard into her eyes.

She blinked back tears and nodded.

He took his hand from her mouth slowly and moved over to guard the door.

She wiggled her jaw painfully and sniffed, trying to regain some dignity. In all her life, no one had dared to treat her this way. Her father might be a gentle minister, but when the occasion arose, he could stand up to the worst ruffian in Boston. In the city's North End, everyone respected the Reverend Jeremiah Harris. Even the worst criminals had never assaulted her family. How she longed for Papa now. She sniffed again to keep from crying. But when Winnie put an arm around her, she sobbed into her friend's shoulder.

In a short time, the burly man returned and shoved Gemma into the room. Her eyes blazed with anger and anguish, and when she saw Juliana and Winnie, she cried out and ran to them. The three women clung to each other. The two men left the room, locking it behind them.

"Oh, Miss Harris, I'm so sorry," Gemma said. "I never expected you to get into trouble helpin' me. I jus' thought you'd call the police."

"Never mind," she said. "Jim-Jim knows where we are. He went to get your young man and the white man who was with him."

Gemma's eyes widened. "Cordell and Mr. Beauchamp are coming?"

Juliana emitted a squeaking gasp. "Mr. Beauchamp?" How was he involved in all this? If Dupris was his partner...

"Umm, uh, oh my." Gemma's cheeks grew pink.

Juliana gulped down her fear. "Tell me, dear. You must tell me, you know. What is Mr. Beauchamp to you?"

Gemma hung her head. "Mr. Beauchamp was...is...I work for him, takin' care of his mama."

Juliana thought she would drop to the floor in a faint. André had *owned* Gemma. He was the one she was afraid of. He was the one who had taken this innocent child and...no, she could not think of it. What a fool she had been to think he was different from other southern men. And after all this, would she learn he was in partnership with Dupris in this horrible place, too?

She slumped down onto the cot, ignoring her revulsion over the dingy linen. But she could not ignore her aching jaw or smarting cheek. With a gentle touch, she checked her injury and was relieved that the skin was not broken. That beast had struck her! How dare he?

"Miss Harris?" Winnie sat beside her and touched her back.

Juliana shook her head. "I'll be all right. We have to think of a way to get out of here. We're near the back of the building. Perhaps we can sneak out." She stood and marched across the room to try the only door. The lock was secure. She searched behind the crates for a window and found a row of tiny ones near the ceiling. But even if they could reposition the boxes and climb up, the openings were too narrow for Winnie, the smallest of them.

She and her two friends sat wordlessly on the cot until the last bit of daylight disappeared. In the near-pitch darkness, a dull ache filled Juliana's soul. How could she have thought André...Mr. Beauchamp...was any different? Just yesterday, he sat in church looking for all the world like a fine Christian gentleman. Once when she had glanced back, his eyes had been lifted toward the cross above the altar, and he seemed filled with heavenly joy. What a hypocrite.

The noise of a key in the lock startled them all. Gemma had been dozing, and she awoke with a start. They clung to each other and whispered prayers.

The burly man entered holding a lantern, and Dupris followed. He regarded the women as one would a herd of sheep.

"The blond one will bring a good price in Rio. We'll send the darkie along to tend her. This one..." He pointed at Gemma. "She needs some training, but she'll learn what she has to do."

Gemma blew out a noise of disgust. "I will *not*."

"You don't work, you don't eat," Dupris said. "That goes for all of you." He turned to the other man. "Get one of these crates ready. We'll send these two out tonight." ✾

CHAPTER TWENTY-NINE

✷ ✷ ✷

André and his three companions raced over the short distance to the Shady Moon Restaurant on Bourbon Street. Two young women with painted faces called out to him from the balcony, but he didn't acknowledge them. Again he realized that half his party, Curtis and Jim-Jim, would not be permitted inside. Cordell could go in only if he acted as André's servant.

"Jim-Jim, try to find a police officer. Curtis, I would welcome your help, but you'll have to wait here."

"I understand." Curtis gathered the reins of the three horses and moved them to the side of the street.

"Oh, Lawd, Mister André." Jim-Jim pointed to a little bay mare nearby. "That's Miss Amelia's horse. Miss Juliana done rode her over here."

André willed away the queasy feeling in his gut, the one he'd had to suppress before every battle he had fought in the war. Things were about to get ugly. The outcome was uncertain, yet retreat was unthinkable.

He and Cordell strode across the narrow street and entered the glass double doors. The blended aromas of roasted chicken and heavy perfume met his nostrils.

"Good evening, sir." The maitre d' came from behind his desk to give André a slight bow but ignored Cordell. "What's your pleasure this evening?"

"I'm André Beauchamp, one of Mr. Dupris's business partners." Even as he said the words, André knew this was no longer true. After tonight, he would break all ties to the man.

"Why, of course, Mr. Beauchamp. Unfortunately, Mr. Dupris is not available right at this moment. Perhaps we can find something to entertain you until he is." He lifted one eyebrow in a suggestive manner.

"Never mind that." André's temper threatened to overpower his logic, but releasing it would solve nothing. "I have reason to believe a young lady who is very important to me might have entered this establishment by mistake. I want to look around."

"Oh, no sir. There's no young *lady* here." The man's eyes shifted slightly. "I've been on duty all night and—"

André grabbed his shirt front and lifted him to his toes. "Get Dupris. Now," he said through clenched teeth and then shoved him away.

The man regained his balance and nervously straightened his shirt and cravat. "Now, Mr. Beauchamp, please, this is a decent establishment. We—"

André stepped closer and towered over the man. "I said—"

"Mr. Drummond, you need some help?" A brawny man looking out of place in his black suit approached from a side room.

"Hank, please show these men out." The maitre d' adjusted his jacket, still trying to reclaim his dignity.

"I'm not leaving until I see Dupris." André took a step toward the brawny man and spoke in an icy, controlled tone. "Now get him before I tear this place apart."

Hank reached for André, but Cordell blocked him. The larger man shoved Cordell out of the way, but he quickly rebounded and seized Hank's right arm while André grabbed the left. Hank shook off Cordell and raised his fist to strike André.

"Gentlemen, please…" Drummond wedged his way between them and sent darting glances toward the dining room. "Go peacefully, I implore you. I'll tell Mr. Dupris about your concerns."

"I said I'm not leaving." André turned toward the dining room just as three Yankee officers emerged. Dread seized him. How could he and Cordell overcome all these men? *Lord, help.* God had failed him in the war. Would He help him now?

"What's going on out here?" A young lieutenant about André's age seemed to be the leader of the group.

"Why, nothing at all." Drummond stepped between André and the officers. "Just a little misunderstanding. This gentleman is leaving now."

"I'm *not* leaving until I find Miss Harris." André would go down fighting, and he knew Cordell would do the same.

"Is she a young lady about this tall with blond hair?" The lieutenant held his hand at just the right level for Juliana's height.

"Yes." This was a good man. André read it in his eyes. "Where did you see her?"

"Mr. Dupris took her back to his office. She was looking for a friend and thought she had come here." The lieutenant looked past

André at the maitre d'. "Is there any reason you cannot call Mr. Dupris up front right now?"

Drummond blanched and shot a look at Hank. "Uh, very well. Hank, go tell Mr. Dupris…"

Hank grunted and disappeared behind the door from which he had emerged.

"I don't trust him." André looked at the soldier and almost laughed at the irony of having a Yankee for an ally in this desperate moment.

"Neither do I." The lieutenant glared at Drummond before turning back to André. "I tried to warn the young lady, Miss Harris, is it? But she insisted Mr. Dupris could be trusted because he's your partner. Why would a nice young lady—from Boston, by her accent—come in a place like this? Shouldn't she rely on her menfolk for such matters?"

André shook his head. "Long story." But the man had assessed his Juliana accurately. Foolish, brave girl. And he loved her all the more for it. "Are you with me?" He indicated the door Hank had used.

"We're with you, sir," the lieutenant and his companions chorused.

Shoving Drummond out of the way, André barged through the door and strode down the hallway lit by dim gaslights. He opened doors and called, "Juliana!"

"Gemma!" cried Cordell.

"Juliana! Gemma!" the soldiers echoed.

Screams and scuffling sounds came from the farthest room in the corridor. The men rushed as one, and André flung open the door. A large man held Juliana's wrists and was trying to kiss her. She fought him like a tiger with her long fingers extended like claws.

"Juliana!" André yanked the man from her and slammed his fist into his nose. Blood splattered from the wound.

The man sprang back, but before he could strike André, he saw the other men and shoved his way past them, holding his bleeding nose as he went. "Dupris!" he shouted.

André pulled Juliana into his arms. "Thank God, you're safe!" She stiffened and stared at him as if in shock. "It's all right, darlin'. I'm here. You're safe."

Cordell held Gemma, who sobbed into his shoulder. Winnie hugged herself and grinned her delight.

"Mr. Beauchamp," the lieutenant said, "let's get these women out of this snake pit and safely home."

The group crowded into the hallway only to be met by Dupris.

"Goodness gracious, what on earth is goin' on here?" he said.

"Don't say a word." André longed to knock the man to the floor, but he didn't want to release Juliana. "Get out of the way."

"Why, André, I took this little lady and these women out a side door just over an hour ago and sent them safely on their way. One of my men must have nabbed them and brought them back. It's a good thing you came to the rescue."

"Liar!" Gemma screamed. "Liar! You did it! You was gonna sell us all!"

André's heart surged with pride at her courage, even as he sickened at her words. How he wanted to strangle Dupris.

"Now, gentlemen, surely you see these girls are overwrought."

"*Ladies,* Dupris," the lieutenant growled. "All of them are ladies."

André looked down at Juliana in the dim hallway. Her left cheek bore a nasty bruise with clear finger indentations, and her eyes were unfocused. He could hold his anger no longer. Stepping over to Dupris, he slammed a fist into his chin. Dupris's head snapped back, and he dropped to the floor in a sitting position against the hallway wall.

"Gentlemen, ladies," the lieutenant said, "shall we be going?"

Each member of the party stepped over Dupris, and more than one foot struck his extended legs.

"You'll regret this, Beauchamp. You Yankee lover, you're nothing without me."

André stopped and turned back. A thousand return insults came to mind, but he would not give the man such satisfaction. He wouldn't even waste spit on him. Instead, he just shook his head and turned away.

The entire group trooped through the restaurant, causing no little stir. Patrons called out questions, and the girls who worked there watched nervously and whispered to each other. But by unspoken agreement, neither André nor the lieutenant felt the need to explain or cause further trouble.

Outside, Winnie rushed to Curtis, who enfolded her in his arms. André helped Juliana onto her horse, then mounted Rénard. She did not seem able to command the little mare, so he gathered the reins. Cordell put Gemma on the dappled gray and jumped up behind her.

Jim-Jim shuffled his feet uncertainly. "Ya'll want to take this'n?" he asked the officers.

The lieutenant shook his head. "No, we have our horses down the street." He stepped over to André. "Sir, may we escort you safely home?"

André surveyed his little band and glanced across the street at the Shady Moon. The women on the balcony watched them with sober expressions, and the two bouncers stood with arms crossed by the front door.

He stuck out his hand to the lieutenant. "I'm André Beauchamp, sir, and I would be pleased to accept."

The officer shook his hand. "Frank Sanders, sir. These men are Archer and Brande. Shall we go?"

The solemn procession reached the Beauchamp home within the hour. Curtis and Winnie refused to go home until they knew Miss Harris was all right. André sent Jim-Jim to the Randolph house to inform them of her whereabouts and to request a carriage, for he would not take her there until she had recovered from her shock. All the way to his house, he kept glancing at her, at one moment enraged by the welt on her fair cheek, in the next, disheartened by her troubled, unfocused stare.

Aunt Sukey wept with joy as she gathered Gemma into her arms. *"Lawdy, Lawdy, I thank You, Jesus."*

Noticing Juliana's shock, she insisted that the young lady lie down on the drawing room couch and sent Gemma for cool water and some cloths to tend her injury. Seated beside Juliana, André watched her with growing dismay. She stared at the ceiling with the same vacant gaze Mama wore.

Aunt Sukey offered the soldiers some of her lemon cake and coffee, which they eagerly accepted. After eating their fill, they bade André goodbye.

"This evening's been more entertaining than anything I've done in New Orleans," Lieutenant Sanders said on his way to the door. His companions voiced their agreement.

Once they departed, André hoped Curtis and Winnie would leave as well, for he longed to talk with Juliana. But for the sake of her reputation, he asked them to stay as chaperones.

"Mr. André," Gemma said, "What can I do to help?"

André gave her a brotherly smile, and this time she did not cringe because of his attention. "Are you all right, sweet girl?" He glanced at Cordell, and his face warmed with shame. "Forgive me. Are you all right, Gemma?"

"Yessuh, I'm fine. I was scared those men was gonna carry me off for good, but everything's fine now." She smiled at Cordell and leaned into his embrace. "Everything's real fine."

André nodded his approval. "I'm very happy for you." More than happy. These two deserved happiness. Thank the Lord those thugs had not assaulted Gemma. Yet that very thought stirred guilt for what he had done to Gemma in his callow, heartless youth.

"Shall I git your mama to come down?" she asked.

André started. "Mama? No, she isn't well enough."

"Well, maybe she could jus' come sit here in the room. We know mos' folks don't consider coloreds as fittin' chaperones. Miz Felicity will be all right for a little bit until we can git Miz Harris home."

"All right, then."

André paced the drawing room while Gemma and Winnie fetched Mama. When they brought her into the room, she appeared slightly dazed but also pleased to see him. He led her to an overstuffed chair and eased her down into it.

"A party. How nice." Her dressing gown was fresh and crisp, and her thin hair was brushed into a slender braid down her back. "Why, Cordell, you were just upstairs with me a few minutes ago. How did you get changed so quickly?"

The happiness André had felt upon seeing her vanished at those words. Would her delusions never go away? Cordell appeared as perplexed as he. Gemma stared intently at an old, faded watercolor that hung on the wall and hummed, "Mm-mh."

With this pretense for proper company, André could wait no longer. He went to the couch and knelt down beside Juliana. Her bruised cheek had begun to darken, stirring a mixture of compassion and rage within him.

"Juliana, can you sit up? Will you try? Jim-Jim will be here soon with the carriage so we can take you home." He gently brushed back a few tangled hairs from her forehead.

She opened her eyes and stared at him. "Don't touch me." Her raspy voice shocked him as much as her words. She edged away from him, and he shrank back.

"But…"

"Don't touch me." She pulled herself up to a sitting position and pressed against the back of the couch. "Get away from me."

André thought his heart would burst on the spot. "Darlin' Juliana, it's me, your André. Please don't do this."

Her eyes blazed with raging clarity, and her lips tightened. "You are not *my* André. You are an unscrupulous monster."

He stood and stared around the room. "Gemma, what happened to her? Did they—"

"No suh, no suh, not at all." Gemma seemed as startled as he was. "That Mr. Dupris jus' slap her down real hard, and that's enough to knock a lady like Miss Harris off balance in the head."

"I am not off balance in the head." Juliana addressed her remark to André. "But I do want to go home. Now."

At a loss for words, André stared at her for a moment. Then he strode from the room and out the front door to watch for the Randolph carriage.

What in heaven's name had just happened in there? ✳

CHAPTER THIRTY

✶ ✶ ✶

*J*uliana sat stiffly on the couch in the Beauchamps' drawing room, still stunned by the terrifying events of the evening. When André—Mr. Beauchamp—had burst into the storage room where she had been imprisoned with Gemma and Winnie, she thought for the briefest moment he was in league with Dupris. The last thing she recalled was her relief when he struck the horrid man who tried to kiss her. She had no idea how they had gotten here to the Beauchamp home, but now at last she was able to think clearly.

How had she gotten herself into this mess? She would never regret trying to save Gemma, but her own foolishness brought a blush of shame to her smarting cheek. Why had she thought she could do it without help? Many of the things she had heard at Papa's mission made so much more sense now. The depravity of some men was a bottomless pit, and they harbored no respect for decent women—much like André Beauchamp. Oh, he wore the trappings of decency, but in his heart he was no better than Mr. Dupris.

She looked across the room at the woman Mr. Beauchamp had called "Mama." Although she appeared fragile and slight, Juliana could see that her son resembled her. They had the same blue eyes and youthful appearance.

Mrs. Beauchamp gazed back. "Come here, child. I don't have my spectacles, and I'd like to see you closer." Her words flowed out in a slow but elegant English accent, as if she had come from an aristocratic family.

What was the ailment that kept her confined to this house? Had Mr. Beauchamp imprisoned his own mother? Juliana shooed away the thought. No one could be that evil.

She crossed the room and sat in a chair beside her. "Good evening, Mrs. Beauchamp." She lifted one frail hand and gently squeezed.

"Good evening, my dear. You must be Miss Harris. Juliana."

Juliana gasped. "Yes, ma'am. How did you know?"

A fond look filled her face. "My son told me about you. I can see he has excellent taste. What a pretty young lady you are."

"Thank you." Juliana forced a smile. This woman's eyes exuded honesty and goodness, even if her gaze was a bit unsteady. She would do nothing to disillusion her about her son. Yet something troubled her about the woman's manner. Why was she so lethargic?

"Please forgive me if I'm a poor hostess." Mrs. Beauchamp frowned and rubbed her eyes. "Cordell just gave me my medicine a short while ago. It always makes me so sleepy." She exhaled a weary sigh. "Perhaps I should go back to bed."

Juliana turned to the light-skinned Negro who had helped to rescue her. "You're Cordell?"

"Yes, ma'am." He nodded and then shook his head. "But I didn't give her any medicine. She just has these spells."

A tiny spark lit Mrs. Beauchamp's eyes but quickly faded as if in defeat. She sighed again. "I really should retire for the evening. Would you please excuse me?" She reached toward Gemma, who hurried to help her up.

Mrs. Beauchamp lifted her slender fingers to caress Juliana's cheek. "Dear me, you've been injured. You must see to this. A piece of cold meat for a compress, perhaps. Etty should be able to help you." She leaned on Gemma and slowly walked from the room.

Etty? The Randolphs' Etty? Had she, like Jim-Jim, once been a Beauchamp slave?

Suddenly weary, Juliana longed to lie back down on the couch and go to sleep. She looked across the room where Reverend Adams and Winnie stood talking in a corner.

"Come sit with me." She beckoned them toward the nearby chairs.

"Thank you, Miss Harris," he said, "but coloreds don't sit down in a white lady's drawing room."

"What nonsense. Frederick Douglass sat in my mother's drawing room more than once and had fine conversations with my parents. He convinced my father to become an abolitionist."

Admiration filled the five Negro faces in the room.

"You come from good people, Miss Harris," Reverend Adams said.

A commotion just outside the room drew their attention.

"Where is she?" Amelia's voice sounded in the entry hall. "Juliana, where are you?"

"Please, Miss Randolph, there's no need—" Mr. Beauchamp said.

"Just take us to her," thundered the voice of a man—Dr. Mayfield.

Juliana thought she would weep for joy. They had come to take her home.

Amelia rushed into the room and pulled Juliana into her arms. "My dear, my dear, what has he done to you? Jim-Jim told us you were kidnapped."

"Miss Harris." Dr. Mayfield put his hand on her shoulder. From his hovering posture and earnest expression, she could see he longed to embrace her, too. "Are you all right? Please set my—our—minds at ease about this night's happenings." He sent a glaring glance Mr. Beauchamp's way.

Juliana could not be so unjust as to blame Mr. Beauchamp for danger of her own making. "I tried to rescue one of my students. She was seized by horrid men and taken to a…" She could not speak the word "brothel."

"Dear lady, I understand," Dr. Mayfield said. "What about him?" He nodded toward Mr. Beauchamp.

Only now did Juliana see the look of devastation on his face. Compassion and gratitude welled up inside her. She squelched the compassion.

"Mr. Beauchamp, Cordell, and some splendid army officers rescued Gemma and Winnie and me." She could offer one more kindness. "They brought us here to recover. For that, I thank you, Mr. Beauchamp. Your hospitality has been generous." She turned back to Dr. Mayfield and Amelia. "Shall we go?"

Dr. Mayfield offered his arm, and she took it.

"Juliana…Miss Harris." Mr. Beauchamp still appeared stricken. "If you please, permit me to speak with you alone just for a moment." He swallowed hard and held out his hand in a beseeching gesture. "Please."

"Mr. Beauchamp, I shall be pleased if I never speak with you again as long as I live."

"But why?" He started to take a step toward her, but Dr. Mayfield moved as if to block him, so he stopped. "We have been friends. What happened? What offense did I commit against you?"

Amelia looped her arm in Juliana's free one. "You shot my father, and the only reason you have not been arrested is that you must be paying off the corrupt New Orleans police. There, I said it. Don't try to deny it."

Mr. Beauchamp glanced at her, stiffened, then looked back at Juliana. "Do you believe this abominable lie?"

She turned away, unable to bear the icy rage written across his face. How dare he be offended?

Dr. Mayfield steered her toward the drawing room door.

"Miss Harris." Mr. Beauchamp's tone reflected his hauteur.

She turned back. His blue eyes cut into her soul.

"If you think I could shoot a man down in cold blood, then perhaps this is the best course for both of us."

She shuddered away the unpleasant feelings that swept through her back. She would challenge him with her suspicions.

"Indeed, what shall I think of a man who keeps his own mother in a constant stupor with laudanum?"

"Laudanum?"

He looked as if he had been struck. Had he practiced that expression of shock in case he was ever actually accused?

"Take me home," she whispered to Dr. Mayfield.

With Amelia following, they left their stunned host behind. Jim-Jim awaited them outside in the phaeton, and they soon rattled homeward over the rutted streets. Exhausted from the day's misfortunes, Juliana bounced limply against her fellow passengers until Dr. Mayfield steadied her with a strong embrace.

But these were not the arms she wanted around her. This was not the voice she wanted to murmur reassurances to her. She ached for the man who had bravely rescued her this night, who had struck down her attacker, who more times than she could count had rescued her. *He* was her hero, her gallant knight. But that was all wrong.

She had come to this wicked southern city to educate Negroes, to help them salvage their lives from the horrors of slavery forced upon them by greedy, fiendish men.

But why, Lord, why oh why did I have to fall in love with the very worst kind of slave owner?

Against his will, his heart compelling him, André followed Juliana out of the house. The too-solicitous Mayfield helped her into the carriage and wedged in beside her, with Amelia Randolph on the other side. André wanted to punch the doctor. As for Miss Randolph, he hardly knew what to think. He never would have shot her father, even though he hated the man. Where had she come up with that idea?

Then he remembered. After he had heard about Mama's fall, he had ridden past them on poor old Max. As he raced home from the docks, it might have appeared he had come around the corner from the Randolph house. And because of that error in their judgment, Juliana thought him capable of murder.

No, that made no sense. Their friendship had grown after that fateful day. When they spoke in the park, her eyes had been free of judgment or even suspicion. Something else had turned her against him, some other lie even more heinous than her mad accusation about his giving Mama laudanum.

Would Curtis know? Or Gemma? As the carriage pulled out of the driveway, André hurried back into the house. He found the others in the kitchen enjoying some of Aunt Sukey's lemon cake. Their conversation stopped the moment he entered the room. All of them, even Cordell, stood up from the table, and their relaxed posture became stiff. Not like naval subordinates who came to attention when an officer entered the room but rather like former slaves uncertain of their present place. While he once would have thought it appropriate, André now felt as uncomfortable as they appeared. When he talked about his "people" being a part of his family, did they simply mouth their agreement with him but feel very different?

"Mister André," Aunt Sukey said, "what can I do for you? I have another cake we ain't ate from. Can I serve you some of that one?"

"Don't cut into the new cake. Just give me the last slice of that one and a cup of coffee."

Her eyes lit up. "Yessuh." She quickly obeyed. "Here you go."

He sat at the table. "Sit down, all of you. I have some things to figure out, and you're the only ones who can help me."

Winnie's dark eyes were so round with wonder that André almost laughed. From her slender but sturdy build and her behavior, he guessed she had been a field slave like Curtis, one who wasn't used to being around white people. Whose slave had she been? Did it matter now that she was free?

"What can we do for you, boss?" Cordell's servant act grated on André's nerves.

He stuck a forkful of lemon frosting in his mouth, savoring the way it melted down his throat. "Mm-mm, Aunt Sukey, this can't be beat."

"Yessuh, that's my specialty." Her delight at the compliment shone in her smile. As he had often thought before, he imagined that she must have been beautiful when she was young.

"Gemma," he said, "what happened to Miss Harris today? Why would she suddenly change her opinion of me? Did Dupris tell her some sort of lie about me?"

Gemma's cheeks grew pink, and she averted her eyes. "Um, well sir, I don't know for sure about that." She chewed her lip and played with a ribbon on her blouse.

"Gemma, pay attention. This is important to me. Did she say anything? Ask anything?"

Gemma swung her head from side to side. "Oh, Lawd, Mr. André, I don't know for sure, but it might be my fault. When Miss Harris figured out you was my...my old massuh, she jus' got real quiet and wouldn't talk about it. But I could tell it troubled her. I'm so sorry."

André leaned toward her and frowned. "That can't be all. She knew about—" He glanced at Curtis. "She knew Curtis had been my—" The word stuck in his throat. Gratitude toward Curtis surged through him for not trying to turn Juliana against him. "She realized things had changed. Why would knowing about you upset her?"

Gemma burst into tears. "Oh, Mr. André, I'm so sorry. When they was bringing me home last week, when I was asking her all those things for you, I sort of mentioned…" She gulped in a great sob. "I tol' her your daddy, not by name, o' course, bought me for your birthday present when I was twelve and you turned sixteen. I never thought she'd know you was the one."

Sickened, André shoved away his cake. How could he have claimed to be a Christian while being a party to such a thing? How could he have used this sweet girl that way? And how could a pure young lady like Juliana be expected to bear such knowledge? From everything he had heard, Southern women knew to look the other way about these things. Fortunately, his own father had never…or had he? If he could give his son such a gift, what did he himself do?

André stared across the table at Cordell, who had settled an understanding and affectionate smile on him. André then glanced up at Aunt Sukey, whose eyes brimmed with tears. She brushed at them and turned away. André looked from one to the other and suddenly he knew. This was why they stayed. This was why they claimed to be family. They were.

And Cordell was his brother. ✸

★ ★ ★ ★

André shoved back from the table and strode from the room. He felt as if he was suffocating. He must have air. Out on the narrow front lawn, he stared up at the stars, trying to grasp what he had just realized.

Father, what a hard legacy you've left me. How can I sort all this out?

Grief continued to press on his lungs and stifle his breathing. Perhaps he was talking to the wrong father.

"God," he whispered, *"I've turned a blind eye to Your truth, haven't I? Just like every other man in the South."*

Most white slave owners claimed to be Christians yet insisted they were the superior race. That had been their excuse for brutally using their chattels, both men and women. And he had embraced every part of it. What hypocrites! What vile sinners!

He envisioned Curtis kneeling before him, begging not to be beaten. Why had he tried to kill the overseer? A chill swept down André's back at the memory.

"Please, boss, don't do this," Curtis had cried. "He done took my baby sister and ruined her. Please, boss, you and me gone fishin' together. You been my friend. Help me. Lawd, help me."

Today André had saved the woman he loved from brutal assault. Why had Curtis been wrong for trying to do the same thing? Simple. He hadn't been.

"If you don't control them, they'll rise up against you," Father had said. Knowing of their boyhood friendship, he had forced André to hold Curtis. He then forced Elgin to lay on the whip. If he had required André to do the beating, maybe it never would have happened. Still, something had hardened within his soul that day. Was it too late to reclaim it?

He heaved out a great sigh and inhaled a long breath to clear his mind. Few southern men would ever admit their culpability in all of this. In the clandestine meetings he had attended, most were seeking ways to subvert Reconstruction and prevent Negroes from seizing any rights, especially voting. Despising the Freedmen's Bureau, they blocked every advance their former slaves tried to make. What could one man do against all that?

André started back to the house. Beyond the hedge, he heard several horses approaching at a gallop. Curiosity softened the emotional weight on his chest. He turned, expecting to watch them ride past his house.

Instead, the riders reined their horses at his house and barely stopped in time to keep from knocking him down. He counted six men, two with lanterns, all brandishing pistols, and all of them masked. Raw fear swept through him. Would they shoot him down, here and now?

Lord, help.

"Beauchamp," the leader called out, "this is a warning. Tell your lady friend to close down her schoolhouse, or she'll wish she had." The man sounded like Stevens.

"You better decide who your friends are," called another. "We don't need Yankee and darkie lovers around here." That was Baxter's voice.

Cordell ran out of the house with Curtis right behind him. "Mr. André, we're here to help." He shoved a rifle into André's hands and showed his own. Curtis held the sword from over the study fireplace.

André nearly fell over in relief, but his battle experience seized control.

"Get off my property, you cowards."

The men cursed and shouted crude and angry words at his backers.

"You think these darkies can help you? We'll make sure they learn their lessons good and proper." Dupris could not hide his Creole accent behind that handkerchief.

"I said get off my property." André raised his rifle and pointed it at his former partner's heart.

The men looked at each other as if conferring silently. Their nods signaled their agreement. One lifted his pistol toward André, but Curtis stepped forward and slapped his arm with the flat of the sword. The gun fired, Curtis jerked backward against Cordell, and both fell to the ground. As André prepared to return fire, another weapon sounded in the distance, striking one of the riders on the arm. He sent up a cry and a curse as blood sprayed out across the lawn. André's hurried shot missed his moving target.

"They've got guards!" the leader yelled. "Let's get out of here."

As they turned their horses to ride away, one of the men threw his lantern toward the house, but it fell short and shattered against a stone planter, igniting a small patch of dried shrubbery. The flames briefly illumined the bright blood on Curtis's black coat.

"André?" Blake Sutter's voice sounded through the darkness. "You all right?"

"I've got a man shot here. Can you send for that Yankee doctor over at the Randolph place?"

"Will do."

André fell to his knees beside the unconscious Curtis. *"Dear Lord, have mercy."* In his anguish, those were the only words André could choke out.

✦◄►◙❀◙◄►✦

Juliana sat on the gallery outside her bedroom. The night was clear, and stars sparkled above her. The breeze had strengthened over the past hour, so perhaps a storm would arrive before morning. Three muted pops sounded in the distance, startling her. She sent up a quick prayer that it was not gunfire, though it sounded like it. Why would anyone be shooting at this time of night in this elegant neighborhood?

Other than those few sounds, the night had been peaceful once she had disengaged herself from Amelia and Dr. Mayfield. After they returned from Mr. Beauchamp's house, both of her friends had hovered over her like worried mothers until she pleaded to be left alone.

Yet even in her solitude, how could she sort out the day's events when nothing made sense to her? All her accidental meetings with Mr. Beauchamp and all the answers to her prayers for God's guidance seemed to make His will clear: they were meant to be friends and probably more. Now she could see that had been wishful thinking, and she was a foolish, romantic girl for wanting it to be otherwise. Her heart ached at the loss of her fond hopes for the future *and* her loss of Mr. Beauchamp.

She could not think of returning to the school tomorrow. Perhaps next week she could face her students again.

In the dim light of the gas lanterns lining the street, she could see a man running her way. It appeared to be the Sutters' butler, Eben, but she couldn't be sure until he reached the house and pounded on the door beneath her gallery. Jerome answered, and Eben huffed out his message.

"Man's been shot over to the Beauchamp house. Need the doctor. Please come quick."

André!

Juliana hurried downstairs just as Dr. Mayfield was gathering his hat and bag and told him of the shooting. "Don't bother to saddle the horse," he said to Jim-Jim. "Just a bridle, and I can ride her."

"I want to go with you." Juliana gripped his arm.

Disappointment clouded his expression. "You still care for him?"

She choked out a sob. "I would not wish him dead."

"Stay here, Miss Harris. I will bring you word as soon as I can."

He ran out the door, and her heart followed. Dr. Mayfield was a good man. He had gone to treat the wounded man, whoever he might be, even if it was someone for whom he had no respect.

Amelia drew her into her arms, rocking her back and forth. "Isn't Dr. Mayfield remarkable? Steady, kindhearted, wise. A young lady could do no better than choosing him for a husband."

Juliana pulled back and kissed Amelia's cheek. "I agree. Let us pray the good doctor will see that Helena loves him and would make him a splendid wife."

She ran back up the stairs to weep alone in her room and to beseech God on behalf of André Beauchamp.

⋆⊱⊰❀⊱⊰⋆

Curtis moaned, and relief flooded André's chest. He was alive.

"Steady," he said as he searched for the wound.

"Left shoulder." Cordell pulled aside Curtis's coat to reveal more crimson stains on his white shirt.

Curtis mumbled something and struggled to sit up.

"Lie back," André said. "We're getting the doctor."

"My head." Curtis reached behind his right ear and moaned again.

"He must have hit his head pretty hard." Cordell glanced beyond André. "Could we move him inside in case they come back?" He bit his lip. "I'll clean up the blood if it gets on anything."

André grimaced. "He saved my life. Forget about the bloodstains!"

Cordell shrugged an apology. "Let's get him in, then."

He lifted Curtis around the chest while André gripped his legs.

As they stumbled through the door, Winnie wrung her hands and wailed until Aunt Sukey shushed her. "That don't do no good, girl. Now pull up that rug so we can lay him on the floor."

"No," André huffed out. "On the drawing room couch." He heard their gasps of surprise.

"Gemma, git that piece of oilcloth and some old sheets." Aunt Sukey turned to Winnie. "Girl, you can find water and rags in the kitchen. Ain't no way I'm lettin' that couch git stained with blood."

"I'm not worried about the blood stains." André's muscles screamed at the weight of Curtis's legs while Cordell grunted from his end of the load.

"Well, I am." Aunt Sukey pointed to a wooden chair. "Put him there a minute."

They rested Curtis on the chair until Gemma arrived with the oilcloth and sheets to protect the couch.

They removed Curtis's coat and shirt and staunched the oozing blood with clean rags. In the light of the kerosene lantern, André could see gray scars on his face and shoulders. The reminder of that beating would never go away.

Dr. Mayfield arrived within twenty minutes.

"What happened?" Studying the wound, he ignored André and addressed his question to Cordell.

"He was shot," André said.

The doctor glared at him. "That seems to happen frequently around you, doesn't it?"

If Curtis's life had not depended on the man, André would have thrown him out. Instead, he walked away to stare out the front window. There he prayed for Curtis's recovery and patience for himself not to strike the doctor, should he make another insulting remark. These Yankees seemed determined to think the worst of him.

And Lord, please help Juliana recover from her ordeal. Please help her...

No, he couldn't pray for that. How could he ask God to give him the love of such a pure, good woman? ✸

CHAPTER THIRTY-TWO

✫ ✫ ✫ ✫

"Juliana?" Amelia's muffled call came through the door. "Are you asleep?"

Juliana checked her pin watch. Almost midnight! She set aside her Bible and hurried to open the door. "Has Dr. Mayfield returned?"

Amelia shook her head and hugged Juliana. "I'm so sorry. I never wished this unhappiness for you."

"I know." Juliana brushed her cheeks with a handkerchief. "Did you want something?"

Amelia's face lit up with a happy smile. "Father wants to talk with us. Mother and Helena shaved and bathed him, and he's sitting up in bed. Will you come?"

For the first time since she left the schoolhouse earlier that day, Juliana felt a small measure of happiness. "Yes, of course."

They walked down the long hallway to the other end of the house, where they found Mr. Randolph teasing Helena.

"I think Dr. Mayfield is a fine man, my dear, but perhaps a little too old for you."

"Shh." Helena glanced across the bed at the new arrivals. Even in the dim light of the kerosene lantern, Juliana could see her blush.

"Yes, indeed, Helena." Juliana gave her a merry smile across the bed. "The doctor is everything that is excellent. I happen to know he has a fondness for ginger cookies. Why don't you bake some for him?"

Puzzlement filled the young lady's face, and Juliana almost laughed. Instead, she turned to Mr. Randolph.

"How handsome you look, sir. You'll be out and about in no time."

He chuckled, and then pressed his hand against his wound. "Can't laugh too much yet, but it's getting better."

She inhaled a deep breath to stop the tears this good news brought. "Well, we probably shouldn't tire you. We can talk in the morning."

"I would not think of postponing my expression of deep sorrow over the ordeal you endured this evening." He studied her cheek with a grief-stricken look. "What kind of monster could abduct and strike a delicate young lady like you?"

She put her hand up to her face. Cold compresses had lessened the swelling, and her teeth remained intact. *Thank You, Lord.* The ladies of the house had given her all the sympathy she needed. "It was an experience I shall endeavor to forget. Please, for my sake, do the same. Now, should we not leave you to your rest?"

"Please stay, if you will, Juliana. I need to speak with you and Amelia." He turned to Mrs. Randolph, who sat in a chair on the opposite side of the bed. "My dear, will you and Helena excuse us?"

She looked as if she had been prepared for the request. "Of course, my dear. Helena, you must go to bed. You've been with Father since early this morning."

"Yes, ma'am." Helena did not look pleased, but she kissed her father and left the room. Mrs. Randolph cast one more sad glance at Juliana's face before she went out.

Mr. Randolph asked Amelia and Juliana to bring their chairs close. "I did not wish to distress Mrs. Randolph or Helena, for they have been near hysteria over your unfortunate ordeal, Juliana. But I see in you and my eldest daughter great strength and courage. If it will not add pain upon pain, I feel the need to confide in you both before another misfortune overcomes this house while I am unable to protect you all."

"You may say whatever is on your mind, sir." In spite of her words, Juliana wondered how much more she could endure in one day.

"You have my gratitude, dear girl." He shifted in his bed. "Sergeant Wallace returned again today to ask me if I could recall anything at all to help him find the man responsible for…" He tapped his chest just above the wound.

"Did you remember something?" Amelia sat up on the edge of her chair. "Did you see who it was?"

He frowned and shook his head. "Not for certain. He was standing in the shade of the magnolia trees across the street, so I could not even discern whether he was a white man or a light-skinned Negro. However, I do recall that he wore a brown straw hat pulled down close to his eyes, and his frock coat was light brown or perhaps tan. I remember the color because Mrs. Randolph always says a true gentleman's frock coat shouldn't be any color but black."

Juliana endeavored to keep a tremor from her voice. "Do you recall whether he was short or tall or stout or...?"

Mr. Randolph's eyes twinkled. "My, my, Juliana, you sound just like Sergeant Wallace—a true detective." He coughed and held his chest for a moment before continuing. "I would say he's close to six feet tall, judging by the level of the tree branch near him. He's not stout, by any measure, but has a sturdy physique and an almost military bearing."

Amelia shot a triumphant glance at Juliana but quickly changed it to a silent apology. "If you noticed his bearing, you must have considered whether or not he is someone of our acquaintance."

He tapped his fingertips together and blew out a long sigh. "I must admit he does call to mind someone I know." His frown deepened. "I just cannot believe he would try to kill me."

"André Beauchamp," Amelia said.

Mr. Randolph's eyes grew red, and he gazed across the room vacantly. "There was a similarity, but I don't know for certain. I just don't know."

"Well, I do." Amelia's face took on a hard look. "And with Dr. Mayfield's knowing what kind of pistol the bullet came from, we should have no trouble finding out if Mr. Beauchamp owns that kind of gun."

Mr. Randolph continued to stare across the room. "You cannot imagine the terror I felt at seeing that gun aimed at me. I could think only of my wife and girls, and I prayed for God's mercy." His voice broke slightly, and he cleared his throat. "As you can see, He did grant mercy."

Juliana's heart felt like a cold, dead rock within her. So it was true. André was the would-be murderer. Everything within her rebelled against the thought, and yet she knew she must accept this awful reality.

Amelia reached out to squeeze her hand. "Please know that I take no pleasure in this. For your sake, I would rather have been wrong."

Juliana nodded.

"What's this?" Mr. Randolph shifted in his bed to look directly at her. "Do you know this man?"

She nodded again, and her tears now flowed freely.

Amelia reached over and pulled her close. "Mr. Beauchamp tried to form an attachment with Juliana."

Juliana leaned against her friend but found no comfort in her embrace.

"Ah, I see." Mr. Randolph focused on her. "Hmm. I suppose that would make sense if he were eager to finish the job he began that day. Dear girl, I am so sorry. You're too fine a lady for such chicanery from a callous young man." He grunted out his disgust. "His father would be ashamed."

"His father—" Amelia spat out then stopped.

"Was a fine Christian man," he finished for her. "He just could not see the error of his ways regarding slavery and other issues of states' rights." He suddenly appeared as if the last of his energy had deserted him. "But he did not plot against General Butler, and he did not deserve to hang."

"You're tired, sir." Juliana dabbed her wet cheeks with her handkerchief. "We should leave you to your rest."

"If I am…not awake in the morning," he said to both of them, "will you notify Sergeant Wallace about what I told you?"

Did Mr. Randolph still expect to succumb to his injuries? "Yes, of course." Juliana stood and kissed his cheek. "But I would imagine you'll be able to do it yourself."

She excused herself, leaving Amelia to help her father settle in for the night. How she longed to fall asleep and not wake up for a week. In the hallway, she found Jerome awaiting her.

"Miz Juliana, Dr. Mayfield is in the drawin' room wantin' to talk to you."

She cringed inside. Would he tell her Mr. Beauchamp had died of his injuries? Why, oh why, did she still care? Yet she must go down and learn the worst.

"Miss Harris." Dr. Mayfield's dark blue eyes exuded the utmost kindness, which almost undid her fragile emotions. "I must hasten to tell you that your…your Mr. Beauchamp is uninjured. The man those criminals shot was a Negro by the name of Curtis."

She fell toward him, and the world turned black.

✦

"You gave us a scare, old man." André sat beside Cordell's bed, where they had taken Curtis after the doctor removed the bullet.

Curtis gave him a sickly smile. "Mm-mm. Don't reckon I like this being shot. Makes a fella think twice about things." He glanced across the room where Winnie slept in a chair, and his expression warmed.

"She wouldn't leave," André said. "What I can't figure out is how a nice girl like her would fall in love with a lunkhead like you."

Wincing, Curtis let out a soft laugh. He touched the back of his head. "Did they shoot me here, too?"

"No, you hit the edge of a stepping-stone when you fell."

He grunted. "Guess you oughta take that stone out and let the grass grow over the place. I think there's a scripture verse about that in Psalms 102 or 103."

André grinned. "I might do that."

Curtis stared at him for a moment. "You a good man, boss."

André shook his head and cleared his throat. "Now don't start that."

"No, suh, I mean it."

André clenched his teeth to grip his emotions. He took a deep breath. The two of them smelled rank. Nothing like a night of adventure to stir up a sweat. One of his old naval officers used to say that a sailor who didn't smell of sweat wasn't worth his salt.

When he felt that he could speak without choking up, he leaned toward Curtis. "Will you forgive me?" It was the hardest thing he had ever said, yet once the words were out, a weight lifted from his chest.

Curtis's eyes widened. "Suh?" His shock mellowed to understanding. "Yessuh, I have already done that."

"I owe you my life."

Curtis continued to look at him. "Not meaning to contradict you, boss, but it's the Lord we owe our lives to."

André chuckled softly. "Well, that's true."

Curtis punctuated his grin with a little grimace of pain. "Like I said, you're a good man, Mr. Beauchamp."

André gently gripped his uninjured shoulder. "And you are, too, Reverend Adams."

Curtis yawned. "It's gonna be a new day soon."

"That's right. It is."

Not until Curtis fell asleep did André realize he meant something more than the coming dawn. A new day was coming for the South. But would it bring good or more evil? Would the Yankees who were forging Reconstruction feel the need to condemn and punish the South for its past, much as Juliana condemned him? Had they not been punished enough?

How ironic that this man, who had been so terribly wounded by his hands, had granted him forgiveness long before André asked for it. Would that Juliana, for whom he had done only good, could extend to him similar grace, no matter how unworthy he was.

But she would never be able to look beyond his past. He had seen it in her lovely dark and unforgiving eyes. ✳

★ ★ ★ ★

"Easy now." André stood on one side with Cordell on the other as they helped Curtis down from the borrowed wagon. Winnie hovered like a nervous mother hen, clucking and wincing with each of Curtis's groans of pain. They carried him into her narrow shotgun house, where he would spend his convalescence, and laid him on a battered cot in the front room.

"That Yankee doctor said he would come over to see how you are today." André stood back while Winnie and her mother fussed over the injured man.

"That's mighty good of him." Curtis spoke through clenched teeth. The morphine was wearing off. "Mighty good of you, too." His smile looked more like a grimace.

"Let me know if you need anything, you hear?" André patted his good shoulder.

Curtis slumped back against a tattered pillow and exhaled another groan. "I left my Bible at your place. It's in my coat pocket."

"I can have someone bring it over tomorrow."

Disappointment clouded Curtis's face, but he nodded. "Thank you, suh."

"Or I can go back and get it now." André's chest tightened. He needed to get to the warehouse to supervise the loading of the *Bonnie June.* But he owed Curtis this much.

"No, no suh, that's all right."

"Now you hush, sugar," Winnie said. "If the man wants to do it, you let him."

André chuckled. They were leaving Curtis in good hands. As for the loading, Cordell could handle that.

While Cordell returned the wagon to its owner, André rode Rénard back across town. This morning, he had been so occupied with moving Curtis that he hadn't checked on Mama. That would be the first thing he did when he got home.

A dull ache still filled his chest from the previous night's bizarre happenings. He wondered if he would be making a mistake to sail to St. Louis right now. Even with Cordell's promises to take care of everything, he hated to leave Mama and the rest of the family. Would Dupris try more of his tricks? Last night Blake Sutter, finally on his feet but still weak, had hobbled over to find out what all the commotion had been about. He too promised to keep an eye on André's house. Perhaps he should accept Blake's advice to take care of business and trust the Lord to take care of the Beauchamp household.

Riding up the street toward his house, he noticed as always how much the place needed repairs. When he returned the Bible, maybe he would ask Curtis to contact old Percy and ask him to start to work as soon as possible.

He left Rénard tied to the hitching post outside the back door and entered the kitchen, savoring the aroma of Aunt Sukey's baking.

Maybe he would have a fresh slice of bread and molasses before going to the warehouse.

The moment he stepped into the kitchen, Aunt Sukey gasped and dropped the spoon she had been using to stir a pot of soup.

"Lawdy, Mr. André, what you doin' back so soon? Is everythin' all right?" Her voice sounded shrill, and she lifted her apron to fan herself.

"Don't mind me, Auntie." He still could not get used to her nervousness. "I didn't mean to startle you. I just came to get Curtis's Bible out of his coat pocket. Did Gemma manage to wash out the blood and mend that bullet hole? I can take it with me if she has. I'm going to check on Mama first."

André crossed the kitchen to the back hallway, but Aunt Sukey hurried over to block his path.

"You don' want to go up there, Mr. André." Her eyes were round with fear, and she trembled. "Miz Felicity's sleeping. I'll git Gemma for you, and we can see about that coat."

André gripped her shoulders. "What's the matter, Auntie? Are you still upset about what happened last night?"

She shook her head. "No suh, but…"

He gently moved her out of his way and proceeded up the stairs. She followed right behind him.

"Don' know why you gotta disturb her right in the middle of her nap." Her voice was loud enough to wake someone next door.

"Well, hush then, Auntie." Was she losing her mind?

Feeling Aunt Sukey at his shoulder, he opened Mama's bedroom door quietly and peered in.

"What in blazes!" André threw the door all the way open. "Who are you?"

The man he had seen in church just two days before sat beside Mama on the *chaise lounge* and was spooning something into her mouth. The light-skinned Negro dropped the spoon in Mama's lap and gasped. "Mr. Beauchamp!"

"Who are you?" André raised his voice.

The man appeared dumbstruck, but Mama frowned at him.

"Why, André, you've known Cordell all your life."

Ignoring her, he strode across the room and grasped the man's fancy white shirt front. "Who are you? What are you feeding my mother?" A sick feeling filled his stomach. He knew the answer to his question. *Laudanum!* He would strangle this man here and now.

"Please, sir." The man gripped André's wrists and tried to wriggle free. Although he was as tall as André and well-proportioned, his strength did not match his size, and he could not break free.

Aunt Sukey tugged at his arm. "Please, Mr. André, please, this is my boy, my son. Let him go. Let him go."

André shoved the man away and turned to her. "What are you talking about? Your boy? You have one son—Cordell. Who's this?"

Aunt Sukey and the man clasped each other, eying him fearfully.

"I thought I jus' had one boy, too. They tol' me my first baby died, the one I had by ol' Mr. Beauchamp. But your grandmother, ol' Miz Beauchamp, sold him off to free coloreds. They adopted him and sent him to school, and here he is, come back to me." Her eyes flickered with pride.

Her words slammed into André's heart. What more would he learn about the evil in his family? He knelt beside Mama and caressed her cheek.

"You all right, Mama?"

"Yes, dear, but I don't like that medicine Cordell gives me every day."

André stood, stepped toward the man, and grabbed his shirt front again. "What have you done to her? Why were you keeping her drugged?" And how could he have been so blind not to see what was happening? Juliana had spotted it right away.

For the briefest instant, he saw the same arrogance on the man's face that he had seen in church.

"Mr. André, please," Aunt Sukey said, "let me tell you all about it."

"You? You would do this to my mother after all of her kindnesses to you?"

Aunt Sukey gulped, and her light brown cheeks grew pink. "We didn't do her no harm, suh. It was to keep her from killin' grief after your papa…" She stopped and eyed Mama. "You know."

"For over two years?" André shouted, his voice almost breaking. "You think she's so weak she can't bear the truth? Who gave you the right to do this? Why didn't you ask me?"

"André, please don't shout." Mama put her hand to her temple. "Maybe I'd better have some of my medicine after all."

He knelt beside her again and cupped her face in his hands. "No, Mama, no more. You're not going to have it ever again."

Her confused expression sent blinding rage through him again. He stood and lunged at the man, grabbing his neck with both hands. "Who put you up to this?"

The man's light face grew red as he struggled to breathe. Behind him, André heard Aunt Sukey cry out and Mama plead with him. He slammed the man against the wall, where he slid down to the floor.

"Who?" André's tone turned cold as he tried to contain his fury.

The man felt his neck and gasped for air. Aunt Sukey knelt beside him.

"It was ol' Mr. Beauchamp." Her eyes pleaded for understanding. "He say she needed it." She looked at her son. "Ain't that right, Bernard?"

"Yes, ma'am. My father told me to do it…for her own good."

The look in Bernard's eyes seemed far too sly for André to believe him. And why had he punctuated the assertion by calling Augustus his father? Great heavens! That meant this man was his father's brother and André's uncle.

"I've been looking out for your mother all this time because he told me to."

Bernard adopted an injured look—an artificial injured look. But from Aunt Sukey's pleased expression, André could see she believed him.

André strode across the room, flung back the drapes, and threw open the windows. "From now on, I want fresh air in here." Why was he giving them orders? He would no longer permit either of them near Mama.

He walked over to Aunt Sukey and glared directly into her eyes. "Who else knows about this? Gemma? Cordell? Who?"

Again, she shook violently. "Jus' Gemma. Bernard tol' me not to tell Cordell." She glanced at her son. "Ain't that right, Bernard?"

André turned his glare on the man. "You knew he would figure you out, didn't you?"

Bernard appeared offended. "Why, Mr. Beauchamp, there's nothing to figure out. After my brother François was hanged, my father regretted his treatment of both his white son and his free son of color—me. He has been trying to find a way to bring us all together as a family." He puckered his lips in a petulant expression. "It was I who suggest that he buy that ship for you."

Liar.

"Oh, Mr. André, can't you see how good this is?" Aunt Sukey stared at him with pleading eyes. "Mos' whites don' have nothin' to do with their colored relations. Mr. Augustus is doin' a fine thing, a real fine thing."

The pathos in her face cut into André's heart. She had never had a choice in any of this. She had been used by one man and then had been passed on to his son. Yet she always made the best of things. If she had raised Bernard, he might have turned out to be as good a man as Cordell. How happy she must have been to rediscover a lost child. But he could see she was blind to her older son's cunning.

What was this man's game anyway? What game was Augustus playing to send him over here? He couldn't even go to confront the old man for fear of leaving Mama.

"Aunt Sukey, go over and get Mrs. Sutter. Tell her I need her to sit with Mama."

She winced. "Yessuh." She cast a worried glance at her son and then hurried out.

"You." He turned to Bernard. "Get out and don't come back."

"Why, nephew, what a thing to say—"

"I said get out." André feared he would kill the man if he didn't leave.

"Of course." Bernard must have seen his peril, for he straightened his sack coat, lifted his chin, and departed.

Mama softly sighed, and André knelt beside her again.

"That was strange indeed, wasn't it?" She shook her head ruefully. "My poor boy, having to hear such awful things."

André studied her for a moment. "Did you understand what that was all about?" If she didn't, he would do everything in his power to keep her from learning about Father's wicked behavior.

Mama frowned. "Why, André, I'm not a fool, in spite of what you think." She looked at him tenderly. "You see? I wasn't befuddled when I told you Cordell was giving me medicine."

Regret pummeled him. He had treated her like a child and ignored the truth right in front of his face. "No, Mama, you weren't. I'm the one who's been the fool."

She patted his cheek. "Well, never mind. Everything will be fine now."

André nodded. Maybe she was right. To do his part to make it so, he would cut all ties with Augustus as soon as he returned from St. Louis. Let the old man pull the puppet strings on his newly reclaimed son. His grandson would start dancing to his own tune.

⁕⹃⹌⁕⹃⹌⁕

"This description could fit many men, Miss Randolph." Sergeant Wallace stood in the drawing room with notepad in hand. Of medium height, the pleasant, determined young man still towered above Amelia. "But I'll question Mr. Beauchamp about the tan frock coat and pistol. If he's our man, you can be sure I'll be able to tell. These murderers always give themselves away. Anyone can see it."

Juliana cringed at his words. If that were true, why had she not been able to discern Mr. Beauchamp's evil side?

"I'm counting on you not to let him get away with this crime." Amelia gave the officer a pleading look. "He might come back to finish it."

He shifted his stance and cleared his throat, clearly smitten. "I shall not let you down, miss."

"Oh, thank you, Sergeant. You will have my undying gratitude."

After she showed him out, she returned to the drawing room.

"Juliana, please reconsider your decision about teaching. The children love you so much, and you have skills I do not possess."

Juliana set aside her embroidery to focus on her friend. "Give me a little time. I don't want the children to see my bruised face."

Amelia sat beside her and seized her hand. "But don't you see? This will stir their hearts to see what you suffered to save a friend. You will inspire them to similar self-sacrifice."

Juliana laughed without mirth. "I would not wish for them to follow my example in this. I only made the situation worse." Her laugh became genuine. "You've changed your mind since last night when you scolded me for trying to find Gemma and for entering the Shady Moon."

Amelia made a face. "Well, I am all in favor of making the best of a bad situation. If you can use this"—she pointed to Juliana's injury—"to inspire the children, why not do so?"

"Oh, do cease your badgering. I shall go. But it will be just as much to find out about how Reverend Adams is faring as it is to show off my war wound."

"There, I knew I could convince you to be sensible."

Juliana smiled at her friend. Last night after she woke up from her childish swoon, Dr. Mayfield had informed them that Reverend Adams would recover from his wounds. Since then, Amelia had done her best to cheer Juliana. But her heart continued to ache. Until this matter of the shooting was solved for certain, her normal routine would be difficult to follow. Until then, she could dream, could hope, could pray that Mr. Beauchamp was innocent. She almost wished the sergeant would never solve the crime. ✻

✶ ✶ ✶ ✶

"*Y*our mother will be fine, André." Mrs. Sutter sat beside Mama in the drawing room. "You go on and do what you have to do."

"We can take her over to our place if necessary." Blake leaned on his walking cane. He was thin, but his color and posture had greatly improved.

André studied Mama's sallow complexion. *Lord, please help her to recover from that laudanum.*

"What do you think, Mama? Should I go to St. Louis or stay here and take care of you?"

A bit of her old personality sparkled in her eyes. "I'm not a child, and neither are you." She took Mrs. Sutter's hand. "My dear friend will help me recover. You manage your business and make me proud of you."

He chuckled. "Do you want to stay here or go next door?"

"Oh, I do want to stay in my own home." She glanced toward the door and sighed. "Considering all that Aunt Sukey has meant to us through the years, I still trust her. But perhaps I'm not the best judge of such things at the present time."

"You don't have to decide right now, Miss Felicity," Blake said. "We're not going any time soon."

Gratitude welled up in André. "We'll be in a lot of trouble if I don't make this trip. Thank you for easing my mind."

A frown passed over Blake's brow, but then he smiled and nodded. "Happy to do it, friend. That's what neighbors are for."

André studied him for a moment. Many of their acquaintances had lost everything in the war. "How are you making out?"

Blake shrugged. "Could be better. But let's not worry about that today. The Lord said, 'Sufficient to the day is the evil thereof.' He'll lead us step by step."

Mrs. Sutter's smile looked forced, as if she was putting on a brave face.

André stepped over to Blake and gripped his shoulder. "I'm in the market for a new partner. What about you?"

Blake shook his head. "I can't do that to you. I don't have any money to invest, and I won't let you carry me." He glanced at his mother, asking permission with lifted eyebrows. She nodded her consent. "The honest truth is that we're broke. We'll probably have to sell both the house and plantation just to survive." He released a heavy sigh. "If only the Yankees hadn't cleaned out the plantation. They took everything. Paintings, furniture, silver—"

Mrs. Sutter gasped. "No. Not everything. When we heard that the Yankees had taken New Orleans, I buried the silver. All of it." She laughed. "How could I have forgotten?"

"Mama." Chuckling, Blake eased himself down into a chair. "What am I gonna do with you? All this time, and you didn't remember the silver?"

"I've been tending a sick man, my dear."

"Ah, yes." Blake gazed at her tenderly. Then he looked at André. "If it's still there, you've got yourself a partner."

André stuck out his hand. "Partner." At last, someone he could trust without reservation. If his trip to St. Louis turned a healthy profit, he could break off from Augustus as soon as he returned.

Blake's handshake was firmer than André expected. "Get to work, then. You have many mouths to feed."

André smothered a laugh. "Don't go planning to sit around much longer. I'm sailing out tomorrow and should be home before Christmas. I expect you to put more than capital in our little operation."

"Yes *sir*." Blake saluted him.

"Army," André muttered in mock derision. "Here's how a *navy* man salutes." He returned the gesture with a bit more finesse. At least he thought so.

Trusting Mama to their care, André grabbed his new straw hat and strode across the back yard to the stable. Because of all the delays, he had sent Gemma to remove Rénard's saddle and give him some water and shade. But Rénard stood saddled in his stall. With a snort of disgust, he approached the horse. Was Gemma going to let him down too?

Sudden shuffling sounded behind him, and dark cloth was flung over his head, knocking off his hat. He struggled, but many strong hands grasped him, and he could not strike out. Ropes quickly bound his arms and legs. He shouted but realized no one would be able to hear him through the heavy fabric. Kicking backward with one booted foot, he met flesh, and a man shouted a curse.

"Shut up," another voice ordered. "Get him on the horse."

Ropes now bound his ankles, and he was tossed across Rénard and secured. With no hands to brace him, he bounced hard against the saddle and felt the air go out of him.

Lord, help me!

It was his last conscious thought.

⁕⊦⊣⊹⊛⊢⊦⊧⁕

"Horrible. Just horrible. Augustus, how could you have let them treat your grandson so brutally?"

Jacinta's rich, memorable voice filtered through the fog in André's head. His ribs and lungs ached. In fact, very little of his body remained free of pain. He felt a cool compress on his throbbing temples and reached up to touch the gentle hand that applied it.

"Miss Jacinta," he mumbled. He was lying on some sort of bed or couch, and she sat beside him.

"Shh, it's all right. You're safe here." Her lovely face became clear as he blinked his eyes. She wore a sweet, sad smile.

"He will survive." Augustus peered over her shoulder. "His injuries will be far worse if the police find him—he'll be sure to suffer a particular injury around his neck."

"What?" André's mind quickly cleared. He rubbed his forehead and tried to rise. Jacinta stood and helped him sit up on the drawing room couch. "What are you talking about?"

Augustus sat down across from him. "They'll hang you, boy. Don't you know that?"

A twinge of concern passed through André. "Hang me? For what? I signed the oath of allegiance to the United States. Are they going to prosecute Confederate officers after all?"

Augustus snorted unpleasantly. "Don't you pay attention, boy? You're the prime suspect in the shooting of Charles Randolph, that Yankee_____." He ended with a rude slur.

Relief filled André, and he looked at Jacinta. "Ma'am, I do hope you'll refuse to forgive this old buzzard for using such language in your presence."

She bent her head toward Augustus. "Can you blame him? Randolph conspired against Augustus's son and caused him to be hanged."

André snorted. "His son? Ah, yes, François, the one he disowned, not Bernard, the one he sold and then reclaimed after someone else reared and educated him." He glared at Augustus but decided to refrain from further accusations.

"I'll not answer to you for anything, boy. But I will try to save your miserable life."

"Oh, Augustus," Jacinta said, "haven't we talked about this? André is a dear, brave young man. He is your heir. If nothing else, will you show some respect for a Confederate hero?"

His heir?

The old man's face seemed to droop suddenly, and at last he looked his age. He heaved out a deep sigh. "I'm sending you to South America, to Chile where Jacinta has family. They will receive you, and the American authorities can't reach you there."

"I'm not running away. Why should I run? They have no evidence against me. In fact, I have witnesses to verify I was nowhere near the Randolph house that day." Even as he said the words, André realized his error. He had ridden near the scene of the shooting on his way home after learning that Mama had fallen. Yet her injury wasn't nearly as bad as he had been told. An icy chill swept down his back.

"Someone set me up."

Augustus slowly nodded. "My man at police headquarters learned that someone found a tan frock coat and a gun bearing François's initials. They brought these two items to the police this morning. The coat had a tailor's mark, and the tailor said he made it for François just before the war. Furthermore, because tan frock coats are unusual, Charles Randolph identified it as the one the gunman was wearing. If my men hadn't brought you here, you'd be in jail right now."

"That's no kind of evidence. I lost that coat weeks ago. And the gun—" Realization slammed him. He stood and paced the room. "...disappeared from my collection. But who?" Cold fear filled André's chest. Who in his household would have or could have stolen the gun? Bernard! André's eyes shot to his grandfather, who had now gone pale.

The old man groaned. "Bernard."

Jacinta gasped. "Of course." Her wide-eyed expression of horror revealed her distrust of the man.

At the memory of seeing him at Mama's side, André could not contain his rage. He stood over Augustus and shouted, "It's your fault. You sent him there to keep my mother drugged with laudanum. You could have killed her." He moved back, fearing he would strike him. "What did she ever do to you? She loved your son more than you ever did." He coughed out a caustic laugh. "I despise you, you pitiful old man." He stepped close again. "I'll keep my word to you for my mother's sake. I'll take the cargo to St. Louis, take my cut of the profits, but then we're through."

"Laudanum?" Augustus pressed his hand over his heart. "What laudanum?"

Jacinta rushed to his side. "Are you sick, my love? What is it?"

"Yes, I'm sick, sick at heart for all of this." He patted her hand. "But do not fear. Augustus Beauchamp will never succumb to such weakness." His pale face hardened. "I will see to Bernard."

He stood and walked near to André. "I swear to you that I did not send him to harm Felicity. He begged to visit his mother, and I permitted it as long as he kept it a secret and advised me on your activities."

"I told you," Jacinta said. "He wants André out of the way so that he can be your heir. And now he has given the police enough evidence to accomplish his ends."

Augustus gripped André's shoulders. "You must believe me. I never meant her harm. My only error was in trusting my…Bernard." His stare bored into André's eyes, demanding his acceptance. "I will arrange safe passage for you. You must be on a ship to Chile tonight."

André pulled away and wandered over to the front window. Out on the street beyond Augustus's front gate, gaslight lanterns illumined the roadway. Carriages clattered past, and people on foot hurried about with the last business of the day or the first business of the evening.

"Lord, what shall I do? Elijah fled Jezebel. Shall I flee my false accuser?"

Juliana's fair face came to mind. He desperately wanted her to know he had not harmed Charles Randolph. If he ran away, he would never convince her of his innocence.

He turned back to Augustus.

"The only place I'm going is St. Louis. Tomorrow at dawn. Now, may I have my hat and my horse? I have business to attend to before I sail."

Augustus lifted a pleading hand. "Be sensible, boy…André. The Yankees won't believe you're innocent. I will protect you. Just give me the chance. I will be as a father to you."

André smiled and shook his head. "I already have a Father." He glanced upward.

Jacinta caught his gesture and nodded her agreement.

Augustus slumped into his chair, and then stiffened against the carved protrusion in its back. "Send for his horse."

"And my hat?"

"We do not have it." Augustus's eyes narrowed. "There are some missing pieces to all of this that I cannot place." He waggled a long, bony finger at André. "But I will."

André shrugged. "Do as you wish. I'll send you a report when I return some time before Christmas." He turned to leave, then looked back. "Don't send your henchmen after me again. From now on, I'll be armed."

The old man was saying something as André left the room, but his body ached and he was tired of the whole affair. Despite the apparent evidence, the authorities could never convict him of shooting Randolph. The Lord was on his side. Of that he was certain. ✳

✦ ✦ ✦

*S*eated at the head of the table in his formal dining room, André ate ham, eggs, biscuits, and molasses, his favorite breakfast, yet it tasted bland. Strange how his loss of trust in Aunt Sukey and Gemma affected every detail of his daily life. If Cordell hadn't served himself from the same platter and quickly downed his food, André might have feared it was poisoned. This sort of thought had plagued everything he had done for the past twenty-four hours.

"Here's the list of contacts." Cordell sat beside him and checked the plans for the trip upriver. "I made certain these"—he held up one large sheet of paper—"have no acquaintance with Dupris, at least as best we can tell." He held up another sheet. "These might be all right, but be careful."

André took the page, forcing himself to concentrate. His temples throbbed with a dull headache. He had left far too many details to Cordell's management, much as a commanding officer depended on reliable subordinates to accomplish objectives. Now he saw what a fool he had been not to be more involved in his own business. If Augustus knew about this, as he seemed to know everything, no wonder he had so little respect for him.

He read over the names and locations. "It will be interesting to see how some of these merchants receive a former Confederate officer."

Cordell chuckled. "I wouldn't worry. They'll be too happy to get their coffee and silk to mind who ships it to them."

André eyed him. This was the old Cordell, his lifelong, trusted friend and confidant. Yet hadn't Aunt Sukey been like a second mother to André? He rubbed his eyes to force away the vision of Bernard spooning laudanum into Mama's mouth.

Cordell gripped André's forearm. "Don't worry. You can do this." He tapped the paper. "Everything's right here."

He gave Cordell a curt nod and handed back the paper.

Cordell shoved the stack of information into a leather folder and clasped it shut. "You're ready to go." The note of confidence in his voice faded as he finished. "What is it, André? You're wearing that look that says you're not too sure about all of this."

André leaned back in his chair to study him. "Oh, I'm confident you've put together a good plan." Yes, that much was true.

Cordell frowned, drawing his arched eyebrows into a line that resembled Bernard's.

André felt his chest tighten. This was why his farsighted mother had been fooled.

"André, I promise you before my Lord that I will look out for your interests. I won't betray your trust."

"I've always believed that."

"You can keep on believing it." Cordell's gaze was steady and clear. He glanced away for a moment and then rested his chin on his hand. "I'll keep that Bernard fellow out of the house, and I'll make sure Mama understands why."

"You're not claiming him as your brother?"

Cordell shrugged. "I'll think about it. I don't know the man, but from what you tell me, I don't think I'll like him a whole lot." He grinned at André in his old familiar way. "Besides, I have a brother."

Against his will, André's heart warmed. "So have I."

Cordell frowned again. "André, if you can, would you please forgive Mama? She's always loved you. But just think about how it must have felt for her to find out her dead baby was alive after all these years. How happy she must have been."

"But why didn't she tell me about him?"

Cordell grunted. "During our slave days we did a lot of things our masters didn't know about just so we could survive. Being free won't change that right off. Until people here in the South accept us as full human beings—full United States citizens, and let us take a full part in society, we still might have to dissemble sometimes." He gave him a sheepish grin. "Now, I'm not saying that's right before the Lord. I'm just saying that's how it's going to be."

"I suppose so." An old memory, once bitter, filled André's mind. "Tell me something. Back in '61 when we were packing up and leaving the naval academy, that fellow Jacobs tried to talk you into going north to freedom. He was ready to knock my head off to help you. Why didn't you go with him?"

Cordell shuffled the *Daily Crescent* newspaper and then took a sip of coffee. "When you and I first went up to Maryland, I knew my chances of running away were better up there than down here. But the Lord put a verse from First Corinthians, Chapter Seven on my heart. Every time one of those midshipmen kicked me or called me a bad name,

I hung on to God's command in that passage to remain in the condition I was in when I became a Christian, even if that meant remaining a slave. The next part of the verse says, 'if thou mayest be free, use it rather,' so I could have figured out how to run away like Frederick Douglass did back in '45. But how could I leave my mama down here by herself?"

André's heart swelled with affection and pride. "You're a good man, Cordell, and I'm proud to call you my brother to anyone who'll listen."

Cordell leaned toward him with a frown. "Don't get yourself in trouble now, you hear?"

André stared down his nose and smirked. "Just because you're the older brother doesn't mean you get to give the orders."

Cordell stood and handed the leather folder to him. "Just two orders today. Say goodbye to your mama, and let's head on down to the docks."

André took the folder. "Aye, aye, sir." He shoved back from the table and started for the staircase.

"André?"

He turned back.

"Make sure you carry your Colt. I loaded it and set out some extra bullets."

André gave him a mock salute and strode up the stairs two at a time. He had expected the police last night. When they hadn't come, he decided they weren't going to. Maybe Augustus bribed someone. Maybe they found the evidence lacking. What did it matter? Let the authorities figure out who shot Charles Randolph. He was on his way to St. Louis at last.

Mrs. Randolph had helped Juliana apply powder to hide her ugly purple and yellow bruise, but it still showed through. When she entered the classroom, all the children stared at her, their eyes round with wonder and alarm. Some of the older girls openly wept at the sight of it. Twelve-year-old Jack became so angry that he stepped outside for a few minutes to regain his composure. At the back of the classroom, Reverend Adams sat supported by Winnie, and both wore determined expressions. The place where Gemma usually sat was vacant.

After the first flurry of emotions, Juliana and Amelia settled the class down, and Reverend Adams offered a prayer that they all would learn their lessons that day.

By noon, the normal buoyancy of children redirected their attention to other things. Without a backward glance, they ran out to eat their dinner and play in the back yard. Only little Pearl remained inside because of a cold. She lay sleeping on a tattered blanket behind the teachers' desk. Juliana and Amelia joined the adults at the back of the room for dinner.

"Reverend Adams," Amelia said, "shouldn't you go home and rest?" She poured each of them a cup of coffee made on the Ben Franklin stove.

"I been tellin' him that." Winnie held his hand, and her dark face clouded with worry. "But he don't listen."

"Now, honey, use the right grammar." His eyes twinkled even as he winced in pain. "Say 'He *doesn't* listen.'"

Winnie chuckled. "There you go. He admits it."

Juliana laughed with her.

Amelia said, "tsk," but she also smiled.

"My father always says a person can find humor in almost any situation, no matter how difficult," Juliana said. "But I do think you should go home and rest, Reverend Adams." She took a bite of her cold chicken and a sip of coffee.

"I'll go home directly. I just want to set an example for the children. I keep telling them they're going to need a great deal of courage as they grow up. I saw a little bit of that need the other night at Mr. Beauchamp's house. A lot of white Southerners are filled with hate and will do anything they can to stop us from learning and voting and becoming responsible citizens of the United States." Those last words rolled out in sonorous tones, as if he loved saying them.

Juliana shuddered at the thought of such hatred. "But with the army still present throughout the South, surely they realize how futile resistance is. Reconstruction will be good for everyone in establishing a new order and helping former slaves to fit into society. Sensible people will prevail. They must prevail." Even as she said the words, she felt a twinge of doubt. Her own ordeal had punctured her confidence.

"We can only pray that will be so. The people of Faubourg Tremé are willing to work hard to bring themselves up in this world. This school is just the beginning of what we can accomplish—" He stopped. "My, the children are getting loud."

Screams that exceeded playful noises came from the play yard. Juliana hurried to the back door but could not open it.

"It's blocked," she cried.

"The front door is, too." Amelia pulled on the doorknob and then pounded on it. "Let us out!"

The sound of cursing, shouting voices filtered into the room. A front window shattered, and a lantern smashed to the floor. Kerosene splashed widely and burst into flames near a wooden bench. A second lantern ignited paper and books.

"The children!" Reverend Adams staggered to the back window. With Winnie's help, he raised it. "Run, children, run and hide," they yelled.

Amelia's skirt had begun to smolder where she had come too close to the flame, and Juliana doused the flame with a ladle of water from the drinking pail.

"We must get out of here." Stinging smoke filled her lungs. Would they all die? She ran to the unbroken front window. Masked men on horseback leveled guns at the front of the building.

"This way." Reverend Adams called them to the back window. "You go first." He shoved Winnie through the tall opening with his good arm. "Ladies, hurry!" His voice resonated with urgency.

Juliana and Amelia crawled out in turn, landing in a heap on the ground. Just as Reverend Adams stuck his leg out, Juliana stood up.

"Pearl!"

He disappeared back inside and soon brought the coughing child to hand out to them. Amelia grasped Pearl and ran toward the back fence. Again, the minister put one leg through the window.

Amid the women's cries for him to hurry, horsemen rounded the back corner of the schoolhouse firing their guns. One man shot toward the window. Reverend Adams drew back inside but fire drove him out again.

Winnie and Juliana grabbed his arms and pulled him through the opening just as several gunshots sounded behind them. His body went limp, but they managed to drag him to the ground and yards away from the burning building.

"Stop! Oh, stop it!" Juliana screamed at the gunmen. "Why are you doing this?" She blocked their aim on Reverend Adams. They would have to kill her to get to him. Smoke stung her eyes and throat, but she must not let them shoot again.

The men shouted vile curses at her. One rider bumped her with his horse and leaned over her, his hot whiskey-breath almost knocking her over. "That's what uppity darkies get for trying to take over what don't belong to them. You tell these black sons of Ham that this is what happens to any of their menfolk who try to stir up their worthless hides to think they're equal with whites."

He leered at her, and she shuddered so hard that her knees almost gave out.

"As for you, missy, you'd better go back to where you came from. We've had enough of you Yankees—"

"Let's get out of here." Another man, whose voice sounded horribly familiar, shouted at the leader.

"Just shoot her," a third man called. "Don't leave witnesses."

"They'll hang us for shootin' a white woman," the first man responded. "Too bad she didn't die in the fire." To Juliana, he said, "Just remember what happened here. We're gonna keep these darkies in their place, and there's nothing you can do to stop us." He turned his horse and rode away, followed by the others.

Juliana could barely control her violent trembling enough to return to Reverend Adams. Winnie sat weeping and moaning on the ground with his head on her lap. She looked up at Juliana.

"He's gone." Her vacant stare and expressionless tone revealed her state of shock.

Juliana knelt beside Reverend Adams's body and started to press her ear to his chest. Then she saw the wound to the back of his head, where blood poured out.

"Yes," Juliana whispered. She began to tremble, and rage shot through her. "Murderers!" she screamed. "Wretched murderers!"

Amelia! Where was she? Juliana had last seen her racing away with Pearl. She scanned the yard and then dashed to the back fence and searched up and down the alley. Whimpering drew her attention to the far corner of the yard. Behind the outhouse, Amelia sat rocking Pearl, who clung to her and sobbed. She rose and carried the child to Juliana, who embraced them both as they watched the schoolhouse inferno destroy all their hard work and dreams.

Gradually, children emerged from their hiding places and gathered together. Adults came running from neighboring houses and formed a bucket line from the pump down the street to the burning schoolhouse. But their attempts seemed futile for the task.

Jack hurried to Juliana. "Miss Harris, what's gonna happen now? Will you still help us?"

"I don't know what's going to happen, Jack."

His posture slumped, mirroring her despair. How could she make hopeful promises when she felt so defeated?

"The reverend said it wouldn't be easy, so we have to be brave." He touched her shoulder. "Please don't give up on us." He glanced at his sister, still in Amelia's arms, and sprinted away to take his place on the bucket line.

Juliana's eyes stung from the heat of the fire, but she could not look away. Did this murder and burning foreshadow the doom of all their hopes for Reconstruction? Was this kind of madness the legacy that southern white men wanted to pass on to their children?

Dear God, please don't let it be so. ❋

CHAPTER THIRTY-SIX

✷ ✷ ✷ ✷

"I'll meet you at the *Bonnie June*." André rode beside Cordell on their way to the wharf. "I want to stop by the warehouse and get Father's silver-handled cane."

"Sure thing." Cordell reined his dappled horse toward the right while André veered left.

The early afternoon sun shone warm and bright, a harbinger of a good voyage to come. André pulled in a deep breath. The smell of the river air lifted his spirits as he anticipated being in command of a ship again, especially because the steamboat was so much like his blockade-runner. Fortas, his navigator, had traveled the Mississippi for years, and that would make up for his own lack of river experience. In spite of the concerns at home and his aching heart over Juliana, he eagerly anticipated this beginning of a grand new life.

When he returned, maybe he could find a way to win her heart. Thinking of all the times they had encountered each other, he could only surmise that God had planned their "accidental" meetings. Once he cleared himself of the false accusations, surely then she would receive him. They could begin their friendship again and plan when they wanted to keep company, which for him would mean every day. Somehow, however, he must find a way to diminish Miss Randolph's poisonous influence over Juliana. But all of that was in the future. Now he must concentrate on the task before him.

He rode Rénard toward the warehouse, taking one last glimpse of the city before his three-month absence. Near the French Quarter, black smoke rose in a plume above Faubourg Tremé. Some poor soul probably caught his wooden shotgun house on fire just trying to cook a meal. Those flimsy hovels should be against the law.

Were the slave quarters on our plantation any safer?

André shook his head and grunted. The list of slave owner offenses never seemed to end.

He found the cane in the locked cabinet in his office. This one was his favorite. He kept it there to carry when he did business on the docks. Now as he traveled, it would contribute to the distinguished style of his black suit and silver cravat. He took out a handkerchief and rubbed a bit of tarnish from the silver horse's head handle and gave the cane a twirl. He would make a jaunty picture. A man with a cane always appeared confident and well-bred.

He gave the handle a little twist and pulled a sword from the stick. Along with the Colt in his shoulder holster and the Bowie knife in a sheath strapped to his calf, he was fully armed and prepared for any ruffians he might encounter along the river.

Back in the saddle, he urged Rénard to a brisk trot, wending his way between cargo crates, wagons, and robust stevedores who filled the docks. Despite rundown warehouses and many faltering or ruined businesses, New Orleans was becoming a bustling port again, and he was in the thick of it. What a satisfying feeling it gave him, as if good things were about to come his way.

Ahead at the *Bonnie June,* he saw Cordell with ten or more uniformed men. Were they police or soldiers? Panic enveloped him. They had come to arrest him at last. He reined Rénard to a halt a hundred feet from the ship. At the same moment, they spotted him and seemed to be waiting for his next move.

What now, Lord?

Should he run for it? Ride to Augustus and accept his offer of sanctuary in Chile? Lose them in the maze of the French Quarter and find a way to head out west? No plan took root in his mind, but a deep and certain peace filled his breast. He gently nudged Rénard forward with his heels and rode toward the group.

"Good afternoon, gentlemen. May I surmise you have not come to wish me bon voyage?"

"André Beauchamp?" The police sergeant who appeared to be in charge held his hand on the gun strapped to his belt.

André tipped his hat. "I am he."

"Mr. Beauchamp, keep your hands where I can see them."

André lifted both hands with palms upward and held them at waist level. "May I dismount, sir?" He used his strongest southern inflection and steadily stared at the police sergeant. The man's expression did not change. Was he a Yankee? Why hadn't André escaped when he had the chance?

Because I'm innocent!

"Take him off the horse." The sergeant waved several men toward him. They rushed to obey.

Rénard whinnied and reared up. André was forced to grip him hard with his knees and grasp the saddle.

"Don't let him get away," the sergeant shouted.

One man grasped Rénard's reins and three officers pulled André from the saddle. They roughly searched him, ripping his new black frock coat and seizing his cane and pistol.

"Have a care, you fools." The protest involuntarily escaped his lips.

"It will go in my report that you resisted arrest, Mr. Beauchamp. You would do well to cooperate from now on." The sergeant pointed to an enclosed, horse-drawn wagon with City of New Orleans Police painted on the side. "Tie him up and take him away."

One officer pulled André's hands behind him and tied them with rough ropes.

"You're making a mistake," cried Cordell. "Mr. Beauchamp hasn't done anything wrong. He hasn't broken the law."

The sergeant whirled around and poked a finger into Cordell's chest. "Boy, I told you to keep your mouth shut."

"André!"

"Pray, Cordell. Pray."

Lifted and thrust into the wagon, André couldn't keep his balance. He landed on his side with a groan, and the bruises from last night's abduction cried out in complaint. Surely this time a rib had broken.

The wagon door slammed shut, and a loud click announced it was locked.

As the wagon clattered over the rocky and rutted dirt streets, André struggled to sit up against the bench on one side. Dust filtered in to clog his lungs and raked his lungs as he painfully coughed it out.

Why hadn't he fled? What madness made him think these people would be reasonable?

The once friendly afternoon sun now heated the wagon like an oven. Sweat poured from André's face, but no breeze entered the small space to cool him.

"God, why are You doing this to me? Help me, please. I swear I'll…" No, he would make no promises. *"I'm just asking for mercy, Lord. Mercy and justice."*

He pulled his knees up and hung his head.

"Mercy and justice, Lord, mercy and justice," he repeated along the endless road to the police station.

At least he hoped that was where they were taking him.

⁕

Juliana picked at her roast beef and mashed potatoes smothered with gravy. The aroma tempted her, but the fire had scorched her throat, making it hard to swallow. Further, her stomach threatened to return anything she might eat. Glancing across the table, she saw that Amelia was having a similar problem.

"Juliana, you must eat." Mrs. Randolph gazed at her with loving concern. "And you, too, Amelia. You both must keep your strength up. We don't know what the coming days will bring."

"Now, Eleanor, don't prod the young ladies. They have endured enough this day." Mr. Randolph had returned to his place at the head of the table and as head of the house. Yet the lines around his eyes revealed his weariness. "This tragedy was the work of wicked men. They will be caught and punished."

"How can you say that?" Amelia dabbed at her tears with a napkin. "You didn't see the hatred in their eyes. Not one of these Southerners can be redeemed. They would have killed the children if they hadn't run away to hide."

Mr. Randolph propped his forehead on his hand and groaned. "My poor daughter. I despair to think of what you and Juliana have suffered." He looked up. "Yet I wonder if they waited until the children were playing outside before they locked you inside the house." His voice trembled as he spoke. "Perhaps they only wished to harm…"

Juliana shivered at the memory. Never in her life had she felt such terror, not even when Dupris had struck her and threatened to sell her into slavery. "Or perhaps they knew that there would be a public outcry if they murdered ch-children. Poor Reverend Adams." She pressed her handkerchief to her mouth to keep from sobbing anew. "Such a good, wise man. How I hope they catch those dreadful men." Her heart wrenched within her at the terrible memory.

"Would anyone in this city care about that?" Helena had been silent for most of the meal, and her former coolness to Juliana had been replaced by warm glances and sympathetic smiles.

"Why, isn't that the whole purpose of the Freedmen's Bureau?" Mrs. Randolph asked. She glanced toward the door. "Yes, Jerome, what is it?"

The butler stood just inside the room. "Excuse me, ma'am, but Miss Juliana has a visitor…a gentleman. Shall I tell him to wait in the drawin' room?"

"Is it Dr. Mayfield?" Helena scooted her chair back until her mother's "tsk" and raised eyebrows corrected her. She stared down at her plate and pouted.

"Surely not that horrid Mr. Beauchamp." Amelia's eyes narrowed.

Juliana almost laughed at their conjectures, but her heart felt too heavy. She doubted Mr. Beauchamp would dare to show his face at this house ever again. With a glance to include Mrs. Randolph, she turned to Mr. Randolph. "May I receive him?"

He appeared weaker to her, as if the dreadful happenings of the last two days had at last overwhelmed him. "I will go first and see who it is."

"No, please." Juliana could not bear to see him exert any more energy. "Jerome will be with me."

With permission granted by her host and hostess, she rose and walked toward the drawing room, realizing that she was not prepared to greet guests.

Even before the fire died down, the people of Faubourg Tremé insisted that she and Amelia go home to safety. Both of them had taken full baths, put on fresh clothes, and brushed their hair with cleansing powder. Yet Juliana could still smell smoke. Her visitor would simply have to endure it. She felt a moment of nervous antici-pation as she approached the drawing room. Who could be visiting her now?

A tall, distinguished-looking gentleman of fifty-some years stood by the fireplace. His light brown hair was handsomely graced with strands of silver, and a look of expectancy filled his bright blue eyes.

"Daisy!" He strode across the room with arms extended.

"Papa!" Juliana ran to her father's arms. Safe in his strong embrace, she could at last surrender all claims to her own strength. She wept into his shoulder, not asking what miracle had brought him to New Orleans just when she needed him most.

✦✦✦✦✦

"Daisy?" Amelia laughed softly, as though afraid to find humor in anything after the day's events. Seated in the drawing room with the others, she leaned toward Papa. "Reverend Harris, why on earth do you call her Daisy?"

Papa chuckled, and his deep, warm laugh sent reassurance surging through Juliana's heart. "Because she was as pretty as a daisy when she was born. And because her older sisters could not pronounce her first name, Dorcas." He took Juliana's hand and held tight. "I shall endeavor to remember to address you by your middle name, as all your new friends do."

"We are grateful for the crates of clothing you've brought." Mrs. Randolph sipped her tea and then set her cup down on the coffee table. "I shall write to thank the kind-hearted donors, but would you also convey our gratitude to them when you go home? Many needy people will be clothed by their generosity."

"It will be my pleasure, Madam," Papa said. "The Christian people of Boston are eager to help in any way that they can."

Gradually, through his grasp, Juliana could sense a release of the tension that had gripped him when he saw her bruised cheek and smelled the smoke still clinging to her, when she told him of the last two terrible days—the death of the remarkable Reverend Adams and the burning of the schoolhouse.

"Sir," Mr. Randolph said, "your daughter does credit to you and your wife. She is a kind and courageous young lady."

"Thank you, sir." Papa bowed his head slightly in acceptance of the compliment. "My Daisy, my Juliana, has always been an independent young lady, even as a small child. I could not keep her in Boston with her sisters and brother. She was determined to serve the Lord in a more challenging city, as though we did not have enough to do there at home." Papa's eyes glowed with affection. "When my son-in-law Isaiah spoke so highly of your family's hospitality to him during the war, she knew she would find kindred souls with whom to minister here in New Orleans."

"After hearing of the events of the past several days," Mr. Randolph said, "do you regret your decision to trust her to our care?" His appearance had improved the moment Papa had arrived, as though another man's presence in the house bolstered and renewed his flagging strength. Now the lines on his face once again deepened with concern.

Papa studied his host's face for a moment. His expression was one Juliana knew well—the very picture of Christlike kindness and love. In that pause before he answered, he was praying for God's wisdom. Now he shook his head. "No, my friend, I do not regret it. When we received the telegram from Juliana informing us that you had been shot, I felt God's urging to come to New Orleans, for I wished to ascertain that we had not misunderstood His leading for her. Not once have I felt that we erred. The Almighty has taken far better care of her than either of us could, although I must admit her injury is shocking." He brushed her cheek with the back of his hand. "But when I realize she could have disappeared from that wicked establishment without anyone knowing her whereabouts, I see His faithful protection."

Mr. Randolph sighed, clearly relieved. "Thank you, sir. We love her as one of our own daughters, but I fear I have been a poor protector. I continue to wonder if I could have avoided the shooting."

"Oh, Father, how could you possibly have avoided it?" Amelia sat up on the edge of her chair. "Reverend Harris, my father is not the only Unionist who's been shot. Even though our army has occupied the city for over three years, they haven't been able to protect us all the time." She huffed out her irritation. "I'll never understand why General Butler turned law enforcement over to civil authorities back in '62 when it should be Union soldiers with that power. We have been the target of surreptitious assaults and even murder. At least this time we have a competent police detective on the case." She sent a triumphant glance around the room. "The gunman has been identified, and Sergeant Wallace has assured me they would arrest him today and charge him with attempted murder."

Juliana swayed in her chair, and Papa glanced at her with a questioning look. She had no need to answer him. She could see that he read her distress, for he sent back a subtle wink of reassurance and the minutest of nods. Dear, dear Papa. He always understood.

But could he help to mend her broken heart? ✸

CHAPTER THIRTY-SEVEN

✯ ✯ ✯ ✯

"Who is this young man who has won your heart?"

Papa's gentle voice carried through the now-empty drawing room. He studied Juliana with his searching stare, the one that always uncovered the truth. At least she and her sisters and brother thought so. No matter what the situation, each had learned it did no good to dissemble, for Papa's wisdom and love always prevailed.

She glanced beyond him toward the closed drawing room door. Helena had a bad habit of eavesdropping and might have lingered behind after the rest of the family retired. Satisfied that she and Papa were alone, Juliana at last permitted herself a few tears of weariness.

"I didn't mean to love him, Papa, and I never tried to see him. Yet everywhere I went, he happened to be there, too." She told him of meeting André on the docks, at the dry goods store, at the opera and church, and even in the park. "We discussed the serious differences in many of our opinions and agreed that our friendship must proceed carefully." She picked at the crocheted doily on the arm of her chair. "But when I comprehended what a wicked slave master he had been,

I could no longer think of accepting his attentions, no matter what my heart felt."

"Yet you still feel some attachment to him." Papa reached over and took her hand.

She nodded. "When he rescued me from that...that b-brothel, I thought my heart would shatter. I knew in that moment that I loved him completely, and yet for what he had done to Gemma when she was just a child and his helpless slave, I despised him at the same time. I was so devastated that I couldn't think straight."

"Hmm." Papa rubbed his hand across his chin and frowned. "Do you think he is a Christian?"

She released a quiet, unladylike snort. "Oh, I'm sure he thinks he is. All of those wretched slave owners claimed to be Christians."

Papa chuckled. "Oh, my little Daisy, listen to what you're saying."

Juliana pressed her lips into a line for a moment as she considered her words. "But how could they be Christians and yet keep other people in cruel bondage, beating them and misusing young girls?" She blushed to mention such a thing to him. "They even called slavery a 'peculiar institution,' which is enough proof to me that deep down they knew it was wrong."

He shook his head, as if he had difficulty understanding it, too. "I suppose it is because the heart is deceitful above all things and desperately wicked, just as the prophet Jeremiah says. Even we Christians can excuse any habit or action when changing our ways might prove inconvenient or costly."

Her own foolish actions came to mind. "I have observed this, too. Now you can see why I cannot follow my heart. I cannot permit myself to love such a complete reprobate."

He tilted his head and raised an eyebrow in a questioning expression. "A reprobate? Did you not tell me less than an hour ago that he saw to the care of your friend, Reverend Adams, after he was wounded?"

"Well, yes," Juliana pondered the idea for a moment. Did that kindness prove André might alter his views toward Negroes? Suddenly, she longed to ask him, longed to know if he would grieve when he learned of his former slave's tragic murder.

"Then might he not repent of his cruelties and immoralities?"

"I suppose so." Her heart began to feel lighter. "Oh, I hope so."

"Will you forgive him for his past if he does?"

Certainty swept through her. "Yes, yes, I will. How can I fail to forgive him when I have not always done the right thing myself?"

Papa smiled his approval of her words. "It's important to realize that so that we avoid self-righteousness." Then his expression turned grave. "Do you suspect that this man whom you love could have shot our Mr. Randolph?"

She envisioned André's blue eyes, much like Papa's in clarity and honesty. He had not hidden from her his bitterness against Mr. Randolph, yet his demeanor never revealed any guilt in regard to the shooting. Had she been wrong to accept Amelia's assertion?

"I fear I cannot trust my own judgment in this."

Papa appeared to consider her words for a moment. "Of all our children, your mother and I have always trusted your judgment the most."

Juliana felt a surge of happiness fill her breast. She had never known that.

"Otherwise," he said, "we would not have permitted you to come to New Orleans." He stared across the room for a moment and then turned back to her. "I cannot grant you permission to obey your heart's longings until I meet this man. Will you give me leave to visit him?"

Relief flooded her weary body and mind. She rose from her chair to throw her arms around him. "Oh, Papa, would you do that for me?"

◆═┝╢◈╟┥═◆

Dawn sent a dim light into the jail cell where André sat slumped against the stone wall. His wrists stung from rope abrasions, his ribs ached, and he had refused the disgusting slop they had served for supper the night before. The stifling air reeked of every sort of human stench, and several of his cell mates lay on the floor sleeping off their drunkenness with loud snores. Vermin crawled on some of them. A seedy looking miscreant stared at him across the fifteen-foot space and snickered.

"Say, Dandy, what are you in for, overdressing?"

The man's chortling laugh reminded André of a grunting pig. Rather than rise to the challenge of the insult, he ignored him. Somehow the guards had failed to find the knife strapped to his leg, so if the man attacked him, he would have a way to protect himself.

He had slept little during the night, partly because of the pain in his body and partly because of the grief in his heart. He had done a poor job of caring for his family, and now the one thing he had thought would be successful had failed as surely as if the *Bonnie June* had sunk with her cargo. Would Augustus find another captain? Would he decide that Bernard should take his place? And what of Juliana? No, he could not let himself think of her, for he had no doubt she would find happiness with the Yankee doctor. Mama's care was now his deepest concern. Who would look out for her if he was sent to prison?

All through the night he had prayed for each matter that troubled him, but in the deep darkness before dawn, he had grown weary of his battle against despair. Once again he could only send up a silent cry, *Dear Lord, where are you?*

Now a shaft of sunlight shone through the small window above the jail cell. Somehow its bright warmth seeped into his soul and brought a glimmer of hope, although nothing had occurred to warrant it.

No matter what happens, I will trust You, Lord. I know You will care for Mama.

"Beauchamp!" The jailer banged through the outer jail door and approached the barred space where André sat with his fellow prisoners. "You got company." The short, burly jailer rested one hand on his holstered gun and stuck a key in the lock. "Out." He jerked his head toward the exit door.

André stepped out of the cell. "Who is it?"

"I ain't your butler." The man spit tobacco through the vertical bars into the putrid chamber pot on the other side. "This way."

He shoved André toward the door, then down a hallway and into a small room. "Don't try anything" was his parting comment before locking the wooden door.

André glanced around. The gray-walled room was furnished with a bare wooden table and several plain chairs. The only window had iron bars outside the glass. Even if no barriers existed, he would not have attempted to escape. He would face the charges against him and prove them wrong. However, he did try to open the window to let out some of the room's stale cigar smell, to no avail.

This must be where prisoners conferred with their lawyers. Had Augustus's snitch told him about his arrest? After André's rudeness last night, did the old man care? He would not count on it. Rather, he would cling to that mysterious ray of hope that had pervaded his soul only moments ago in the cell.

André rubbed his eyes and slumped down into one of the chairs. He yawned, crossed his arms on the table, and laid his head down, trying to ignore the pain in his ribs. He had no idea how much time passed before the sound of a key in the lock snapped him awake. He pulled in a deep breath to clear his head and staggered to his feet. Then he dropped back down again.

Charles Randolph entered, followed by another man.

"What do you want, Randolph?" Had the man come to taunt him? Was this his lawyer or a prosecutor?

"Good morning, Mr. Beauchamp." Ignoring André's question, Randolph sat across the table. The other man leaned against the wall by the window, his arms crossed.

"Just knock on the door when you want out, Mr. Randolph," the jailer said.

"Thank you, sir." Randolph nodded to the departing officer and then looked across the table at André. "Your demeanor makes it clear you have no use for me, and yet there was a time when your father and I were the best of friends."

André snorted his disgust. "Friends do not falsely accuse innocent men."

Randolph leaned forward, his thin, pale visage exuding sorrow. "I swear to you, André, I did not conspire against François. It is true that when Louisiana seceded, he and I broke off our friendship. But I never had cause to accuse him of the Butler conspiracy. Why would I wish to destroy a man whose friendship I hoped to regain when the conflict ended? Did no one ever tell you that I tried to prove his innocence to the authorities?"

André sat back, glaring at Randolph and glancing at his companion. He tried to maintain a severe expression, as when he had questioned recalcitrant sailors on his ship. But the sincerity on Randolph's face cut through his façade. A stream of peace flowed into his chest and flooded his whole being. In that moment, he knew the truth: this man had not brought about his father's hanging, even though all suspicions pointed to him.

"I came here today," Randolph continued, "because of that deep friendship with your father. To honor his memory, I have forgiven you for"—he cleared his throat, as though loathe to speak the word—"for the shooting. Furthermore, I will do all I can to make certain the charges against you are dropped."

André blinked once and looked him directly in the eyes. "But I didn't shoot you."

Randolph leaned forward again. "I saw you, André, just as surely as I see you now. You stood across the street from my house, raised your pistol, and aimed right at me. Your face may have been hidden by shadows and a broad-brimmed straw hat, but your posture and form and clothing could not be mistaken."

André straightened in his chair and looked evenly into Randolph's eyes. "Sir, I swear to you before God and this witness that I did not shoot you." *Bernard!* André clenched his jaw and balled his fists. It had to be more of Bernard's work. But why would he shoot Randolph?

Randolph glanced over his shoulder at the other man. "What do you think? Am I mad? Is he telling the truth?"

The man moved to place his hands on the table and bent forward. His intense stare almost unnerved André, but he refused to flinch. In fact, something about the stranger inspired his confidence. He stood and reached out to him.

"How do you do, sir? I am André Beauchamp."

The man stood tall and firmly clasped his hand. "Pleased to meet you, Mr. Beauchamp. I'm Jeremiah Harris."

André almost staggered back a step, almost sat down. But with a quick, bracing breath, he held firm. "Reverend Harris? Juliana's... Miss Harris's father?" He was babbling. *The man must think me a fool.*

"One and the same." The minister continued to hold André's hand in a firm grasp, and his eyes, clear and honest, held his attention with a genuine, reassuring smile.

André forbade himself to tremble under his scrutiny, but every part of him felt like an awkward schoolboy. He'd had the honor of meeting President Jefferson Davis and General Robert E. Lee. But never in his life had he met a man whose good opinion he craved more.

Reverend Harris freed his hand and clapped André on the shoulder. "Sit down, my friend."

Those four words supplied all that André needed to know. A rush of joy filled him. Juliana still cared for him. Otherwise her father would not be here. He released a deep, quiet sigh of relief. The glimmer of hope he had felt earlier had not been for naught.

The minister pulled up a chair. "What can we do to help you?"

André rested his forearms on the table to relieve the pressure on his ribs. "The evidence they have, my coat and gun, were stolen. I've no doubt that my housekeeper's son took the gun, but I'm perplexed about my frock coat." False evidence, but far more condemning than André's former suspicions about Randolph.

He searched his memory. When did he first miss the coat? He had worn it to work and had taken it off due to the heat.

"Dupris!"

Randolph jolted. "Dupris? What's that criminal got to do with it?"

"He came to my warehouse to offer me a partnership on the same day you were shot. While I was out, he must have stolen it from my office and passed it off to the gunman so he could appear to be me."

Randolph grunted. "I hope you had the good sense to turn that partnership down. The man is a crook and a turncoat."

André let the first remark pass. "Why a turncoat?"

Randolph grimaced. "I hesitate to say this, André, because it hasn't been long since we stood on opposite sides. With political matters as they are in the city, sometimes it's difficult to remember we are not still at war. However, I must tell you that I feel certain Dupris spied for both sides during the conflict, using whatever would give him the best advantage and profit."

"I'd heard that rumor." André glanced at Reverend Harris, whose look showed he knew André was holding something back. He would have to watch this man with a probing stare. He had a right to scrutinize his daughter's suitor, but André would solve his father's murder and his own betrayal by himself. His first move would be to find out where Augustus stood in all of this. The second would be to discover how Bernard and Dupris were connected. The third would be to make all the right people pay for Father's death.

"Are you still willing to help me gain my freedom?" He looked at Randolph and then the minister.

"I'll be proud to do it." Randolph stood slowly, wincing no doubt from pain, and shook André's hand. He walked to the door, knocked for the jailer, and requested escort to the police chief.

Reverend Harris rose to follow.

André reached out to touch his arm. "May I speak with you alone for a moment?"

"Certainly." He sat back down, and his face lit with interest. "What may I do for you?"

André swallowed hard. Perhaps this was not the proper time to speak to him, but he might not have another chance.

"Reverend Harris, sir, we have not met under the best of circumstances, but I must tell you…that is, I…" He cleared his throat. "I am very fond of your daughter, and I crave your good opinion. Will you give me a chance to prove to you that I am a man of character, that I am innocent of the charges laid against me?" His mouth was dry by the time he finished the question.

Reverend Harris clapped him on the shoulder. "Mr. Beauchamp, if you are innocent, God will provide a way for you to prove it. You do seem to be a decent fellow, so much so that I'll do everything I can to help you clear your name."

Profound relief filled André's breast. "Thank you, sir. I could not wish for anything more from you." *Except your permission to court your daughter.* ✳

★ ★ ★ ★

Amelia leaned into Juliana's arms on the drawing room couch and gripped her hand. "Please read the letter, Mother."

Seated in the adjacent chair, Mrs. Randolph held a thick brown envelope that had arrived a few minutes before. "Are you certain you don't want to wait until your father returns?"

Amelia glanced toward the door, as if he might walk through though it, although he had been gone less than an hour. "No, I want to hear it now."

"It might be happy news." Helena sat on the other side of Amelia and held her sister's other hand.

"We can hope so." Juliana tried to sound cheerful, but she had written many letters to families of men who had died at the mission, often returning to loved ones the tokens they had carried into battle. Amelia had said the handwriting on this one was unfamiliar, which bode ill for announcing any happiness.

Mrs. Randolph broke the seal and pulled out a small picture.

Amelia gasped and reached for her tiny portrait. "This was the memento I gave to Captain Billings." She sniffed back a sob and looked at her mother. "The letter?"

Mrs. Randolph unfolded it and brushed away tears. "Juliana, would you please? I fear I cannot make out the writing."

Juliana took the letter and read.

Der Mis Randuf,

I rite to you today with hevy hart. My comandin oficer capin Billins died at Andersonville prison last Janary 12 or 13. He ast me to send this picher back to you an to say he loved you. He was a brav man an I was proud to serv under him. He was at pece with God when he died.

I wud have rit sooner but I hav not yet recoverd from my ordele. They say they wil punish the prison comander for what he done.

My wif has rit this for me, as I lost my rite hand.

God bless you, brav lady.

Your servant, Junius Bedford, Ohio

Much practice at the mission had enabled Juliana to decipher ill-formed and misspelled words. She also had learned how to restrain her tears of sympathy when others were suffering. But this time, she joined the Randolph ladies in sobbing out her sorrow over a good man's death, even though she had never known him. Once again, she wondered how men who claimed to be Christians could behave as cruelly as the commander of the Andersonville Prison, where hundreds of Union soldiers had starved to death.

"I did love him," Amelia said through her tears. "I truly did."

Juliana ached for her. Amelia also loved Blake Sutter. How difficult it must have been to have a divided heart.

"He was a fine man," Mrs. Randolph added.

"Miz Randolph?" Jerome stood at the drawing room door. "You and Miz Juliana has a guest. A lady, ma'am. May I show her in?"

Juliana traded a look with her hostess. Should they receive a visitor at a time like this?

As if sensing their concern, Amelia squeezed Juliana's hand and nodded to her mother. "It's all right. You both know I was expecting this news about Captain Billings. Please receive your guest. I need to be alone right now."

Juliana looked to Mrs. Randolph to respond.

"Very well. Amelia and Helena, you may be excused. Jerome, please show the lady in."

Amelia took her letter and linked her arm in Helena's. "Come, sister. I'm going to my room, and you have mending to do."

They left the room through the side door. Helena peeked back toward the opposite door only once on the way out.

Juliana followed Mrs. Randolph's example and stood to greet the visitor. The older woman gasped softly when Jerome ushered in Mrs. Beauchamp and Gemma. Juliana's heart lilted upon seeing them, but she remembered the decorum she had learned in her mother's parlor and waited for her hostess to speak first.

"Felicity." Mrs. Randolph hurried across the room and embraced Mrs. Beauchamp. "How nice to see you. How good of you to come." The emotion in her voice resonated within Juliana.

"Eleanor, my friend." Mrs. Beauchamp's English-accented voice sounded far stronger than it had two nights ago. "What a joy it will be to revive our friendship now that the war is over." She clasped Mrs. Randolph for a few moments while both wept softly.

Juliana crossed the room to embrace Gemma, but stopped short when Gemma took a backward step and stared down at the floor. The beautiful young woman wore a plain brown skirt, a white blouse, and a flour sack apron. Her lovely black hair was pulled back into a severe bun and covered with a scarf, as required by the old Black Codes. Juliana's annoyance sparked, but she worked to stifle it before pulling Gemma into a quick embrace.

"Miss Amelia and I have missed you, Gemma." Her voice trembled. "Have you been practicing your reading?"

Gemma's eyes widened. She glanced at Mrs. Beauchamp, who smiled and gave her a little nod. She looked back at Juliana with a shy grin.

"Yessum, I have. I read to Cordell every night, and he helps me speak proper…properly."

Juliana took a deep breath, not trusting herself to say anything until Mrs. Randolph set the tone for this visit. She would bide her time and extricate Gemma from her slave-like position one day soon.

"Please sit down." Mrs. Randolph waved one hand toward the cozy grouping of chairs and a settee near the fireplace.

"Come along, Gemma," Mrs. Beauchamp beckoned to her. "You may stand behind me." She chose a blue damask chair and sat on it like a duchess, smiling serenely at Juliana. "I fear I was not a good hostess the other night, Miss Harris. In addition to visiting Eleanor, I came to apologize to you."

"Thank you, ma'am." Juliana sat on the settee. "I'm so happy to see both you and my good friend. Gemma, come sit with me."

Mrs. Randolph gasped. "Juliana—"

"Please forgive my ignorance, Miss Harris." Mrs. Beauchamp raised her eyebrows, but her aristocratic smile remained. "I have never been to Boston. Is it customary there for servants to sit with you when you have visitors?"

Heat flamed up Juliana's neck and across her face. "No, ma'am." Mother would be mortified by her error and her rudeness.

"You know, of course, that we English abolished slavery in 1807."

"Yes, ma'am."

Mrs. Beauchamp's expression softened. "I understand that prior to the war you were an abolitionist. That is very admirable. The slavery issue has always troubled me." She gazed off across the room. "When I married my François, we planned to settle in England, where the economy was and still is structured quite differently than in these southern states. But his business did not go as planned, so we returned to his Louisiana. He acquired property from his mother's people, including slaves. I loved my husband, but I hated it all." She shook her head and stared down at her hands. "That does not excuse me for being a part of it."

"Miz Felicity, 'scuse me, ma'am," Gemma said, "but you always treated us real good. We all love you." Her fair face grew pink. "I'm sorry for speakin' out, but Miz Harris needs to know that."

Mrs. Beauchamp looked over her shoulder to give Gemma a little smile and nod. Her bearing bore not a whit of hauteur, only gentility and grace. She turned back to Juliana.

"I am explaining all of this to you because a certain person of our mutual acquaintance informed me of your concerns."

Juliana's embarrassment cooled under her kind gaze, even as her heart lightened. Not only had André told his mother about her, but he had addressed her deepest apprehension about him. Might this not betoken a change of opinion? "Please forgive my rudeness, Mrs. Beauchamp."

"We will not mention it again," Mrs. Beauchamp said. "However, I do want to ask you a favor."

"Yes, ma'am?"

"Our Gemma has great potential." A twinkle lit her eyes. "Since she will soon be married to a bright young businessman, she needs to continue her education. Will you see to that?"

Shame filled Juliana once again. She had condemned Mrs. Beauchamp without giving her a chance to reveal her true nature. What had Papa said about self-righteousness?

"Oh, yes, ma'am. I would be delighted to do that."

Mrs. Beauchamp winced suddenly and put her hand to her temple. "Mm. Forgive me, but my head…"

Gemma leaned over the back of the settee and touched her shoulders. "Miz Felicity, are you sure you don' want your medicine? I could run home and fetch it."

She shook her head. "Never again, Gemma. These headaches will go away soon. At least I hope so." Looking at Juliana, she said, "I understand I have you to thank for realizing I was being drugged."

"Yes, ma'am." Juliana would search as soon as possible for a remedy for Mrs. Beauchamp's pain that would not create another malady.

"Now, Eleanor," Mrs. Beauchamp said in her lovely accent, "we have dominated your drawing room long enough with this conversation. Shall we send these young girls out while we reclaim our friendship?"

Mrs. Randolph nodded her agreement. "I have waited for this moment, Felicity."

"Come, Gemma." Juliana rose quickly and reached out her hand. "Let's look at my pattern book. We both could use new clothes."

✦┉┅╫╢❀╟╫┅┉✦

"You don't need to go with me, Reverend Harris." André stood with the minister and Mr. Randolph outside the police station. "I'm just going to visit my grandfather to find out what he knows about all of this."

Reverend Harris set his hand on André's shoulder. "Son, I wonder about the wisdom of your going now. You couldn't have slept well in there." He nodded toward the building behind them. "Why not go home, rest, and put on fresh clothes." He pointed to André's torn lapel and dirt-stained suit.

"I won't be able to rest until this is settled." André avoided his stare and looked toward the nearby carriage where Jim-Jim sat waiting. "You should take Mr. Randolph home." Turning to the other man, he added, "I'm sure coming here hasn't been easy on him."

Randolph gave him a weary nod and put his hand on his chest. "I do believe I should return home, gentlemen. But I can drive you wherever you need to go on the way."

"No need to bother. I'll just walk," André said. "Good day, gentlemen. Thank you again for seeing to my release." Cane in hand, he started walking in the direction of the French Quarter.

"I'll return to your kind hospitality shortly, Mr. Randolph," Reverend Harris said. "Mr. Beauchamp, one moment." He fell in step beside André. "You must let me accompany you."

André stopped. "Sir, I am grateful for your concern, but…"

Reverend Harris stared into his eyes with an intense frown. "I feel strongly that I must go with you whether you wish it or not."

André studied his expression and, for the second time in their two-hour acquaintance, felt compelled to trust him. Yet he could not involve a minister, especially Juliana's father, in the trouble that would no doubt arise when he confronted Augustus. He sighed with frustration and shook his head. "Juliana will never forgive me if you're injured or worse trying to help me."

Reverend Harris put on an expression of wounded pride. "Young man, I've been in a few skirmishes in my lifetime. Don't count me out because of a few gray hairs *or* my occupation."

"Why, no, sir, I didn't mean you're incapable—" Now he had done it, insulted the man whose good opinion meant the world to him.

The minister laughed heartily and clapped him on the shoulder. "Of course you didn't. Now, we're wasting time. I'm eager to see the French Quarter again after all these years." He took André's arm and turned him in that direction. They soon fell into step, covering ground quickly.

"You've been to New Orleans before?" André found the man could keep up with his long stride.

"Back in '37, I came west with a broken heart and went home with this." He pointed to a pale, jagged scar on his tanned left cheek. "And a small measure of wisdom about human nature."

André looked at him with renewed respect. Perhaps it would be a good thing to have this man behind him when he confronted Augustus.

He would find out soon enough. ✳

CHAPTER THIRTY-NINE

✶ ✶ ✶

Without much effort, André grabbed the bars and crashed open Augustus's front gate and, to the dismay of the young boy guarding it, strode toward the house with Reverend Harris close behind.

"Massuh, please," the boy cried, "I'll be in a heap of trouble."

"I'll vouch for you," André called over his shoulder. He took the inside stairs two at a time, then hurried down the hallway.

The startled butler began to block him but apparently decided it was wiser to stand back against the wall. "Sir, please…"

"Is the old man in the drawing room?" Even as he asked the question, André could hear raised voices coming from the room. He open the door hard and entered.

Clearly alarmed, Augustus and Jacinta jumped to their feet. Bernard, who had been standing before them, seemed even more frightened. He started toward the opposite door.

"What's the meaning of this?" Augustus quickly regained his dignity and took a step toward the two men.

André pointed his cane at Bernard. "Get back in here and sit down."

"You'll not give orders in my house." Augustus's voice resonated with authority.

Bernard cringed but did not flee. His wide-eyed stare darted from one man to the other, and he fanned himself with a straw hat—André's hat! Had the spider at last invited the fly in for a mint julep? André glanced at Jacinta, whose pleased expression seemed to confirm his guess.

"Miss Jacinta." André gave her a deep bow. "I beg your pardon for this intrusion. I have some things to discuss with Mr. Beauchamp. Will you please excuse us?"

She smiled serenely. "Should you not have as many in your camp as possible?" She walked over and reached out to him. "Welcome."

André took her hand and kissed it. "I defer to your wisdom, dear lady." He glanced at his older companion, whose pleasant smile contrasted with the ready energy of his posture. "May I present Reverend Harris?"

She turned to the minister and presented her hand to him. "Welcome, Reverend Harris."

"I am honored, Miss Jacinta." The minister performed the proper honors.

"You have completed your rituals," Augustus said. "Now you may leave until I send for you."

"I'm not leaving until we have a little discussion." André eyed Bernard, who had begun to edge toward the door again. "Sit down, *uncle*."

"André…" Augustus raised a finger as if to scold.

Jacinta glided back to Augustus's side and grasped his hand. "We owe it to him to hear what he has to say."

Augustus frowned at her, but André could see his hesitancy. At last the old man gave her a decisive nod of his head. In a sudden and strange transformation, his regal posture lost its rigid, defensive stance and became that of a gracious host. He walked to Reverend Harris and extended his hand. "Welcome, sir. May I assume you are my worthless grandson's future father-in-law?"

Reverend Harris chuckled as he accepted the offered hand. "I'm honored to meet you, Mr. Beauchamp. As to my becoming André's father-in-law, that remains to be seen."

Augustus grunted out a short laugh. "Come sit down, then. If I must listen to the boy, I want to be comfortable."

The minister accepted the invitation, but André remained standing. The shifty look in Bernard's eyes concerned him, and he wanted to be prepared for anything that might happen.

"Well," Augustus said, "speak up, boy. What's troubling you? Why aren't you on your way up to St. Louis?"

"Don't act as if you didn't know," André said. "I was arrested yesterday for the Charles Randolph shooting. If it hadn't been for Reverend Harris and Randolph himself speaking up for me, I'd still be in jail awaiting that hanging you hoped for."

"Randolph?" Augustus's eyebrows lifted in genuine shock. Then he snorted. "Why would that Yankee care whether you live or die? He was responsible for François' death."

André exhaled a heavy sigh of disgust. "You'll never convince me that you ever cared about my father after he failed to be your toady." He waved his hand in an impatient gesture toward Bernard. "This is what you wanted in a son, someone who would do your bidding, no matter what you told him to do."

Augustus didn't look at Bernard. "I told you the other day, my son's death made me realize my…" He seemed unable to find the right word.

"Failure?" André offered.

Augustus grimaced. Jacinta, seated in the chair beside him, caressed his hand.

"Yes, my failure as a father. I am still offering to be as a father to you if you will give me the chance to do so." His expression had lost its arrogance, and he now appeared wounded.

"What about me?" Bernard stepped close, waved his hand roughly toward André, and hovered over the old man.

Jacinta moved closer to Augustus while Bernard continued shouting.

"Why do you want this *boy*, as you call him? I'm your blood just as surely as he or François, maybe even more so. I've done everything you told me. I've committed perjury, I've stolen, I've even tried to avenge my brother—"

"Silence!" Augustus moved Jacinta aside and sent him a warning look.

Bernard straightened, and his lips curled upward in a sneer. "Yes, *massuh*."

André traded a look of surprise with Reverend Harris.

"You shot Randolph." André stared at Bernard.

"What if I did?" His sneering face no longer resembled Cordell's kind visage.

André turned to Augustus. "And you would have let him frame me for it."

"No, I swear it, no." Augustus blanched. "Until Randolph remembered the description, I never thought they would find the gunman." He glared at Bernard. "You stole André's gun." It was a statement.

Bernard wilted under the look. "Yessir."

André guessed he didn't dare lie to Augustus.

"And the tan frock coat." Augustus said.

"No sir. That I got from Dupris—" He gasped and looked around the room, his eyes filled with horror.

"Dupris?" André saw the pieces coming together. Dupris, the reputed turncoat. Dupris, the conspirator. Dupris, his father's anonymous accuser.

"Dupris? You've been in league with that…" Augustus spouted a denigrating epithet. He turned to Jacinta. "You were right, my love. Bernard has been out to destroy André since he returned from the war."

"He has conspired against you even before that, my darling. He must have helped Dupris plot against François."

Augustus looked ill now. "And to think, I wanted him to kill an innocent man to avenge my son." He raised a shaking, accusing finger toward Bernard. "Get out of my house, you worthless toad."

"No." André took a step toward Bernard. "I'm going to wring the whole story out of him."

Bernard pushed aside his sack coat, pulled out a large knife, and yanked Jacinta up into his grasp. With the blade to her throat, he backed toward the door. "Don't move. Don't follow me. If you do, I'll kill her."

André drew the short sword from his cane and moved closer, sensing Reverend Harris right behind him.

"Jacinta," Augustus cried. He tried to rise but fell back in his chair, his hand on his heart.

"Augustus." She breathed out his name like a reassuring caress. With a glance sideways and down, she instructed her would-be rescuers, then twisted away from the knife and to the floor. A strangled gasp escaped her.

André lunged forward and thrust the sword into Bernard's arm. Bernard roared as the knife fell from his grasp. Reverend Harris seized it, and the two men wrestled him down and away from Jacinta's body. Several servants came running into the room.

"Tie him up." André relinquished his place to two capable men. He hurried over to Augustus, who knelt on the floor moaning and cradling Jacinta. A lacey curtain of blood across her fair neck formed a grotesque necklace.

"*Grandpère.*" He knelt beside the old man. "Let me see." He drew out his handkerchief and gently dabbed the edge of the wound. "Look, it's not deep. I think she fainted."

Augustus shook his head as if to clear it. "Yes, yes. She's all right." His voice sounded weak. "You're all right, my love."

Jacinta blinked and gave him a weak smile. He tried to lift her to the couch, but at André's insistence, he surrendered the task to younger arms.

With her safety assured, Augustus stood and turned to Bernard, who had ceased his useless struggle against the servants.

"Why did you betray me? I would have sent you to safety in Chile. I would have given you everything you needed."

Wincing in pain, Bernard glowered at him. "Everything but your name."

Augustus lifted his chin. "Why would I give you my name? You have no strength of character, nothing I would recognize as worthy of a Beauchamp." His lip curled in a sneer. "You failed every test I gave you."

"Father—" Bernard cried.

"Don't ever address me by that title." Augustus's regal voice reverberated throughout the room. He waved his hand with an imperious air and spoke to his servants. "Take him to the police."

"Wait," André said. "If you take him now, word will get to Dupris. I'm going after him."

"Not alone, my friend." As once before, Reverend Harris set a hand on André's shoulder, and his eyes held a hint of warning.

André studied the minister's expression. "I'll be all right."

"Yes, but will Dupris?"

André shifted uncomfortably. This man read him well. "Maybe so. Maybe not."

"I'm going with you." His voice resonated with authority.

"All right, then. Come along." Renewed exhilaration surged through André. He hoped for a long, close friendship with this wise man.

"André, Reverend Harris." Augustus sat on the couch cradling Jacinta.

The two men faced him.

"I am pleased to know that Miss Harris was unharmed in yesterday's fire."

"What?" Alarm filled André. "What fire?"

"I'll tell you as we go," Reverend Harris said.

With Augustus's promise to hold Bernard until they had arranged for Dupris's arrest, the two men departed. In the short blocks from Augustus's house to the Shady Moon, the minister told André of the previous day's disaster at the schoolhouse.

"Fortunately for me, I had my daughter safely in my arms before I heard about the tragedy." Reverend Harris shook his head. "It is beyond my comprehension how some men can be so evil as to destroy the benevolent works of others. I grieve for the good man who died simply because he wanted to read and to help educate his people."

Curtis! André forbade himself to succumb to sorrow. He knew who had done it. Would that he could disentangle himself from Reverend Harris right now. He would put an end to Dupris's masked assaults and attempted kidnappings and murders. With each thud of his footsteps on the pavement, he longed to tread his adversary under foot as he would a worm, for that's all Dupris was.

As they neared their destination, André saw several uniformed men a block from the Shady Moon. He turned to the minister. "Do you see those Yankee, eh, Union soldiers?" He pointed down the street. "I think we'll need them. Will you ask them to come?"

Reverend Harris gave him a skeptical glance but nodded. "Don't do anything foolish, André."

"I won't. I just want to make sure no one warns Dupris."

Once the minister hurried away, André entered the restaurant. Only a few customers patronized the dining room side. More sat in the saloon.

A different maitre d' from the one he had previously encountered stood guard near the front door. He scanned André's disheveled appearance with a sneer of distaste. "May I help you?"

"Will you please tell Mr. Dupris that a riverboat captain is interested in his plans for a floating casino?"

The man considered his words and became more agreeable. "Yes, of course. I'll tell him you're here. May I give a name?"

"François *le plus jeune.*" *François the younger* should confuse the man sufficiently.

"Thank you, Mr. Lepplejune." The man rushed away.

Within minutes, Dupris entered the lobby. "Beauchamp. What do you want? Did you get some sense in your head about our partnership?" His arrogant demeanor ate into André's gut. This was the man responsible for his father's death. This evil incarnate had threatened André, murdered Curtis, and kidnapped and nearly killed Juliana.

"No, but I did want to give you a little reimbursement." André reached into his coat and pulled out his gun. "Something to even our accounts." He stretched out his arm and took aim directly at Dupris's heart.

Dupris backed up. "Now, don't go doing something stupid." His voice wavered nervously.

The maitre d' started to turn away.

"Don't move." André felt awash in sweat. His eyes stung from it. His right arm trembled slightly. Could he do it? Could he put an end to this man's evil? Repay him for Juliana's suffering and Curtis's death?

Dupris turned and took a few steps.

André fired into the floor just beyond him. Women screamed and patrons shoved back chairs to take cover. "Don't move." André growled out the words again. He had to kill him. He had to pay him back. *God, help me. I don't want to be a murderer, but...*

"André, no." Reverend Harris' voice sounded behind him. The minister came close and slowly removed the gun from his hand. "The soldiers are here. I've explained our accusations. They'll take him to the police station and give us a chance to prove it all, including the lies that brought about your father's hanging. The army will want to question him about that."

André breathed out his relief.

"Thank God." ✽

CHAPTER FORTY

✯ ✯ ✯ ✯

"With several days of rest, Mr. Randolph will be fine." In the entry hall of the Randolph house, Dr. Mayfield addressed the Randolph ladies and Juliana. "I hoped he would want to go outdoors to enjoy this fine autumn weather, but today's visit to the police station was more strenuous than what I had in mind."

"Thank you, Dr. Mayfield," Mrs. Randolph said. "Now won't you join us for dinner? I believe Flora will have your favorite lamb stew prepared in just half an hour."

"Well..." In his dark blue army uniform, the doctor appeared as handsome as Juliana had ever seen him. His face glowed with expectation. "I do wish to speak to Miss Harris. Perhaps afterward, I can dine with all of you lovely ladies." He scanned the group, smiled, and settled his gaze back on his hostess. "With your permission, ma'am?"

"Of course." Mrs. Randolph waved her hand toward the drawing room. "Please make yourself at home. Come along, Amelia, Helena."

Helena turned toward the drawing room, but Amelia caught her by the arm and pulled her in the direction of the staircase. "This way, sister."

"Oh!" Helena pouted but did not resist.

Juliana pursed her lips to keep from laughing. Poor Helena.

"May I escort you?" Dr. Mayfield offered his arm to Juliana, and she accepted.

In the drawing room, he seated her on the couch, then sat beside her and held both of her hands. "Dear Miss Harris, I won't dissemble, nor will I attempt to be poetic." He cleared his throat and frowned. "How I wish I could offer you some sonnet of Shakespeare or, better still, Miss Browning, for their words would be far more appealing than my own."

Juliana felt her heart sinking. He was going to propose. If only Helena would return. She tried to loosen her hands from his grasp, but he held on firmly.

"Please permit me to speak directly. From the moment I met you, I have…have…um, this is very difficult."

"Then perhaps we should speak of something else." Juliana searched her mind for a suitable topic to redirect him, but nothing came to mind. No one had ever proposed to her, and she despaired to cause this good man any pain.

"No, no, I mustn't put it off. I shall soon be leaving the army and New Orleans, and I must have your response because…"

"Leaving the army. My, my. And going on to a bright new future, I suppose. Have you decided where you'll set up your private practice?"

He cleared his throat again. "No, not yet. It all depends upon our discussion today."

"Our discussion?" Juliana could not think of a single diversion. She saw such determination in his eyes that she decided to get it over with. "Why would that be?"

He laughed softly. "Why, surely you must know of my high regard for you."

She gave him a little smile. "I have great respect for you as well."

His smile broadened in response. "Well, then, you'll not be surprised when I say...when I ask you...Miss Harris, will you do the honor of becoming my wife?"

She did not answer right away but considered her words carefully. "Dear Dr. Mayfield, I shall not dissemble either. I admire you as both a physician and a Christian friend. However, I cannot accept your proposal. My..." She looked down, not able to watch the growing dismay on the kind, familiar face she had grown so fond of. Yet she must not give him any indication that she might change her mind. "My heart belongs to another."

After a few quiet moments, he released her hands and rose to stand in front of the fireplace and stare at the pastoral painting above the mantle. "Deep within me, I believe I knew that. Still, I hoped."

She watched the brave struggle on his countenance. "I shall forever be grateful to you for your medical instructions. The doctors at my father's mission were often in a hurry and could not take time to broaden my knowledge. They complimented my skill, as it was, but I suppose they thought me too young to learn more than simple nursing."

He turned to her. "What a shame. You are more than competent. You have taught me to trust your feminine instincts. I shall miss that."

"Thank you."

He came to kneel in front of her. "Dear Miss Harris, do promise me one thing."

She hesitated. "If I can."

"You have the most beautiful white teeth I have ever seen. Please, please take care of them as I suggested so that you may retain your beautiful smile, which brings so much happiness to others. Use that toothbrush I gave you, and do not forget to floss."

She clasped his hands and laughed with delight. "Oh, yes, Dr. Mayfield, I will. I will."

He glanced beyond her toward the door, then bent forward and kissed her on the lips. She sat stunned when he followed that by leaning closer and whispering in her ear. "It will be a fortunate man who wins your hand, dear friend."

Juliana pressed back into the couch to distance herself from his uncharacteristic and unsuitable advance. The loud slam of the front door echoed all the way into the drawing room, and she gasped out her relief.

"That must be Papa." And André? How she hoped so.

Papa walked into the room, and Dr. Mayfield quickly stood.

"What just happened?" Papa's frown of puzzlement unnerved her.

"What do you mean?" She rose from the couch and stood apart from the doctor. Had Papa seen the kiss? Her cheeks blazed with embarrassment.

"Uh, Reverend Harris, I presume." Dr. Mayfield reached out his hand as Papa approached. "I'm Robert Mayfield. Your daughter may have told you about me."

Papa shook his hand. "Yes. How do you do?" Not giving him a chance to answer, he looked at Juliana. "Mr. Beauchamp was on his way in here just ahead of me. He stopped at the door, then turned around and left."

Juliana gasped. "That means he saw…" She glared at Dr. Mayfield. "You did that on purpose."

He gulped and had the grace to look ashamed. "I cannot reconcile within myself that he is the right man for you."

Papa narrowed his eyes. "Sir, did you just propose to my daughter?"

Again, the poor doctor gulped. "Yes sir, I did. I know I should have asked your permission—"

"It wouldn't have mattered. Juliana's heart is set." Papa wore his stern expression, the one rarely seen on his kind face.

"Please forgive me, Miss Harris, Reverend Harris. I behaved like a cad."

Juliana felt so cross that she abandoned good manners to shrug and give him a curt nod.

At the doctor's apology, however, Papa's expression grew considerably more understanding. He took the other man's arm and led him toward the door. "I have a prescription for a broken heart, one that I benefited from as a young man. Go out west to the frontier and…"

They left the room, and she could not hear the rest of Papa's advice. So he once suffered a broken heart. In observing his devotion to Mother, she never would have guessed.

She dropped back down on the couch and sighed. Surely André would come back. If not, she would send Papa to explain it all.

She might even go with him and tell André herself.

The *Bonnie June* sailed southward on the Mississippi River on its way home to New Orleans. Trusting the helm to his able first mate, André sat in his cabin with Curtis's Bible before him, open to his favorite verses in Psalm 23. "The Lord is my Shepherd. I shall not want." He had no need to read the words, for they were engraved in his heart. Often during the war, he had recited, "Yea, though I walk through the valley of the shadow of death, I will fear no evil, for Thou art with me." After his short and desolate lapse of faith, he once again appreciated the reassurance of God's promises and the comfort of His presence. He had really needed it for these past three months.

The sting of losing Juliana had softened, but he knew he would never forget her. Why she had chosen Mayfield, he still could not understand. If her acceptance of the doctor's proposal had been less enthusiastic, he might have asked her where he had gone wrong, how he had failed her. But the delight on her face told him everything he needed to know. In spite of their shared attraction, she obviously preferred a Yankee husband, one who undoubtedly held all the same views.

If only she could know how his views had changed, how he had come to realize the wickedness of the ideas he had grown up with. He recalled the faith learned at his father's knee and wondered how such a sincere and godly man could have been so wrong about certain essential issues of life, especially those concerning the humanity of their slaves. How humbling to see that he himself had for so long been guilty of the same errors—sins, if called by the right name.

When he returned to New Orleans, he might go into politics. How else could he help to effect a change in the social system that sought to keep certain groups of people downtrodden? The structure of society must change, of course, or the South would forever be a place of turmoil.

Surely men of intelligence would be able to see the value of educating Negroes and bringing them into the economic system. After all, ever since New Orleans was first settled, free men and women of color had owned businesses, some earning great wealth, separate but somewhat parallel with whites, except that they could not vote. Why should anyone doubt their abilities to function fully in the new order? If anyone questioned his thinking, he could point to Cordell as a first-class example of a Negro with business acumen.

André laughed to himself. If not for the lovely Miss Harris— along with Cordell, Gemma, and Curtis—his thinking might never have changed. Whereas he once had fought to protect the southern way of life, he would now work to demolish it.

Lord, help us, your people, to see the way things should and must be.

He put Curtis's Bible in his valise. On his return, he would take it to Winnie and tell her what a comfort it had been to him.

He left his cabin and reclaimed his place at the helm just in time to steer the *Bonnie June* around the last big bend in the river before reaching home port. Sailing past familiar landmarks, he felt an aching contradiction—joy over returning home from a successful trip and sorrow that the woman he loved was lost to him forever.

Just after dawn, the steamship glided into its berth at the Dumaine Street wharf. Cargo was unloaded, and passengers disem-barked. Recalling Miss Harris's dismal arrival at the port, André made certain each person, especially the ladies, had transportation to their destination.

By early afternoon, the crew had secured the vessel. He supervised their pay and walked home to regain his land legs.

As his house came into view, he noticed the improvements right away. He had instructed Cordell to hire Percy to repair and paint wherever necessary. The results were impressive. He started to enter through the front door but decided not to break custom. When he came into the kitchen, Aunt Sukey gasped and dropped her spoon into a pot of gumbo.

"Lawdy, Mister André, what you doin' home?" She seemed more like her old self than last summer, but he still read hesitancy in her eyes.

André had long ago forgiven her deception. He gave her a quick hug of reassurance. "We sold the whole load sooner than expected and shipped a full cargo for export back to New Orleans." He took a spoon from the silver case and dipped into the pot on the stove. "Mmmm. Best gumbo in Louisiana."

Aunt Sukey beamed. "Thank you, suh."

"How's Mama. Is she upstairs or out shopping?" How he had prayed every day for her full recovery.

"Why, she's over at the Randolphs' house for the weddin' this afternoon. You oughta go over. They was saying they wished you could be there."

A knife twisting into his belly could not have hurt more than this news. What irony that he had arrived just in time for her wedding. "No, I think I'll just rest. It's been a good trip, but tiring."

"Now, André, don't think I can't see what you're thinkin', jus' like when you was a boy. You need to let bygones be bygones. Nobody over at the Randolph house has anythin' against you, and you got no cause to have anythin' against them."

He regarded her for a moment. Maybe she was right. At least by seeing Miss Harris married, he could put an end to it all.

"Thanks, Auntie. I'll go." He gave her a quick kiss on the cheek. After a quick cleanup and shave, he walked the five blocks to the house of his former enemy.

Every step brought him closer to the gallows of his dreams.

✦❖❀❖✦

Juliana dabbed away tears of happiness. Posing for a photographer in the drawing room, Amelia made such a lovely bride, and Blake was the handsomest of grooms. They had said their vows at Christ Church, and now the entire wedding party was gathered in the Randolph home for a reception.

The loud "poof" and flashing blaze of the photographer's lighting powder startled them all, but then they laughed, even as they waved away the smelly smoke that resulted.

"Felicitations and good wishes," the photographer said. "I'll have these pictures for you in a week."

While he gathered his large camera and other equipment, the family and their friends adjourned to the dining room, where pink punch and a tall white wedding cake awaited them.

Juliana mingled with the others, enjoying every moment of the occasion. She teased Helena about her plans to go out west to Colorado, asking if there might be a certain doctor she would look up once she got there. She traded cozy glances with Mrs. Beauchamp, whose company she had enjoyed several times a week for the past three months. And she looked with joy at her fully recovered host, who in turn gazed with pride at his lovely daughter, the bride.

Jerome, dressed in his new black suit and crisp white shirt, managed the serving of guests with quiet efficiency. When Etty approached him to whisper a message, he scanned the room and found Mr. Randolph. The two exchanged words, and Mr. Randolph beckoned to Juliana.

"We have another guest, but I believe you are the person who should greet him. Do you mind?"

Juliana's heart seemed to jump within her. Could André be back from his trip? "Not at all. Thank you."

She hurried out to the entrance hall but stopped at the sight of him. How handsome he looked. How tall and fit. How *depressed!* She approached him with what she hoped was an encouraging smile. Her heart pounded wildly.

"André," she breathed out. "Welcome." What a thing to say, when she really wanted to proclaim her love to him.

His posture was stiff, and he gave her a disapproving look. "Should you address me by my Christian name? What will your new husband think?" A tone of censure resounded in his voice.

She laughed. "Husband? The only husband I will have is you." Then she gasped. What a saucy thing to say. But Papa had told her André had asked to court her. Would he now think her shameless?

André's face took on a boyish look of confusion. "What about your Dr. Mayfield? I saw you accept his proposal."

She laughed again, recalling the doctor's mean trick. "I was promising him that I would brush my teeth."

André grinned. Then he chuckled. Then he laughed out loud.

"Oh, my beautiful Juliana, what a comedy of errors. All these months of despair for nothing."

"If you had not been in such a hurry to go to St. Louis, we would have been able to correct those errors. Poor Mr. Randolph suffered a relapse, and we could not leave him. Then later that evening, Papa and I searched for you, but you had already sailed away."

"But I was responsible to my investor and my crew. I had to go."

She looked up at him and decided she could gaze into those clear blue eyes for the rest of her life. "We shan't find something else to disagree on, shall we?"

He grinned. "Only for sport, my lady love." He grasped her hand, pulled her into the drawing room, and shut the pocket doors behind them.

When he drew her into his arms, she willingly complied.

"Miss Harris, would you do me the honor of becoming my wife?"

"Mr. Beauchamp, I would be delighted."

This time, when he kissed her—right on the lips—it was perfectly proper. Of that she was certain. ✳

READING GROUP DISCUSSION QUESTIONS

1. In July 1862, early in the Civil War, the Union Navy conquered Confederate forts at the mouth of the Mississippi River, taking New Orleans without firing a shot. Not only did this give the Union control of the mighty waterway, it protected the city from physical devastation such as that suffered by much of the South during the war. After the war, however, many political factions vied for control of the city, which led to political devastation that deeply affected the course of history for more than a century. White southerners were desperate to reestablish their power and way of life and to keep newly-freed blacks in a subservient position. Opportunistic carpetbaggers from the North sought riches and a foothold in the strategic Mississippi port city. Compare that political upheaval to the physical and political devastation left by Hurricane Katrina in 2006. Do you think New Orleans is still suffering from the effects of the pre-Civil War, slave-based economy of the South? If so, what do you think it will take to change that? What part should Christians of all colors take in this process?

2. Unlike today, in the mid-1800s American society as a whole had a high consciousness of God's movement in the affairs of mankind. When the Civil War pitted brother against brother, friend against friend, and Christian against Christian, each side believed its cause was God's will. Is it possible for true Christians in all integrity to find themselves on opposite sides of major issues? Are there issues today that divide true believers in Christ as seriously as states' rights/slavery did in the 1800s? What are those issues?

3. André Beauchamp returns home from fighting for the Confederacy in the Civil War to find his family in ruins. Although his home is undamaged, his father has been hung for a crime André feels certain he did not commit; his mother seems lost in a dream world; his only brother has died of yellow fever; and the family's cotton plantation is bankrupt. How does André respond? Is his response reasonable? How would you respond under similar circumstances? How does André change through the course of the story? What/who causes those changes?

4. Juliana Harris comes from a family of abolitionists, and she supports the cause with missionary zeal. Now that the war is over, she feels strongly that God has punished the South for holding people in slavery. Are her feelings justified? What does she learn through meeting real southerners? Do her feelings change? In what way? How does Juliana grow to maturity in other ways?

5. After the war, both former slaves and free persons of color thought they would now be given full citizenship and the right to vote. Why did their struggle for these rights require well over another century to be successful? Do African-Americans and other minorities where you live have the same rights as white Americans?

6. It has been said that the Union won the Civil War on the battlefield, but the South won the war of ideology. Is this true? In what ways? Are there problems in today's society that reflect the scars inflicted by that national tragedy? What can Christians do to effect a change for the better?

7.   Reverend Curtis Adams has forgiven André and his family for their cruelties to him and his family. Why does he not seek revenge? Would you consider him a Christ-figure in this story? In what ways? How does his forgiveness affect André?

8.   Before learning the truth about who shot him, Charles Randolph forgives André unconditionally based on his friendship with André's father. Then Randolph goes so far as to say he will see that the charges against André are dropped. How does this parallel Christ's forgiveness based on His relationship with His Father?

9.   Why did Cordell stay with André when they left the Naval Academy at the beginning of the war? Why did he stay with Mrs. Beauchamp after his master's death? Do you think these were wise decisions? What would you have done?

10. How had Cordell's loyalty affected André? Considering all that happened in the South after the war, do you think that André and Cordell could ever safely acknowledge their relationship in public?

11. What does Gemma represent in this story? Is she a tragic figure or a triumphant one? At the end of the story, how do you think her life will change? What will the future hold for any children she and Cordell may have after they marry?

An Interview with Author
Louise M. Gouge

1) **When did you first realize that you wanted to be a writer? Was there anything in your childhood that influenced you to become a writer?**

    Like most children, I always had my own imaginary little world. Then, when I was ten years old, Mary Martin appeared on black and white television playing Peter Pan. If you'll forgive the pun, that's when my fantasies really took flight because it was such a happy tale. I wanted to make up stories like that, too. I loved to write in school, often turning ordinary term papers into fiction that incorporated my research. There was always a story simmering in my imagination. But my children were all in school when I finally began to write seriously.

2) **Although you have written several novels, what inspired you to specifically write a historical trilogy of the post Civil War era?**

    The Civil War was such an important turning point in United States history because it defined what we would become as a nation. In this series, I wanted to explore why Reconstruction failed and why we still suffer the consequences of that failure. As with my school term papers, I show my historical perspective and research best through fiction.

3) **Knowing that you have several writing awards to your credit, please share with us which novelists and other writers have influenced your writing and in what ways?**

    Charlotte Brontë was my first strong influence. In my opinion, her *Jane Eyre* is not only a perfect romance novel but also an eloquent social and spiritual commentary. DiAnn Mills is a prolific and talented author whose "expect an adventure" style has shown me how to use just the right amount of research rather than doing an "information dump" on my readers. Francine Rivers has one of the most powerful spiritual voices in today's Christian fiction. Every one of her novels deeply moves me and brings me closer to God. I hope to emulate these three authors so that God's message can be clear, deep, and exciting in my stories.

4) **Why did you write *Then Came Faith* rather than some other story?**

André Beauchamp has been on my mind for some time, so I had to write his story. I imagined a young Christian man who deeply believes in the southern cause and who has valiantly fought in the Confederate Navy. When the South loses the war, he wonders why God had abandoned His people. Add to that his personal losses of property, slaves, and family, and it becomes the perfect setup for a Christian to question his faith very seriously and ultimately to become embittered. Of course the heroine in this story must be his exact opposite. Juliana Harris not only has been a staunch abolitionist, but she also believes God had punished the South for perpetuating the evil institution of slavery. With two such different people living in my imagination, how could I not write their story?

5) **Your characters are distinctive, multi-faceted, and even endearing at times. What inspired the development of the plot and characters in your story? Are they based upon themes and people you already know?**

Addressing the question of themes: because I was a child in the Civil Rights era, I've always wondered why things did not turn out better for this nation after the Civil War and why the Civil

Rights movement was even necessary. I have come to understand that national identities are formed through the choices that individual people make. In this country, the generation after the Civil War failed to take up the torch and "fix" the racial divide, failed to bring African-Americans fully into American society, so that all of us could work together to build the greatest nation this world has ever known. We are still suffering because of that. We had a chance to become a beacon to a world where tribal and ethnic identities often wreak havoc and destruction. But we failed. By placing my characters in the post-Civil War, I show that many Americans had great hope for a better world, and there is still a chance we can overcome that failure.

6)   **You have a way of taking the reader right into your literary landscape—in this case the post Civil War era. How much research did you use to set the mood and ambiance of 1865 New Orleans?**

Once upon a time, before television, radio, and movies, people enjoyed novels that were filled with great historical and scenic details. They would sit around the hearth listening to the family patriarch reading a great novel such as *Moby Dick* or *A Tale of Two Cities,* from which they learned about a world they did not know. Today, we know all that stuff just by watching the Discovery or History channels. In today's novels, we readers want an author to throw in just a few details of setting and history to give us the picture. Then tell us all about the people: their struggles, their hopes, their triumphs and tragedies. That's what we're concerned with because that's what touches the core of our unchanging humanity. So I go to the heart of the human issues involved in my story and intersperse the history around it.

7) **How would you describe your writing style—not your literary style—but the actual writing itself? What kind of techniques do you use?**

I park myself in front of my computer and start putting words on the page. Sometimes I delete, and sometimes I save. But all of this comes after first imagining my characters, my basic plot line, and my themes.

8) **Many novelists say ending the novel is the most difficult part of writing. Why do you think that is, and how do you know when you have reached the end of your story?**

I think this is all about feelings. If I've solved all the problems and my characters look forward to happily-ever-after, how do I end with a nice little punch line? I want my readers to feel satisfied, so once those two problems are solved, I usually put in a sweet little kiss to seal the romance. Or, in one case, I had my hero and heroine merely reaching out to hold hands. It just felt right.

9) **There's obviously more to a novel than just an entertaining read. What do you want readers to take away from *Then Came Faith*?**

I believe God speaks to every believer's heart about His truth. My prayer is that my readers will listen to God rather than to their all-too-human "conscience" or to whatever is popular or expedient in their time or their social group. I pray that they will be Christ's representative in their sphere of influence, however large or small that may be. If I have created characters who live by these ideals, perhaps my readers will gain the courage to "go forth and do likewise."

10) **We've talked about the novelists who have most influenced you as a writer, so now let us make the question a little more personal. Who is the one person most influential in your life today?**

At the risk of sounding predictable or corny, I would say that my husband of 41 years is the most influential person in my life. He has worked very hard to make it possible for me to write. He comes home every day and asks to read what I've written, which means he holds me accountable. And he cooks! Not only when I have a deadline, but most of the time. What a guy! He *sets me free* to indulge in my art and fulfill my soul's desires.

11) **In conclusion, tell us something personal about Louise Gouge that most people may not know?**

Shortly before I met my dear hubby, I was a single girl in Denver, Colorado. This was 1964, the year of the Beatles' first U. S. tour. I had a friend who worked security at the Beatles concert at Red Rocks amphitheater, and he took me back stage because he knew I was not a screamer. I stood within five feet of the Fab Four. But "Imagine" this: I now stand hand-in-hand with the Fab ONE, my Savior, Jesus Christ, and that's really "Something."

LOUISE M. GOUGE earned her BA in English/Creative Writing at the University of Central Florida in Orlando and her Master of Liberal Studies degree at Rollins College in Winter Park, Florida. Her novel, *Ahab's Bride,* Book One of Ahab's Legacy, (2004) was her master's thesis at Rollins College. *Hannah Rose,* Book Two of Ahab's Legacy, was released in 2005, and *Son of Perdition,* Book Three of Ahab's Legacy, was released in February 2006. *Then Came Faith* is the first in a historical fiction trilogy featuring the post-Civil War era.

To her credit, Louise is the recipient of several writing awards, including the Inspirational Readers Choice Award for Historical Fiction, the Road to Romance Reviewer's Choice Award, placing second with the prestigious American Christian Fiction Writers Book of the Year, placed first in the esteemed Inspirational Readers Choice Award, and garnering a rare four star review from Romantic Times Bookclub Magazine.

While writing Christian fiction is her primary occupation and labor of love, Louise is also an adjunct professor of English and Humanities at Valencia Community College in Kissimmee, Florida. Having received her advanced education in middle age, she tries to inspire her younger students to complete their own education early. For her older students, Louise hopes that her experiences prove that it is never too late for them to work toward their dreams. (Her first novel was published after she turned fifty!) In the classroom, she attempts to live out her Christian faith both in words and in action.

Louise has been married to David Gouge for forty-one years. They have four grown children and five grandchildren.

Her favorite Bible verse is "He shall choose our inheritance for us" (Psalm 47:4), a testimony to her belief that God has chosen a path for each believer. To seek that path and to trust His wisdom is to find the greatest happiness in life.

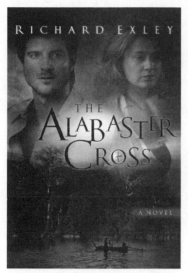

0-9785-370-3

Trapped in a world of anger, 29-year-old Bryan Whittaker cannot move on with his life until he takes a journey into his past…a dangerous journey that will lead him into the heart of the Amazon Rain Forest. Instead of the revenge he seeks, Bryan finds Diana and through her love he is able to make peace with his past and find redemption.

If you've ever struggled to restore a broken relationship, you will identify with Bryan's journey as he strives to make peace with his past.

0-98751-371-1

Luke Hatcher is the pride of Magnolia Springs, Louisiana. The perfect kid, he's the star of the high school baseball team and is on his way to LSU after graduation on a full scholarship—destined for the big leagues. Little did he know that a simple dare from his high school sweetheart would change his whole life.

A riveting novel that celebrates the God who gives second chances. If you've ever looked back on your life, feeling you threw away a golden moment, you will walk away from this passionate story cheering and with a renewed outlook on your own life.

Additional copies of this book and other titles by
Emerald Pointe Books are available from your local bookstore.

If you have enjoyed this book, or if it has impacted your life,
we would like to hear from you:

Please contact us at:

Emerald Pointe Books
Attention: Editorial Department
P.O. Box 35327
Tulsa, OK 74153

Emerald Pointe Books